*Be tantalised by their smouldering good looks,
wooed by their fiery passion, and excited by the
emotional power of these strong and sexy men…*

Marrying
the Italian

Three fabulous, emotional novels by bestselling
authors Melanie Milburne, Caroline Anderson
and Margaret McDonagh

Marrying
the Italian

MELANIE MILBURNE
CAROLINE ANDERSON
MARGARET McDONAGH

First published in Great Britain 2012
by Mills & Boon, an imprint of Harlequin (UK) Limited,
Eton House, 18-24 Paradise Road, Richmond, Surrey TW9 1SR

MARRYING THE ITALIAN
© by Harlequin Enterprises II B.V./S.à.r.l 2012

The Marcolini Blackmail Marriage, *The Valtieri Marriage Deal* and *The Italian Doctor's Bride* were first published in Great Britain by Harlequin (UK) Limited.

The Marcolini Blackmail Marriage © Melanie Milburne 2009
The Valtieri Marriage Deal © Caroline Anderson 2009
The Italian Doctor's Bride © Margaret McDonagh 2006

ISBN: 978 0 263 89687 9
ebook ISBN: 978 1 408 97050 8

05-0512

Printed and bound in Spain
by Blackprint CPI, Barcelona

THE MARCOLINI
BLACKMAIL MARRIAGE

BY
MELANIE MILBURNE

Melanie Milburne says: "One of the greatest joys of being a writer is the process of falling in love with the characters and then watching as they fall in love with each other. I am an absolutely hopeless romantic. I fell in love with my husband on our second date, and we even had a secret engagement—so you see it must have been destined for me to be a Mills & Boon® author! The other great joy of being a romance writer is hearing from readers. You can hear all about the other things I do when I'm not writing and even drop me a line at: www. melaniemilburne.com.au."

Melanie Milburne writes for Modern™ and Medical™ romance!

To Pauline Samson for all the work she does for swimming in Tasmania and nationally. She has sat on various pool decks tirelessly timing both mine and other people's swims for the National Aerobic Trophy. Winning it in 2007 was a great achievement for such a small but dedicated club, but really all the credit must go to Pauline for there is only one thing worse than swimming eight hundred metres of butterfly and that is sitting there timing it!

CHAPTER ONE

IT WAS the very last thing Claire was expecting. She stared at the lawyer for several seconds, her brain whirling, her heart suddenly beating too fast and too hard. 'What do you mean, he wouldn't agree to it?' she said.

The lawyer gave her a grim look. 'Your husband flatly refused to sign or even to accept the papers for a divorce,' she said. 'He was absolutely adamant. He insists on a meeting with you first.'

Claire gnawed at her lip for a moment. She had hoped to avoid all contact with Antonio Marcolini during his lecture tour of Sydney. It wasn't supposed to happen this way. Five years had passed; a divorce after such a long separation was surely just a matter of a bit of paperwork? Leaving it in the lawyer's hands was meant to make it easier for her to move on.

She *had* to move on.

'Unless you have specific reasons not to meet with him, I suggest you get it over with—and soon,' Angela Reed advised. 'It may well be he wants to end things on a more personal note, rather than formally through the legal system. Ultimately he will not be able to prevent a divorce, of course, but he could make things drag on—which would incur even more legal fees for you.'

Claire felt a familiar twist of panic deep inside at the thought of more bills to pay. She was sailing far too close to the wind as it was; a long drawn-out legal process would just about sink her. But why on earth would Antonio want to see her after all this time? The circumstances under which their relationship had ended were hardly conducive to a friendly cup of coffee and a chat about old times.

She took a deep breath and met the lawyer's speculative gaze. 'I guess one face to face meeting won't hurt,' she said, with a sinking feeling deep in the pit of her stomach.

'Think of it as closure,' Angela said, as she pushed back her chair and rose to her feet, signalling the consultation was at an end.

Closure, Claire thought wryly as she made her way out to the street a short time later. That was why she had activated the divorce proceedings in the first place. It was well and truly time to put the past behind her. She owed it to herself to embrace life once more.

The phone was ringing as she unlocked the door of her flat and, dropping her bag and keys on the lumpy sofa, she picked up the receiver. 'Hello?'

'Claire.'

Claire gripped the phone in her suddenly damp hand, trying to suppress the groundswell of emotion that assailed her as soon as she heard the smooth, even tones of Antonio's accented voice. Oh, God, if this was how she was going to be just listening to him, how on earth was she going to cope with seeing him? Tiny beads of perspiration broke out on her upper lip; her heart was hammering and her breathing becoming shallow and uneven.

'Claire.' He repeated her name, the velvet stroke of his deep tone making every pore of her skin lift beneath the layers of her winter-weight clothes, and the blood to kick start in her veins.

She swallowed tightly and, closing her eyes, released his name on a stuttering breath. 'Antonio…I was…er… just about to call you…'

'I take it you have spoken with your lawyer?' he asked.

'Yes, but—'

'Then you will know I will not take no for an answer,' he said, as if she hadn't spoken. 'No meeting, no divorce.'

Claire felt her back come up at his arrogance. 'You think you can order me about like some sort of puppet?' she asked. 'Well, damn you, Antonio. I am not—'

'Face to face, Claire,' he said, in the same indomitable tone. 'I believe there is no better way to do business.'

Claire felt tiny footsteps of ice-cold fear tiptoe up her spine at his words. 'I—I thought you were here for a lecture tour, not to socialise with your soon to be ex-wife,' she said, trying for a cool and unaffected tone but failing miserably.

She glanced to where she had left the newspaper announcing his arrival, lying open, even though every time she walked past, it drove a stake through her heart to see his handsome features smiling as if everything was right with his world.

'It is true I am spending the next three months in Australia, lecturing and operating for the charity I began in Italy,' he said.

It had not been the first time Claire had read about his charity, called FACE—Facial and Cranial Endowment—which raised millions of dollars for the surgical reconstruction of patients with severe facial injuries. She had followed the progress of some of the cases he had operated on via his website, marvelling at the miracles he performed for his patients. But then miracles only seemed to happen to other people, Claire reminded herself bitterly. Her brief marriage to Antonio had taught her that if nothing else.

'But I must say I find it rather strange you did not expect me to want to see you in person,' he continued.

'I find it inappropriate, given the circumstances,' she returned a little coldly. 'We have nothing to say to each other. I think we said it all the last time we were together.'

And how, Claire thought as she recalled the bitter words she had thrown at him. Angry, bitter words that had done nothing to ease the pain of her loss and the final barbarous sting of his betrayal. He had been so cold, so distant, and clinically detached in that doctor way of his, making her feel as if she had no self-control, no maturity and precious little dignity.

'I beg to differ, Claire,' he countered. 'The last time we were together you did the speaking, and all the accusing and name-calling, if I recall. This time I would like to be the one who does the talking.'

Claire's already white-knuckled fingers tightened around the phone, her heart skipping in her chest. 'Look, we've been separated for five—'

'I know how long we have been separated,' he interrupted yet again. 'Or estranged, as I understand is the more correct term, since there has been no formal division of assets between us. That is one of the reasons I am here now in Australia.'

Claire felt her stomach tilt. 'I thought you were here to promote your charity…you know…to raise its profile globally.'

'That is true, but I do not intend to spend the full three months lecturing,' he said. 'I plan to have a holiday while I am here, and of course to spend some time with you.'

'Why?' The word came out clipped with the sharp scissors of suspicion.

'We are still legally married, Claire.'

Claire clenched her teeth. 'So let me guess.' She let the words drip off her tongue, each one heavily laced with scorn. 'Your latest mistress didn't want to travel all this way so you are looking for a three-month fill-in. Forget it, Antonio. I'm not available.'

'Are you currently seeing anyone?' he asked.

Claire bristled at the question. How he could even *think* she would be able to move on from the death of their child as he had so easily done was truly astonishing. 'Why do you want to know?' she asked.

'I would not like to be cutting in on anyone else's territory,' he said. 'Although there are ways to deal with such obstacles, of course.'

'Yes, well, we all know how that hasn't stopped you in the past,' she clipped back. 'I seem to recall hearing about your affair with a married woman a couple of years back.'

'She was not my mistress, Claire,' he said. 'The press always makes a big deal out of anything Mario and I do. You know that. I warned you about it when we first met.'

To give him credit, Claire had to agree Antonio had

done his very best to try and prepare her for the exposure she would receive as one of the Marcolini brothers' love interests. Antonio and Mario, as the sons of high-profile Italian businessman Salvatore Marcolini, could not escape the attention of the media. Every woman they looked at was photographed, every restaurant they dined at was rated, and every move they made was followed with not just one telephoto lens, but hundreds.

Claire had found it both intrusive and terrifying. She was a country girl, born and bred. She was not used to any attention, let alone the world's media. She had grown up in a quiet country town in Outback New South Wales. There had been no glitz and glamour about her and her younger brothers' lives in the drought-stricken bush, nor did Claire's life now, as a hairdresser in a small inner-city suburb, attract the sort of attention Antonio had been used to dealing with since he was a small child.

That was just one of the essential differences that had driven the wedge between them: she was not of his ilk, and his parents had made that more than clear from the first moment he had brought her home to meet them. People with their sort of wealth did not consider a twenty-three-year-old Australian hairdresser on a working holiday marriage material for their brilliantly talented son.

'I am staying at the Hammond Tower Hotel.' Antonio's voice broke through her thoughts. 'In the penthouse suite.'

'Of course,' Claire muttered cynically.

'You surely did not expect me to purchase a house for the short time I will be here, did you, Claire?' he asked, after another short but tense pause.

'No, of course not,' she answered, wishing she hadn't been so transparent in her bitterness towards him. 'It's just a penthouse is a bit over the top for someone who heads a charity—or so I would have thought.'

'The charity is doing very well without me having to resort to sleeping on a park bench,' he said. 'But of course that is probably where you would like to see me, is it not?'

'I don't wish to see you at all,' Claire responded tightly.

'I am not going to give you a choice,' he said. 'We have things to discuss and I would like to do so in private— your place or mine. It makes no difference to me.'

It made the world of difference to Claire. She didn't want Antonio's presence in her small but tidy flat. It was hard enough living with the memories of his touch, his kisses, and the fiery heat of his lovemaking which, in spite of the passing of the years, had never seemed to lessen. Her body was responding to him even now, just by listening to his voice. How much worse would it be seeing him face to face, breathing in the same air as him, perhaps even touching him?

'I mean it, Claire,' he said with steely emphasis. 'I can be at your place in ten or fifteen minutes, or you can meet me here. You choose.'

Claire pressed her lips together as she considered her options. Here would be too private, too intimate, but then meeting him at his hotel would be so public. What if the press were lurking about? A quick snapshot of them together could cause the sort of speculation she had thankfully avoided over the last five years.

In the end she decided her private domain was not ready to accept the disturbing presence of her estranged husband. She didn't want to look at her rumpled sofa a few days hence and think of his long, strong thighs stretched out there, and nor did she want to drink from a coffee cup his lips had rested against.

'I'll come to you,' she said, on an expelled breath of resignation.

'I will wait for you in the Piano Bar,' he said. 'Would you like me to send a car for you?'

Claire had almost forgotten the wealth Antonio took for granted. No simple little fuel-efficient hire car for him—oh, no—he would have the latest Italian sports car, or a limousine complete with uniformed chauffeur.

The thought of a sleek limousine pulling up to collect her was almost laughable, given the state of her own current vehicle. She had to cajole it into starting each morning, and go through the same routine at the end of the day. It limped along, as she did, battered and bruised by what life had dished up, but somehow doggedly determined to complete the journey.

'No,' she said, with a last remnant of pride. 'I will make my own way there.'

'Fine. I will keep an eye out for you,' he said. 'Shall we say in an hour?'

Claire put the phone down after mumbling a reply, her heart contracting in pain at the thought of seeing Antonio again. Her stomach began to flutter inside with razor-winged nerves, her palms already damp in apprehension over what he had already said to her, let alone what else he had in store.

If he didn't want a divorce, what did he want? Their marriage had died, along with the reason it had occurred in the first place.

A giant wave of grief washed over her as she thought about their tiny daughter. She would have just completed her first term in kindergarten by now—would have been five years old and no doubt as cute as a button, with her father's dark brown eyes and a crown of shiny hair, maybe ink-black and slightly wavy, like Antonio's, or chestnut-brown and riotous like hers.

Claire wondered if he ever thought of their baby. Did he lie awake at night even now and imagine he could hear her crying? Did his arms ache to hold her just one more time, as hers did every day? Did he look at the last photograph taken of her in the delivery suite and feel an unbearable pain searing through his chest that those tiny eyes had never opened to look at his face?

Probably not, she thought bitterly as she rummaged in her wardrobe for something to wear. She pulled out a black dress and held it up for inspection. It was three or four seasons old, and far too big for her, but what did it matter? She wasn't out to impress him. That was the job of the supermodels and socialites he partied with all over Europe.

CHAPTER TWO

THE HAMMOND TOWER HOTEL was close to the city center, with stunning views over the harbour, and the sail-like wings of the iconic Sydney Opera House visible from some angles. But, unlike the other hotels the Hammond competed with, it had an old-world charm about it; the art deco design and furnishings and the immaculately uniformed attendants made Claire feel as if she was stepping back in time, to a far more gracious and glamorous era that few modern hotels could rival, in spite of their massive stainless steel and glass towers.

Claire left her car with the valet parking man, trying not to wince in embarrassment when the engine coughed and choked behind her as he valiantly tried to get it to move.

The doorman on duty smiled in greeting and held the brass and glass doors open for her. 'Good evening, madam,' he said. 'Welcome to the Hammond.'

'Thank you,' Claire said with a polite smile in return, and made her way towards the plush Piano Bar on legs that felt uncoordinated and treacherously unsteady.

Antonio was sitting on one of the leather sofas and got to his feet when he saw her approach. Claire felt her breath hitch in her throat like a bramble brushing against soft fabric. He was so commandingly tall; how could she have forgotten how petite she'd always felt standing in front of him? He towered over her, his darker than night eyes probing hers without giving anything away.

'Claire.'

That was all he said, just her name, and yet it caused a reaction so intense Claire could barely get her brain to work, let alone her voice. Her gaze consumed him greedily, ravenously, taking in every detail of his features in that pulsing nanosecond of silence. Would he touch her? she wondered in a flash of panic. Should she make the first move so as to keep things on her terms? Or should she lift each cheek in turn for the kiss she had learned was commonplace while living in Italy? Or stand stiffly, as she was doing now, her arms by her sides, the fingers of her right hand tightly clasped around her purse, her heart thumping like a bass drum as she delayed the final moment when she would have to meet his black-as-pitch gaze?

He had barely changed. He still had no signs of grey in his raven-black hair, even though he was now thirty-six years old, and his skin was still tanned, his jaw cleanly shaven. The classic lines of his Italian designer business suit did nothing to hide the superb physical condition he was in. Broad-shouldered and lean-waisted, with long, strong legs and narrow hips—all speaking of a man who took his health and fitness seriously, in spite of the long hours he worked.

'A-Antonio…' She finally managed to speak his

name, but it came out barely audible and distinctly wobbly. She could have kicked herself for revealing how much his presence unsettled her. Why couldn't she be cool and sophisticated for once? Why did she have to feel as if her heart was in a vice, with someone slowly but surely turning the handle until she couldn't breathe?

'Would you like to sit down?' He gestured towards the sofa he had just vacated.

So polite, so formal, Claire thought as she sat down, keeping her legs angled away from his as he resumed his seat.

'What would you like to drink?' he asked as the drinks waiter came over.

'Something soft…mineral water,' she said, clutching her purse against her lower body like a life raft. 'I'm driving.'

Antonio ordered her a mineral water, and a brandy and dry for himself, before he sat back to look at her. 'You have lost weight,' he said.

A spark of irritation came and went in her blue-green eyes. 'Is that a criticism or an observation?' she asked.

'I was not criticising you, Claire.'

She folded her arms in a keep-away-from-me pose. 'Look, can we just get this over with?' she asked. 'Say what you want to say and let me get back to my life.'

'What life would that be, I wonder?' he asked, leaning back, one arm draped casually over the back of the sofa as his dark gaze ran over her lazily.

She narrowed her eyes at him, two points of colour firing in her cheeks. 'I have a life, Antonio, it's just I choose not to have you in it.'

Antonio smiled to himself. She had such a cutting

tongue when she thought she could get away with it. But now he was here he had ways and means to bring her to heel, and bring her to heel he would. 'We have things to discuss, Claire,' he said. 'We have been apart a long time, and some decisions have to be made about where we go from here.'

'I can tell you where we go from here,' she said. 'We go straight to court and formally end our marriage.'

He paused for a moment, taking in her flashing blue-green gaze and the way her soft-as-a-feather-pillow mouth was pulled into a tight line. The skin of her face was a pale shade of cream, with a tiny dusting of freckles over the bridge of her *retroussé* nose, giving her a girl-next-door look that was captivating. He had already noted how every male head had turned when she had come into the bar. She was either totally unaware of the effect she had on the male gaze, or she very cleverly ignored it to enhance her feminine power.

'What if I told you I do not want a divorce?' he said after a measured pause.

She put her mineral water down with a sharp little thwack on the nearest coffee table, her eyes going wide as she stared at him. 'What did you say?'

He gave her an indolent half-smile. 'You heard me.'

She sucked in a breath and threw him a flint-like glare. 'That's too bad, Antonio, because I *do* want one.'

Antonio kept on pinning her with his gaze. 'Then why have you not done anything about it before now?'

She shifted her eyes from his. 'I...I couldn't be bothered,' she muttered in a petulant tone. 'You were out of sight and out of my mind, as far as I was concerned.'

'But now I am back you suddenly want to put an

end to our marriage?' he snapped his fingers. 'Just like that.'

She looked at him with icy disdain. 'Our marriage ended five years ago, Antonio, and you damn well know it.'

'And why was that?' Antonio asked, not bothering to disguise his simmering anger this time. 'Because you wanted to blame someone for anything and everything and I was the nearest scapegoat?'

She glared at him heatedly. He could see a pulse leaping in her neck, and how her fingers were so tight around her purse. Each and every one of her knuckles looked as if the tiny bones were going to break through the fine layer of her skin.

'You betrayed me,' she said in a low hard tone. 'You betrayed me when I was at my lowest point. I will never forgive you for that.'

Antonio clenched his jaw, the pressure making his teeth ache. 'So you are still running with that fairy story about me being unfaithful to you in the last few months of our relationship, are you?'

Her eyes flashed with pure venom. 'I know what I saw,' she hissed at him in an undertone, so the other drinkers in the bar wouldn't hear. 'You were holding her in your arms, so don't bother denying it.'

'I would not dream of denying it,' he said. 'Daniela was and still is a close family friend. You know that. That is something else I told you when we first met.'

'Yes, but you neglected to tell me you were her lover for the eighteen months prior,' she tossed back. 'A minor detail but a rather important one, I would have thought.'

Antonio put his drink down. 'I did not want to upset

you with talk of my ex-lovers,' he said. 'It did not seem appropriate since you were without similar experience.'

'Yes, well, I certainly got all the experience I needed living with you for almost a year,' Claire said, with an embittered set to her mouth.

His eyes warred with hers for a tense moment. 'Why don't you say it, Claire?' he said. 'Why don't you tell everyone in this bar what it is you really blame me for?'

Now she had made him so blisteringly angry Claire wasn't sure she knew how to handle it. She was used to him being cold and distant, clinically detached, with no hint of emotion ever showing through his mask-like expression.

She became aware of the interested glances of the other guests in the bar and felt her face begin to crawl with colour. 'Would you mind keeping your voice down?' she asked in a terse whisper. 'People are staring at us.'

'Let them bloody well stare.'

Claire cringed as she heard someone snicker close by. 'Could we at least go somewhere a little more private?' she said in desperation.

Antonio got to his feet. 'Come with me,' he said, and set a brisk pace towards the lifts situated on the other side of the marbled foyer.

Claire followed at a slower pace, on account of her heels, stepping into the lift he was holding for her, moving to the back of it, as far away from him as the space allowed.

She watched as he swiped his security pass for the penthouse floor, her nerves jumping and leaping beneath her skin as the doors whooshed closed and the lift began to climb each floor.

The silence apart from the mechanical whirr of the lift was palpable; it seemed to grow teeth, snapping at her where she stood in her corner.

Claire could feel her heart thumping irregularly, the blood racing through her veins at breakneck speed. She felt the faint knocking of her knees, and the on-off clench of her insides as the lift finally came to a smooth halt.

Antonio held the doors open for her and she slipped past him, her breath locking in her throat as she caught a faint trace of his lemon-based aftershave, an evocative fragrance that brought a host of memories to the forefront of her brain. Memories of her body pinned beneath his, her skin smelling of him, the taste of him salty and sexy in her mouth, all her muscles relaxed in the afterglow of their shared passion. Each vision made her body glow with heat; she could feel the creep of colour in her cheeks and wondered if he knew what had put it there.

He unlocked the door of his suite with the security card and silently gestured for her to enter, his dark eyes unreadable as they followed her every movement. Claire lowered her gaze and moved past, the gentle swish of her skirt brushing against his trouser legs, making her even more acutely aware of him.

The sound of the door closing behind her made her skin pepper all over with goosebumps, and to disguise her reaction she took a leisurely wander over to the bank of windows, looking down at the view as if that alone was what she was there for.

She sensed him come up behind her, the hairs on the nape of her neck rising to attention one by one. She suppressed a tiny shiver, and concentrated on watching a brightly lit ferry go under the Harbour Bridge.

'So you want a divorce?' he said, as if she was an employee who had just asked for a raise that was not going to be forthcoming.

Claire turned and faced him combatively. 'You can't deny me one, Antonio. We've been separated for too long for you to contest it.'

'I realise that,' he said, holding her gaze with the dark intensity of his. 'And if that is what you want then I will grant you one. But only after the three months of my stay.'

'I'm not sure I'm following you,' she said, frowning at him guardedly. 'Are you suggesting some sort of temporary reconciliation?'

His eyes continued to watch her steadily. 'I would like us to try again, Claire,' he said. 'This time on your territory, not mine.'

Claire felt the stungun-like blows of her heart inside her chest cavity as his words gradually filtered through her brain. 'You're serious about this…aren't you?' she said. 'My God, Antonio, you are out of your mind if you think I would agree to something like that.'

His expression had more than a hint of intractability about it. 'Three months is not a long period of time, Claire,' he said. 'If things do not work out then what has been lost? This way we can both be assured we are making the right decision.'

She sent him a querulous look. 'As far as I am concerned I made the right decision when I caught that plane back home to Sydney.'

'You made that decision in the heat of the moment, after a particularly harrowing time,' he returned.

Claire gaped at him in rapidly rising rage. 'That's

how you refer to her now, is it? "A particularly harrowing time"?'

He drew in a breath as he raked a hand through his hair. 'I knew you would be like this,' he said. 'It is impossible to discuss anything with you without you twisting everything I say to imply I did not care about our daughter. Damn you, Claire, you know that is not true. I wanted her more than anything.'

Claire clenched her jaw, her emotions beginning to spiral out of control. Yes, he *had* wanted their baby; it was just his wife he hadn't wanted as part of the bargain. 'Say her name, for God's sake. Say her name—or have you forgotten it? Is that it, Antonio?' Her voice rose to a shrill level. 'Have you forgotten all about her?'

He set his mouth. 'Do not do this, Claire. It will not bring her back.'

Claire swung away, biting the inside of her mouth to stop herself from becoming hysterical as she had so many times in the past. He was so good at keeping his emotions at bay, which made her loss of control all the more humiliating. How she hated him for it. How could he stand there so coldly and impersonally, assuming she would fall in with his plans, as if by crooking his little finger she would run back to him as if nothing had happened?

'I am serious about this trial reconciliation, Claire,' he said into the thrumming silence.

She turned back, her eyes flashing at him defiantly. 'Well, I hate to inform you, Antonio, but you've got your work cut out for you—because the very last thing I will ever agree to is resuming the position of your wife. Not for three months, not for three weeks, not even for three days.'

He gave her a long, studied look, his dark eyes centred on hers. 'You might want to rethink that position after you have spoken with the authorities about the situation one of your half-brothers has just landed himself in.'

Claire felt her eyes rounding in alarm. 'W-which one?' she asked, silently praying it wasn't Isaac. *Oh, please God don't let it be Isaac.* Callum was no angel, having had a few run-ins with the law in the past, but he was on the straight and narrow now. Isaac, however, was the vulnerable one—young and hot-headed, and fiercely loyal at times, which had got him into trouble more often than not.

'Isaac,' Antonio answered.

Claire swallowed, and hoped the despair wasn't showing on her face. 'What has he…um…allegedly done?' she asked with a lift of her chin.

He slanted one brow in a wry manner. 'I see you are no stranger to the legal vernacular when it comes to the behaviour of your sibling.'

She drew in a breath and forced herself to hold his gaze. 'I am the first to admit Isaac has some behavioural issues,' she said. 'But I fail to see what they have to do with you.'

'Actually, his behaviour on this occasion has everything to do with me,' he said, with a purposeful glint in his dark eyes. 'And you too, when it comes to it.'

Don't ask, Claire tried to warn herself, but even so the words left her lips in a stumbling stream. 'What do you mean?'

'Your brother took it upon himself to steal my hire car from the hospital car park earlier this afternoon and take it for a joy-ride,' he said.

Oh, dear God, Claire thought in rising despair. Of all the cars in Sydney, why pick Antonio Marcolini's? She knew Isaac was still in the city; he had come down from the country to go surfing with some friends. He had come to see her only a couple of days ago. He had stayed overnight, and she had given him some money to put towards a new wetsuit.

'Um…was there any damage?' she asked, with a thread of hope holding her voice almost but not quite steady.

'None that three months living with me as my wife will not rectify,' he said, his eyes boring into hers with steely intent.

Claire stared at him, her heart doing a pretty fair imitation of her car's recalcitrant engine on a cold morning. *'You're blackmailing me to come back to you?'* she choked out.

'The word blackmail implies a lack of choice,' he said, with an enigmatic tilt of his lips that was close to a smile. 'In this instance I am giving you a choice, Claire. You either return to our marriage for the duration of my stay in Sydney or I will press charges against your brother. What is it to be?'

CHAPTER THREE

CLAIRE felt the arctic-cold water of shock trickle drop by chilling drop down her spine as she stood gaping speechlessly at the man she had once loved more than life itself. What he was suggesting was unthinkable. But the alternative was even more horrifying. If Isaac went to prison, or even a detention centre, how could she ever forgive herself, knowing she'd had the means to prevent it? Callum had once described some of the things that went on in remand centres, and none of them had anything to do with justice.

But returning to the marriage that had brought her such heartache and unmitigated despair was surely going to test her limits. How on earth would she do it? What strength of character would she need to draw on to see it through?

Hatred clogged her veins as she sent Antonio a castigating glare. 'You've really surpassed yourself this time, Antonio,' she said. 'I thought your callous, unfeeling treatment of me in the past set the benchmark, but this is way above that. You couldn't have thought of a better revenge than this.'

He responded coolly. 'I am merely offering you an escape route which will be of benefit to all parties concerned.'

Claire rolled her eyes again, only because she knew it would annoy him. 'Pardon me,' she said, 'but I fail to see how *I* could possibly benefit from this outrageous plan of yours.'

Anger flickered in his gaze as it pinned hers. 'Have you ever thought of the sort of damage your brother could have done this afternoon?' he asked.

Claire lifted her chin. 'So your precious prestige hire car got a scratch or two? So what?'

His mouth stretched into a thin, flat line of fury. 'Do you have any idea of how many faces I have had to reconstruct over the years?' he ground out. 'Beautiful, perfect faces, permanently damaged by fools like your brother, whose idea of fun is to do burnouts and wheelies in city streets with no thought or regard to whoever else might be on them. That is what my life's work is all about, Claire. Not that you have ever shown a moment's interest, of course.'

'That is just so typical of you,' she threw back. 'I gave up my whole life for you and your career—not that you ever noticed. I was stuck at home day after miserable day, with only your mother and very occasionally your father dropping in just often enough to remind me none too subtly how I wasn't good enough to be their precious firstborn brilliant surgeon son's wife.'

His jaw tightened like a clamp. 'That is not how my mother tells it,' he bit out. 'She tried her utmost to help you settle in, but you refused to give an inch.'

'Here we go again,' Claire said with a curl of her lip.

'Her version and mine—and you still can't make up your mind which one to believe.'

Antonio thrust his hands into his trouser pockets in case he was tempted to pull her into his arms and kiss her into submission. She was so damned infuriating. No one could make him angrier than she did. He was master of his emotions, he always had been—and needed to be during the long hours of complicated surgical procedures where a cool, calm head was essential. But five minutes with Claire in this mood was enough to set his blood on the boil.

The very fact she had demanded a divorce the moment he stepped foot in the country showed how much of a gold-digger she had become. He could not stomach her getting half of his inheritance. He would do anything to prevent it. She had already taken enough. It still infuriated him to think of her demanding money from his mother the day she had left him.

Their blazingly hot affair had suddenly changed gear when she had informed him she was carrying his child. He had stood by her, marrying her promptly even though he had always had some misgivings over the true state of her feelings. She had claimed to love him, but he had always suspected it was the lifestyle she had fallen in love with, not him at all. From the little she had told him, he knew she came from a relatively poor background. Money had been scarce and luxuries almost unheard of. She had certainly acted a little starstruck on more than one occasion. Her wide-eyed wonder at the way he and his family lived had amused him at first, but after a while he'd realised he had become a passage for her to a new life, a life where each day wasn't a struggle for survival. That was until fate had stepped in with its most devastating of blows.

Thinking of that time always twisted his insides. He had been so busy, so very distracted. The surgical career pathway was strenuously demanding at the best of times, but juggling the needs of a young wife during an unplanned pregnancy and long hours of study and operating had been crippling, to say the least. His mother had told him many times how she had found Claire still in her dressing gown, moping about the villa, unwilling to make the slightest effort to adjust to being a surgeon's wife. Claire had obviously expected him to be at her beck and call, a nine-to-five sort of husband, when he had been anything but.

His own feelings he hated examining too closely, although he had to admit if he had loved her half as much as he had lusted after her maybe things would have been different. Love was a word he had never been quite comfortable using when it came to Claire, or indeed any other woman he had been involved with. He had decided long ago he was not the falling in love type.

The trouble was he still wanted her. He had never stopped wanting her. It was like a thrumming pulse in his body every time he was near her. His blood pounded in his veins as he thought of the ways she had pleasured him in the past. What she had lacked in experience she had made up for in enthusiasm. He had never had a more satisfying lover. Something about Claire and her responses to him, and his to her, made him feel as if he would never be content until he got her out of his system once and for all. And this was the perfect opportunity to do it.

'Claire,' he said locking his gaze with hers, 'is it

possible for us to put aside the past for a moment and discuss this like mature adults?'

The look she sent him was contemptuous. 'I fail to see what is mature about forcing me back into your life when you didn't want me in it in the first place,' she said. 'All you really wanted was an heir, and I once I failed to provide one you moved on to the next person who could.'

Antonio silently counted to ten to control his temper. 'So I take it your decision is to send your brother to prison? Is that correct?'

She turned away from him, folding her arms across her chest like a shield. 'You know I would do anything to stop that happening,' she said. 'No doubt that's why you're playing that particular card from the deck.'

'This is not a game, Claire.'

She turned to look at him again, her expression cynical. 'Isn't it?'

He blew out a gust of breath. 'I am thirty-six years old,' he said. 'I want to settle down at some point, but I cannot do that until things are finalised between us one way or the other.'

Claire felt a sensation akin to a sharp pain beneath her ribcage. 'So…' She ran her tongue over the sudden dryness of her lips. 'So you're thinking of getting married to someone else…once we get a divorce?'

His eyes gave little away, his expression even less. 'That is not an unlikely scenario,' he answered. 'I have been thinking about it a lot lately.'

'Are you…' Claire swallowed against the aching restriction in her throat. 'Are you planning on having children?'

Again his expression was shuttered, totally and frustratingly unreadable. 'It is a goal of mine, indeed of most people my age, to have a child or two if it is at all possible.'

'Then I'm not sure why you are wasting your time on our relationship, given it has already failed once,' she said, holding his gaze with an effort. 'Wouldn't you be better placed looking for a replacement wife, instead of trying to refashion the one you've got and don't really want?'

'I do not recall saying I did not want you,' he said, with a look that would have ignited tinder. 'On the contrary, you would not be here right now if that was not my primary focus.'

Claire's eyes widened, her heart skipping a beat. 'So…so what you're saying is…you still want me… as in…*sex*?'

A corner of his mouth lifted in a smile that set her pulse racing out of control. 'You find that surprising, *cara*?' he asked.

'Actually, I find it totally insulting,' she tossed back, desperate to disguise her reaction to him. 'You haven't spoken to me in five years, other than via an occasional terse e-mail in the first few months of our separation, and now you're expecting me to dive headfirst into your bed. What sort of woman do you think I am to agree to something as deplorable as that?'

'You do not have a current lover, so I do not see why this will not work between us—for the time being at least.'

Claire narrowed her eyes in outrage. 'How do you know I don't have a lover? Have you done some sort of background search on me?'

'You are still legally married to me, Claire,' he said. 'I believe it is very much my business to know if you are involved with anyone at present. Particularly if we are to resume a physical relationship.'

'That is a very big if,' she said, folding her arms. 'Anyway, what about you? How many women have *you* had during our separation?'

'I have had the occasional date, but nothing serious.'

Claire wanted to believe him, but knowing him as she did, or at least had, she couldn't imagine him remaining celibate for five years. He was a full-blooded male, healthy and virile, with a sex drive that had left her shuddering in his arms each and every time. She could feel that virility and potency now. The sensual spell he cast was woven around her like an invisible mist. She couldn't see it but she could feel it dampening her skin, making her aware of his maleness as no one else could. She could feel her breasts stirring against the lace of her bra, the tightness of her nipples reminding her of how his hot, moist mouth had suckled on her, his teeth tugging at her in playful little bites that had made her toes curl. Her belly quivered, the hollow ache of her womanhood pulsing with longing to be filled with his length and thickness again and again, driving her to the cataclysmic release she had silently craved for every one of the days, months and years they had spent apart.

It shamed her to be confronted by her own weakness where he was concerned. What sort of gullible fool would she be to go back for a second helping of betrayal and heartbreak?

He had never wanted their relationship to be anything other than a short-term affair, but her accidental pregnancy had changed everything. It had taken her almost a month to summon up the courage to tell him. Claire still remembered the total look of shock on his face when she had. But then to her surprise he had insisted they get married. It was only later she'd realised it had not been because he loved her, but because he had wanted an heir.

Claire had always known Antonio wasn't anywhere near as serious about her as she was about him. She had heard the adage far too many times to ignore it: Italian men slept with foreigners, but when it came to settling down they married their own countrywomen. But even so she had been caught up in the fairytale of it all: having a handsome man who lavished her with gifts and took her on exciting dates, not to mention one who initiated her into the heady pleasures of the flesh. It was all like a dream come true to a shy country girl from the Outback of Australia.

Claire had always been so careful with men in the past. She hadn't wanted to repeat the mistakes of her mother, pregnant and abandoned at a young age, spending most of her life looking for love in all the wrong places, and going on to have two other children, none of whose fathers had stayed around long enough to have their names registered on the birth certificates.

Claire hadn't slept around like most of her peers. Instead she had saved up the money from the three part-time jobs she'd juggled in order to put herself through hairdressing college. She had graduated as student of the year, and spent the next year or so saving for a holiday abroad, wanting to see the world before she settled into an upmarket salon.

But then she had met Antonio.

He had come in for a haircut, and as Riccardo, her

flamboyant boss, had been double-booked due to a mistake one of the apprentices had made, he had asked her to wash and cut Antonio's hair for him.

Claire had smiled up at the tall, gorgeous-looking man, introducing herself shyly. 'I am so sorry about the mistake in the appointment book,' she said. 'Riccardo has spoken to you about me filling in for him?'

Antonio smiled. 'It is not a problem,' he said. 'You are from England, *si*?'

'No.' She felt herself blushing and gushing. 'I'm actually Australian, from Sydney...well, really the country, not the city...a rural district...you know...cows and sheep...that sort of thing.'

'Ah, Australia,' he said, taking the chair she held out for him. 'I have distant relatives there. In fact my younger brother has been there several times. I have been promising myself a trip out there some time. It is the land of opportunities, *si*?'

Claire draped the cape around his impossibly broad shoulders, her nerves fizzing as her fingers accidentally came into contact with the raspy skin along his jaw. 'Um...yes...I guess so. If you're prepared to work hard,' she said, trying to avoid meeting his coal-black eyes in the mirror.

'Do you speak Italian?'

'*Non parlo Italiano,*' she said with an apologetic grimace. 'But I would like to learn. I've been thinking about taking some classes.'

He met her eyes in the mirror and held them. 'I will give you a lesson for free if you agree to have dinner with me tonight.'

Claire's fingers stilled amongst the silky strands of his

sooty black hair. 'Um…I'm not sure if Riccardo agrees with his staff fraternising with clients,' she faltered.

'He will agree when it comes to me,' Antonio said, with the sort of easy confidence that would have presented itself as arrogance in anyone else.

'Would you like to come over to the basin?' she asked, trying for cool and calm but not quite pulling it off.

Antonio rose from the chair, his height yet again dwarfing her. 'Riccardo must think a lot of your skill if he has shunted one of his best clients into your hands,' he said. 'Will I be safe?'

Claire responded to his flirting as any other young woman would have done. 'Only if you behave yourself, Signor Marcolini,' she said with a smile. 'I make a habit of keeping all of my customers satisfied—even the most demanding ones.'

'I am sure you do,' he said, and put back his head so she could wash his hair.

Claire had to drag herself out of the past to concentrate on the here and now. She didn't want to remember how it had felt to run her fingers through his hair, to massage his scalp for far longer than any other client before or since. She didn't want to remember how she had agreed to have dinner with him—not just that night but the following night as well. And she certainly didn't want to remember the way he had kissed her on their third date, his mouth sending her into a frenzy of want that had led to her lying naked in his arms only moments later, his body plunging into hers, her muffled cry of discomfort bringing him up short, shocked, horrified that he had inadvertently hurt her…

No. Claire shoved the memories back even further. It

had been the first time he had hurt her, but not the last. And there was no way she was going to think about the last.

'I find it hard to believe you have been without a regular bedmate for the last five years,' she said, voicing her doubts out loud.

'Believe what you like,' he said. 'As in the past, I have no control over the unfathomable workings of your mind.'

Claire ground her teeth. 'You know, you are really going to have to dig a little deeper on the charm front to get me back into your bed, Antonio.'

He gave her an imperious smile. 'You think?'

She took a step backwards, her hands clenched into fists by her sides. 'What do your parents and brother think of your dastardly little scheme to lure me back into the fold of the Marcolini family?'

A shadow passed through his dark eyes. It was just a momentary, almost fleeting thing, and Claire thought how she could so easily have missed it. 'My father unfortunately passed away a couple of months ago,' he said, with little trace of emotion in his voice. 'He had a massive heart attack. Too many cigarettes, too much stress, and not enough advice taken from his doctors or his family to slow down, I am afraid.' He paused for a moment, his dark eyes pinning hers in a disquieting manner. 'I thought you would have read about it in the press?'

'I…I must have missed it,' she said, lowering her voice and her gaze respectfully. 'I am so sorry. Your mother must miss him greatly. You must all miss him…'

'My mother is doing the best she can under the circumstances,' he said after another slight pause. 'My brother Mario has taken over my father's business.'

Claire brought her gaze back to his in surprise.

'What? You mean your father didn't leave you anything in his will?'

An indefinable look came into his eyes. 'Mario and I are both partners in the business, of course, but due to my career commitments I have by necessity left most of the corporate side of things to him.'

'I am sure your brother was shocked to hear of your intention to look me up while you are here,' Claire commented with a wry look.

Antonio continued to hold her look with an inscrutable one of his own. 'I have spoken to my brother, who told me rather bluntly he thinks I am a fool for even considering a rematch with you. But then he has always been of the philosophy of one strike and you are out. I am a little more…how shall I say…accommodating?'

Claire could just imagine his playboy younger brother bad-mouthing her to Antonio. His parents had been the same—not that Antonio would ever believe it. That last degrading scene with his mother had been filed away in Claire's do-not-go-there-again-file in her head. She had kept the cheque in her purse for weeks, folded into a tiny square, frayed at the edges, just as her temper was every time she thought of how she had been dismissed, like a servant who hadn't fulfilled the impossible expectations of her employer. But then she had finally cashed it, without a twinge of conscience. As far as she was concerned it had been money well spent.

'How do you know it was my brother who took your car?' Claire asked, looking at Antonio warily. 'You've never met any of my family.' *Thank God*, she thought. What he would make of her loving but totally unsophisticated mother was anyone's guess, but her brothers—

as much as she loved them—were way beyond the highbrow circles Antonio moved in.

'When the police caught him he identified himself,' Antonio said. 'He made no effort at all to cover up the fact he was my young brother-in-law.'

Claire felt her stomach drop.

'Wh-where is he?' she asked. 'Where is my brother now?'

'I have arranged for him to spend a few days with a friend of mine,' he said. 'He runs a centre for troubled youths on the South Coast.'

She clenched her fists by her sides. 'I want to see him. I want to see my brother to make sure he's all right.'

'I will organise for you to speak to him via the telephone,' he said, and reached for his mobile.

Claire sank her teeth into her bottom lip as she listened to him speak to his friend before he handed her the phone. She took it with a shaking hand and held it up to her ear, turning away so he wouldn't see the anguish on her face, nor hear what her brother had to say.

'Isaac? It's me, Claire.'

'Yo, sis. What's up?'

Claire mentally pinched the bridge of her nose. 'I think you know what's up,' she said, stepping further out of Antonio's hearing and keeping her voice low. 'Why did you do it, Isaac? Why on earth did you take Antonio Marcolini's car?'

Her brother muttered a filthy swear word. 'I hate the way he treated you. I thought it would help. Why should he drive around in such a cool-dude car when yours is a heap of rust?' he asked. 'Rich bastard. Anyway, I thought you were going to divorce him?'

Claire cringed as the sound of her brother's voice carried across the room. Turning away from Antonio's livid dark brown gaze, she said, 'I'm actually considering…um…getting back with him.'

Her brother let out another swear word. 'Get *out*. Jeez, why didn't you tell me that the other day?'

'Would it have made a difference?' she asked.

There was a small silence.

'Yeah…maybe…I dunno. You seemed pretty cut up about that article and the photo in the paper.'

Claire squeezed her eyes shut. Why hadn't she thrown it in the rubbish, where it belonged? 'Look, I just want you to promise me you'll behave yourself now you've been given this chance.'

'Don't 'ave much choice, locked up here,' he grumbled.

Claire frowned. 'You're locked up?'

'Well…sort of,' Isaac said. 'It's some sort of youth reform centre. It's kind of all right, though. The food's OK, and they've given me a room to myself and a TV. The head honcho wants me to think about teaching some of the kids to surf. I might take it on; I've got nothing better to do.'

'Just stay there and do as you're told, Isaac,' she pleaded with him.

'So you're dead serious about getting back with the Marcolini bloke, huh?' Isaac asked.

She lowered her voice even further, but even so it seemed to echo ominously off the walls of the plush suite—just as her brother's damning words had. 'Yes,' she said. 'I am as of this moment going to return to Antonio and live with him as his wife.'

CHAPTER FOUR

CLAIRE handed back Antonio's phone with a look of grim resignation on her face. 'Would you like me to lie down on the bed now, so you can get straight down to business?' she asked. 'Or would you like me to perform a strip show and really get your money's worth?'

Anger flared like a struck match in his dark eyes. 'There is no need to prostitute yourself, Claire,' he said. 'We will resume a physical relationship only when I am convinced it is what we both want. Right at this moment I can see you would much rather rake your nails down my face than anything else.'

Claire felt relief tussling with her disappointment, making her feel disconcerted over what it was she actually felt for Antonio. She had told herself so many times how much she hated him, and yet standing before him now she found that hatred proving frustratingly elusive. Other feelings had crept up on her—dangerous feelings of want and need. She could feel the traitorous beat of her pulse, the hit and miss of her heartbeats reminding her of the sensual power he still had over her.

'So…' She tried to keep her voice steady and her expression coolly detached. 'This three-month reconciliation… Am I supposed to move in here with you, or do I get to keep my own place?'

'You are renting at present? Is that correct?' he asked.

Claire wondered again how he knew so much about her current circumstances when their contact had been so limited. In the first weeks after she had left he had called and left message after message on her mobile, but she had deleted them without listening. He had e-mailed her several times, but she had not responded, and in the end had changed her e-mail address and her mobile number. She had assured herself if he really wanted to contact her he would find some way of doing so. But after some months had gone by, and then a couple of years, and then another couple, she'd resigned herself to the fact he had well and truly moved on.

'Claire?'

'Um…yes,' she said. 'I'm renting a place in Glebe, not far from the salon.'

'Do you own the salon outright?'

She frowned at him. 'What, do you think I am made of money or something?' she asked. 'Of course I don't own it outright. I work for a friend, Rebecca Collins.'

Antonio searched her features for a moment. 'So if you do not own a share in the salon, and you rent where you live, what exactly did you do with the money my mother gave you?' he asked.

Her shoulders went back and her blue-green eyes flashed flick knives of resentment at him. 'So she told you about that, did she?' she asked.

'She reluctantly informed me of it a couple of weeks after you left,' he said, keeping his expression deliberately shuttered.

'I looked upon it as a severance payout,' she said. 'After all, you no longer required my services once you'd hooked back up with Daniela Garza.'

Antonio ignored that little jibe to ask, 'Is that why you refused to accept money from me, even though I offered it repeatedly in my e-mails and phone calls?'

She gave him another castigating glare. 'Do you really think I would have accepted money from you after what you did?' she asked.

His lip curled in disdain. 'And yet you demanded it from my mother.'

Shocked, she stared at him with wide eyes. *'What* did you say?'

He let a three beats of silence pass.

'I think you heard what I said, Claire,' he said. 'You blackmailed my mother, forcing her to pay you a large sum of money to stop you going to the press about your marriage to me.'

She was looking at him as if he was speaking another language. But Antonio was well aware of how manipulative she could be, and still had his suspicions about her plans to take him for what she could get. Yet no one looking at her now would think her guilty of such a scheme. Her eyes were wide, feigning shocked innocence, her mouth trembling and her face pale.

'You have not answered my question,' he said.

Her back visibly stiffened, although her tone sounded calm and even. 'What question is that?'

'What did you do with the money?'

She let out her breath in a long hissing stream. 'What do you think I did with it?'

He frowned at her darkly. 'I would have given you money, damn it, Claire. But you always refused it.'

She turned her back on him. 'It was less personal taking it from her,' she said. 'I didn't want anything to do with you.'

'So what did you do with it?'

She turned after a moment, her expression as cold as the night air outside. 'I spent it on myself,' she said, with that same razor-sharp glint in her eyes. 'That's what gold-diggers do, isn't it, Antonio?'

He drew in a breath as he reined back his temper. She was deliberately goading him, as she had done so many times before. Yes, he had proof she had blackmailed his mother, even though she now staunchly denied it, but he understood how she would have seen it as some sort of payback for him not being there for her in the way she had wanted him to be.

He had come to a time in his life now where he wanted to put down roots. His father's sudden death had no doubt got a lot to do with it—not to mention his mother's deterioration since. And, since his brother Mario had no intention of settling down and producing a Marcolini heir, it was up to Antonio to make some important decisions about his own future. He could not move on until he had tied up the loose and frayed ends of the past. God knew he owed it to his beautiful little daughter, who hadn't even had the chance to take her first breath.

Antonio swallowed against the avalanche of emotion he felt whenever he pictured that tiny, perfect, lifeless face. He had helped so many people during the long, arduous course of his surgical career. He had saved lives, he had changed lives, he had restored health and vitality to people who had stared death or disfigurement in the face—and yet he had not been there when his daughter and Claire had needed him most.

It tortured him to think he might have been able to do something. Claire had gone into labour far too early. He had ignored the signs when she had mentioned her concerns that morning. He had no excuse, not really. The truth was he had been distracted with the case scheduled first on his list that day. A young girl of only seventeen, who had just landed herself a lucrative modelling contract, had been involved in a horrific traffic accident some weeks earlier. Antonio hadn't seen anyone quite so damaged before. He'd had to concentrate on preserving crucial facial nerves during surgery that would decide whether she would ever smile her beautiful smile at the camera again. He had perspired beneath his surgical scrubs; it had run like a river down his back as he'd worked with his dedicated team for twelve, nearly thirteen hours, to put her face back together the best they could—hoping, praying she would still be able to live the life she had mapped out for herself.

And he had done it. Bianca Abraggio was still modelling today—her face her fortune, her gorgeous smile intact, her life on track, while Antonio's was still in limbo.

'I do not recall referring to you at any time as a gold-digger,' he said.

She lifted her chin, her eyes flashing at him like shards of blue-green glass. 'You didn't need to. Your family made it more than clear that's what they thought I was.'

'Look,' he said, dragging a hand through his hair, 'I admit they were not expecting me to produce a daughter-in-law for them quite so soon. I was in the middle of my final fellowship training and—'

She cut him off. 'They never accepted me. They thought I wasn't good enough for you. I was a foreigner. I couldn't even speak their language. Not to mention I spoke with a broad Australian accent.'

'That is not true,' Antonio said. He had seen time and time again how both of his parents had tried their level best to get on with Claire, but she had been so fiercely independent they had eventually given up trying to include her. 'Anyway, it was not up to them, it was up to me who I spent my time with. It is still up to me.'

'What would *you* know of how it was for me?' she asked. 'I couldn't bear going through it all again. It has taken me this long to move on.'

Antonio could feel his frustration building, and couldn't quite disguise it in his tone. 'Get used to it, Claire, because you and I are going to spend the next three months together—otherwise you will be personally responsible for sending your brother to jail where he belongs.'

She glared at him furiously. 'I thought you had devoted your life to saving the lives of others?' she said. 'If you send my brother to prison you might as well be signing your name on his death certificate. He won't last a day inside. He'll get bullied or beaten up or something. I know he will.'

The look he gave her was merciless. 'Then do not make me do it, Claire, for I will if I have to. It is in your hands. Do not forget that.'

She threw him a hateful glare as she snatched up her

purse from where she had flung it earlier. Fighting to control her anger was like trying to rein in a bolting horse with nothing but piece of string. She had never thought it was possible to hate someone so intensely— especially someone she had loved so much before. Antonio was a ruthless stranger now, a man without mercy, a man who was prepared to go to unbelievable lengths to have her bend to his will.

'When do you wish to start this ridiculous charade?' she asked.

'Have you had dinner?' he asked.

'Um…no, but I'm not hungry.'

'There is a very fine restaurant within a block of here,' he said. 'I suggest we have dinner together, so as to ease back into our relationship.'

'I don't think I could eat a thing.'

'It looks like you have not eaten a thing in days.'

She gave him a cutting look. 'Is there anything else you would like to criticise me about while you're at it?' she asked.

Antonio's eyes glittered determinedly as they held hers. 'One thing I would like to make very clear from the outset,' he said. 'You can say what you like to me when we are alone, but while we are in the presence of other people I expect you to act with the dignity and decorum befitting your role as my wife.'

'Yes, well, that's all it's going to be,' she snipped back. 'An act—and not a particularly attractive one.'

'I will make sure there are certain compensations,' he said. 'A generous allowance, for one thing, which will mean you can cut back your hours at work—or quit altogether while I am here.'

She stood as stiff as a broom handle. 'You can keep your stupid allowance, and I am *not* giving up my job for you,' she said. 'I want to maintain some element of independence.'

'If that is what you want then I have no issue with it,' he said. 'I just thought you might be glad of a break from the long hours you work. You certainly look like you could do with one.'

Claire knew she had dark shadows under her eyes, and she was at least a couple of kilos lighter than she should be, but did he *have* to make her feel as if she had just crawled out from beneath a rock?

'Would you like me to get a paper bag to place over my head before we are seen in public together?' she asked. 'No doubt I fall rather short of the glamorous standard of the legions of other women you have enjoyed over the last five years.'

He held her challenging look for a tense moment. 'I was merely commenting on how stressed and tired you look, *il mio amato*,' he said. 'There is no need to feel as if everything I say to you is a veiled insult.'

Claire had to hastily swallow to keep her emotions in check. Her heart recognised the term of endearment and swelled in response. *My beloved one.* Of course he didn't mean it. How could he? He had never said he loved her. He had not once revealed anything of how he felt about her apart from at the start of their affair, when his desire for her had been so hot and strong it had left her spinning in its wake.

But then he had left her grieving the loss of their baby to find solace in his previous lover's arms. He had always denied it strenuously, and she might have believed his version of events if it hadn't been for Antonio's mother Rosina confirming her son's clandestine relationship.

'Do we have to do this tonight?' she asked now, with a hint of petulance. 'Why can't we meet for dinner tomorrow, or even the day after?'

'Because I have limited time available,' he said. 'I have a large operating list tomorrow, which could well go over time. And besides, I know what you will do if I give you a reprieve. You will more than likely disappear for the next three months so as to avoid further contact with me.'

Claire shifted her gaze so he wouldn't see how close his assessment of her had been. She had been madly thinking of various escape routes, mentally tallying the meagre contents of her bank account to figure a way of covering her tracks until he left the country. But she could hardly leave Rebecca in the lurch—not after she had always been so supportive of her over the years.

'I know how your mind works, Claire,' he said into the silence. 'You would rather walk over hot coals than spend an evening with me, would you not?'

Claire returned her gaze to his, surprised at the bitterness in his tone. What did *he* have to be bitter about? She hadn't destroyed their marriage, he had—and irreparably. 'You surely don't expect me to be doing cartwheels of joy about you forcing your way back into my life, do you?' she asked.

The line of his mouth tightened. 'I can see why you have lost so much weight,' he said. 'It is no doubt due to that chip on your shoulder you are carrying around.'

Claire gripped her purse so tightly her fingers began

to ache. 'You don't think I have a right to be upset?' she asked. 'I'm not an emotional cardboard cut-out like you, Antonio. I feel, and I feel deeply. Not a day goes past when I don't think about her—about how old she would be now, what she would look like, the things she would be saying and doing. Do you even spare her a single thought?'

His eyes darkened, and the tension around his mouth increased, making a tiny nerve flicker beneath the skin of his rigid jaw. 'I think of her,' he said, his voice sounding as if it had been scraped across a serrated surface. 'Of course I think about her.'

Claire bit the inside of her mouth until she tasted the metallic sourness of blood. She didn't want to break down in front of him. She didn't want him to see how truly vulnerable she still was around him. If he reached out to comfort her she would betray herself; she was sure of it. Her arms would snake around his neck; her body would press up against his in search of the warmth and strength only he could give. Her flesh would spring to life, every cell in her body recognising the magnetism of his, drawing her into his sensual orbit, luring her into lowering her guard until she had no defences left. The sooner she was out of this suite and in a public place the better, she decided firmly.

She drew in a scratchy breath and forced herself to meet his gaze. 'I guess dinner would be OK,' she said. 'I missed lunch, and breakfast seems like a long time ago.'

He picked up the security card and slid it into his wallet. 'I will not keep you up too late, Claire. I am still getting over my jet lag.'

Claire noticed then how tired he looked. His dark eyes

were underscored with bruise-like shadows, and the grooves either side of his mouth looked deeper than usual. He still looked as heart-stoppingly gorgeous as ever—perhaps even more so. Maybe it was because she hadn't seen him for so long. She had forgotten how compelling his chocolate-brown eyes were, how thick and sooty his long lashes, and how his beautifully sculpted mouth with its fuller bottom lip hinted at the passion and potency she had tasted there time and time again.

She had to wrench her gaze away from his mouth, where it had drifted of its own volition.

'So…what's this restaurant like?' she asked as they made their way out of his penthouse. 'What sort of cuisine do they offer?'

He reached past her to press the call button for the lift, and Claire felt her breath come to a stumbling halt in her chest. The near brush of his arm had triggered every nerve in her body, until she could almost sense how it would feel to have him touch her again. Her breasts ached for the press of his hands, the brush of his lips, the sweet hot suck of his mouth and the roll and glide and tortuous tease of his tongue. Was she so pleasure-starved as to be suddenly craving the touch of a man she hated? Her mind was playing tricks on her, surely? He had accused her of blackmail, and yet she couldn't quite stop her heart from skipping a beat every time his gaze meshed with hers.

The lift arrived with an almost soundless swish of doors opening, and Claire stepped in, moving to the back, out of temptation's way.

'Come here, Claire,' Antonio commanded.

Claire held her purse like a shield against her traitorous pelvis, where a pulse had begun beating. 'Why?' she asked. 'There's no one else in the lift.'

'No, but as soon as we hit the ground floor there will be. So it is better to start as we mean to go on,' he said.

She frowned at him as suspicion began to crawl beneath her skin. 'How do you know there will be someone there?' she asked.

He held her narrowed gaze with equanimity. 'I took the liberty of releasing a press statement earlier today.'

Claire felt anger rise up within her like a cold, hard substance, stiffening every vertebra of her spine. 'You were *that* sure I would agree to this farce?' she asked.

His eyes glinted as they held hers. 'I was sure you would not like to see your brother face the authorities. I was also sure you would do it for the money.'

The despair she felt at that moment almost consumed her. It was so hurtful to realise how badly he thought of her, how for all this time he'd believed her to be an avaricious opportunist, when all she had ever wanted from him was his love. How could he have got it so wrong about her? Hadn't he seen how much she had adored him? Claire knew she had been a little goggle-eyed at his lifestyle to begin with, but as their relationship had progressed she'd thought she had demonstrated how little his fame and fortune meant to her. Was his heart so hard and impenetrable he was unable to recognise genuine love when he saw it?

'Come here, Claire,' he commanded again, holding out his hand for her.

Claire released her tightly held breath and pressed herself away from the back of the lift, where she had flattened her spine. She took his hand, struggling to hide the way his fingers curling around hers affected her. His hands—his so very clever, life-saving hands—felt strong and warm against hers. They had been one of the first things she had noticed about him all those years ago in Riccardo's salon. Antonio had strong, capable hands—tanned, lightly sprinkled with hair, broad and yet long-fingered, his nails cut short and scrupulously clean from the hundreds of washes he subjected them to in order to operate.

She looked down at their entwined fingers and suppressed a tiny shiver. Those hands had explored every inch of her body. They had known her intimately; they had taught her everything she knew about sexual response. She could feel the warmth of him seeping through her skin, layer by layer, melting the ice of her resolve to keep herself distanced and unaffected by him.

The lift doors opened and a camera flashed in Claire's face as she stepped out hand in hand with Antonio. She cringed, and shielded her eyes from the over-bright glare, but within seconds another journalist had rushed up and thrust a microphone towards her.

'Mrs Marcolini,' the young woman said, struggling to keep up with Antonio's determined stride as he pulled Claire towards the front of the hotel. 'Is it true you are returning to your husband after a five-year estrangement?'

Antonio gently but firmly moved the microphone away from Claire's face. 'Do you mind giving my wife some space?' he asked.

The journalist took this as encouragement, and directed her line of questioning at him instead. 'Mr Marcolini, you are reputed to be here in Sydney for a limited time. Does that mean your new relationship with your wife will be on a set time-frame as well? Or do you intend to take her back to Italy with you once your lecture and surgical tour here in Sydney is completed?'

Claire looked up at Antonio, her breath catching in her throat, but he was as cool and collected as usual, the urbane smile in place, his inscrutable gaze giving no clue to what was ticking over in his mind.

'That is between my wife and I,' he answered. 'We have only just sorted out our differences. Please give us some space and privacy in which to work on our reconciliation.'

'Mr Marcolini.' The young female journalist was clearly undaunted by his somewhat terse response. 'You and your wife suffered the tragedy of a stillbirth five years ago. Do you have any advice to parents who have suffered the same?'

Claire felt the sudden tension in Antonio's fingers where they were wrapped around hers. She looked up at him again, her heart in her throat and the pain in the middle of her chest so severe she could scarcely draw in a much needed breath.

'The loss of a child at any age is a travesty of nature,' he answered. 'Each person must deal with it in their own way and in their own time. There is no blueprint for grief.'

'And you, Mrs Marcolini?' The journalist aimed her microphone back at Claire. 'What advice would you give to grieving parents, having been through it personally?'

Claire stammered her response, conscious there were women out there just like her, who had been torn apart by the loss of a baby and would no doubt be hanging on every word she said. 'Um…just to keep hoping that one day enough research will be done to make sure stillbirths are a thing of the past. And to remember it's not the mother's fault. Things go wrong, even at the last minute. You mustn't blame yourself…that is the important thing. You mustn't blame yourself…'

Antonio, keeping Claire close, elbowed his way through the knot of people and cameras. 'Just keep walking, *cara*,' he said. 'This will die down in a day or two.'

'I can't see why our situation warrants the attention it's just received. Who gives a toss whether we resume our marriage or not? It's hardly headline material.'

Antonio kept her hand tucked in close to his side as he led the way down the sidewalk to the restaurant he had booked earlier. 'Maybe not here in Australia,' he said. 'However, there are newshounds who relay gossip back to Italy from all over the world. They like to document whatever Mario and I do—especially now we are at the helm of the Marcolini empire.'

'So what is Mario up to these days?' Claire asked, not really out of interest but more out of a desire to steer the conversation away from their unusual situation. 'Still flirting with any woman with a pulse?'

Antonio's smile this time was crooked with affection for his sibling. 'You know my brother Mario. He likes to work hard and to play even harder. I believe there is lately someone he is interested in—an Australian girl, apparently, someone he met last time he was here—but so far she has resisted his charm.'

'Yes, well, maybe he could try a little ruthlessness or blackmail,' she said. 'Both seem to run rather freely in the Marcolini family veins.'

He turned to face her, holding her by the upper arms so she couldn't move away. 'I gave you a choice, Claire,' he said, pinning her gaze with his. 'Your freedom or your brother's. You see it as blackmail, I see it as a chance to sort out what went wrong between us.'

She wrenched herself out of his hold, dusting off her arms as if he had tainted her with his touch. 'I can tell you what went wrong with us, Antonio,' she said. 'All I ever was to you was a temporary diversion—someone to warm your bed occasionally. You had no emotional investment in our relationship until there was the prospect of an heir. The baby was a bonus, and once she was out of the equation, so was I.'

Antonio clenched and unclenched his fingers where hers had so recently been. He could still feel the tingling sensation running up under his skin. 'I fulfilled my responsibilities towards you as best I could, but it was never enough for you. So many men in my place would not have done so. Have you ever thought of that? I stood by you and supported you, but you wanted me to be something I am not nor ever could be.'

She sank her teeth into her lip when it began to tremble. Moisture was starting to shine in the blue-green pools of her eyes, making him feel like an unfeeling brute for raising his voice at her. How on earth did she do it to him? One wounded look from her, just one slight wobble of her chin, and he felt the gut-wrenching blows of guilt assail him all over again.

He let out a weighty sigh and captured her hand again, bringing it up to his mouth, pressing his lips warmly against her cold, thin fingers. 'I am sorry, *cara*,' he said gently. 'I do not want to fight with you. We are supposed to be mending bridges, *si*?'

She looked at him for a stretching moment, her eyes still glistening with unshed tears. 'Some bridges can never be mended, Antonio,' she said, pulling her hand out of his.

Antonio held the restaurant door open for her. *Let's just see about that*, he thought with grim determination, and followed her inside.

CHAPTER FIVE

A FEW minutes later, once they were seated at a secluded table with drinks, crusty bread rolls and a tiny dish of freshly pressed olive oil placed in front of them, Claire began to feel the tension in her shoulders slowly dissipate. She could see Antonio was making every effort to put her at ease. His manner towards her had subtly changed ever since that tense moment outside the restaurant.

The earlier interaction with the press had upset him much more than she had thought it would. He was well used to handling the intrusive questions of the paparazzi, but this time she had felt the tensile strain in him as he had tried to protect her. It had touched her that he had done so, and made her wonder if his motives for their reconciliation were perhaps more noble than she had first thought.

The waiter took their orders, and once he had left them Antonio caught and held Claire's gaze. 'Did you blame yourself, Claire?' he asked, looking at her with dark intensity.

Claire pressed her lips together, her eyes falling away

from his to stare at the vertical necklaces of bubbles in her soda water. 'I don't suppose there is a mother anywhere in the world who doesn't feel guilty about the death of her child,' she said sadly.

He reached for her hand across the table, his long, strong fingers interlocking with hers. 'I should have arranged some counselling for you,' he said, in a tone deep with regret.

Claire brought her eyes back to his. 'Would you have come to the sessions as well?'

His eyes shifted to look at the contents of his glass, just as hers had done a moment or so earlier. 'I am used to dealing with life and death, Claire,' he said, briefly returning his gaze to hers. 'I lost my first patient, or at least the first one I was personally responsible for under my care, when I was a young registrar. It was unexpected and not my fault, but I blamed myself. I wanted to quit. I did not think I could carry on with my training. But my professor of surgery at the time took me to one side and reassured me that a surgeon is not God. We do what we can to save and preserve lives, but sometimes things go wrong. Things we have no control over.'

'Is that why you chose plastic surgery rather than general surgery?' Claire asked, wondering why she had never thought to ask him that before.

'I was never really interested in plastics as such,' he answered. 'I understand how many people are unhappy with the features they are born with, and I fully support them seeking help if and where it is appropriate, but I never saw myself doing straight rhinoplasty or breast augmentations or liposuction. Reconstructive work has always appealed to me.

Seeing someone disfigured by an accident or birth defect reclaiming their life and their place in the world is tremendously satisfying.'

'I've seen some of the work you've done on your website,' Claire said. 'The before and after shots are truly amazing.'

He picked up his glass, his expression somewhere between quizzical and wry. 'I am surprised you bothered looking at all. I thought you wanted me out of sight and out of mind.'

She twisted her mouth. 'I guess intrigue got the better of me. From being an overworked registrar when we met to what you are now—a world leader in reconstructive surgery… Well, that's a pretty big leap, and one I imagine you might not have achieved if I had stayed around.'

A frown tugged at his dark brows. 'That seems a rather negative way of viewing yourself,' he said. 'The early years of surgery are punishing, Claire. You know that. It is like any other demanding profession. You have to put in the hard yards before you reap any of the rewards.'

'I suppose some of the rewards, besides the financial ones, are the hordes of women who trail after you so de-votedly,' she put in resentfully.

He made an impatient sound at the back of his throat. 'You really are determined to pick a fight every chance you get, are you not? Well, if it is a fight you want, you can have one—but not here and not now. I refuse to trade insults with you over a table in a public restaurant.'

Claire twisted her hands beneath the table, her stomach tightening into familiar knots. 'I don't see that it is necessary for me to move in with you,' she said, nervously moistening her dry lips. 'Surely we can just see how it goes from day to day? You know…go on the occasional date or something, to see if things work out.'

He looked at her with wry amusement. 'Come now, Claire, surely we have moved well past the dating stage, hmm? You have shared my bed and my body in the past. I am quite sure you will not find it too difficult to do so again, especially since there is financial gain to be had.'

Claire had to look away from his taunting gaze. She felt shattered by his chilling assessment of her. He was treating her like a gold-digger, someone who would sleep with him for whatever she could get out of the arrangement. 'I don't want your money,' she said stiffly. 'I have never wanted it.'

He put his glass down so heavily the red wine splashed against the sides, almost spilling over the rim. 'That is not quite true, though, is it, Claire?'

She twisted her hands even more tightly together, forcing herself to hold his accusatory gaze. 'I wanted your time,' she said. 'But you were always too busy to give it to me.'

'I gave you what I could, Claire,' he said, frowning at her darkly. 'I know it was not enough. You did not always get the best of me; my patients back then and now still have that privilege. Most truly dedicated specialists feel the same way. We have lives in our hands. It is a huge responsibility, for they are all someone's son or daughter, husband or wife, brother or sister.'

'What about your own daughter, Antonio?' she asked, tears filling her eyes. 'The specialist you recommended I see failed to get there on time, and so did you. I felt let down. You both let our baby down.'

Antonio hated going over this. They had done it so

many times in the past and it had achieved nothing. All it did was stir up a hornets' nest of guilt in his gut. 'Leave it, Claire,' he said. 'We have to let the past go and move forward. It is the only hope we have to get things right this time around.'

Claire pushed her barely touched food away. 'We wouldn't even be sitting here now if I hadn't asked you for a divorce. You couldn't stand the fact that I'd got in first— just like you couldn't stand the fact that I was the one who left you, not the other way round. And now you have the audacity to use my brother to blackmail me into being with you. I can't believe how ruthless you have become.'

'Your brother has nothing to do with this,' he said, releasing a tight breath. 'I was going to contact you in any case and suggest a trial reconciliation. He just gave me the means to make sure you agreed to it.'

Claire sat in stony silence, wondering whether to believe him or not. He had certainly taken his time about contacting her; she had heard nothing from him for years. But then she began to wonder if it had something to do with the death of his father. Could Antonio have an ulterior motive for chaining her to his side? Suspicion began to make her scalp prickle. No wonder he had looked at her with such fury in his gaze while she had been talking to Isaac, and when she had questioned him about whether his father's estate had been divided between his brother and himself. She was starting to think Antonio would do anything rather than divide up his assets—even if it meant reconciling with his runaway wife.

'You have been on my mind a lot over the years, Claire,' he said into the silence. 'When this offer to come to Australia came up I decided it was a perfect opportunity to see if anything could be salvaged from what was left of our relationship. You had not pressed for a divorce, so I felt there was a chance you might still have feelings for me.'

'Well, you were wrong,' Claire said, tossing her napkin to one side and glaring at him as her anger towards him raced with red-hot speed through her veins. 'I feel nothing for you.'

He held her caustic look without flinching. 'That is not true, *cara*. You feel a lot of things for me. Anger and hate to name just two of them.'

'And that's not enough to send you and your blackmailed bride scheme packing?' she asked, with vitriol sharpening her voice to dagger points.

'Not until I know for sure there is no hope,' he said, with an intransigent set to his features. 'And the only way to find out is to start straight away—from tonight.'

Claire felt her eyes flare in panic. 'You can't mean for me to spend the night with you? Not yet. I'm not ready. It's too soon.'

He gave her an imperious smile, like someone who knew the hand they were about to spread out on the table was going to be a royal flush. 'You want to pull out of our deal?' he asked, reaching for his mobile. 'I can call Frank and tell him the police will be there in half an hour to pick up your brother and press charges on him.'

Claire clenched her hands beneath the table again. 'No, please,' she choked. 'Don't do that… I…I'll stay with you…'

His dark eyes travelled over her face for a pulsing moment. 'I will not force myself on you, Claire,' he said.

'You surely do not expect me to act so boorishly towards you, do you?'

She compressed her lips, waiting a beat or two before she released them. 'I'm not sure what to think...' she confessed. 'We're practically strangers now...'

'Even strangers can become friends,' he said. 'If nothing else, would that not be a good outcome of this three-month arrangement?'

Her eyes were wary as they met his. 'I can't imagine us exchanging Christmas cards and newsy e-mails, Antonio. Besides, we come from completely different worlds. I honestly don't know what I was thinking, getting involved with you in the first place.'

'Then why not tell me about your world?' he said. 'You hardly ever mentioned your family when we were together. You did not even want them to come to our wedding, though I offered to pay for their flights. I have never even seen a photograph of any one of them.'

Claire felt a tide of colour creep into her cheeks. 'They are my family, and I love them,' she said, knowing she sounded far too defensive. 'They're not perfect—far from it—but things have not been easy for any of them. My mother in particular.'

'What is she like?' he asked. 'You told me so little about her in the past.'

She tucked a corkscrew of curls behind her left ear, wondering where to begin. 'She's had a hard life. She lost her mother when she was in her early teens, and I guess because she felt so rudderless got pregnant at sixteen. Like a lot of other girls left holding the baby, she looked for love in all the wrong places, with each subsequent relationship producing a child but no reliable father. As the eldest and the only girl I kind of slipped into a pseudo-parenting role from an early age. My brother Callum is doing OK now, after a bit of a wild time in his teens, but it's Isaac I worry about. He's a little impulsive at times. He acts before he thinks.'

'He is young, and will eventually grow out of it if he is pointed in the right direction,' Antonio said. 'Frank Guthrie will be a good mentor for him. It sounds like your brother needs a strong male influence.'

Claire lifted her eyes back to his. 'Where did you meet this Frank guy?' she asked. 'I don't recall you mentioning him in the past.'

'I operated on his brother Jack about eighteen months ago,' he said. 'He was involved in a head-on collision just outside of Rome. There was a lot of facial damage. We had to put plates and screws in his forehead and cheeks, and rebuild both of his eye sockets. He was lucky to survive. No one thought he would come through, and certainly not without heavy scarring or disfigurement. I got to know Frank, who had flown over to be with him. He spent a lot of time at the hospital, so we often had a coffee and a chat after my ward rounds.'

'It must be very rewarding, seeing people recover from something like that,' she said. 'Your parents...I mean your mother...must be very proud of you.'

He gave her a wry half-smile. 'My father made it very clear when I first announced I was going to study medicine that he would have preferred me to take up the reins of his business. And my mother complained for years about the long hours I work. But I have always wanted to be a surgeon for as long as I can remember.'

Claire picked up her soda water again. 'How is your mother coping after your father's death?' she asked.

A shadow passed through his gaze as it met hers. 'She is doing as well as can be expected under the circumstances,' he said.

Claire was even more certain now that his father's death had everything to do with Antonio contacting her about this trial reconciliation. There would be certain expectations of him as the firstborn son of a wealthy businessman. An heir would be required. But he could hardly provide one whilst still legally married to his estranged wife.

A divorce between them had the potential to be messy, and no doubt very public. In their haste to marry close to six years ago, when Claire had announced her pregnancy, there had been no time for drawing up a prenuptial agreement. Antonio could not be unaware of how the family laws in Australia worked. She would be entitled to a considerable share of his wealth, including that which he had just inherited upon the death of his father, even though they had been living apart for so long.

She toyed with the edge of the tablecloth, struggling to keep her expression shuttered in case he saw how confused she was. It would be different if she still loved him. She would take him back without hesitation. But her love for him had died the day she had seen him in Daniela Garza's arms.

Or had it?

Claire looked at his face, her heart giving an unco-ordinated skip as her gaze came into contact with his coal-black eyes. She had been aware of a disturbing undercurrent the whole time they had been together this evening. Every time her eyes met his she felt the zap of attraction—unwilling, almost resentful, but no less unmistakable, and it definitely wasn't one-way. Her body recognised him as her pleasure-giver. She had not known such pleasure before or since, and while she imagined in her most tortured moments he had experienced physical ecstasy with many other women, she was more than aware of his ongoing desire for her. She could see it in his eyes, in the way they locked on hers for a second or two longer than necessary. She had felt it in the way his fingers had wrapped around hers in that possessive way of his, their warmth seeping into the coldness of hers. She could only imagine what would happen if he should kiss her at some point. Her lips could almost sense the gentle but firm pressure of his, and her tongue snaked out to try and remove the sensation. She didn't want to remind herself of all she had felt in his arms. She had locked away those memories. They were too painful to recollect.

They were far too dangerous to revisit.

'Have you finished playing with your meal?' Antonio asked.

Claire put down the fork she had been using to move around the seafood risotto she had been vainly trying to push past her lips. 'I guess I'm not as hungry as I thought I was,' she said, her shoulders going down on a sigh.

He took out his wallet and, signalling the waiter, placed his credit card on the table in anticipation of the bill. 'I will give you a night of reprieve, Claire,' he said. 'Go home and get a good night's sleep. If you give me a spare key to your flat I will send someone over tomorrow to shift your things to my suite at the hotel.

Do not worry about your lease or the rent for the next three months. I will see to that. All you need concern yourself with is stepping back into your role as my wife.'

He made it sound so simple, Claire thought as she drove back to her flat a short time later. All she had to do was pack a bag or two and slip back into his life as if she had never been away.

Even more worrying—how many nights would pass before he expected her to slip between the sheets of his bed?

CHAPTER SIX

THE salon was fully booked the following day, and it seemed as if every single client of Claire's had seen the press item documenting her reunion with Antonio Marcolini. All were intent on expressing their congratulations and best wishes. She smiled her way through each and every effusive comment, hoping no one would see through the fragile façade she'd put up.

Claire had refrained from telling Rebecca, her friend and employer, the finer details of her reconciliation with Antonio. How could she tell her closest friend that her estranged husband had more or less blackmailed her back into his life for the next three months?

But Rebecca must have sensed something in Claire's demeanour, and, cocking her head on one side, gave her a penetrating look. 'Claire, are you sure you're doing the right thing?' she asked. 'I mean, according to the papers he's only here for a limited time. What happens when he leaves at the end of August? Is he expecting you to go back to Italy with him?'

Claire bit her lip as she turned to fill the kettle in the small kitchen at the back of the salon. 'We haven't got around to discussing those sorts of details,' she said. 'We're taking it one day at a time, to see how things work out between us.'

Rebecca folded her arms, giving Claire a cynical look. 'So at any point he could just say *Forget it, it's over, I want a divorce.* Aren't any alarms bells ringing in your head?'

Claire puffed out a sigh. 'Look, I know it sounds a bit shaky, but he…*we* both feel it's worth a try. As he said, we were on his territory last time, and emotions were running high when we parted—or at least mine were. This way we can see if there is anything left to rebuild what we had before…before…things went wrong…'

Rebecca gave Claire's nearest arm a squeeze. 'If you need some time off to sort things out, just tell me,' she said. 'I can get Kathleen to come and fill in for you. She's been asking for the occasional day now her son's at preschool. You wouldn't be putting me out—not at all.'

'Thanks, Bex,' Claire said, with an attempt at a convincing smile. 'I'll see how it goes for now.'

Not long after her last client had left the salon door opened, and Claire looked up to see Antonio come in. She felt the ricochet of her reaction ripple its way through her as her eyes met his. Her stomach felt light and fluttery, her heart began to race, and her breathing intervals shortened.

Conscious of Rebecca's speculative look from the behind the reception desk, Claire was uncertain whether to greet him with a kiss or not. For five years she had thought of his kisses—those barely-there nibbles that had made her spine loosen, or the slow, drugging movement of his lips on hers that was a prelude to a drawn-out sensual feast, or the sexy sweep and thrust of his tongue, or the fast-paced pressure of his mouth grinding against hers as desire raced out of control.

No one had kissed her since him, Claire realised with a little jolt. She couldn't even bear the thought of anyone else claiming her lips. It didn't seem right, somehow, and not just because technically she was still married to him.

She looked up into his face, her heart giving a little kick against her breastbone when his gaze dropped to her mouth.

He slowly bent down and brushed his lips against hers, a light touchdown that made her lips instantly hungry for more. She opened her eyes to find his were half closed in a broodingly sexy manner, his focus still trained on her mouth. She moistened her dry lips with the tip of her tongue, her heart going like a piston in her chest as his mouth came back down.

It was a firmer kiss this time, purposeful, and with just the right amount of passion to awaken every nerve of awareness in Claire's body. Lightning bolts of feeling shot through her, tightly curled ribbons of need unfurling deep inside her, making her realise how desperately she still wanted him.

'Ahem…' Rebecca's discreet but diplomatic reminder that they were not alone came just as Claire had started to wind her arms around Antonio's neck.

She stepped out of his hold with a rush of colour. 'Sorry, Bex, I forgot to introduce you,' she said. 'Antonio, this is Rebecca Collins. Bex, this is Antonio Marcolini…my…er…husband.'

Claire watched as Antonio took Rebecca's hand with a smile that would have melted stone. It clearly went a long way to melting any cynical animosity Rebecca had felt previously, for she smiled back widely, congratulating him on coming to claim Claire.

'I'm so happy for you both,' she said, just short of gushing. 'I hope it all works out brilliantly for you. I've told Claire if she needs time off to spend with you, then that's fine. I have back-up. She needs a holiday in any case. She works far too hard as it is.'

Antonio drew Claire closer with one of his arms about her waist. 'I am looking forward to spending some downtime with her once the first rush of my lecture tour is over,' he said. 'I thought we might go on a second honeymoon in a few weeks' time, to somewhere warm and tropical and totally private.'

Claire fixed a smile on her face, her body already on fire at the thought of spending tonight with him in his hotel suite, let alone days and nights at a time in a tropical paradise.

There hadn't been time for a proper honeymoon the first time around. Claire had been suffering with not just morning sickness but all-day sickness, and Antonio had been sitting his final exams. Looking back, she wondered how they had lasted the year even without the tragedy of losing their baby girl. It seemed from the start everything had been pitted against them. Although in time Antonio had seemed to look forward to having their child, Claire had still felt his gradual pulling away from her. His increasing aloofness had made her overly demanding and clingy, which had achieved nothing but to drive him even further away. When she'd failed to produce a live heir he had let her go with barely a protest. That was what hurt the most. He hadn't fought for her. She had secretly hoped he would follow her back to Australia, demanding she come back to him, somehow circumventing the obstacles she had put in his way, but he had not.

Until now.

Antonio led Claire outside a few minutes later, to where she had parked her car. '*This* is your car?' he asked, frowning at her.

Claire lifted her chin. 'It gets me from A to B,' she said, adding silently, *Mostly*.

She could tell he was angry, but he seemed to be working hard to control it. 'Claire, if you have been having trouble making ends meet why did you not contact me?' he asked with a brooding frown.

She shifted her eyes from his. 'I didn't want your money,' she said. 'I just wanted to get on with my life.'

No, Antonio thought with a bitter twist of his insides. She hadn't wanted *his* money, but she had thought nothing of taking his mother's. If it took him every day of the three months he was here he would find out what she had done with it.

He gave her car—and that was using the word loosely—another scathing look. She clearly hadn't been spending up big in that department. In fact, there was no indication from what he had seen so far that she lived anything but a low-key life. She owned no real estate, either private or commercial, and her work at the salon was permanent, not casual. She dressed well, but if there was anything new and crafted by a high street designer in her wardrobe he had yet to see it. The black dress she had worn the evening before he had recognised as one he had bought for her in Paris. But then someone as naturally beautiful as Claire did not need the trappings of *haute couture* to showcase her assets. He had seen her in nothing but her creamy skin and he could hardly wait to do so again.

'I forbid you to drive this heap of rust,' he said, taking her keys from her hand before she could stop him.

She glared at him. 'Give me my keys!'

He pocketed them and, capturing her outstretched hand, led her back down the street. 'I will have someone move it later,' he said. 'And I will have a new car delivered to the hotel for you tomorrow.'

She trotted alongside him, tugging at his hold, but his fingers tightened. 'I don't want a new car,' she said. 'I don't want anything from you.'

He shot her a trenchant look as he turned her round to face him. 'If I want to buy my wife a new car, I will. For God's sake, Claire, you are driving around in a death trap. Does it even have airbags?'

She pulled her mouth tight. 'No, but—'

He swore viciously and continued striding towards his own car, parked in a side street. 'I suppose you have done it deliberately?' he said, using his remote to unlock the upmarket vehicle.

'What the hell is that supposed to mean?' she asked.

His eyes lasered hers. 'Do you have any idea of what the press would make of you driving around in that coffin on wheels? For God's sake, Claire, I am here to teach other surgeons how to repair the sort of damage people get from being drivers and passengers in unworthy road vehicles such as yours.'

'It's not an unworthy vehicle,' she said. 'It passed its registration inspection last year.'

He clicked the remote control device once they got to his car. 'How?' he asked with an indolent curl of his lip. 'Did you bribe the mechanic by offering *him* a service?'

The blue in her eyes burned like the centre of a flame as they warred with his. 'Only someone with your disgusting moral track record would think something like that,' she bit back furiously.

He held the passenger door open for her. 'I am not going to discuss this any further,' he said. 'You are not going to be driving it any more and that is final.'

Claire waited until he was behind the wheel before she spoke through tight lips. 'If you think by buying me a flash new car it will get me back into your bed, then you are not only wasting a heck of a lot of money but your time as well.'

He sent her a challenging look. 'I could get you into the back seat right now, Claire, and have you writhing beneath me within seconds.'

Claire felt her face fire up, and a traitorous pulse began deep and low in her belly. 'You would have to knock me out first,' she said with a derisive scowl.

He laughed and gunned the engine. 'I am looking forward to making you eat every one of those words, *tesoro mio*.' He thrust the car into gear. 'Every single one of them.'

Claire sat with a mutinous set to her mouth, but inside her stomach was quivering at the thought of becoming intimate with him again. When he looked at her in that smouldering way she felt as if she was going to burst into flames. Heat coursed through her. She was annoyed with herself for being so weak. What sort of wanton woman was she, to be allowing herself to fall all over again for his lethally attractive charm? Hadn't she learned her lesson by now? He was using her to keep her hands off his money. He thought far more of his inheritance than he did of her. He didn't care one iota for her. He never had. What other proof did she need? Hadn't she always known it in her heart? As much as she had longed for him to love her, she knew it was not going to happen. Not then, and not now.

Not ever.

After a few minutes of nudging his way through the clogged city streets, Antonio pulled into the parking bay of the hotel. One of the attendants opened Claire's door, while the valet parking attendant took Antonio's place behind the wheel.

Antonio took Claire's hand and led her inside the hotel to the bank of lifts. He didn't speak on the ride up to his penthouse suite, but Claire was aware of the undercurrent of tension building between them. She could feel it in his fingers where they were curled around hers, the warmth and the sensual strength searing into her flesh like a brand.

He swiped his security card and held the door of his suite open for her, waiting until she had moved past him before he closed it with a click that made her nerves jump.

'Relax, Claire,' he said, reaching up to loosen his tie. 'I am not going to throw you to the floor and ravish you, even though I am tempted.'

Claire chewed at her lip and watched as he shrugged off his jacket, his broad chest and lean, narrow hips making her want to press herself against him and feel every hard plane of his body.

He laid his jacket over the back of one of the sofas. 'Your things were brought over from your flat earlier today,' he informed her. 'One of the housemaids has placed them in the wardrobe in my bedroom.'

Claire looked at him with eyes wide with alarm. '*Your* bedroom?' she asked. 'You mean you expect me to share your bed...like...' she gulped before she could stop herself '...straight away?'

He gave her a bland look. 'Is that going to be a problem for you?'

She let out her breath in a gust of outrage. 'Of *course* it's a problem!'

'It is a big bed, Claire,' he said. 'I am sure I will hardly notice you are there.'

'Thanks,' she said with a resentful glare. 'That makes me feel as if I should just cover up all the mirrors right now, in case they shatter to pieces if I so much as happen to glance into them.'

His dark eyes glinted with amusement as he closed the distance between them. He pushed up her chin to lock gazes with her. 'You are searching for compliments, *si*?' he asked. 'Then I will give you one.' He brought his mouth down to hers, his lips moving against hers in a leisurely fashion, exploring, tasting and teasing.

Claire couldn't hold back her response when his tongue stroked the seam of her mouth for entry; she opened her lips on a sigh, her body sagging against his as he pulled her into his hardness. His tongue explored her thoroughly, reacquainting himself with every contour of her mouth, leaving her breathless with need when he finally lifted his mouth from hers.

'Now,' he said, with that same glint of amusement darkening his eyes, 'do you feel beautiful and desirable again?'

Claire looked into his eyes and felt her resolve slip even further away. Her mouth was still tingling all over from the sensual assault of his, her heart-rate so hectic she could feel it pumping against her breastbone.

She was unable to move out of his embrace, her body locked against the rock-hard wall of his, the unmistakable probe of his erection sending her senses into overdrive.

She lowered her eyes to look at his mouth, her belly giving a little flip of excitement when she saw his tongue move out to sweep over his lips, as if he was preparing to kiss her again.

She drew in a breath as his head came down, a soft whimper escaping from her lips just before his mouth sealed hers. The pressure was light at first, but within moments it subtly increased, his tongue going in search of hers, taking the kiss to a whole new level of sensuality as his groin pulsed against hers with growing need. She could feel the rigid outline of his erection, the length of him so familiar it felt like coming home. She rubbed herself against him, relishing in the feel of him, the way he groaned deep and low in the back of his throat as his hands cupped her bottom to bring her even closer.

His kiss became even more fervent, and her response was just as fiery as their tongues duelled and danced with each other. Her breasts felt achingly alive, tense and tingling with the need to feel his hands and mouth on them.

His hands moved from her bottom to slide up under her top, his palms deliciously warm as they skated over her quivering flesh. He unhooked her bra and she let out a breath of pure pleasure when his hands cupped the weight of her breasts, his thumbs pressing against the tight buds of her nipples.

He lifted his mouth from hers and brought it to her naked breast, that first moist stroke of his tongue evoking a sharp cry of delight from Claire's throat. He suckled on her then, softly at first, his teeth scraping gently, before drawing on her with hot, wet need. The raspy skin of his jaw was like fine sandpaper over her silky skin, but it only made her need for him all the more unbearable. She writhed impatiently against him, her body telling him what she was too proud to admit out loud. Desire flowed like a torrid flame, licking along her veins, igniting her passion to fever-pitch, making her breath come in short sharp gasps as his hands moved down between their pressed bodies and cupped the swollen heat of her feminine mound. Even though two layers of fabric separated his hand from her, Claire nearly exploded with need. He stroked her through her clothes, slowly, tantalisingly, until she was arching her back, desperate for more.

'You want me, *cara*?' he asked as he brought his mouth within a breath of hers.

Claire couldn't speak, and whimpered instead, her teeth nipping at his full bottom lip in tiny, needy bites.

He smiled against her lips. 'I want to hear you say it, *mia moglie poco passionale*—my passionate little wife. Tell me you want me.'

'I want you,' she said without hesitation this time. 'Oh, God, I want you.'

The light of victory shone in his eyes, but instead of bringing his mouth back down to hers he released her and, turning his back, strode casually across the room to the mini bar. 'Would you like a drink?' he asked over one shoulder.

Claire stared at him speechlessly, her arms crossing to cover her naked breasts, her heart feeling as if it had slipped from its rightful position in her chest. He couldn't have orchestrated a more devastating way to demonstrate how weak she was where he was concerned. Kissing her into submission only to walk away as if the erotic interlude had had no effect on him at all.

'No, thank you,' she said, and with fumbling fingers tried to do up the buttons on her blouse. But her vision suddenly blurred, making the simple task impossible.

'Here,' he said, coming back over to where she was standing. 'Let me.'

Claire's heart thumped harder and harder as his steady fingers slowly but surely refastened each tiny button, her mouth trembling slightly when he got to the last ones, between her breasts. She dragged in a breath, the expansion of her chest bringing his fingers into contact with the slight swell of her right breast.

His eyes meshed with hers for a pulsing moment. 'It *will* happen, Claire,' he said, sliding his hand to the nape of her neck in a light but possessive touch that sent another shiver of sensation racing up and down her spine.

She swallowed again, not sure she would be wise to contradict him, given what had almost happened moments earlier.

It will happen.

Oh, how those words set her senses on full alert! She could almost feel him plunging inside her, the length and breadth of him filling her, stretching her, making her shatter into a thousand pieces of ecstasy. How many times in the past had she been his willing slave to sensuality? One look, one touch, and she had been on fire for him, her body feeling as if it was going to explode with pleasure as soon as he nudged her trembling thighs apart.

'But then,' he said, moving his hand to trail his fingers down the curve of her cheek, 'sex was never a problem for us, was it?'

Claire compressed her lips, her eyes skittering away from his. She was not going to fall for that again, to openly admit her need of him just so he could gloat over the sensual power he still had over her. He wanted to grind her pride in the dust, but she was going to do everything possible to thwart him. It would take every gram of self-control, but she would do it.

His hands settled on her waist, bringing her close to his body. 'We were good together, were we not, Claire?' he said. 'Better than good, in fact. Do you remember the way you used to relieve me with your mouth?'

Claire's whole body quivered in response to his erotic reminder of how she had pleasured him in the past. She had been an eager learner and he had taught her well. She had done things with him she had never thought she would do with anyone. The carnal delights he had given and taken still made her blush. His eyes had always scorched her with one look—just as they were doing now.

'Don't do this…' she said, struggling to keep her voice even.

He gave her a guileless look. 'Don't do what?' he asked.

She moistened her lips, hardly realising she was doing it until she saw his eyes drop to her mouth and follow the movement. 'You're trying to destroy my pride. I know you are. It's all a game to you, isn't it? Making me admit I still want you just so you can leave me dangling.'

'I am entitled to recall our most intimate moments together, am I not?' he asked. 'I can hardly erase them from my memory. I just have to look at that soft full mouth of yours and I want to unzip my trousers and push your head down.'

'Stop it,' Claire said, putting her hands over her ears to try to block the incendiary temptation of his words. 'Stop doing this. It won't work.'

He pulled her hands away from her head and brought her up close, pelvis to pelvis, his hot, hard need against her soft, moist ache. 'What are you frightened of, *cara*?' he asked. 'That you might discover you do not hate me as much as you claim? Is that it?'

Claire refused to answer. She clamped her lips together, glaring at him, her heart pounding with a combination of anger and out-of-control desire.

'The fact is you do *not* hate me, Claire,' he said. 'You just hate the fact that you still want me.'

'I do hate you,' she said, wrenching out of his hold. 'You slept with that—'

'Damn you, Claire.' He cut her off. 'How many times do I have to tell you there was nothing going on between us?'

'Your mother told me,' Claire said, putting up her chin at a combative height. 'She told me you had been lovers for a long time and were planning to marry, but that I had ruined everything by falling pregnant. She said you would never have married me if it hadn't been for my accidental pregnancy. She said that Daniela had been unofficially engaged to you for years.'

Antonio felt every muscle in his body tense. He had broken things off with Daniela a couple of months before he had met Claire. Daniela had taken it well, having come to the conclusion herself that their relationship had run its course. She had seemed to understand his need to focus on his career. Yes, they had once or twice laughed off their respective parents' none-too-subtle hints that a marriage between them would be more than agreeable, but he had never been in love with her, and as far as he could tell she had not been in love with him.

The afternoon Claire had seen them together had been as innocent as it had been coincidental. He had been having a quiet non-alcoholic drink with a colleague, both being on call, when Daniela had turned up, having seen him from the street outside. His colleague had left after a half an hour and Daniela had stayed on, expressing her concern over how Antonio was coping with the strain at home. It had been no secret he and Claire were having problems after the stillbirth of their baby. The last couple of months had been particularly dire, with Claire's shifting moods. He had done everything in his power to help her, but it had seemed nothing he said or did was what she wanted. She had oscillated between bouts of hysterical accusation and cold stonewalling, shutting him out for days on end.

Daniela had been supportive, and, knowing him as she had for so many years, had understood his private and internal way of processing the pain of his grief in a way Claire had not been ready or willing or even able to understand.

When Claire had come across them in the foyer, hugging as they had said goodbye, she had immediately misconstrued the situation. Daniela had made a diplomatic exit, but Claire had drawn him into a blazing row out on the street, which had been interrupted by an emergency page from the hospital, where one of his patients had begun bleeding post-operatively. By the time he'd got home the following morning, after more than twelve hours of horrendously difficult surgery, Claire had packed her bags and left.

As to what Claire had just intimated about his mother, there was no way Antonio could verify that now. As far as he knew Claire had demanded a large sum of money from his mother, and once his mother had written the cheque Claire had taken it and left the country. He had arrived at the airport just as her plane had taken off. The anger he had felt at that moment had carried him through the weeks and months ahead, and it had been refuelled every time Claire had refused to answer her phone or respond to his e-mails. Pride had prevented him chasing after her, even though not a day had gone past when he hadn't considered it. He knew it had been stubborn of him, leaving it so long, but he was not the type to beg and plead. He had finally accepted she had moved on with her life, and he had more or less done the same. It had only been when she had started the divorce process that he'd realised what was at stake—and not just his money. They had unfinished business between them, and this time around it was going to be done on his terms and his terms only.

'Perhaps you misunderstood what my mother said,' Antonio offered. 'Her English is not quite as good as it could be.'

Claire's blue-green eyes sent him a caustic glare. 'I know what I heard, Antonio,' she said. 'And besides, your mother speaks perfectly understandable English. Why don't you ask her what she said to me that night? Go on—call her up and ask her. Put the phone on speaker. She can hardly deny it with me standing right here listening to every word.'

Antonio sent splayed fingers through his hair again, releasing a breath that caught on something deep inside his chest on its exit. 'I do not wish to upset my mother right now,' he said. 'She has not been well since the death of my father.'

She gave a disdainful snort. 'You Italians really know how to stick together, don't you? I know blood is thicker than water and all that, but Marcolini blood is like concrete.'

'It is not about taking sides, Claire,' he said. 'The issues that brought about our estrangement need to be addressed by you and me personally. I do not want to drag in a jury on either side to complicate things any further.'

'What about Daniela?' she asked. 'Have you spoken to *her* lately?'

'No, not lately,' he answered. 'She got married about a year ago, to a friend of one of my cousins who lives in Tuscany. She is expecting a baby; I am not sure how far along she is now—pretty close to delivery, I should think. I have not spoken to her since my father's funeral.'

Claire tried to ignore the deep stab of pain she felt every time she heard of someone else's pregnancy. She seriously wondered sometimes if she would ever be able to feel happy and hopeful for another mother-to-be. How could they be so complacent, so assured of a healthy delivery? Did they really think a good diet and moderate exercise would guarantee them a live baby? She had done all that and more, and look where it had led. She had gone home empty-handed, shattered, shell-shocked. Every tiny bootie and delicately embroidered and knitted outfit had screamed at her from the walls of the beautifully decorated nursery she had seen to herself: where is the baby for all this stuff?

There had been no baby.

Instead there had been a tiny urn of ashes which Claire had carried all the way back to Australia, to give her daughter the interment she felt her baby deserved.

'If my mother somehow misinformed you about my relationship with Daniela, I am deeply sorry,' Antonio's voice broke through her painful thoughts. 'The only excuse I can offer on her behalf is that she was probably concerned our marriage was on the rocks, and thought it would help you to come to some sort of decision over whether or not to continue with it.'

Claire hugged her arms close to her chest, her teeth savaging her bottom lip as she thought about Antonio's explanation for his mother's behaviour. It sounded reasonable on the surface. Their marriage certainly hadn't been a rose-strewn pathway, and they hadn't exactly been able to hide it from his family. Claire cringed at the thought of how often she had sniped at Antonio in their presence towards the end.

Doubts started to creep up and tap her on the shoulder with ghost-like fingertips. What if she had got it totally wrong? What if what she had seen that day had been exactly as Antonio had tried to explain it at the time?

Claire's own insecurities, which had plagued her

from the beginning of their hasty marriage, had made her vulnerable to suggestion. She had immediately jumped to the conclusion Daniela and Antonio had enjoyed a mid-afternoon tryst in the hotel that day. She had not for a moment considered any other explanation. But then maybe she hadn't wanted to? Claire thought in retrospect. Maybe Antonio was right about his mother. Rosina Marcolini had been concerned her daughter-in-law was miserably unhappy, and had been so from the start. She had probably assumed Claire was no longer in love with her son, so had given her a way out of the situation. Rosina had obviously told her son it was Claire who had asked her for money, not she who had offered it, but proving it now was going to be difficult—unless she could challenge his mother face to face.

Claire looked up at Antonio. 'When you didn't come home at all that night I assumed you were with Daniela.'

He frowned at her. 'But don't you remember I got an emergency page to go back to Theatre?' he asked. 'When I saw how bad things were with the patient I asked one of the theatre staff to call you to let you know I was going to be late. She tried several times to call, but each time it was engaged or went through to the message service. In the end I told her to give up, as I did not want to be distracted from the difficult case I was working on. The patient was in a bad way and I needed to focus.'

Claire bit her lip again. She had been so angry and upset she had turned her mobile off and left the landline off the hook. It had only been after Antonio's mother had dropped by and had that short but pointed conversation with her that she'd decided to pack her bags and leave.

Antonio came closer and took her hands in his. 'I

got home at six in the morning to find you had gone,' he said. 'I lost valuable time thinking you had gone to stay with one of the friends you had made from the Italian class you attended. By the time it was a reasonable hour to call one of them to check you had already boarded the plane. I got to the airport just in time to see it take off. I was angry—angrier than I had ever been in my life. I could not jump on the next plane to follow you as I had patients booked in for weeks ahead. So I decided to let you go. I thought perhaps some time with your family would help you. God knows nothing I did ever seemed to work. But when you consistently refused to take my calls I realised it was over. I thought it was best you got on with your life while I got on with mine.'

Claire lowered her gaze to look at their linked hands. There were no guarantees on their current relationship. He had not made any promise of extending their reconciliation beyond the three-month period. She knew he desired her, but then he was in a foreign country without a mistress at the ready. What better way to fill in the time than with his wayward wife—the one who had got away, so to speak? A man had his pride, after all, and Antonio Marcolini had more than his fair share of it. Claire had done the unthinkable to him. Walking out on him without once begging to be taken back.

This set-up he had orchestrated might very well be a cleverly planned plot to serve his own ends. He knew a divorce would be costly; he no doubt realised he had to keep her sweet as so much was now at stake—his father's millions, for one thing. A temporary affair would stall divorce proceedings for several months.

Long enough for him to find some way out of handing her millions of dollars in settlement.

She pulled her hands out of his. 'I think you did the right thing in leaving me to get on with my life,' she said. 'We both needed time to regroup.'

'Perhaps,' he said, looking at her for a long moment. 'But five years is a long time, Claire.'

'Yes, and I needed every minute of it,' she said, with another lift of her chin.

His mouth thinned. 'How many lovers have there been? How many men have come and gone from your bed?'

Her eyes flashed at him. 'I hardly see what business that is of yours.'

He reached for her hands again, tethering her to him with long, strong fingers. 'How soon did you replace me?' he asked, holding her gaze with the searing heat of his.

She tried to get out of his hold but his fingers tightened. 'Why do you want to know?' she asked, glaring up at him.

His jaw tensed, a nerve at the side of his mouth pulsing like a miniature hammer beneath his skin. 'Have you had casual affairs, or something more permanent?' he asked.

'There's been no one permanent,' Claire said, tugging at his hold again. 'Now, let me go. You're hurting me.'

He looked down at his hands around her wrists and loosened his hold without releasing her. His thumbs began a slow stroke of the underside of each wrist, making her spine lose its rigid stance. Claire closed her eyes against the tide of longing that flowed through her. His body was so close she could feel its tempting warmth. The urge to feel his hardness against her again was suddenly irresistible, and she tilted towards him before she could stop herself. It was a betraying movement, but she was beyond caring. For some reason his demonstration of jealousy had stirred her, making her wonder if he felt something for her after all. It had been so long since she had felt anything but this aching sadness and emptiness inside. Would it be so very wrong to succumb to a moment of madness? Making love with Antonio would make her forget everything but the magic of his touch, how he could make her feel, how he could make her body explode time and time again with passion. It was what she wanted; it was what they both wanted.

Antonio held her from him. 'No, Claire,' he said firmly. 'Not like this. Not in anger and recrimination.'

Claire looked up at him in confusion. 'I thought your whole idea was to get me back into your bed as quickly as possible?'

His expression left her little to go on. 'I am not denying my intention of resuming a physical relationship with you, Claire, but if I were to follow through on your invitation just now I am sure you would hate me all the more tomorrow.'

She raised her brows at him. 'Scruples, Antonio?' she asked. 'Well, well, well—who would have thought?'

He stepped away from her, his mouth once again pulled into a taut line. 'If you would like to shower and change, we have a charity function to attend this evening,' he said. 'The dress is formal. You have just under an hour to get ready.'

Claire frowned. 'You expect me to come with you?'

His look was ruthlessly determined. 'I expect you to be by my side, as any other loving wife would want to be. No public displays of temper, Claire, do you understand?'

She pressed her lips together in resentment, not trusting herself to speak.

'I said, do you understand?' he repeated, pinning her with his coal-black gaze.

She lifted her chin. 'I hate you, Antonio,' she said. 'Just keep thinking about that tonight, while I am hanging off your arm and smiling at the cameras like a mindless puppet. I *hate* you.'

He shrugged off her vitriol as smoothly as he did his jacket; he hooked his finger under the collar of it, his eyes still holding hers. 'Just think how much more you are going to hate me when I have you begging in my arms, *tesoro mio.*'

Claire swung away from him, anger propelling her towards the bathroom. She slammed the door behind her, but even under the stinging spray of the shower she could still feel the promise of his words lighting a fire beneath her skin. Every surface the water touched reminded her of how he had touched her in the past: her breasts, her stomach, her lower back and thighs, and that secret place where the tight pearl of her womanhood was swollen with longing for the friction of his body. She hated herself for still wanting him. It made her feel like a lovesick fool who had no better sense than to get her fingers burned twice. That she had been a lovesick fool the first time round was more than obvious to her now. Antonio had probably been laughing at her gaucheness from the start of their affair. She had been a novelty to him—a girl from the bush, an innocent and naïve girl who had been knocked off her feet by his sophisticated charm.

Claire turned off the shower and reached for a towel with grim determination. She would show him just how much she had grown up and wised up over the last five years. He might think he could cajole her back into his bed as easily as he had the first time, but this time around she was not going down without a fight.

CHAPTER SEVEN

ANTONIO was flicking through some documents on his lap when Claire came out of the bedroom, close to forty-five minutes later. She felt his gaze run over her, taking in her upswept hair, the perfection of her understated make-up, and the flow and cling of her evening dress, in a fuchsia-pink that highlighted the creamy texture of her skin and the blue-green of her eyes.

He put his papers to one side and rose to his feet. 'You look very beautiful, Claire,' he said. 'But you have forgotten something.'

Claire frowned and put a hand up to check both her earrings were in place. 'What?'

He picked up her left hand. 'You are not wearing your wedding and engagement rings.'

Claire felt her stomach go hollow. 'That's because I no longer have them,' she said, not quite able to hold his look.

He brought up her chin with the end of his finger, locking his gaze with hers. 'You sold them?' he asked, with a glint of anger lighting his eyes from behind.

'No,' she said, running her tongue across her lipgloss. 'They were stolen not long after I got back from Italy.

My flat was broken into one day when I was at work. My rings were the only things they got away with. The police said the burglars had probably been disturbed by someone and took what they could and bolted.'

His finger stayed on her chin for several heart-chugging seconds. 'Were the rings covered by an insurance policy?'

'No…I couldn't afford it, and—'

'That is not true, though—is it, Claire?' he said, with that same glitter of simmering anger in his diamond-hard gaze. 'You could well afford it, but you chose to spend the money my mother gave you on other things.'

Pride made Claire's back stiffen. 'So what if I did?' she said. 'What are you going to do about it?'

His hand dropped from her face as if he didn't trust himself to touch her. 'We will be late if we do not leave now,' he said tersely.

Claire followed him out to the lifts. The smooth ride down was conducted in a crackling silence. As soon as the doors swished open he put a hand at her elbow and escorted her to a waiting limousine. She pasted a stiff smile on her face for the benefit of the hotel staff and their driver, but inside she was seething. Acting the role of his reconciled wife was going to be much more difficult than she had first imagined. There was so much bitterness between them, so much ingrained distrust and resentment.

Antonio leaned forward to close the panel separating them from the driver. As he sat back one of his thighs brushed Claire's, and she automatically shifted along the seat.

He gave her a smouldering look that sent a shiver

down her spine. 'You did not find my touch so repulsive an hour or so ago, Claire.'

She sent him a haughty glare in the vain hope of disguising her reaction to him. 'I must have been out of my mind. I can think of nothing I want less than to sleep with you again.'

He smiled a lazy smile as he moved closer, until he was touching her thigh to thigh, his hand capturing one of hers. Claire flinched at his touch, and he frowned and looked down at the faint bracelet of fingertip bruises he had unknowingly branded her with earlier.

His smile disappeared and a heavy frown furrowed his brow. He picked up her other hand and turned it over, ever so gently. '*I* did this?' he asked in a husky tone as he met her eyes.

Claire swallowed tightly. His touch was achingly gentle now, his fingers like feathers brushing over the barely-there bruises. His eyes were so dark, intensely so, as if the pupils had completely taken over his irises. Her heart began to thud, in an irregular rhythm that made her chest feel constrained.

'It's n-nothing…' she said with a slight wobble in her voice. 'I probably knocked myself against something…'

He was still frowning as he looked back at her wrists. 'Forgive me,' he said, low and deep. 'I had forgotten how delicately you are made.'

Claire held her breath as he lifted each of her wrists in turn to his mouth, the soft salve of his kisses stirring her far more deeply than the words of his apology could ever do. His lips were a butterfly movement against her sensitive skin, a teasing of the senses that made her realise how terribly unguarded she was around him.

Her heart shifted inside her chest like a tiny insect's wings, beating inside the narrow neck of a bottle.

His eyes came back to hers, his fingers loose as they held her hands within his. 'Do they hurt?' he asked in a gravel-like tone.

She shook her head, still not trusting herself to speak. She felt choked-up, emotion piling right to the back of her throat in a great thick wad of feeling she couldn't swallow down, no matter how hard she tried. Her eyes began to burn with the effort of keeping back tears, and she had to blink rapidly a couple of times to stave them off. This was the Antonio she had fallen so deeply in love with all those years ago. How was she supposed to resist him when he sabotaged her resolve not with force but with tenderness?

Antonio released her hands with a sigh. 'We have to sort this out, Claire. I know you think I have engineered this to my advantage, but we both have to be absolutely sure about where this ends up.'

Claire could already guess where it was going to end up. She was halfway there already: back in love with him, back in his arms, dreaming of a happy ever after when there were no guarantees she would ever have a nibble at the happiness cherry again. She could almost taste the hard pip of reality in her mouth. He didn't love her. He had never loved her the way she longed to be loved—the way her mother had never been loved, even after three desperate tries to get it right. Was Claire facing the same agonising destiny? A life of frustrated hopes? Girlhood dreams turned to dust as thick as that lining the roads of the Outback where she had grown up?

The limousine purred to a halt outside a convention

center, and within moments the press were there to capture the moment when Antonio Marcolini and his wife, newly reconciled, were to exit the vehicle.

Claire thought she had hidden her discomfiture well as she got out of the car with Antonio by her side, but somehow, in the blur of activity and the surging press of the crowd, she met his gaze for the briefest of moments and realised she had not fooled him—not even for a second.

He offered her his arm and she looped hers through it with a smile that tugged painfully at her face. 'Do we have to do this?' she whispered with a rueful grimace. 'Everyone is looking at us.'

He picked up a tendril of her curly hair and secured it behind her ear. 'We have to, *cara*,' he said, meshing his gaze with hers. 'We need to show ourselves in public as much as possible.'

Claire drew in a scratchy breath and, straightening her shoulders, walked stride by stride with him into the convention center. But for some reason she felt sure he hadn't been referring to the glamorous evening ahead, but more about the night that was to follow…

The table they were led to was at the front of the ballroom, where the other guests were already seated. Each person stood and greeted Antonio formally, before turning to greet her with smiles of speculative interest.

Drinks were served as soon as they sat down, and Claire sipped unenthusiastically at a glass of white wine as convivial conversation was bandied back and forth around her. She smiled in all the right places, even said one or two things that contributed to the general atmosphere of friendliness, but still she felt out on a ledge. She didn't belong here—not amongst his colleagues, not amongst his friends. She had never belonged, and somehow sitting here, with the lively chatter going on around her, it brought it home to her with brutal force. Even listening with one ear to one of the women at the table describing the latest antics of her toddler son felt like a knife going through Claire's chest. Her mind filled with those awful moments after her baby had been delivered, the terrible silence, the hushed whispers, the agonised looks, the shocking realisation that all was not as it was supposed to be.

'Claire?'

Claire suddenly realised Antonio was addressing her, his eyes dark as the suit he was wearing as they meshed with hers. 'Would you like to dance?'

She sent the tip of her tongue out to sweep away yet another layer of lipgloss. 'Dance?'

He smiled—Claire supposed for the benefit of those around them, watching on indulgently. 'Yes,' he said. 'You were very good at it, I seem to remember.'

Claire lowered her gaze to stare at the contents of her glass. 'I haven't danced for ages…'

'It does not matter,' he said, taking her by the hand and gently pulling her to her feet. 'This number is a slow waltz. All you have to do is shuffle your feet in time with mine.'

She had a lot more to do than shuffling her feet, but after a while Claire relaxed into it, relishing the feel of Antonio's arms around her as he led her in a dance that was a slow as it was sensual. Each step seemed to remind her of how well-matched their bodies were, the union of male and female, the naturalness of it, the ebb and flow of moving in time with each other as if they had been programmed to respond in such a way. His thigh pushed hers backwards, hers moved his forwards, and then they moved together in a twirl that sent the skirt of her long dress out in an arc of vivid pink.

'See?' Antonio said, smiling down at her as he led her into another smooth glide across the floor. 'It is like riding a bike, *si*? You never forget the moves.'

Claire could feel her body responding to his closeness. His pelvis was hard against hers, with not even the space for a silk handkerchief to pass between their bodies. She felt the stirring of his body, the intimate surge of his male flesh that made her ache for his possession all over again. She tried to convince herself it was just a physical thing: he was a virile man, she was a young healthy woman, and the chemistry that had brought them together in the first place had been reawakened. Sex with an ex or an estranged partner was commonplace. The familiarity of the relationship and yet that intriguing element of forbidden fruit made resisting the urge to reconnect in the most elemental way possible sometimes unstoppable. She could feel that temptation now; it was like a pulse deep in her body, a rhythm of longing that would not go away no matter how much she tried to ignore it.

'You are starting to tense up on me,' Antonio said. He ran his hands down the length of her spine as the number came to an end, and an even slower, more poignant one took its place. 'Relax, *cara*, there are people watching us.'

How could she possibly relax with his hands resting in the sensitive dip of her spine like that? Claire felt as if every nerve was set on super-vigilance, waiting for the stroke and glide of his next touch. Her belly quivered and her skin lifted in a fine layer of goosebumps as she met his dark, intense gaze.

'I'm not used to such big crowds these days,' she said. 'I haven't been out for ages. Compared to you, I live a very quiet life.'

He rested his chin on the top of her head as they moved in time with the music. 'There is nothing wrong with living a quiet life,' he said. 'I sometimes wish mine was a little less fast paced.'

Claire breathed in the scent of him as they circled the floor again. It felt so right to be in his arms, as if she belonged there and nowhere else. The trouble was she wasn't sure how long she was likely to be there. He seemed very intent on sorting out the train wreck of their previous relationship, but his motives for doing so were highly suspect.

It was so hard to tell what Antonio was thinking, let alone feeling. He had always been so good at keeping his cards close to his chest. She, on the other hand, wore her heart on her sleeve and had done so to her own detriment. She had made herself far too vulnerable to him from the outset, and now she felt as if she was doing it all again. He knew he had her in the palm of his hand. He knew she would not do anything that would jeopardise her brother's well-being. That was his trump card, and she was too cowardly to call his bluff, even though she dearly wanted to.

But even without the threat of Isaac facing the authorities, Claire suspected she was in too deep now to extricate herself. She couldn't quite get rid of the nagging fear she had got her wires twisted over his alleged affair with Daniela Garza. If so, she had ruined both of their lives by impulsively leaving him. The very thing she lectured her brother Isaac on time and time again was the very thing she most hated in herself: acting before thinking. How would she ever be able to forgive herself if she had got it wrong?

Antonio skilfully turned her out of the way of another couple on the dance floor, his arms protective around her. 'You look pensive, *cara*,' he said. 'Is something troubling you?'

Claire worried her bottom lip with her teeth, finally releasing it to look up at him. 'If you weren't having an affair with Daniela, why didn't you share the same bed as me after we lost the baby? You never came to me—not once.'

His expression tightened, as if pulled by invisible strings underneath his skin. 'That was because I thought it better to leave you to rest for the first couple of days, without me taking calls from the hospital late at night and disturbing you. It was clear after a while that you did not want me to rejoin you. You seemed to want to blame me for everything. I was damned no matter what I did, or what I said or did not say.'

Claire felt the dark cavern of her grief threatening to open up and swallow her all over again. He was right— she *had* blamed him for distancing himself. But hadn't she done the very same thing? She had been so lost, so shell-shocked at her loss, it had made it so hard for her to reach out to him for comfort. She had wanted to, many times, but when he'd taken to sleeping in the spare room, or staying overnight at the hospital, she had lain in the sparse loneliness of the bed they had shared and cried until her eyes had been almost permanently red-rimmed and swollen.

She had never seen him shed a single tear for their tiny daughter. She knew people grieved in different ways, but Antonio and his family had all seemed much the same in dealing with the stillbirth. They'd simply got on with their lives as if nothing had happened. Apart from the first day after Claire came out of hospital the baby had never been mentioned—or at least not in Claire's presence. There had been a brief christening in the hospital, but there had been no funeral. Antonio's parents had not thought it appropriate, and in the abyss of her grief she had gone along with their decision because she had not wanted to face the heartbreaking drama of seeing a tiny coffin carried into a church. It had only been later, once she was back in Australia, that she had felt ready to give her daughter a special place to rest.

The music had stopped, and Claire grasped at the chance to visit the ladies' room to restore some sort of order to her emotions. She mumbled something to Antonio about needing to touch up her lipgloss and, conscious of his gaze following her every step of the way, made her way to the exit.

She locked herself inside one of the cubicles in the ladies' room and took several deep breaths, her throat tight and her eyes aching with the bitter tears of regret.

For all this time she had relished placing the blame for the collapse of their relationship on Antonio. She had so firmly believed he had betrayed her. But in hindsight she could see how immature and foolish she had been right from the start. She had been no more ready for marriage than he had; she had been too young—not just in years, but in terms of worldly experience. He at least had had the maturity to accept responsibility for the pregnancy, and he hadn't even insulted her by insisting on a paternity test, as so many other men might have done. How had she not realised that until now? He might not have loved her, but at least he hadn't deserted her. He had stood by her as much as his demanding career had allowed.

Was it really fair to blame him for not being there for the delivery? He was a surgeon, for God's sake. He had the responsibility of other people's lives in his hands every single day. She hadn't even asked him why he hadn't made it in time. She had jumped to the conclusion that he had deliberately avoided being there because he hadn't wanted the baby in the first place— which was yet another hasty assumption she had made. He might have been initially taken aback by the news of her pregnancy, but as the weeks and months had gone on he had done his best to come with her to all of her prenatal appointments and check-ups. She had even caught him several times viewing the ultrasound DVD they had been given of the baby, wriggling its tiny limbs in her womb. He had bought a baby name book for her, and had sat with his hand gently resting on her belly as they looked through it together.

Claire had never realised how physically ill remorse could make one feel. It was like a burning pain deep inside, gnawing at her, each savage twinge a sickening reminder of how she had thrown away her one chance at happiness. Yes, they had experienced a tragedy, one that neither of them would ever be able to recover from fully, but this was the only opportunity she would get to do something to heal the disappointment and hurt of the past. It was optimistic, and perhaps a little unrealistic, to hope that Antonio would fall in love with her this time around, but she had three months to show him her love was big enough for both of them.

When she came out a few minutes later, Antonio rose from the table to hold out her chair for her, his dark eyes moving over her features like a searchlight, a small frown bringing his brows together. 'Is everything all right, *cara*?' he asked. 'You were away for so long I was about to send someone in to find you.'

Claire shifted her gaze and sat down. 'I'm fine; there was a bit of a queue, that's all.'

The woman seated opposite leaned forward to speak to her. 'I read about the reconciliation with your husband in the paper this morning. I am sure you'll be very happy this time around. I've been married to John for thirty-five years this September. We've had our ups and downs, but that's what marriage is all about—give and take and lots and lots of love.'

Claire stretched her mouth into a smile. 'Thank you. I am sure there will be plenty of hard work ahead, but, as you say, that is what marriage is all about.'

'My husband is a plastic surgeon as well,' the woman who had introduced herself as Janine Brian continued. 'He's very impressed with some of the new techniques Antonio is demonstrating. You must be very proud of him. He has brought new life and hope to so many people all over the world.'

'Yes…yes, I am,' Claire said, glancing at Antonio, who was now deep in conversation with one of the other guests at the table. She felt her breath lock in her throat as he turned his head to look at her, as if he had sensed her gaze resting on him.

She couldn't stop staring at him; it was like seeing him for the very first time. She marvelled at how handsome he looked in formal dress, how his tuxedo brought out the darkness of his eyes and hair, and how the stark whiteness of his dress shirt highlighted the deep olive tone of his skin. His mouth was tilted at a sexy angle, as if he knew exactly where her thoughts were leading. How could he possibly know how much she wanted to explore every inch of his body as she had done so often in the past? Could he see the hunger in her eyes? Could he sense it in the way her body was tense and on edge, her hands restless and fidgety, her legs crossing and uncrossing under the table? Desire was an unruly force in her body. She felt it running like a hot river of fire beneath her skin, searing her, branding her inside and out with the scorching promise of his possession.

'You two are just so romantic,' Janine said with an indulgent smile. 'Look at them, John.' She elbowed her husband in the ribs. 'Aren't they the most-in-love couple you've ever seen?'

Claire felt a blush steal over her cheeks as Antonio came back to sit beside her. He placed an arm around her shoulders, drawing her close. 'I was a fool to let her get away the first time,' he said. 'It will not be happening again, I can assure you.'

'Well, you know what they say: there's nothing better than making up in the bedroom,' Janine said. 'That's how we got our three kids, wasn't it, darling?'

'Janine…' John Brian frowned.

'What did I say?' Janine frowned back.

'It is OK, John,' Antonio said, giving Claire's shoulder a little squeeze. 'Claire and I cannot expect everyone to be tiptoeing around the subject of children for the rest of our lives.'

Janine Brian's face fell. 'Oh, dear...I completely forgot. John did tell me about... Oh, how awfully insensitive you must think me. I'm so, *so* sorry.'

Claire gave the distressed woman a reassuring smile, even though it stretched at her mouth uncomfortably. 'Please don't be upset or embarrassed,' she said. 'Each day has become a little easier.'

The conversation was thankfully steered in another direction when the waiter appeared with the meals for their table. Claire forced herself to eat as if nothing was wrong for Janine's sake, but later she would barely recall what it was she had eaten.

After the meals were cleared away, Antonio was introduced by the chairman of the charity. Claire watched as he moved up to the lectern, which had been set up with a large screen and data projector. After thanking the chairman and board members, Antonio spoke of the work he carried out in reconstructive surgery under the auspices of FACE. He showed pictures of some of the faces he had worked on, including several from Third World countries, which the charity had sponsored by bringing patients to Rome for surgery to be performed.

Claire looked at one of the young children he had worked on. The little girl, who was seven or eight, had been born with hyperteliorism, a congenital condition which presented as a broad face with wide, separated eyes and a flat nose. Fixing it required major cranial-facial reconstruction, with a team of three surgeons: a neurosurgeon, a facial maxillary surgeon and a plastic surgeon. In this case it had been Antonio. The team had operated for twelve hours to give the little girl a chance at a normal life, without shame or embarrassment over her unusual appearance. The before and after photographs were truly amazing. So too were the happy smiles of the child's parents and the little girl herself.

Once Antonio had finished his presentation he took some questions from the floor before returning to the table to thunderous applause.

The band began to play again and Antonio reached for Claire's hand. 'Let's have one more dance before we go home,' he suggested.

Claire moved into his arms without demur, her own arms going around his neck as his went around her back, holding her in an intimate embrace that perfectly matched the slow rhythm of the ballad being played.

'I thought you handled Janine Brian's little slip very graciously,' Antonio commented after a moment or two.

She looked up at him with a pained expression. 'Thank you,' she said. 'But you're right in saying we can't expect people to avoid the subject of babies all the time. I have friends with little ones, and I have taught myself to enjoy visiting them, even babysitting them without envy.'

He looked down at her for a beat or two. 'That is very brave of you, Claire.'

She gave him another little grimace before she lowered her gaze to stare at his bow tie. 'Not really… There are days when it's very hard…you know…thinking about her…'

Antonio felt the bone-grinding ache of grief work its way through him; it often caught him off guard—more lately than ever. Being with Claire made him realise how much losing a child affected both parents, for years if not for ever. The mother bore the brunt of it, having carried the baby in her womb, not to mention having the disruption of her hormones during and after the delivery. But the father felt loss too, even if it wasn't always as obvious as the mother's. Certainly the father hadn't carried the child, but that didn't mean he didn't feel the devastation of having failed as a first-time father.

Antonio had grown up with an understanding of the traditional role of husband and father as being there to protect his wife and children. He might have gone into marriage a little ahead of schedule, due to the circumstances of Claire's accidental pregnancy, but when their baby had died it had cut at the very heart of him. He had felt so helpless, swamped with grief, but unable to express it for the mammoth weight of guilt that had come down on top of it.

He wondered if Claire knew how much he blamed himself, how he agonised over the 'what if' questions that plagued him in the dark hours of the night. He still had nightmares about arriving at the delivery suite to find her holding their stillborn baby in her arms. A part of him had shut down at that point, and try as he might he had never been able to turn it back on. He felt as if he had fallen into a deep, dark and silent well of despair, locked in a cycle of grief and guilt that to this day he carried like an ill-fitting harness upon his shoulders.

The music changed tempo, and even though she didn't say a word Antonio felt Claire's reluctance to stay on the dance floor with him. He could feel it in her body, the way she stiffened when he drew her close. Whether she was fighting him or fighting herself was something he had not yet decided. But then he had the rest of the night to do so, and do so he would.

He felt a rush of blood in his groin at the thought of sinking into her slick warmth again. The tight cocoon of her body had delighted him like no other. It made his skin come alive with sensation thinking about her hands skating over him the way they'd used to, tentatively, shyly, and then boldly once her confidence with him had grown. The feel of her soft mouth sucking on him that first time had been unbelievable. He had felt as if the top of his head was going to come off, so powerful had been his response. He wanted to feel it all again, every single bit of it—her touch, her taste, the tightness of her that made his body tingle for hours afterwards.

'Time to go home?' he asked as he linked his fingers with hers.

Her cheeks developed a hint of a blush. 'Yes…if you like…' she said, her gaze falling away from his.

Antonio led her back to the table, from where, after a few words of farewell to the other guests, he escorted her out to the waiting limousine. It would take them back to his hotel, where she would have to share his bed in his arms or spend the night alone on the sofa.

It would be interesting to see which she chose.

CHAPTER EIGHT

IT WAS a mostly silent trip on the way back to the hotel.

Antonio looked at Claire several times on the way, but each time she had her gaze averted, and her fingers were restless as they toyed with the catch of her evening purse.

'Do I unsettle you so much, *cara*?' he asked, as the car purred to a smooth halt outside the hotel.

She turned her gaze on him, a shadow of uncertainty shining in their ocean-blue and green depths. 'A little, I guess,' she confessed as he helped her out of the car.

Antonio led her into the hotel, his hand at her elbow, his stride matching her shorter one. He pressed the call button for the lift, and as he waited for it to come turned to look at her. 'I told you, Claire, we will not resume a physical relationship until we are both ready. I am not going to force myself on you. You can be absolutely sure of that.'

She rolled her lips together as she lifted and then dropped her gaze again. 'I'm not sure what I want... that's the problem...I feel confused right now...'

He tipped up her chin with the end of his index

finger. 'I want you,' he said. 'I think you know that. That is something that has not changed in the last five years.'

'But is this right…what we're doing?' she asked, the tip of her tongue sneaking out to sweep over her lips. 'It seems to me we're back together for all the wrong reasons.'

The lift came to a stop at Antonio's penthouse floor, and he held the doors open with his forearm for Claire to move past.

He swiped his key and led her into the suite, closing the door behind him. 'We have a past, Claire,' he said, securing her gaze with his. 'We have to deal with it one way or the other.'

She bit her bottom lip, her throat moving up and down over a little swallow. 'But is this the right way?' she asked. 'What if we make more problems than we've got now?'

'Like what?' he asked, pulling at his bow tie.

She gnawed at her lip again, releasing it after a second or two to say, 'I don't know…it's just I don't want any misunderstandings to develop between us.'

He tossed his bow tie and his jacket on the nearest sofa. 'The whole point of this exercise is to see if what we started out with is still there, hidden under the sediment of our separation,' he said heavily. 'I do not want to go through the messy process of a divorce only to take the same unresolved issues to another relationship.'

Claire felt her heart clamp with pain. 'So this arrangement you've orchestrated between us is basically an experiment?' she asked, frowning at him.

He held her look for a moment before he blew out a sigh. 'I want to get on with my life, Claire. You need to get on with yours. Neither of us can do that until we work through this.'

She pulled herself upright and faced him squarely. 'So what you're really saying is you need to have a three-month affair with me to see if there is anything worth picking over before you move on to the next woman you want to get involved with. Is that it?'

He gave her a brooding look. 'No, that is not it at all.'

Claire felt as if her hopes and dreams were about to be shattered all over again. Would she ever be anything more than a fill-in for him? Was it too much to ask him to care something for her?

Her rising despair made her voice come out sharper than she had intended. 'Then what the hell is it about, Antonio? I just don't know what you want from me.'

He took her gently but firmly by the shoulders, his dark eyes almost black as they pinned hers. 'I think deep down you know exactly what I want from you, *cara*,' he said and, swooping down, captured her mouth with the searing warmth of his.

Claire had no hope of resisting such a potently passionate kiss. Flames of need licked along her veins, sending her heart-rate soaring as Antonio's tongue probed for entry, the hot searching heat of him making her whimper in response. She could feel her lips swelling under the pressure of his, her body melting into his embrace as he pulled her closer. She felt the erotic ridge of his erection against her—a heady reminder of all the passion they had shared in the past and how earth-shattering it had been.

His mouth continued its sensual assault on her senses as his hands went from her waist to her lower back, the gentle pressure of his hand against her lumbar region bringing her right up against the hard probe of his arousal. Her belly quivered at that intimate contact, her legs becoming unsteady as a raging tide of desire flooded her being.

His kiss became deeper and more insistent, and Claire responded with the same ardour. She took his full bottom lip in her teeth, gently tugging, then sucking, and then sweeping her tongue over it in a caress that brought a groan from deep inside him.

His hands pressed her even harder against him; even the barrier of his clothes did not lessen the sensation of feeling the potent length of him so close to the heart of her need. Her body was already preparing itself; she could feel the slick moistness gathering between her thighs, her breasts tight and aching for the feel of his mouth and hands.

His kiss became even more urgent as she moulded herself against him, his tongue more insistent as it mated with hers.

She reached between them and shaped him with her fingers, her mouth still locked under the scorching heat of his. He made another guttural sound of pleasure, and she increased the pace of her stroking, up and down, glorying in the licence to touch him, to feel him pulsing with such intense longing for her.

He dragged his mouth from hers, looking down at her with eyes so dark with arousal they looked bottomless. 'Are you sure this is what you want, *cara*?' he asked in a husky tone. 'We do not have to continue with this if you do not feel ready.'

Claire moistened her passion-swollen lips as she held his gaze. 'I'm not sure about anything,' she said. 'I can't seem to put two thoughts together in my head when you are around.'

His wry smile was intoxicatingly sexy. 'Then maybe we should not think, but instead concentrate on feeling,' he said, moving his hand to the zipper at the back of her dress and slowly but surely sliding it down until the satin pooled at her feet.

Claire felt her breath catch as his dark gaze ran over her, taking in her naked breasts, the flat plane of her stomach, the slight flare of her hips and the tiny black lace panties she was wearing.

Her breathing almost stopped altogether when he trailed a fingertip down between her breasts, circling each one before he bent his head and took each tightly budded nipple in his mouth. It was torture and pleasure rolled into one, and the sparks of fiery need shooting up and down her spine at the rasp of his tongue made every rational thought fly out of her head.

He lifted his head and, locking his gaze on hers, sent his fingertip down to the cave of her belly button, and then lower, tracing over the cleft of her body through the lace that shielded her. 'Take them off,' he commanded in a toe-curling tone.

Claire kicked off her heels and peeled off the tiny lace garment, her heart kicking in excitement as he began to undress. Becoming impatient, she helped him with the buttons of his shirt, stopping every now and again to press a hot, moist kiss to his chest, then lower and lower, until she came to the waistband of his trousers.

He shrugged his shirt off and stood with his thighs slightly apart as she undid his belt, pulling it through the loops until it joined her dress on the floor.

She heard him draw in a breath as her fingers pulled down his zipper, and then she felt him jerk in awareness when she peeled back his underwear to touch him skin on skin.

He was like satin-covered steel under her fingertips, and so aroused he was seeping with moisture. She blotted it with her fingertip and then, lifting her eyes to his, brought her finger up to her mouth and sucked on it.

'*Dio*, you are driving me crazy,' he growled, as he heeled himself out of his shoes, his trousers and underwear landing in the same heap as his belt and her dress.

Claire drew in an uneven breath as he walked her backwards towards the bed, his hands on her hips, the heated trajectory of his body setting her alight all over again. She could smell his arousal, the hint of salt and musk that was as intoxicating as the notes of citrus she could pick up from his aftershave.

'Tell me to stop, Claire, otherwise I will not be able to,' he groaned as his mouth brushed against hers.

She linked her arms around his neck, pushing her pelvis against his. 'I don't want you to stop,' she said in a breathless whisper. 'It's been such a long time…'

'You are right about that,' he said as he eased her down on the bed, his eyes devouring her all over again before he joined her. 'It has been far, far too long.'

Claire shivered as his long, strong legs brushed against her smooth ones. The arrant maleness of him had always made her heart race with excitement. The hardness of his body against her dewy softness made her feel light-headed with anticipation. She arched her spine in invitation, aching for him to pin her body with his, to drive her towards the paradise she craved.

'Not so fast, *cara*,' he said, stroking his hands over her belly, thrillingly close to where she pulsed for him.

'You know how it was between us before. It was always much more intense when we took our time.'

Claire sucked in a breath as he bent his head to her breasts, his mouth and tongue inciting her passion to an almost unbearable level. The hot trail of his kisses continued down her sternum to the tiny dish of her belly button, and then over the faint stretchmarks on both of her hips, before moving to the throbbing core of her body. Her breath skidded to a halt in her chest as his fingers gently separated her, the tender, honeyed flesh opening to his stroking touch. He set a slow but tantalising rhythm, each movement bringing her closer and closer to the release she could feel building and building inside her. Then she was there: her back lifting off the bed, her senses soaring out of control, as wave after wave of ecstasy smashed over her, rolling her, tossing and tumbling her, until she felt totally boneless, limp with satiation.

Claire reached for him, her fingers circling his hardness before she slithered down to brush her mouth against him. She felt a shudder go through him when she traced him with the point of her tongue. He was still in control—but only just. His breathing was choppy and uneven, each and every one of his muscles taut with tension as she drew him into her mouth, tasting him, tantalising him with the butterfly caress of her tongue.

'No,' Antonio growled suddenly, and pulled her away. 'I want to come inside you. I have waited so long for this.'

Claire felt her insides tremble with excitement as his body settled over her, one of his thighs nudging hers apart, his weight propped up on his elbows as he drove into her with a deep groan of satisfaction. She felt the skin of his back and shoulders lift in a shiver as her body grabbed at him hungrily, the rocking motion he began setting her alight all over again. Electrifying sensations shot through her with each stroke and smooth glide of his body in hers. She felt the tremors begin deep inside her, the ripples of reaction rolling through her as he increased his pace, each deep thrust taking her higher and higher. She felt as if her body imploded, so forceful was the release he evoked. It rocketed through her like a torpedo, making every nerve hum and sing with sensation.

Antonio's breathing quickened, his thrusts now so deep and so purposeful Claire could feel the exact moment his control finally slipped. With a deep groan he burst inside her, his body shuddering against hers as pleasure coursed through him, her tight body milking him until he collapsed in satisfaction above her.

She kept stroking his back, her fingers dancing over his muscled form, hoping the magical spell of sensuality would not be broken too quickly.

Antonio was right: this was the part they had always got right. It was the other details of their relationship they had tripped over: the involvement of relatives, the demands of his career and the loss of her independence, not to mention the vicissitudes of life, which in their case had been particularly cruel.

Antonio shifted his weight to look down at her. 'It has not changed, has it, *cara*?' he said, brushing a damp curl back from her forehead. 'Although perhaps I am wrong about that; it *has* changed—if anything it has got better.'

Claire trembled under his touch, her body acutely aware of his, still lying encased moistly in hers. 'What if it's not enough, Antonio? Physical attraction will eventually burn itself out. Then what will be left?'

His eyes were dark as pitch as they held hers. 'It has not burned out yet, in spite of our five-year hiatus. As soon as I saw you again I realised it. I wanted you back in my bed no matter what it took to get you there.'

'This can't go anywhere,' she said, dropping her gaze from his in case he saw too much of what she was feeling. She was like a toy he had decided to play with for a limited time. She had to keep reminding herself this was not for ever. He was only here for three months.

'It can go where we want it to,' he said. 'For as long as we want it to.'

Claire felt a prickle of alarm run over her bare flesh as she brought her gaze back to his. 'I'm not sure what you're saying,' she said, flicking her tongue out over her lips. 'This is temporary…isn't it?'

His gaze went to her mouth, halted, and then lifted back to hers. 'Are you on the pill?' he asked.

Something dark and fast scuttled inside Claire's chest, making her feel breathless, as if the faceless creature of fear had buried itself in the chambers of her heart. 'Um…no…' she said, unable to hold his gaze.

He nudged her chin up with the point of his finger, his dark eyes drilling into hers. 'No?'

She rolled her lips together, trying to think where she was in her cycle. 'I'm not on it at the moment…' she said, grimacing slightly.

He kept his gaze steady on hers for several heart-chugging seconds. 'Do you think you are in a safe period?' he asked with an unreadable expression.

'Yes,' she said, even though she was not quite sure. It would be disastrous if she was to fall pregnant by him, setting off another heartbreaking cycle of waiting and hoping, and yet…

Oh, God, the thought of another chance at being a mother was so very tempting. Maybe this time it wouldn't end in tragedy, in spite of the information she had sought on the internet. She had learned that after a previous incident of placental abruption the chances of a second occurring was between ten and seventeen percent. The statistics stated that whereas one out of one hundred and fifty deliveries cited a case of placental separation, the severe form, where foetal death occurred, was only one in five hundred.

It was all a matter of chance…

'Are you sure?' Antonio asked, his gaze now darkened with intensity.

She nodded and eased herself away from him, hugging her knees to her chest to affect some measure of decency. 'But even if we had used a condom there's no guarantee it would have prevented a pregnancy,' she said. 'That's how it happened the last time, if you remember?'

'Yes, but only because you had not been taking the pill long enough for it to be effective,' he said.

Claire felt resentment rise up in her like a viper wanting to strike at its tormentor. 'So you're blaming me for what happened in the past, is that it? It was my fault for being so naïve in thinking I was covered when I wasn't? We would not have had to go through any of what we went through if I had taken the time to read the leaflet in the box? Is that what you are saying?'

A deep crevasse appeared between his brows. 'I did

not say that, Claire. An unplanned pregnancy can happen to anyone.'

She still felt herself bristling in spite of his response. 'Then what exactly *are* you saying?'

It seemed a long time before he answered. 'This is probably not the right time to bring up the subject of babies.'

Claire felt the faint hope she had secretly harboured in her chest deflate at his words. He was after a good time, not a long time. He was at a loose end in a foreign country. No wonder he had looked her up—hooked up with her in a blackmail bargain that would see him as the only winner at the end. He wanted no ties, no lasting consequences of their brief encounter. Just like last time he wanted a short, hot, full-on affair to compensate for the punishing hours he worked.

He also wanted revenge, she reminded herself. He wanted to have things on his terms this time. He would be the one to walk away, not her.

'I can't do this,' she said, springing off the bed to snatch up a bathrobe hanging on the back of the door. She thrust her arms through the sleeves and tied the waistband securely before she faced him again. 'I can't do casual, Antonio. I'm not built that way.'

'This is not casual, Claire,' he said, locking gazes with her. 'We are still married.'

She frowned at him, her heart fluttering in panic. 'What do you want from me?' she asked in a broken whisper.

'I want you, Claire,' he said with an intransigent look as he stepped towards her. 'This is not over. You know that. What happened in that bed just minutes ago proved it beyond any shadow of a doubt.'

Claire tried to back away from him but came up against the wall. 'What happened in that bed was a stupid mistake on my part,' she said, flattening her spine against the cold hard surface behind her. 'I got carried away with the dancing and the wine. I wasn't in my right mind. You should have known that.'

He lifted one brow in a perfect arc of derision. 'It seems to me it is only my fault when you do something you later regret,' he said.

'You're trying to make me fall in love with you, aren't you?' she asked.

He came closer, his eyes meshing with hers. 'Is that your biggest worry, *cara*?' he asked as he trailed his index finger down the curve of her cheek, before tracing over her top lip in a nerve-tingling caress.

Claire's biggest worry was how she was going to prevent a repeat of what had just occurred between them. The sex had been mind-blowing and blissfully satisfying. Even now she could feel her body responding again to his nearness. It didn't help that she was totally naked beneath the bathrobe she was wearing. She could feel the way her breasts were pushing against the soft fabric, her nipples still swollen and sensitive from his mouth. She could feel the moistness of his essence between her thighs. She could even smell the fragrance of their coupling—an intoxicating reminder of how she had fallen apart in his arms and how easily it could happen again. She was hard-wired to respond to him. No one else could affect her the way he did. The intimacy they had shared had only intensified her longing. She could feel it building in her; it was like an on-off pulse deep inside.

She was acutely aware of how he was watching her,

with that dark, intelligent gaze of his, noting every nuance of her expression, every movement of her body as it stood so close to his.

He placed his hands either side of her head, on the wall behind her, not just trapping her with the brackets of his arms but with his eyes as well. 'Would falling in love with me be a problem?' he asked.

Claire ran the tip of her tongue over her lips, her chest rising and falling on an uneven breath as she looked into his deep dark gaze. 'It…it would only be a problem if it wasn't reciprocated.'

His eyes went to her mouth. 'If we fall in love then we will not need to go through a divorce,' he said, bringing his gaze back to hers. 'A good solution, *si*?'

She tightened her mouth. 'For you, maybe, but not for me,' she said. 'I'm not going to move back to Italy with you.'

He measured her with a cool, appraising look. 'You might not have a choice if you have conceived my child,' he said. 'I am not prepared to be separated by thousands of kilometres from my own flesh and blood.'

Claire felt her heart lurch, panic fluttering like startled wings inside her chest. 'If I have fallen pregnant there is no guarantee it will end in a live birth,' she said, trying to ignore the blade of pain that sliced through her at admitting it out loud. 'If you want to become a father you would be well advised to pick someone who is capable of doing the job properly.'

His eyes held hers for a tense moment before he dropped his hands from the wall. 'I am aware of the statistics, Claire,' he said. 'But with careful monitoring it may not happen again.'

'I am not prepared to risk it,' Claire said. 'If we are going to continue this farcical arrangement I want you to use protection. I will see my doctor tomorrow about arranging my own.'

Antonio watched as she pushed herself away from the wall, her arms around her middle like a shield, her eyes flashing resentment and pent-up anger against him.

He could still feel the tight clutch of her body around him, the way she had convulsed to receive every drop of his seed. He wanted her so badly it was a bone-deep ache inside him; it had never gone away, no matter how hard he had tried to ignore it. And she wanted him, even though she resented it and did her best to hide it. Her body betrayed her just as his had. And it would betray her again. Of that he was sure.

CHAPTER NINE

CLAIRE slipped past Antonio to the plush bathroom and closed the door firmly behind her. She considered locking it, but upon inspecting the device recognised it was one of those two-way models which could be unlocked from either side of the door—no doubt installed as a safety feature, in case a guest in the hotel slipped and fell in the bathroom. She realised the only lock she really needed was a lock on her heart, but as far as she knew no such item existed. She was as vulnerable to Antonio as she had ever been—maybe even more so now she had experienced such rapture again in his arms.

She stepped into the shower stall, hoping to wash away the tingling sensations Antonio's touch had activated, but if anything the fine needle spray of the shower only made it worse. Her whole body felt as if every nerve beneath her skin had risen to the surface. Every pore was swollen and excited at the anticipation of the stroke and glide of his hands, the commandeering of his mouth. She touched her breasts. They felt full and heavier than normal, and her nipples were still tightly budded, the brownish discs of her areolae aching all over again for the sweep and suck of his mouth.

Her hands went lower, over the flat plane of her belly and down to the cleft of her body where he had so recently been. She felt tender and swollen, still acutely sensitive, the intricate network of nerves still humming with the sensations Antonio had evoked.

She turned the water off and reached for a fluffy white towel. But even after she was dried off and smothered all over with the delicately fragrant body lotion provided, she felt the tumultuous need for fulfilment racing through her body.

The hotel suite was large, but it only contained one bed—and Claire knew she would be expected to share it with Antonio. Because of their history, she also knew there would be no demarcation line drawn down the middle of the mattress.

Antonio was a sprawler. She knew there would be no hope of avoiding a brush with a hair-roughened limb or two. It would be a form of torture, trying to ignore his presence. If it was anything like in the past he would reach for her, drawing her close to him, like two spoons in a drawer, his erection swelling against her until she opened her thighs to receive him as she had done so many times before.

Her mind began to race with erotic images of how he had taken her that way: the breathing of him against her ear as he plunged into her wetness, the pace of their lovemaking sped up by its primal nature, the explosion of feeling that would make her cry out and make him grunt and groan as each wave of ecstasy washed over them, leaving them spent, tossed up like flotsam on the shore.

Claire exchanged the towel for the bathrobe and, tying the belt securely around her waist, took a steadying breath and opened the door back into the suite.

Antonio was sitting with his ankles crossed, a glass of something amber-coloured in his hand. 'Can I get you a drink, Claire? You look as if you need something to help you relax.'

She gave him a brittle glance. 'The last thing I need is something that will skew my judgement,' she said. 'What I need is a good night's sleep—preferably alone.'

His mouth tilted at a dangerously sexy angle. 'There is only one bed, *tesoro mio*. We can fight over it, if you like, but I already know who will win.'

Claire knew too. That was why she wasn't even going to enter into the debate. She eyed the sofa. It looked long enough to accommodate her, and certainly comfortable enough. She would make do. She would *have* to make do—even if it meant twice-weekly trips to a physiotherapist to realign her neck and back as a result.

Antonio got to his feet in a single fluid movement. 'Do not even think about it, Claire,' he said, placing his drink down with a clink of glass against the marbled surface. 'Our reconciliation will not be taken seriously if the hotel cleaning staff come in each day and see we have not been sleeping in the same bed.'

Claire fisted her hands by her sides and glared at him. 'I don't want to sleep with you.'

He gave her an indolent smile. 'Sleeping is not the problem, though—is it, *cara*?' he asked. 'We could sleep in the same bed for weeks on end if we were anyone other than who we are. Our bodies recognise each other. That is the issue we have to address in sharing a bed: whether we are going to act on that recognition or try to ignore it. My guess is it will continue to prove impossible to ignore.'

I can ignore it, Claire decided—although with perhaps not quite the conviction she would have liked, given what had occurred less than an hour ago.

Antonio pulled back the covers on the bed. 'I will leave you to get settled,' he said. 'I am going to have a shower.'

She clutched the edges of the bathrobe tightly against her chest. 'Do you expect me to stay awake for you—to be ready to entertain you when you get back?' she snipped at him.

He smoothed the turned-back edges of the sheet before he faced her. 'I expect no such thing, *cara*,' he said. 'You are tired and quite clearly overwrought. Perhaps you are right. I should not have taken advantage of your generous response to my attentions. I thought we both wanted the same thing, but in hindsight perhaps I misjudged the situation. If so, I am sorry.'

Claire captured her bottom lip, chewing at it in agitation. He made it sound as if he had ravished her without her consent, when nothing had been further from the truth. She had practically ripped the clothes off his body in her haste to have him make love to her. She had been as out of control as he had, her need for him like an unstoppable force—a force she could still feel straining at the leash of common sense inside her, waiting for its moment to break free and wreak havoc all over again.

'It's not your fault...' The words slipped out in a breathless rush. 'I shouldn't have allowed things to go so far. I don't know why I did. I don't think it was the wine or the dancing...it was just...curiosity... I think...'

His brows arched upwards again. 'Curiosity?'

Her tongue darted over the surface of her lips, her gaze momentarily skittering away from his. 'I guess, like you, I wanted to know if it would be the same…you know…as it had been before…before things went wrong…'

He came closer and, using his finger, brought up her chin so her eyes met his once more. 'We cannot change what happened,' he said. 'Our past is always going to be there, whether we continue our association or not. We will both carry it with us wherever we go in the future, and whoever shares our future will have to learn to accept it as part of who we are.'

Her eyes misted over. 'Hold me, Antonio,' she whispered as her arms snaked around his middle. 'Hold me and make me forget.'

Antonio held her close, lowering his chin to the top of her silky head, breathing in the freshly showered flowery fragrance of her as his body stirred against her. He wanted her again, but he was conscious that this time her need for him was motivated by a desire for solace, not sensual fulfilment. He closed his eyes and listened to her breathing, feeling the slight rise and fall of her chest against his, every part of him aching to press her down on the bed and possess her all over again.

He'd had to rein in such impulses before. In the weeks following the loss of their baby he had thought the best way to help her heal would be to mesh his body with hers again—to bring it back to life, to start again, to reignite the passion that had flared so readily from the moment they had met. But she had been so cold, so chillingly angry, as if he had deliberately orchestrated the demise of their daughter. Her reaction had been like an IV line plugged into the bulging vein of his guilt, hydrating it, feeding it, until it had flowed through every pore of his body, poisoning him until he finally gave up.

Antonio stroked the back of her hair, the bounce of her curls against his fingers making the task of holding her at bay all the more difficult. She was crying softly, so softly he would not have known it except for feeling the dampness of her tears against his bare chest. He was used to tears. How many patients had fallen apart in his consulting rooms over the years? Time and time again he had handed them tissues and spoken the words and phrases he'd hoped would make the burden they faced a little easier to bear. And most times it had worked. But it hadn't worked with Claire. Not one word he had spoken had changed anything.

He knew his feelings were undergoing a subtle change, but he wasn't ready to examine them too closely. He had been trained to see things from a clinical perspective. He had seen for himself how often emotions got in the way, complicating the decision-making process. What he needed was a clear head to negotiate his way through the next few months.

Divorce was a dirty word just now. It had always been a dirty word in his family. His parents were of the old school, their religious beliefs insisting on marriage being 'until death do us part'. His father's will might easily have been remade in the years since Claire had left, but Salvatore had done nothing. Antonio had told himself it was a simple oversight—like a lot of people his father hadn't expected to die so soon—but he wondered if there had been more to it than that.

Antonio hadn't been particularly close to either of his

parents since late adolescence. His desire to be a surgeon had not been met with the greatest enthusiasm, and he had subsequently felt as if he had let them down in some way, by not living the life they had mapped out for him. He had been assured of their love growing up, and certainly they had done everything possible to support him during his long years of study, but the chasm that divided them seemed to get bigger as each year passed.

His father had only once spoken to him about Claire's desertion. Antonio had still been too raw from it all; he had resented the intrusion into his personal life, and after a heated exchange which had caused months of bitter stonewalling between them eventually his father had apologised and the subject had never been raised again. His mother too had remained tight-lipped. Over the last five years he could not recall a single time when she had mentioned Claire's name in his presence.

Looking back now, he realised he had not handled things well. He had allowed his anger and injured pride over Claire leaving him to blur his judgement. He had been so incensed by her accusation of him having an affair that he hadn't stopped to think why she had felt so deeply insecure, and what he had done or not done to add to those feelings. He had believed her to be looking for a way out of their relationship, and he had done nothing to stop her when she took the first exit.

Antonio put her from him with gentle hands. 'Go to bed, Claire,' he said. 'I will sleep on the sofa tonight.'

She looked up at him, her eyes still glistening and moist. 'I don't want to be alone right now,' she said, so softly he could barely hear it.

His hands tightened on her shoulders. 'Are you sure?'

She nodded, her teeth sinking into her bottom lip. 'Please, Antonio, don't leave me alone tonight. I just couldn't bear it.'

Antonio sighed and slid his hands down the length of her arms, his fingers encircling her wrists. 'You make it so hard to say no, Claire,' he said, looking down at the faint marks he had left on her tender skin. 'Everything about you makes it hard to say no.'

She placed her hands on his chest, looking up at him with luminous eyes. 'I want to forget about the past,' she said. 'You are the only person who can make me forget. Make me forget, Antonio.'

He brought his mouth down to hers in a kiss that was soft and achingly tender. The pressure of his lips on hers was light at first, gently exploring the contours of her mouth. He took his time, stroking her lips until they flowered open on a little sigh. His tongue danced just out of reach of hers, tantalising her, drawing her to him, challenging her to meet him in an explosive connection.

Claire could not resist the assault on her senses; her tongue darted into his mouth, found his and tangled with it boldly, while her lower body caught fire against the hard pressure of his holding her against him. She felt the swollen ridge of his erection through the thin barrier of the boxer shorts he had slipped on earlier. Her hand went down, cupping him through the satin, relishing the deep groan he gave as her fingers outlined his length. She felt his breathing quicken, and slowly but surely lowered the shorts until she was touching him skin on skin, her fingers circling him. Delighted with the way he was pulsing with longing against her, she began to slide her fingers up and down, slowly at first, knowing it would have him begging in seconds—and it did.

He growled against her passion-swollen mouth. 'Please, *cara*, do not torture me.'

She smiled against his lips—a sensual woman's smile, not a shy young girl's. 'You want me to go faster?' she asked huskily.

He nipped at her bottom lip once, twice, three times. 'I think you know what I want, *tesoro mio*. You seem to always know what I want.'

Claire left the bathrobe slip from her shoulders, her eyes watching his flare as he drank in the sight of her naked. His gaze felt like a brand on her flesh; each intimate place it rested felt hot and tingling. Her breasts swung freely as she pushed him back onto the bed, coming over him like a cat on all fours, pausing here and there to lick him, her belly quivering with desire as, each time her mouth came into contact with his flesh, he gave a little jerk of response. His hands bunched against the sheets as she came closer and closer to the hot, hard heat of him. She took her time, each movement drawn out to maximise his pleasure. A little kiss here, a little bite there, a sweep of her tongue on the sharp edge of his hip before she nipped at him with her teeth, each touch of her mouth making his back arch off the bed and a gasping groan came from his lips.

Claire had dreamt of this moment over the years. Alone in her bed, miserably unhappy and unfulfilled, she had dreamed of being with Antonio again, having him throbbing with need for her and only her, just as he was doing now. He was close to losing control. She could sense it in every taut muscle she touched with her hands or lips or tongue. But she still hadn't got to the *pièce de résistance* in her sensual repertoire.

She met his eyes; his were smoky, burning with expectation, totally focussed on her. 'If you want me to beg, then keep doing what you are doing,' he said between ragged breaths. 'But be warned, there will be consequences.'

She gave him a devil-may-care look as she moved down his body with a slithering action. 'I can hardly wait,' she breathed, and bent to the task at hand.

Claire sent her tongue over him first, in a light, cat-like lick that barely touched the satin of his strained flesh. But it was enough to arch his spine. She did it again, stronger this time, from the base to the moist tip, her tongue circling him before she took him in her mouth.

He shuddered at the first smooth suck, his hands going to her head, his fingers digging into her curls, as if to ride out the storm of feeling she was evoking.

Claire tasted his essence, drawing on him all the harder, delighting in the way she was affecting him. She could hear his breathing becoming increasingly rapid, the tension in his muscles like cords of steel as he flirted with the danger of finally letting go.

In the end Claire gave him no choice. She intensified her caresses. Even when he made a vain attempt to pull away she counteracted it, pushing his hand aside as she drew on him all the more vigorously. She heard him snatch in a harsh-sounding breath, his fingers almost painful at they held on to her hair for purchase. He exploded in three short sharp bursts, his body shuddering through it, his chest rising and falling, his face contorted with pleasure as the final waves washed through him.

Claire sat back, a little shocked at how wanton she had been, when only minutes before she had been insisting she was not going to share a bed with him. She had shared much more than a bed now, she realised. The act she had just engaged in was probably the most intimate of all between couples.

She could still remember the first time she had done it. She had been shy and hesitant, wondering if somehow it was wrong, but Antonio had coached her through it with patience, all the time holding back his passion until she had felt comfortable enough to complete the act. It had taken a few tries, but he hadn't seemed to mind. And besides, he had done the same to her—many times. The first time he had placed his mouth on the secret heart of her she had nearly leapt off the bed in reaction, so intense had been the feelings. But over time she had learned to relax into the caress of his lips and tongue, forgetting her shyness and simply enjoying his worship of her body demonstrated time and time again.

Antonio pushed her gently back down on the pillows, his ink-black eyes meshing with hers. 'I owe you,' he said.

Claire felt her belly quiver like unset custard. 'I feel like a hypocrite,' she confessed.

'Why is that?' he asked as he brushed his mouth over her right breast.

She pulled in a sharp breath as her nipple tightened. 'I told you I didn't want to sleep with you, but that is clearly not the case—given what just happened.'

'So, who is sleeping?' he asked, looking at her with a smouldering look.

She began to gnaw at her bottom lip again, her brow furrowing.

'Hey,' he said, stroking her lip with the tip of his index finger. 'Stop doing that. You will make yourself bleed.'

Claire ran her tongue over her lips and encountered his finger. The contact was so erotic she felt a tug deep inside her abdomen.

He was giving her that look—the look that meant she was not going to go to sleep tonight without experiencing the cataclysmic release he had planned for her in return for what she had done to him.

'Lie back,' he commanded deeply.

Claire shivered as she eased back down on the mattress. Her nakedness would barely even have registered in her consciousness if it hadn't been for his searing gaze, drinking all of her in. She saw the way his eyes focussed on her breasts, the way his gaze moved down over her belly to where the triangle of her womanhood was barely concealed by the tiny landing strip of dark, closely cropped curls. It was as close to a Brazilian wax as her pain centres had allowed on her last beauty salon visit, but now she wished she had gone the whole distance. She wanted to please him, to surprise him, to show him she was no longer an innocent girl from the Australian Outback, starstruck by his good looks and status. She was a woman now—a woman who knew what she wanted. And what she wanted was him.

If it was only going to be for three months then she would settle for that. She had dealt with loss before and survived. She had made the mistake of living in the past too long. It was well and truly time to move on, to live in the moment as so many of her peers did. They didn't worry about a few weeks of pleasure with a casual lover. They didn't agonise over whether or not they should sleep with a man they were seriously attracted to. They just did it and enjoyed every minute of it.

Claire's life, on the other hand, had become an anachronism; she had locked herself away in a time warp, not moving on with the times, not dealing with the past, stuck in a blank sort of limbo where her true feelings were papered over most of the time—until Antonio Marcolini had reappeared in her life and turned her world upside down and inside out.

From that first moment when she had heard his voice speak her name on the phone everything had changed. The feelings she had tried to squash had risen to the surface. They were bubbling even now, like volcanic mud, great big blobs of feeling, spluttering, popping with blistering heat, unpredictable, driven by forces outside of her control.

He kissed her mouth lingeringly, deeply and passionately, leaving her in a state of mindless, boneless need. Desire rippled through her as his tongue brushed against hers, calling hers into a sensual duel that left her gasping for more and more of his touch.

He moved his way down to each of her breasts, shaping them, moulding them with the warm broad palms of his hands, before taking each puckered nipple into his mouth. He rolled his tongue over the aching points in a circular motion, before sucking on them, his hot, wet mouth a delicious torture of feeling, sending shooting sparks of reaction to the very core of her being.

'You have such beautiful breasts,' he murmured as he trailed his mouth down to her belly button, circling it with the tip of his tongue. 'Everything about you is beautiful.'

Claire melted under the heat of his words. She had always considered herself an average-looking girl—not ugly, not supermodel material, but somewhere in between. Antonio made her feel as if she was the most gorgeous woman he had ever laid eyes on.

When he separated her tender folds with his fingers she flinched in response. 'Relax, *cara*,' he said softly. 'We have done this many times in the past, *si*?'

She still squirmed a little, her muscles tensing in spite of how gentle he was. 'I'm sorry,' she said on a scratchy breath. 'I'm not sure I can…'

'Do not be sorry, *tesoro mio*,' he said, stroking her inner thighs. 'We can take our time.'

Claire felt her heart swell. He was being so patient with her, just as he had been when they had first met. She had been reticent then, shy and uncertain of how to receive pleasure in such an intimate way, but he had patiently tutored every sensory nerve in her body, bringing every secret part of her to earth-shattering life.

After a moment she began to relax under the gentle caress of his hands. The movements against her smooth skin were slow but sure. It became increasingly obvious to her that he recalled all her pleasure spots. He knew just where to touch, how hard, how soft, how fast and how slow. She felt her body respond with small flutters beneath her skin to begin with, and then, as he stroked against her moist cleft, a wave began to build, higher and higher, gathering momentum, until that final moment when he brushed against the swollen pearl of her arousal again and again, in a soft flickering motion, triggering an orgasm so intense she gasped out in shocked surprise and wonder, her hands clutching at him as she rode out the storm of tumultuous feeling.

When she had calmed, Antonio tucked a springy chestnut curl of her hair behind the shell of her ear, his fingers lingering over the curve of her cheek. She looked so beautiful lying there, her dark lashes like tiny fans over her eyes, her breathing still hectic, her mouth still swollen and blood-red from his kisses.

Would he ever get enough of her to be able to let her go for good? he wondered. Was that why he hadn't pressed for a divorce? Was that why he had let things slide, putting his life on hold in a subconscious hope she would one day return to him? He had used her brother as a tool to get her back in his bed, but now he felt as if he had short-changed himself in some way. She was only with him now because she'd believed she had no choice. Once she realised how much she stood to gain if they were to divorce, would she use it against him in an act of revenge?

He drew her closer into his embrace, his body aching to have her again, but she was drifting off to sleep and he would have to wait. Then he felt her hand reach for him, her soft sigh of satisfaction at finding him hard and pulsing making him snatch in a breath of anticipation. He closed his eyes as she worked her magic on him, every sensitive nerve responding to her touch. He let her carry on for as long as he dared before he pulled her hand away and flipped her on to her back, driving into her warmth so deeply she clutched at him to steady his pace.

'I am sorry,' he said, instantly stilling his movements. 'Have I hurt you?'

'No,' she said, kissing his mouth in little feather-like kisses. 'You just took me by surprise, that's all.'

Antonio smiled against the press of her mouth. 'You took me by surprise too, *cara*,' he said, slowly building his rhythm until she was quivering in his arms.

He closed his eyes and felt himself lift off, the convulsions of her body triggering his own release, making him realise again how much he had missed her and how he would do anything to keep her right where he had her.

In his arms, in his bed, for as long as he could.

CHAPTER TEN

CLAIRE could feel the pain ripping through her, the stomping march of each contraction tearing apart her abdomen. She clutched at her stomach, her eyes springing open when she realised it was flat, not distended.

Sweat was pouring off her—tiny, fast-running rivulets coursing down between her heaving breasts—and the darkness of the strange bedroom only added to her sense of disorientation and deep-seated panic.

'Claire?' Antonio's deep voice came out of the thick cloak of darkness, and she felt the mattress beside her shift as he reached for the bedside lamp.

The muted glow was of some comfort, but Claire could still feel her heart thumping so heavily she was sure it would burst out of her ribcage. She held her hands against her breasts, just to make sure, her breathing coming in choking gasps.

'I…I had a bad dream…' she said through still trembling lips. 'A nightmare…'

Antonio frowned and, hauling himself into a sitting position, reached for her, gathering her close. 'Do you want to talk about it?' he asked against the fragrant silk of her hair.

She shook her head against his chest.

He began stroking the back of her head, her unruly curls tickling his palm. 'Dreams are not real, *cara*,' he said. 'It is just the brain processing a thousand images or more into some sense of order. Some of it makes sense; a lot of it does not. Dreams are not prophetic; they are just the workings of our deep unconscious at rest.'

She pulled back from him and looked into his eyes, hers wide with anguish. 'It's not the first time it's happened,' she said. 'I feel like she's crying out to me. I *hear* her, Antonio. I sometimes hear her crying for me, but I can't get to her.'

Antonio felt his throat thicken. Five years on and he knew exactly what Claire meant. He could fill his days and even his nights with totally mind-consuming work, and yet in those eerie, unguarded moments, late at night or in the early hours of the morning, he could hear her too. A soft mewing cry that ripped at his guts and left them raw and bleeding.

'I'm sorry…' Claire's soft voice penetrated the silence. 'I'm keeping you awake, and you probably have another big theatre list tomorrow.'

He continued stroking her hair. 'Try and go back to sleep, *cara*,' he said. 'I am used to sleepless nights. It is part of my job.'

After a while Antonio heard the deep and even sound of her breathing, but he didn't move her out of his arms. She had her head nestled against his chest, and his left arm was almost completely numb from the press of her slim body, but he didn't dislodge it or her. He lay staring blankly at the ceiling, his fingers still playing with her hair, his heart feeling as if a heavy weight was pressed down upon it.

It wouldn't take her long to realise he had never had any intention of pressing charges against Isaac. Once Claire knew she no longer had a compelling reason to stay with him as his wife, he would have to think of some other way of keeping her chained to his side. Not because of his father's will, not even because of the money she had taken from his mother, but because he wanted to wake up each morning just like this, with her warm and soft against him.

When Claire woke to find she was alone in Antonio's bed she felt a wave of disappointment wash over her. She wasn't sure what she had been expecting. Breakfast in bed with an avowal of love and red roses on the side was the stuff of dreams; it had no relevance to their current set-up.

She flung the covers back and got up, wincing as her inner muscles protested at the movement. It gave her a fluttery, excited sort of feeling inside to remember how passionately they had made love.

Had sex, she corrected herself. This was not about love—at least not from Antonio's point of view. This was about a physical attraction that had suddenly resurfaced.

Claire turned on the shower, a frown pulling at her forehead as she waited for the temperature to adjust.

Yes, but *why* had his attraction for her suddenly resurfaced? He had not sought her out until she had tried to serve those divorce papers on him. And by returning to live with him she had postponed any prospect of a divorce being processed smoothly. This reconciliation was not about working through the issues of the past; this was about a very rich man who did not want his inheritance cut straight down the middle. He could very well string her along indefinitely; she had already demonstrated to him how easily she could be won over. She cringed at how she had responded so freely to him the night before. She hadn't lasted twenty-four hours in his company without caving in to her need of him. How he must have gloated over her ready capitulation. She might even now be pregnant. She would have that whole heartache to go through again—tied to him for the sake of a child, never knowing if he wanted her for her, or for what she could give him.

When she had showered and dressed she found the note he had written next to the tea-making facilities in the suite, informing her he had an early list at one of the large teaching hospitals and would see her for a late dinner at around eight to eight-thirty that evening. There were no words of affection, no *I love you and can't wait to see you* phrases—nothing for her to hang her hopes on. She crumpled the note and tossed it in the bin, annoyed with herself for wishing and hoping for what she couldn't have.

Downstairs in the car park a few minutes later, Claire hoisted her handbag over her shoulder and narrowed her gaze at the parking attendant. 'What do you mean, this is *my* car?' she asked.

The parking valet smiled and handed her a silver embossed keyring. 'It is, Mrs Marcolini,' he said. 'Your husband had it delivered late yesterday. If you would like me to go through all the features with you, I would be happy to explain them—'

Claire plucked the keys from his hand. 'That will not be necessary,' she said with a proud hitch of her chin. 'A car is a car. I am sure I will be able to work out where the throttle and the brakes are.'

'Yes, but—'

She gave the young man a quelling look over her shoulder as she got behind the wheel. She took a moment to orientate herself. The new-car smell was a little off-putting—not to mention the butter-soft leather of the seats. Then there was the dashboard, with all its lights and gadgets, which looked as if it had been modelled on the latest space shuttle from NASA. Maybe she had been a little hasty in sending the helpful assistant on his way, she thought ruefully. After her old and battered jalopy, this car looked as if it needed a rocket scientist to set it in gear, let alone start it.

She took a deep breath and inserted the key that didn't even look like a key into the ignition. The car started with a gentle purr of the engine, its side mirrors opening outwards as if by magic, and the seatbelt light flashing to remind her to belt up.

'All right, already,' Claire muttered, and strapped herself in with a click.

OK, so where was the handbrake? It wasn't in between the driver and passenger seats, so where the hell was it?

The parking valet tapped on the window. Claire pursed her lips and hunted for the mechanism to lower the window, locking all the doors and popping the boot open before she finally located the button with the little window symbol on it.

'There's a foot brake on the left,' the man said with

a deadpan expression. 'And the release is that button on the right, marked brake release.'

Claire mentally rolled her eyes. 'Thank you,' she said, stiff with embarrassment. 'Have a nice day.'

The valet smiled and stepped well back. 'Have a nice drive.'

'Oh, my God.' Rebecca's eyes ran over the showroom-perfect gunmetal-grey of the vehicle Claire had parked outside the salon. 'You're driving a sports car?'

Claire dumped her handbag on the counter and sent her hand through her disordered curls. 'Yes, well, you *could* call it driving, I suppose,' she said wryly. 'Not that I had to do too much. The slightest spot of drizzle has the windscreen wipers coming on without me having to leaf through the manual to locate the appropriate switch. Apparently there's some sort of sensor that detects moisture. Going through the city tunnel, the headlights came on automatically—and turned off again once I was back out in daylight. And just now, parking between that florist's van and that utility, all I had to do was listen to the beeps and watch the flashing red lights as the parking assist device told me when I was getting too close.'

Rebecca let out a whistling stream of air through her teeth. 'Gosh, I wish *my* estranged husband would buy me a sports car. All he has given me so far is a lawyer's bill for the division of assets, most of which *I* own, since I was the only one with a full-time job the whole time we were together.'

Claire hid her scowl as she shrugged herself out of her coat and hung it on a hook in the back room. Rebecca was right. She shouldn't really be complaining about such a generous gift. Most women would be falling over themselves to have been given such a luxurious vehicle. Besides, Antonio had openly expressed his concern over her driving a less than roadworthy car. She didn't fool herself his concerns were for her safety, it was his reputation he was most concerned about—he had said as much at the time. But wouldn't it be wonderful if he had done it out of love for her? Money was no object for him, it never had been, so how could he know what such a gift would mean to her if the right motives had been behind it?

'You have a full list of clients today,' Rebecca said, when Claire came out of the back room into the salon. 'It seems everyone wants to be styled by the woman who has stolen the heart of Antonio Marcolini, celebrity surgeon *extraordinaire*.'

Claire organised her cutting and styling trolley with meticulous care. 'He's just a normal man, Bex,' she said, keeping her gaze averted. 'He brushes his teeth and shaves every morning, just like most other men.'

'So what's it like being back with him?' Rebecca asked. 'I read in the paper you've moved into his hotel suite with him.'

Claire lined up her radial brushes with studious precision. 'That's because my flat is too small. He is used to living in the lap of luxury. A one-bedroom flat in a tawdry inner-city suburb is hardly his scene. Moving in with him seemed the best option—for the time being, at least.'

'Have you done the deed with him yet?'

Claire couldn't control the hot flush of colour in her cheeks. In fact she could feel her whole body heating up at the memory of what she had done to him and what he had done to her.

'Bex, don't ask me questions like that,' she said, frowning heavily. 'There are some things even best mates have to keep private.'

Rebecca perched on the nearest stool and crossed her booted ankles. 'So that's a yes,' she said musingly. 'I thought as much. As soon as he came in here I knew you were a goner. He's hardly the sort of man you could say no to, is he?'

Claire put on her most severe schoolmistress sort of frown. 'This is just a trial reconciliation between us,' she said. 'Nothing has been decided in the long term. Just because he bought me a car it doesn't mean he wants me back for ever. For all I know it could be a consolation prize for when he hotfoots it back to Italy without me.'

Rebecca's forehead creased. 'But I thought you were still in love with him,' she said. 'You are, aren't you? Don't shatter all my romantic delusions, Claire. I'm counting on you to get me back into the dating pool with hope not despair as my personal floating device.'

Claire decided to come clean. 'It's a farce, Bex,' she said on an expelled breath. 'I'm not really back with Antonio. Not in the real sense.'

Rebecca narrowed her gaze. 'But you've all but admitted you slept with him,' she said. 'If that isn't being back together, what is? And what about that kiss in here yesterday, huh? That looked pretty full-on and genuine to me.'

'He's only here for three months,' Claire said flatly. 'There's no way I would go back to Italy with him unless I was absolutely sure he cared something for me, and quite frankly I can't see that happening. He's not the "I love you" type. I had his baby, for God's sake, and he never once said how he felt about me. Doesn't that tell you something?'

Rebecca grimaced. 'I guess when you put it like that…'

Claire blew out a breath. 'His father is dead. He died just a couple of months ago. I have reason to believe that is why Antonio is here now—not just to do the lecture tour, but to see what gives where I am concerned.'

'So what does give?' Rebecca asked with a pointed look.

Claire looked away and started realigning her brushes again, even though they were all neatly spaced on the trolley. 'I'm not sure,' she said, fiddling with a teasing comb, running her fingers across its pointed teeth, the movement making a slight humming noise. 'A divorce has always been on the cards. For all this time I have been waiting for him to make the first move, but he didn't. I decided to take matters into my own hands once I heard he was coming here, but now I wish I had let sleeping dogs lie.'

'Have you ever asked yourself *why* he never asked you for a divorce?' Rebecca asked after a small pause.

Claire continued to turn the comb over in her hands. 'What happened back then was…' She stopped for a moment, thinking about why Antonio had not sought his freedom as soon as he could. If he *had* been involved with Daniela Garza, why wouldn't he have activated a divorce as soon as possible, so he could be with the woman he wanted to be with? Everything pointed to Claire having got it horribly wrong about him. It didn't sit well with her to be in the guilty seat—that was the position she had always assigned *him*.

'Or, more to the point, have you ever asked yourself why you didn't divorce him?' Rebecca added.

Claire let out her breath on a sigh. 'I think you have probably guessed why.'

Rebecca gave her a look. 'So you *do* still love him? I sort of guessed you did. It's the way you say his name and the look you get in your eyes.'

Claire dropped the comb back on the trolley. 'All this time I've been fooling myself I hate him, but I don't. I love him. I have always loved him. I was so convinced he'd been having an affair, but he's always denied it.'

'Yeah, well, men do that, you know.'

Claire chewed at her lip. 'I don't know… Antonio is a good man, Bex. He does a lot of charitable work all over the globe. The more I think about it the more I start to doubt myself. What if I made a terrible mistake? What if he wasn't having an affair? What if he's been telling the truth the whole time? What have I done?'

'Claire, lots of marriages survive an affair, or even the suspicion of one,' Rebecca said. 'If he had one it must be well and truly over now—otherwise he wouldn't be with you, trying to sort things out. Give him a chance. You love him. Isn't that all that matters?'

'I'm not sure if he will ever feel anything for me,' Claire said. 'You can't exactly force someone to fall in love with you. If it happens, it happens.'

Rebecca raised her brows and flicked her gaze to the shiny new car outside. 'Listen, honey, any man who buys a woman a car like that must feel something for her. Just go with the flow for a while. Stop agonising over what you haven't got and enjoy what you have got. Some men are just not able to put their feelings into words; it's their actions you have to listen to.'

Claire glanced back at the car outside and sighed. How she wished Rebecca was right—that Antonio was showing her, not telling her how he felt. But then she remembered how much was at stake for him if they were to divorce. Was the car part of the buttering-up process, to keep her sweet when it came to finally putting an end to their relationship?

'Oh, I almost forgot,' Rebecca said. 'Your mother called. She said she'd left a couple of messages on your mobile but you hadn't got back to her. I think she's a bit hurt you didn't call her about getting back with Antonio. Like everyone else, she read about it in the paper.'

Claire grimaced. 'I turned my phone to silent. I forgot to change it back. Oh, God, what am I going to say to her?'

'Tell her the truth,' Rebecca said. 'Tell her you love Antonio and are working at rebuilding your marriage. She's your mum, Claire. All she wants is for you to be happy.'

Claire wanted it too—so much that it hurt. But her happiness was dependent on securing Antonio's love, and unfortunately that was not in her hands.

Maybe Rebecca was right; she needed to learn to go with the flow, to enjoy what she had for as long as it was there to be had. Antonio might have had less than noble motives for bringing about their reconciliation, but perhaps this window of time was her chance to show him how much she loved him—in spite of how he felt about her…

CHAPTER ELEVEN

CLAIRE didn't go straight back to the hotel from work. She took a detour to the cemetery, stopping to buy a bunch of tiny pink roses first. She cleaned out the brass vase and refilled it with fresh water, arranging the roses with loving care before placing them on her little daughter's resting place. She felt the familiar tight ache in her chest as she looked at the inscription, hot tears blurring her vision so she could hardly read her baby's name.

'Sleep tight, darling,' she said softly as she finally prepared to leave.

The traffic was heavy on the way back, so by the time she got to the hotel it was much later than she had expected.

'Where the hell have you been?' Antonio barked at her as soon as she came in the door.

Claire let her bag slip to the floor. 'I…I was caught up in traffic.'

'For two hours?' he asked, his gaze hard as it collided with hers.

She ran her tongue over her lips. 'How do you know how long it's been?'

'I called in at the salon but you had already left,' he

said. 'I made the trip back here and it only took me fifteen minutes—and that was during peak hour.'

Claire slipped off her coat, trying her best not to be intimidated by his brooding demeanour. 'Thank you for the car,' she said. 'It's lovely. I took it for a bit of a drive.'

'Where to?' The question was accusatory, hostile almost.

'To the cemetery,' she said, holding his dark angry gaze. 'To visit our daughter.'

Claire saw his throat move up and down over a tight swallow, one of his hands scoring a rough pathway through the thickness of his hair as his gaze shifted away from hers.

'Forgive me,' he said in a gruff tone. 'I should not have shouted at you like that.'

'I would have told you where I was going, but I thought you were going to be late,' she said. 'You said so in the note you left for me this morning.'

His eyes came back to hers. 'We got through the list faster than I expected. One of the patients had to be put off until next week due to a clotting problem.'

The silence stretched for a lengthy moment.

Claire broke it by saying, 'I need to have a shower. I feel as if I am covered in hair clippings and dye.' She began to move past him, but he captured her arm on the way past, stopping her in her tracks.

'Claire.'

She looked up at him, the weariness she could see in his face making her heart melt. 'Yes?' she said, barely above a whisper.

'I have something for you,' he said, reaching into his trouser pocket with his other hand.

Claire held her breath as he handed her two velvet ring boxes. She opened the first one to find an exquisite diamond solitaire engagement ring glittering there. The second box contained an equally beautiful diamond-encrusted wedding ring. She knew even before she slipped them onto her finger that they would both be a perfect fit.

She looked up at him again once the rings were in place, but his expression was difficult to read. 'Thank you, Antonio,' she said softly. 'They're truly beautiful. They must have cost you a fortune.'

He gave an off-hand shrug of one of his broad shoulders. 'They are just props,' he said. 'I do not want people to think I am not able or willing to provide you with nice jewellery.'

Claire couldn't help feeling crushed, but tried not to show it on her face. 'I am sure no one would think you a neglectful husband after all the money you have spent on me in the last twenty-four hours.'

His eyes studied her for a pulsing moment. 'Why didn't you tell me you made a large cash donation to the neonatal unit at St Patrick's hospital a few weeks after you returned to Australia?' he asked.

Claire rolled her lips together, wondering how he had found out. She had asked the CEO at the time to keep her name off the records. He had assured her no one would ever know who had made the donation.

'Claire?'

'How did you find out?' she asked.

'There are some secrets that are not so easy to keep,' he said, still with that inscrutable expression on his face.

Claire shifted under his steady gaze, absently twirling

the rings on her finger. 'You seem to have made it your business to find out everything you can about me.' She looked up at him again and asked, 'Should I be checking over my shoulder for a man in a trenchcoat?'

The line of his mouth grew tense. 'I would like you to inform me of your movements in future.'

Claire felt her back come up. 'Why?' she asked. 'So you can monitor my every move like a prisoner being kept under guard?'

'I would just like to know where you are and who you are with,' he said. He paused for a moment before adding, 'I was worried about you this evening.'

'Worried?' she asked with a lift of her brows. 'About my welfare or about whether I had escaped your clutches?'

His jaw visibly tightened as he held her gaze with the coal-black hardness of his. 'If you are harbouring the thought of leaving just remember it will only take one phone call to put your brother behind bars.'

Claire's gaze flicked to his mobile phone. 'You won't be able to hold that particular gun to my head for ever you know,' she said. 'It's already wearing a little thin, don't you think?'

He stepped towards her, tilting up her face, his eyes locking once again with hers. 'As long as it works for now,' he said, and slowly and inexorably lowered his mouth to hers.

Claire shivered as he deepened the kiss, her arms snaking around his neck, her senses firing on all cylinders. His tongue teased hers into a sexy tango, building her desire for him with each sensual movement. She pressed herself closer, her body singing with delight as she felt his arousal growing hot and hard against her. His hands skimmed down her sides, grasping her by the hips and pulling her even closer.

His kiss became more drugging, the sweep and caress of his tongue making her sigh with mounting pleasure. His hands moved from her waist to the undersides of her breasts, his thumbs close enough to rub across her nipples in tantalising back and forth movements that brought another whimper of delight from her in spite of the barrier of her clothes.

'I want you naked,' he said against her mouth. 'Now.'

Claire quivered as his hands cupped her breasts. 'I really need a shower...'

'Good idea,' he said, and lifted her effortlessly in her arms, carrying her through to the bathroom. 'I need one too.'

Claire wasn't sure who undressed who, but it seemed only seconds before they were standing under the hot spray of the shower, his mouth doing knee-trembling things to the sensitive skin at the side of her neck. She tilted her head and closed her eyes in bliss as his lips and tongue began an excruciatingly slow journey towards the swell of her breasts.

She was gasping by the time he got there, her senses screaming in reaction as his teeth gently scraped her sensitised flesh. He took her in his mouth, drawing on her, sucking and licking until every nerve was alive and jumping with feeling. The rasp of his stubbly jaw against her tender skin as he moved to her other breast made her spine tingle and her legs threaten to fold beneath her.

The steady stream of steamy water intensified the sensual feelings of their bodies rubbing against each other. Claire had showered with Antonio in the past, but she could not remember it feeling as exhilarating as this. Even as her excitement was building he was taking his time, as if he wanted to draw out every second of pleasure, and her body was delighting in it. Her anticipation grew and grew, making her breath come in breathless little pants as he came closer and closer to possessing her.

'Now…oh, please now,' she said, pressing herself against his hot, hard heat.

He held her slightly aloft, teasing her with his length at her moist entrance. Just waiting for that first plunge into her tight warmth made her heart race in feverish expectation.

'Tell me how much you want me,' he said, rubbing himself against her.

The erotic motion drove every thought but his imminent possession out of her head. 'Don't make me beg, Antonio,' she gasped as he brushed against her again. 'You know how much I want you. I have never wanted anyone but you.'

His eyes gleamed with male satisfaction as he pressed her back against the shower stall, positioning her for his entry.

Claire closed her eyes as he surged forward, her body accepting him with slick wet heat, her tight muscles clamping around him, drawing him in. He started slowly, but his pace increased until she was breathing as heavily as him, her hands grasping at him to keep her upright as her body began to splinter into a thousand pieces, each one trembling, spinning and quivering in a maelstrom of sensation.

He came within seconds of her, his low, deep grunts of pleasure making her skin pepper all over with goose-bumps as he spilled himself. She felt his body shiver under the pads of her fingertips as she ran them lightly over his back, his taut muscles twitching in the aftermath.

Antonio finally stepped back and brushed the wet hair out of her face. 'I will let you finish up in here,' he said, running a gentle fingertip over a patch of redness on the upper curve of her breast. 'I need to have a shave before I take any more of your skin off.'

Claire looked at her breast, the startling contrast of its creamy softness against the dark tan of his finger making her stomach tilt all over again. She drew in a tight little breath as his fingertip brushed over her nipple, and then another as he circled her areola.

His eyes meshed with hers. 'Did you see your doctor about contraception?' he asked.

Claire felt as if he had just turned the cold water on. She stared at him, her heart-rate not quite steady. 'No...I haven't been able to get an appointment.'

'Where are you in your cycle?'

'I'm not sure...'

His eyes were still locked on hers. 'We have had un-protected sex several times now. Has it occurred to you that you could have already conceived a child?'

She swallowed thickly and, reaching past him, turned off the shower. She stepped out of the cubicle and snatching up one of the big fluffy towels, wrapped herself in it. 'I thought you said the other day it was not the right time to be talking about babies?' she said.

He wrapped a towel around his hips. 'That was then. This is now.'

She eyed him suspiciously. 'So what's changed?' she asked.

'We are older and wiser, Claire. Things could work for us.'

Claire searched his face for some clue to what he was feeling, but his expression was mask-like. 'So…' She paused as she moistened her mouth. 'So what you are saying is…you want to stay married?'

'It was never my intention to divorce you, Claire.'

'Why?' she asked. 'Because it could prove too costly for you now your father has died and left you half of everything he owned?'

Something flickered in his eyes. 'That is why you issued me with the divorce papers, was it not?' he asked. 'You saw a chance to take me to the cleaners in return for all the ways I had supposedly let you down in the past. Do not forget I saw the newspaper article too, Claire. It mentioned the recent death of my father. You did the sums, but fortunately for me your brother took matters into his own hands.'

Claire glared at him, her hands going to tight fists by her sides. 'You bastard. The first I heard about your father's death was when you told me at our first meeting,' she said through clenched teeth. 'You arrogant, unfeeling bastard. Right from the start you set out to seduce me back into your bed, hoping once I was there again I wouldn't want to leave. No wonder you've been buying me expensive rings and a car and talking about babies. You wanted to make me think twice about leaving.'

'There is not going to be a divorce, Claire,' he said, with an intransigent set to his mouth. 'I want you to be absolutely clear about that—especially if there is going to be a child.'

'How can you be so clinical about this?' she asked. 'This is not some business deal. This is my life you're talking about. What if I want to spend it with someone else? Have you thought about that?'

His eyes pinned hers. 'Is there someone else?'

She sent him a resentful scowl. 'Why don't you tell me? You're the one keeping tabs on me.'

'I am not keeping tabs on you,' he said heavily. 'I found out quite by accident you were responsible for that donation. It threw me to think you had not thought to tell me. You allowed me to think you had taken money from my mother to indulge yourself; instead I find that you have been responsible for saving perhaps hundreds of premature babies' lives.'

'I didn't ask your mother for the money. She had written the cheque before she came to see me that night. I am not sure why she continues to insist I demanded it from her.'

Antonio released a sigh. 'There is no point in going over this again. If you say that is how it happened, then I am prepared to leave it at that.'

Her blue-green eyes widened in surprise. 'You believe me?'

'If we are to make a success of our marriage this time around we will both have to learn to trust each other,' he said, dragging a hand through his still-damp hair.

She gave him an ironic look. 'You just accused me of trying to take half your assets. Doesn't that imply a lack of trust on your part?'

He looked at her for a long moment. 'Why, after all

this time, did you wait until now to ask me for a divorce?' he asked.

She captured her lip, chewed at it for a second or two before she answered. 'I believed our marriage to be well and truly over, that's why.'

Even now Antonio wondered if he could believe her. He had blackmailed her back into his bed, but she was right in saying he couldn't hold the threat of her brother's imprisonment over her indefinitely. He should not have held it over her in the first place. Her brother had acted out of a sense of loyalty—the kind of behaviour he had seen in his own brother Mario time and time again.

Antonio's head was still reeling with the shock of finding out Claire had not used that money for her own gain. Five years of brooding anger had been swept away with a single sentence from a virtual stranger who had known more about his wife than he did.

It was like seeing Claire for the first time; he was discovering things about her he had not noticed before. Like how she kissed with her whole body, not just her mouth. And how gentle her hands were, the way they sent electrical charges through him with the simplest touch. How sweet her rare smile was, how it touched him in a way nothing else had done. How her beautiful eyes glittered with anger and defiance one moment, then brimmed with emotion at the mere mention of their baby daughter the next. She was like a movie or a novel he had not understood the first time around. She had layers and sub-plots that made him appreciate her uniqueness in a way he had never done before.

He had never been comfortable identifying his

emotions concerning Claire. He still wasn't sure why. It wasn't as if he'd had a difficult background, or had suffered at the hands of another woman, therefore making it difficult to let his guard down. He just knew he felt something for Claire he had not felt for any other woman.

He tipped up her chin and brushed his mouth with hers. 'It is not over, *cara*,' he said, and unhooked her towel, tossing it to the floor along with his. 'Not by a long shot.'

CHAPTER TWELVE

THREE weeks later Claire came out of the salon's bathroom to find Rebecca looking at her speculatively. 'Are you going to continue to fob me off by telling me it was something you ate, or are you going to come clean?' she asked. 'That is the third time in as many days you've been sick.'

Claire blew out a sigh as she dabbed at her clammy brow. 'I think I'm pregnant. I haven't had a test yet, but the signs are all there.'

Rebecca's eyes opened wide with excitement. 'Wow, Claire—that's fabulous! Have you told Antonio?'

Claire began to chew at her lip. 'No…not yet.'

'You don't think he'll be pleased?'

Claire met her friend's questioning gaze. 'I think he'll be very pleased,' she said. 'It means a divorce will be out of the question—for the time being at least.'

Rebecca frowned. 'But, hon, I thought a divorce was out of the question now anyway. The last couple of weeks you've been happier than I've seen you in years. I thought it was finally working out between you and Antonio.'

'It's true things have been much better between us,'

Claire said, thinking of how attentive and considerate Antonio had been lately. 'He's been lovely towards me—taking me out to dinners and shows, and buying me clothes and stuff. He even offered to drive to Narrabri next weekend to meet my mother.'

'But?'

Claire gave Rebecca an anguished look. 'Don't you see, Bex? It's happening all over again.'

'I'm not sure I'm following you…'

'The one thing Antonio wants is an heir,' Claire said. 'When I fell pregnant before that's why he insisted on marrying me—to give the baby his name. It wasn't about loving me or wanting to spend the rest of his life with me. It was about securing an heir for the Marcolini empire.'

'But, Claire, things might have changed now.'

'Oh, yes,' Claire said with a cynical twist of her mouth. 'They very definitely *have* changed. He is now in possession of half his father's wealth as well as his own, which is no small fortune, let me tell you. He knows if he divorces me he will have to give me a huge cut of it. What better way to keep his money than to lure me back into his life and get an heir in the process?'

Rebecca shifted her pursed lips from side to side for a moment. 'I'm thinking you haven't told him you still love him. Am I right?'

'Oh, Bex, I have to bite my tongue every single day,' Claire choked, close to tears. 'But that's the mistake I made before. I can't make myself so vulnerable again. If we are to stay together I want it to be on equal terms. I want to be loved not for what I can give him, but for me—just me.'

'Claire, it's only been…what…a little over three

weeks or so since you got back together?' Rebecca said. 'And don't forget his feet had barely stepped on Australian soil when you started waving divorce papers under his nose. He's not likely to unveil his feelings in a hurry after something like that.'

'I guess you're right…' Claire said as she sat on the stool at the reception counter and put her head in her hands. 'It hasn't exactly been a textbook reunion.'

Rebecca stood behind her and gave her shoulders a little squeeze. 'Why don't you take a couple of weeks off? You should get some rest in any case. Then, when you're all relaxed and not feeling so unsure of yourself, you can tell Antonio about the baby.'

Claire got off the stool and faced her friend. 'I think I will take a few days off,' she said. 'I don't want anything to go wrong with this pregnancy. I just couldn't bear it.'

Antonio had not long finished his last case when he received a phone call from his brother Mario, back in Rome. He rubbed his hand across the stubble on his jaw as he listened to the news he had been dreading ever since he'd boarded the plane to Australia.

'How long do the doctors think she will last?' he asked as he stripped off his theatre cap and tossed it in the bin.

'It is hard to say—a week, maybe less,' Mario responded. 'She has been asking for you.'

Antonio felt his insides clench. The irony was particularly painful. The last time he had seen his mother she had looked at him blankly, asking the home care nurse who this tall, dark and handsome stranger was. 'I will arrange a flight straight away,' he informed his brother.

'Is your runaway wife coming with you?' Mario asked.

Antonio felt his teeth grind together at his brother's sardonic tone. 'Claire will take some convincing, but, yes, I plan to bring her with me,' he answered. 'And I would appreciate it if you would not mention the past again. We are getting along just fine.'

'So you have so far managed to stop her divorcing you?' Mario asked.

'So far,' Antonio said, thinking of all the times in the last couple of weeks when he had caught Claire looking at him in that covert way of hers, her gaze immediately falling away from his as if she was harbouring a guilty secret.

For all his talk that day of developing trust between them, he could not get past the thought that she might very well be planning the best payback of all. He couldn't quite shake the feeling, no matter how he tried. Even though she shared his bed willingly, with as much if not more enthusiasm as before, she never once mentioned her feelings towards him as she'd used to do so freely in the past. Even her smiles were fleeting and distant, as if her mind was occupied elsewhere. The only place he could get and hold her full attention was in bed. It was there she responded to him without holding back, her body convulsing around his as he claimed her again and again. He had thought his attraction to her would burn itself out, but it had done the very opposite. He wanted her more than he had ever wanted her. His physical need of her was so great at times it was overwhelming. The irony was that it had been all he had wanted from her in the beginning, and yet now, when he was so sure he could have it, he wanted so much more.

When Antonio got back to the hotel Claire was sitting

in the lounge with her legs curled beneath her, a magazine in her lap.

'Hi,' she said, closing the pages as he came in.

'Hi, yourself,' he said, bending down to kiss her briefly.

She looked at him warily once he had straightened. 'Is something wrong?' she asked, unfolding her legs and placing her feet on the carpeted floor, her hands gripping the sofa until her knuckles showed through her creamy skin.

'Claire, I have to return to Italy,' he said without preamble. 'I need to go as soon as possible. I want you to come with me.'

'No,' she said, instantly springing to her feet.

He frowned as she suddenly paled before him, her body swaying slightly. He put out a hand and steadied her. '*Cara*, I did not mean to spring that on you like that, but—'

'I don't want to go.' She cut him off, her face still deathly pale.

'What is wrong?' he asked, still holding her.

'I told you from the start I am not moving back to Italy with you,' she said with a stubborn set to her mouth. 'You can't make me go.'

'I thought we had an agreement,' he said, holding her defiant gaze.

She glared at him, but he could see a nerve flickering at the side of her mouth.

'Don't try and blackmail me, Antonio. It's not going to work. I was speaking to Isaac only yesterday. Your friend has helped him apply for a youth worker's course. He starts in a couple of weeks. He told me you were the one who paid his fees. There is no way you would turn him in now—not unless you don't have an ounce of compassion in your soul.'

Antonio silently ground his teeth as he tried to think of another way to convince her. In the end he decided to try another tactic—to reveal a side of him she had never seen before. 'Claire, my mother is dying,' he said heavily. 'I need to go to her. She is asking for me.'

She shifted under his gaze, her tongue darting out to moisten her lips. 'Go on your own. You don't need me there.'

'I would like you to be there, *tesoro mio*,' he said, scraping a hand through his hair. *I need you to be there.*

'I am quite sure your mother would prefer it if I didn't intrude on such a painfully private moment,' she said, but her voice had lost its hardened edge. Her eyes, too, had softened, bringing out the rich blueness of them.

'The point is my mother will probably not even recognise you.'

She frowned at him. 'What do you mean?'

He released a weary sigh. 'My mother is suffering from Alzheimer's. Up until recently she has been cared for at home by a nurse, but early this morning, Italian time, she suffered a stroke. Her memory of the past, which was already rapidly declining, is now virtually non-existent.'

'But I thought you said she specifically asked for you?' she said.

'She did—which is why it is imperative I go to her,' he said. 'Patients with Alzheimer's can still have short periods of lucidity. I want to see her. It is important to me. I was not there for my father. I did not get to say the things I wanted to say. I did not get to hear the things he wanted to say to me.' He paused for a moment. 'I was not there for you and our baby either. That is something I will regret for the rest of my life. I do not want any more regrets, Claire. Please…do this one thing for me.'

Claire felt her rigid stance begin to crumble. She could see this was a very difficult time for him. He had not long ago lost his father, and now his mother was desperately ill. It was impossible for her to deny him this one request. And hearing him speak of their little baby with such emotion in his voice went a long way to healing the hurt she had carried for so long. Although he had said nothing to her about it, she knew he had gone to visit their daughter's resting place. When she had gone there today, after she had left the salon, she had found a teddy bear dressed in a pink tutu propped up next to a huge bunch of flowers, and a card written in both English and Italian: *With all my love, your devoted Papà.*

It had made Claire realise how private a person Antonio was. He had lived most of his life under the intrusive glare of the paparazzi, and when he grieved he liked to do so alone. If only she had recognised that all those years ago. He was not one to express his feelings to all and sundry. He kept things inside, working through them at his own pace, locking a part of himself away to cope with the difficult issues he had to deal with on a daily basis. How could he handle the welfare of his patients if he was to fall apart emotionally all the time? Patients did not need a surgeon to cry with them. They needed a competent, caring specialist who could think clearly and make good clinical decisions about their condition and how best to deal with it.

It was a shock to realise how little she had known

Antonio in the past—how little she had understood of him as a man and as a gifted surgeon. She had fallen in love with a small part of him, never realising the true depths of his character until now.

'Claire, I do not expect to be away for more than a week or ten days at the most,' Antonio assured her. 'I still have commitments here, although they have had to be rescheduled for when I return.'

'All right,' she said on a little sigh. 'I will come with you.'

He pressed a soft kiss to the middle of her forehead. 'Thank you, *il mio amato*,' he said. 'I will try and make things as comfortable for you as possible.'

The flight to Rome was long, but Claire slept on and off in the executive suite Antonio had arranged on the plane. She woke once during the flight to find him lying fully clothed on top of the covers beside her, staring at the ceiling, his handsome features so drawn with exhaustion her heart went out to him.

She stroked a gentle hand across his stubbly jaw. 'Why don't you get undressed and lie down for a while?'

He turned his head and gave her a rueful smile. 'If I get into that bed with you, sleep will be the last thing on my mind.'

Claire felt her cheeks start to glow. 'Maybe that's exactly what you need right now,' she said softly. 'Maybe it's what we both need.'

He rolled on his side and brushed her hair back from her forehead, his eyes dark and intense as they meshed with hers. She closed her eyes as his mouth came down, the brush of his tongue against hers setting her instantly alight. With her mouth still locked on his, she worked the buttons of his shirt, pulling it off him with impatient fingers. She attacked his belt and trousers with the same passionate intent, aching to feel his body against hers without the barrier of clothes.

Antonio removed the slip of a nightgown she was wearing, kissing her breasts, rolling his tongue over each ripe berry of her nipples, his teeth tugging and his tongue soothing simultaneously, his mouth a hot brand of possession that drove her wild with need.

His erection was thick and throbbing against her moist entrance, his breathing ragged as he fought for control. 'I should put on a condom,' he said, reaching across to rummage in his bag. 'You will not be totally covered by the pill yet. It has only been a couple of weeks, *si*?'

Claire stroked his arm with her fingers, her eyes falling away from his. She had let him think she had gone ahead with the appointment with her doctor, and now she wished she hadn't lied by omission. But telling him about her pregnancy now didn't seem quite like the right time. She wanted to feel more assured of his feelings for her. Anyway, it was very early days; anything could go wrong at this stage. She hadn't even had it confirmed in case she jinxed something. She wanted to wait until she was absolutely sure she wasn't imagining it before she told him.

'I am sure it will be fine,' she said. 'I want to feel you.'

He positioned himself over her and she welcomed him with a gasp of delight, moving with him, catching his rhythm, her body gripping him greedily. He reached between their rocking bodies to stroke the moist centre of her desire, his fingers finding their target with consummate ease. She was so ready for him, her back arching off the mattress to keep him where she wanted him. He drew out the pleasure for her, changing his touch to tease her into a cataclysmic release. She was approaching the summit. He could feel her inner muscles start to contract, her whimpering cries coming faster and faster as she finally let go. It was impossible for him to hold back. He surged forward with several deep, hard thrusts, spilling himself, shuddering with the sensation of ultimate pleasure as it flowed through him in waves.

The deep and even sound of Antonio's breathing had a soporific affect on Claire. Her eyes felt as if they were weighted by anvils, and after a few attempts to keep them open she gave up with a soft sigh, and fell into a dreamless sleep curled up in his arms.

When Claire woke the pilot announced they were due to land.

The journey through Customs was tiresome, due to a security scare that had happened with a tourist a few days ago. Everyone seemed to be on tenterhooks, which was quite understandable, and the checkpoints took much longer than normal, even for those holding an Italian passport.

Although the building was air-conditioned Claire felt clammy and, using a tissue, wiped beads of moisture from her forehead. Antonio glanced at her as they were being ushered through, his gaze narrowing in concern.

'Are you all right, *cara*?' he asked. 'The crowds are annoying, I know, but we will soon be home.'

Home.

He said it so naturally—as if it really was her home as well. But it would never be home for her—not unless she felt loved and accepted by him. She could live anywhere with him if he loved her the way she loved him. His heart was her home and always would be.

The trip to the Marcolini *palazzo* was lengthened by a traffic snarl, but soon enough the familiar sight came into view. The three-storey mansion stood in stately pride, and the lush green of trees and shrubbery, holding a host of hot summer fragrances, reminded Claire of the blisteringly dry and dusty Outback, where her mother vainly tried year after year to coax flowers and vegetables to grow.

The other startling difference from her background was the number of household staff the Marcolinis employed. Housekeepers—both junior and senior—a gardener and a pool maintenance man, not to mention a chauffeur who seemed to be on call twenty-four hours a day.

'Isn't your mother being looked after in hospital now?' Claire asked, automatically lowering her voice to the hushed, whispered tone all the staff she had encountered so far seemed to have adopted.

'No,' Antonio said. 'She expressly wished to be allowed to stay at home with her family around her.'

Claire looked up at the grand marble staircase to see Antonio's brother descending. Taller by an inch or two, he had the same dark good-looks of his older sibling, his body long and lean and toned by the gym and the pool. He had the same dark brown almost black eyes, but while Antonio's were often filled with compassion for the patients under his care, Mario's were hardened with the worldly cynicism he wore like a second skin.

'So the prodigal wife returns,' he said, as he came to

the foot of the stairs where Claire was standing. 'Welcome home, Claire.'

Antonio swore at his brother in Italian, changing back to English to ask, 'How is Mamma?'

'Conscious, but not making much sense,' Mario answered. 'She keeps thinking I am Papà.'

'Yes, well, you look more like him than me,' Antonio said, massaging the back of his neck, where he could feel a knot of tension the size of a golfball. 'Has anyone else been to visit?'

'Daniela came by yesterday, with her husband and baby son,' Mario informed him. 'I am not sure if she will be back,' he added, glancing briefly at Claire.

Claire felt her colour rise and bit down on her lip. Was she for ever to be reminded of her stupid mistake in believing her husband had betrayed her?

'I had better spend some time with Mamma,' Antonio said. 'Has her doctor been today?'

Mario nodded grimly. 'There is nothing you can do, Antonio. You are not her doctor; you are her son. You need to remember that.'

Antonio swallowed the lump of grief that had risen in his throat. 'Can you get Claire a drink and show her to our room? She is tired from the journey. She almost passed out coming through Customs.'

Claire felt her face flame with guilty colour all over again. She was sure Mario thought she had been putting it on, but she did still feel horribly faint and nauseous. A long-haul flight and crossing time zones, even if in the lap of luxury, was not conducive to feeling one hundred percent even without the suspicion of being pregnant. Even the sudden heat after the cool winter in

Sydney took some getting used to. Antonio himself looked ashen and tired beyond description, with dark shadows underscoring his eyes like bruises, but then he was facing the sadness of losing his mother so soon after the death of his father.

'What would you like to drink?' Mario asked as he led the way to the *salotto*.

'Do you have fresh orange juice?' Claire asked.

He gave her his playboy, teasing smile. 'Does Australia have bush flies?'

A reluctant smile tugged at Claire's mouth. She had to admit that Mario, when he let his guard down, could be utterly charming. It was no wonder Antonio would not hear a bad word said against him.

Mario handed her a glass of icy cold orange juice. 'So,' he said, running his gaze over her speculatively, 'you are reunited with my brother.'

Claire lowered her gaze. 'Yes…'

'Let's hope it lasts this time around,' he said. 'He has not been the same since you left.'

Claire took a deep breath and met his hardened gaze full-on. 'I love him, Mario. I know you probably don't believe it, but I do. I've been so stupid. I can't believe how stupid I was back then. I know he wasn't having an affair. I feel so sure of it now. I have never stopped loving him. Not for a moment. I love him so much.'

'Have you told him that?' Mario asked, stalling in the process of lifting his glass to his mouth.

'Have you told me what?' Antonio asked as he stepped into the room behind her.

Claire swung around to reply, but before she could

get the words into some sort of order she began to wobble on her feet, her vision blurring alarmingly. She tried to concentrate, to hold on to consciousness, but her extremities were already fizzing with the sudden loss of blood pressure. She felt herself falling, saw the marbled floor coming towards her with frightening speed. The glass she was holding slipped out of her grasp, shattering into a thousand pieces.

She vaguely registered Antonio's voice calling out, 'Catch her!' but if Mario did so in time she was totally unaware of it….

Claire woke in a darkened room. Her aching forehead was being stroked with a cool damp cloth by Antonio. 'What's going on?' she asked through dry lips. 'Where am I?'

'*Cara*, you hit your head when you fainted,' he said, concern thickening his voice. 'I want you to go to hospital to have it X-rayed. The ambulance is on its way. You could have fractured your skull.'

She felt her vision blurring again, and his words seemed to be coming from a long way off. Her head was pounding as if a construction site had taken up residence inside. She felt a wave of sickness rise in her throat, but managed to swallow it down just as the sound of a siren approached on the street outside.

As the ambulance officers loaded her into the back of the vehicle, Claire turned her head to look at Antonio, whose face was grey with anguish. 'I don't need you to come with me,' she said. 'You should be with your mother. How is she?'

'She is fine for now,' Antonio said, gently squeezing

her hand before tucking it back under the cotton blanket. 'She has even been asking for you.'

She blinked at him, even though it sent another jack-hammer through her skull. 'She's been asking for *me*?' she asked in a shocked whisper. 'She…she knows I'm here…with you?'

'I told her we were together again,' he said. 'I think she wants to say goodbye and to apologise.'

Claire felt her heart contract even as her conscious-ness began to waver alarmingly again. 'Tell her…tell her to wait for me…'

'I will,' Antonio said, leaning forward to press a soft kiss to the paper-white skin of her brow just as her eyes fluttered downwards.

'Come è lei?'

Claire heard Antonio's voice ask how she was. But the answer from the doctor he was speaking with, even though delivered in the rather stilted manner of a non-Italian speaker, she found hard to follow in her disor-dered state, apart from the words for 'mild concussion.'

'Commozione minimo…um…er… Ma non è tutto… Lei è incinta…er…'

'How far along?' Antonio asked next—in English this time, clearly in an attempt to put his struggling col-league out of his misery.

Claire felt a prickly sensation go through her, as if all of her corpuscles had been injected with tiny bubbles of air, each one containing a particle of joy.

So it had been confirmed at last.

She was pregnant.

'Two weeks—maybe three,' the doctor answered

Antonio in English, his lilting accent giving him away as a Scot, obviously on a foreign medical rotation. 'She is obviously sensitive to the change in her hormones. Some women are more so than others, making the symptoms kick in much earlier than normal. The knock on the head will not help the morning sickness, of course, but with adequate rest she should pick up in a few days. I've had a quick look through her records. She will have to be closely monitored, given what happened last time, but it's entirely possible she will have a safe delivery of a healthy wee one this time. We have come a long way in the last five years in maternal health management.'

Claire felt her heart turn over inside her chest as the joy she was feeling began to spread right through her. If everything went right, she would in a matter of months be holding a baby in her arms—alive and breathing. Up until now she hadn't dared think too far ahead. It had been enough to suspect she was carrying Antonio's baby. To find out there was every reason to hope for a healthy delivery was nothing short of a miracle to her.

'*Grazie*,' Antonio said with a hitch in his voice. 'I mean—thank you.'

'No trouble. I am sorry to hear your mother is not well,' the doctor added. 'Perhaps news of a grandchild will be just the tonic she needs right now?'

'You could be right,' Antonio said. 'Thank you again. You have been very kind and attentive. It is greatly appreciated.'

Claire waited until the sound of the doctor's footsteps had faded into the distance before she opened her eyes. Antonio was looking down at her, his dark brown eyes meltingly soft.

'*Cara.*' His tone was gentle. 'The good news is you do not have a fracture of your skull.'

'And…and the bad news?'

He smiled. 'I do not consider it bad news at all. The doctor attending your admission has found you are pregnant. He took a set of routine blood tests and it came up positive. You're pregnant.'

Claire felt the tears rising until they were streaming down her face. She sniffed, and Antonio quickly reached over and plucked a tissue out of the box by her bed. He began to gently mop at her cheeks. 'And here I was, thinking you had gone on the pill,' he said in mock reproach.

'I was going to,' she said. 'I was about to call to make an appointment when I realised I was a couple of days late. I decided to wait and see.'

He began to frown. 'You *were* planning on telling me, were you not?'

'Of course!' she said. 'Surely you don't think…?'

He gave a rueful grimace. 'It would be no less than I deserved. I have not exactly been the best husband to you, have I?'

Claire lowered her gaze, plucking at the sheet with her fingers. 'I haven't exactly been the best wife…'

He picked up her hand and brushed his lips against her bent fingers. 'I cannot tell you how thrilled I am about the baby,' he said. 'It is the best news I could have hoped for.'

She gnawed at her lip for a moment. 'It's not just about keeping your inheritance?'

'It has never been about my inheritance,' he said, his eyes warm and soft as they held hers. 'I love you, *il mio amato uno*. I have been so stupid not to have recognised it for all this time. I was too proud to admit the woman I loved had left me. I should have fought for you, Claire. I realise that now. I should have moved heaven and earth to bring you back to me.'

Claire's heart swelled to twice its size as she fell forward into his arms. 'I love you too,' she sobbed against his broad, dependable chest. 'I've been such a fool. I can't believe I left you. It was so immature of me.'

'Hush, *cara*,' he soothed, stroking her back with a gossamer-light touch. 'You were still hurting. Losing Isabella was…' His voice caught but he went on. 'It was like being locked inside an abyss of grief so thick and dark it was all I could do to get through each day without breaking down completely. People were depending on me—my patients, my colleagues—and yet in all of it the most important person I should have supported was you. But I was too shell-shocked to face it at the time. Every time I looked at the pain in your eyes I felt my heart being ripped open. In the end I just could not bear to think what I had done to you. I got you pregnant. I did not support you the way you needed. And when Isabella did not make it I felt…I *still* feel…it was my fault.'

Claire lifted her eyes to his dark moist ones. 'You said her name…' Her voice came out on an incredulous whisper of sound. 'For the first time *ever* you said her name…twice…'

Antonio's throat moved up and down as he fought to control his emotions. 'I have wanted to so many times, *cara*,' he said. 'But every time I tried to I felt as if a giant hand had grasped me by the throat, squeezing until I could not breathe.'

Claire hugged him tightly, allowing him the chance to let out the grief that in her own ignorance and pain had not been allowed purchase.

It was a long time before either of them could speak, but when they finally came apart she looked into his red-rimmed eyes and felt a rush of sheer joy for the first time in five long, lonely years.

'My mother wishes to apologise in person for misleading you,' Antonio said. 'She really felt she was doing the right thing at the time. She thought you no longer loved me. That is why she gave you the money—to help you get back on your feet. She thought it might help you to cut loose by hinting Daniela and I were still involved. I hope you will find it in yourself to forgive her. I know it is a lot to ask. I am finding it hard to forgive her myself.'

Claire smiled as she stroked his raspy jaw. 'Of course I forgive her—and you must too. I do not want any bad feelings to get in the way of our happiness. Not after so long apart.'

He smiled and kissed her softly on her lips. 'I am the luckiest man on earth,' he said. 'I am over the moon about you being back in my life, about the baby, about being together again, about being a family.'

'Speaking of family,' she said. 'Isn't it time you got back to yours at the *palazzo*?'

'My family is right here,' he said, kissing her passionately. 'And I am not going to be separated from it again.'

* * * * *

THE VALTIERI
MARRIAGE DEAL

BY
CAROLINE ANDERSON

Caroline Anderson has the mind of a butterfly. She's been a nurse, a secretary, a teacher, run her own soft-furnishing business, and now she's settled on writing. She says, "I was looking for that elusive something. I finally realised it was variety, and now I have it in abundance. Every book brings new horizons and new friends, and in between books I have learned to be a juggler. My teacher husband John and I have two beautiful and talented daughters, Sarah and Hannah, umpteen pets, and several acres of Suffolk that nature tries to reclaim every time we turn our backs!" Caroline writes for the Mills & Boon® Cherish™ and Medical™ series.

For Sarah, amazing font of knowledge and maker of the best chocolate cakes in times of need, and for Alastair, Rhea and Eleanor who introduced us to Italy. *Grazie!*

CHAPTER ONE

HE SAW HER through the glass.

He didn't know her—he'd never seen her before in his life—but as their eyes connected, Luca's heart began to pound.

She was beautiful. Utterly gorgeous. Her wide lavender eyes had caught his attention first, and below them a generous mouth, slightly parted, was just begging to be kissed. Her sweater clung lovingly to soft, rounded breasts with just a hint of cleavage to taunt him, but it was something else, something he couldn't define, something fierce and elemental and soul-deep that drew him to her, and he wanted her so much he could taste it.

If he had any sense, he'd keep on walking, because a woman like that just wasn't his style. He liked control—and there was something very uncontrolled about his reaction to her.

But he was in desperate need of a shot of caffeine, this was the best café in the area and the only free seat was at her table. So he went in and walked over to her. He'd just get a coffee and go. How hard could it be?

'*Signorina?*'

She looked up, and her breath jammed in her lungs. It

was the man, standing beside her, a crooked smile on those sexy, unbelievable lips, the dark, intense eyes that had locked with hers through the window glittering with something that if she'd had a shred of sense left would have sent her running, but she couldn't move. Even her lungs had stopped working.

'Are you expecting anyone to join you, or may I take this seat?' His voice was soft, gravelly, warmed by a rich Italian accent, and it trailed over her like the hand of a lover, bringing everything screaming back to life.

She sucked in a breath. 'No—no, I— Please, do.'

She gathered up the books she'd scattered all over the table—a guide to Florence, a phrase book that didn't seem to have any of the questions that she wanted to ask, a couple of tourist information leaflets she'd picked up—and made room for him, and as he sat down, his knee brushed against hers and a hint of spicy citrus cologne drifted over her and made her shiver.

He moved his knee, shocked by the bolt of lightning that had shot through him at the fleeting contact. Hell, this was going to be harder than he'd imagined. He dredged about for something sane and innocuous to say, then his eyes lit on the books. 'Sightseeing?' he asked, disgusted at his corny line, and she gave a little chuckle, but an endearing sweep of colour touched her cheeks.

'Wow. Sherlock Holmes,' she said drily, but there was a teasing little smile playing at the edges of her mouth and he wanted to taste it.

He dragged his gaze back to her eyes. Although her voice was cool and controlled, something in those gorgeous lavender depths told him that the accidental brush of his leg against hers had affected her as much as him, and he felt a kick of something raw and elemental in his gut. His eyes returned to her mouth, and he felt his mouth curve in response to her smile.

'Well, the English-Italian dictionary and the guide book were a bit of a giveaway,' he said, and decided it was time to introduce himself. He extended his hand. 'I'm Luca, by the way.'

'I'm Isabelle.' After a second's pause, she took his hand—only fleetingly, but it was enough. Their gazes locked, heat flared in her eyes and she sucked in a breath and pulled back her hand, to his regret.

Isabella, he thought, saying it in his head in Italian, tasting the word, feeling it surge straight to his groin.

'Signore?' the waitress said. 'What can I get you?'

A room...

He hauled himself back in line. 'Isabelle? May I buy you another coffee?'

'Oh—well, I wasn't—but actually, that would be lovely, thank you. Could I have a latte?'

'Sure.' He added a double espresso and a selection of pastries to the order, and turned back to her. 'So—what brings you to Florence, Isabelle? It's not the best time of year for sightseeing, in January.'

She gave a little shrug. 'I just wanted a break. It's so dreary in London in the winter, and I worked all over Christmas and New Year, so I thought I deserved a treat.'

'I should think so. Weren't you with your family?'

'No—my mother lives in Canada with her husband.'

'And your father? Brothers? Sisters?'

She looked slightly uncomfortable. 'I'm an only child, and I don't have a father.'

He frowned. 'I'm sorry.'

'Why should you be?'

Luca shrugged. 'Because my father is a very important person in my life, as are my mother and my brothers and sisters, and I can't imagine Christmas without them. So— why Firenze?'

It was her turn to shrug. 'I've always wanted to come here, so I thought, Why not? A couple of days—just time to take in a bit of culture, a bit of shopping, some lovely food…' She shrugged again and smiled. 'So here I am.'

'Alone?'

Was it so obvious? 'My friends wouldn't come,' she told him ruefully. 'They didn't mind the shopping, but they weren't interested in traipsing round in the cold looking at mouldy old paintings and statues covered in pigeon poo!'

Luca chuckled, sending shivers down her spine. 'And have you seen much yet?'

She shook her head, trying to drag her eyes off his mouth long enough to concentrate on what he was saying. He really had the most gorgeous mouth.

'Not enough. I only got here early yesterday, and I've done the Ponte Vecchio and the Pitti Palace and a couple of markets, but there's so much more to do today I don't know where to start.' And she was sick of sightseeing alone.

'Would you like a guide?'

She frowned, and for a moment he thought he'd pushed it too far, but then she smiled. 'Why would you want to do that?'

Because I want to spend time with you and I don't care if I have to trudge round every last damned artefact to do it?

He shrugged. 'I know the city inside out, and I can tell you what to see and what not to bother with. And my interview finished early, so I'm free for the rest of the day,' he added.

'Oh—didn't it go well?' she asked, thinking that it explained the rather beautiful suit and wondering what the interview had been for.

'No, it went very well—they offered me the job.'

'But not as a tour guide, I take it?' she suggested, fishing for more information about him, and he gave a deep, sexy chuckle.

'Me? No,' he said with a grin. 'I'm a doctor.'

'Oh!' she said, oddly relieved because doctors she understood. 'So—are you working in the hospital already?'

'No. I had the first interview there yesterday, and I had to go back today for another look round.'

'Interesting job?'

He shrugged. 'I suppose so. Wherever women are having babies the job's essentially the same, though, and I've worked there before, so it's perhaps a bit familiar—not enough of a challenge.'

She tipped her head on one side, fascinated by the coincidence. 'So—you're an obstetrician?'

'Yes—why? Don't tell me—you're pregnant.'

She chuckled. 'No, no chance of that, but I'm a midwife.'

'Really? Hospital or community?'

'Hospital—in the consultant unit, by choice, so I can make things better for women with high-risk pregnancies and try and give them a decent birth experience.'

A brow rose slightly. 'Are you saying that doctors don't?'

She smiled wryly. 'No—but their focus is on something different, and it's easy to get terrified by all the technology. My job's to take away some of the fear and uncertainty and give my mums the labour they want, and it's really rewarding—but that's probably all about to change, because the unit's being refurbished and I'm going to be sent off to some other hospital for months, so who knows what I'll be doing? Anyway, about you—is this a step up? Will you take it?'

'Maybe. But it's not just a career move, it's also a social move.'

'Back to the city of your misspent youth?' she asked teasingly, and he chuckled.

'Perhaps. Actually, since you obviously have an interest, there's something I'd love to show you that I wouldn't show just anybody. It's a bit gruesome but it's interesting. We'll start there, and we can do the mouldy paintings and the pigeon poo afterwards,' he said. 'That is, if you want to?'

She hesitated a second, then gave in. 'Well—since you're offering,' she said, wondering why a man so gorgeous would have nothing better to do all day but spend it with her.

But Luca didn't seem to have any trouble with that idea. He leant back so the waitress could set the tray down and smiled. 'Good. That's sorted. We'll have our coffee, and I'll show you the edited highlights of my city.'

So after they'd finished their coffee and demolished the pastries, he took her to the Museo di Storia della Scienza— the Science Museum—next to the Uffizi, and showed her a room where the walls were lined with fascinating but gruesome old wax models of obstetric complications.

'Oh, horrors!' she said, the professional side of her glad to be working in a modern, well-equipped hospital and her other side, the part that was a woman, just a little bit afraid.

'Now you see why the Italians invented the Caesarean section,' he said with a dry smile, and took her back out into the glorious but chilly winter sunshine. 'Right, the pretty stuff,' he said, heading for the Piazza della Signori by the Uffizi entrance.

Isabelle was awestruck by it all. The city was scattered with amazing and jaw-dropping sculptures in every piazza and public area, so that everywhere she turned she all but fell over another one, and they were all famous. 'It's like a Renaissance theme-park,' she said, making him laugh. 'It's incredible.'

'They're not all originals,' he pointed out. 'You need to see the original David—it's in the Galleria dell'Accademia.'

'Will we have time? We can't possibly see everything!'

'Of course not. I'm cherry-picking—showing you the best bits. Otherwise you'll just get overwhelmed.'

How true, she thought, but it wasn't only the art that was overwhelming, it was Luca, warm and funny and tactile, casually looping his arm around her shoulders to steer her in a different direction, resting his hand on her waist to usher her through doorways, his boyish grin at odds with those very grown-up eyes that were sending an altogether different message.

'Right. The Duomo,' he said after a lightning tour of the Uffizi, and led her through the narrow mediaeval streets to the magnificent cathedral with Brunelleschi's huge terracotta dome that dominated the skyline, then up all four hundred and sixty-three steps between the outer and inner skin of the dome and out onto a little walkway at the very top.

It took her breath away—especially when she glanced down over the curving dome towards the ground so far below.

'Don't look down, look out,' he said quickly, and moved closer to her—so close she could smell the spicy citrus of his aftershave and something else freed by the warmth of his body that made her ache to bury her face in his throat and breathe him in—and turning her with the pressure of his body, his other hand light on her arm, he pointed out the landmarks amongst the higgledy-piggledy terracotta roofs of all the buildings laid out below them.

A waste of time, because all she could feel and smell was him, all she could see was his hand, strong and steady, the long, square-tipped fingers and the light scatter of hair on the olive skin of his wrist tantalising her. What would it feel like to be touched by that hand, to feel it on her skin?

Stifling a whimper, she swayed, and his other arm circled her instantly and hooked her up tighter against him. 'Steady,' he murmured, but her heart just beat faster, because his body was rock-solid and very male, and she just wanted to turn in his arms and kiss him.

'OK?' he asked, and released her carefully, as if he wasn't sure if she'd fall over.

'I'm fine—it's just the height,' she lied, shocked at her reaction, and he slid his fingers through hers and held her hand firmly until they were back inside.

'Have we got time to see the real David?' she asked once they were safely back down, trying to concentrate and not squander the whole day like a lovestruck teenager, and he grinned.

'Feet not tired yet?'

She laughed. 'Don't be silly—I'm a midwife. I put a pedometer on one day and did over nineteen thousand steps. I can walk forever. How about you?'

'Ditto. I'm fine, let's do it,' he said. 'I'd love to show you and we've probably got time. You'll be blown away.'

She was. 'The anatomical detail's amazing,' she said, staring in awe at the statue—the real one, the one Michelangelo's hands had carved lovingly and incredibly skilfully five hundred years ago. 'It's so accurate!'

'Did you know he used to buy corpses and dissect them so

he could learn what happened under the skin? That's why his work is so lifelike—because it's based on real anatomical knowledge. Except the genitalia, of course,' he added softly in her ear, his grin mischievous. 'Pre-pubescent, so as not to shock the matrons and terrify the virgins.'

She suppressed a laugh, and they moved on, but the gallery was closing and they were turned out into the cold and dark of the January evening—and her wonderful day with him was over. She turned to him, hugely reluctant to let it end, needing to show her gratitude somehow.

'Luca, I've had the best day and I've taken so much of your time—would you let me buy you dinner?' she said softly. 'Just as a thank you?'

His mouth twitched. 'You're welcome to my time, *cara*— but I'll buy the dinner. I was going to suggest it anyway. Do you want to go back to your hotel and change?'

He'd agreed? Her heart soared and she beamed at him. 'Actually, I'm starving, so if I'm OK as I am…?'

He laughed softly, sending a delicious shiver down her spine. 'No, you're fine. Better than fine. Most of the women in my life would need at least two hours to get ready, and they'd never confess to hunger.'

'You obviously mix with the wrong sort of women,' she teased, and was surprised by the thoughtful look on his face.

'Maybe I do,' he murmured, and offered her his arm. 'Shall we go?'

She tucked her hand into the crook of his elbow and they turned into the wind, but the cold air struck her face and slid down her neck and she shivered and huddled down into her coat. 'Oh, that's icy. I didn't realise it would be so cold. I should have brought a scarf.'

'Here—have mine,' he said, and draped it round her neck.

'Oh—you'll get cold now!' she said, and then caught the scent of his body on the fine, soft wool and nearly moaned out loud.

'I'm sure I'll survive. It's not far to the place I want to take you, just round the corner.' And it was worth giving up his scarf just to watch her snuggle down inside it with that sensual sigh. 'Here, this is it.'

He opened the door and ushered her in, and the tempting aromas made her mouth water. They'd paused for a light lunch, but it and their coffee this morning were just a distant memory now, and she was more than ready, but it was heaving.

'It's too busy,' she said, disappointed, but Luca just shook his head and looked up, catching the eye of a man with a white apron wrapped around his ample middle, and he beamed and came over to them, arms extended.

'Luca! *Buona sera!*'

'*Buona sera,* Alfredo. *Come sta?*'

Isabelle listened to the warmly affectionate exchange but only caught the odd recognisable word, such as *bambini,* and then Luca switched to English. 'Alfredo, do you have a table?'

'*Si, si!* Of course, for you, my friend. Always.'

And with a bit of shuffling and rearranging, he fitted them in, dragging a table out of the corner and finding another chair.

They sat down, but because they were squeezed in, her leg was jammed against Luca's hard, muscular thigh. 'I'm sorry, I can't move out of your way,' she said, but he just smiled.

'Don't apologise!' he said softly, and she felt heat flood through her. Good grief, what on earth was happening to her? It was only a leg, and yet since the first touch of his knee against hers in the café this morning, every fleeting contact had been enough to send her heart into hyperdrive.

All day she'd been trying to forget it, but he'd made it impossible, constantly brushing into her, touching her—nothing in the least bit questionable, but it had kept her senses simmering all day, and then he'd offered her his arm and wrapped his scarf around her neck, still warm and heavy with the very male scent of his body, enclosing her in his essence, and the small amount of common sense she'd talked into herself had been wiped out in an instant. And now the heat of that solid, well-muscled leg against hers was setting it on fire and burning away the last fragments of reason.

'Relax, *bella*,' he murmured, his teasing eyes dancing. 'I won't eat you.'

Shame, she thought, and shut her eyes briefly at the images that leapt into her mind. Good heavens, this wasn't *like* her! She'd never felt like this, never reacted so violently, so completely to a man's touch.

But it wasn't just his touch, it was his presence, too. She'd felt him at the café before she'd seen him, felt his eyes through the window stroking over her like little fingers of fire. And now, every time he looked at her, there was something there, something hot and dangerous and unbelievably tempting. And she was totally out of her depth. It had been so long since she'd dated anyone she'd forgotten how to do it, and a bit of her wanted to stop the clock and breathe for a few minutes, just to settle everything down again and remind herself why she didn't do this.

But the clock didn't stop, and Alfredo was coming back, weaving between the tables, a bottle of Prosecco in one hand, two menus in the other, and he filled their glasses with a flourish. Luca lifted his and smiled at her. 'Welcome to Firenze, Isabelle.'

'Thank you.' She clinked her glass against his and sipped, the bubbles tickling the back of her throat as she met those hot, dark eyes. 'And thank you for bringing it to life for me. It was fabulous. Much more fun than trailing round alone.'

'My pleasure,' he murmured, his eyes locked on hers.

Oh, help. 'So—what should we eat?' she asked lightly, trying to break the tension, but it lingered for another second.

'The special's always good,' he said after a slight pause, and she dragged her mind back into order.

'Let's go for that, then,' she agreed, and tried to concentrate on the food, but she could hardly taste it. She was too conscious of the pressure of his leg against hers, the warmth in his eyes, the soft sound of his laughter wrapping round her and making her ache because it was so nearly over.

And then at last it came to an end; they'd finished their food, dragged their coffee out indefinitely, and their conversation had finally run dry. The day was officially done.

He set his napkin on the table and smiled wryly. 'Shall we make a move?' he suggested, and she felt a surge of regret.

He held out his hand to her, and after the tiniest hesitation, Isabelle put hers in it and stood up, desperately trying to ignore the sensation that raced up her arm. Her leg was still burning from the heat of his body, and when he'd stood up and moved away, she'd felt the loss of his warmth like an arctic blast. Crazy. He was just a man, just an ordinary man.

No. That was a lie, and she'd never been dishonest with herself. He was gorgeous—witty, intelligent, disarmingly frank, and his body, tall and powerfully built, with those midnight-dark eyes, made her go weak at the knees. His hair was slightly rumpled from the wind; she wanted to touch it, to thread her fingers through it and test the texture, and then draw her hand slowly over his jaw, letting the rasp of stubble graze her palm.

His lips, so firm, so full, made her ache to feel them. On her lips, but also on her cheeks, her eyelids, her throat, her breasts. Everywhere.

Relax, bella. *I won't eat you.*

Oh, lord! She looked away, dragging her eyes off him and bending to pick up her bag from the floor while she gathered her composure.

'I need the Ladies',' she said.

'Good idea, I'll meet you back here,' he said, and she made her way into the sanctuary of the quiet room with relief.

What was *happening* to her? She *never* reacted like this to men! Never in a million years. Or twenty-eight, more to the point. Over a quarter of a century, and no man had ever made her heart beat fast or her skin heat or her body ache with a longing so intense it almost frightened her.

But Luca did. Luca made her body sing with joy at the slightest touch, and when she rejoined him and he rested his hand lightly against her spine to usher her out into the street, she could have been naked the effect on her was so powerful. It was as if he'd touched her intimately, found her secret places and stroked them with the slow, sure hand of a lover.

And now she was being ridiculous! He was just killing time after his interview, indulging in a little mild flirtation, and she'd do well to remember it. It was nothing personal, he was just exercising his natural charm, and there was certainly nothing *intimate,* for heaven's sake! And even if there was, nothing was going to come of it. She was only here for one more night, flying out in less than eight hours! She'd never had a one-night stand in her life, and she wasn't starting now. But she wished there was more time…

'Where's your hotel?' he asked, and she told him.

'That's good, it's just near here.'

He tucked her hand into his arm again, his smile gleaming white against his olive skin in the darkness, and she caught the faint tang of his aftershave and that warm, male scent that was becoming so familiar—the scent that was also drifting up to her from the scarf, snuggled so softly and intimately against her skin, almost as if he was holding her.

She shivered, and he shot her a quick glance. 'OK?'

'I'm fine,' she lied, but she wasn't, because it was the end of their time together and she wasn't sure she'd survive if he simply took her back to her hotel and dropped her off, whatever her scruples, because for some reason this night—no, this man—was different, and if he asked her…

Luca paused outside the entrance, staring down thoughtfully into her eyes, and she reached up and kissed his cheek, her warm breath whispering over his skin and setting it alight. 'Thank you for the most lovely day. You've been so kind, Luca.'

He didn't feel kind. He felt on fire, more alive than he had in years, and extraordinary reluctant to let her go, but there was no way…

'What time's your flight tomorrow morning?'

'I have to be at the airport at five.'

He hesitated, not sure what was happening to him, just knowing he couldn't walk away. Not from this, because this—this was different, and he'd deal with the consequences later.

'It doesn't have to end here,' he said softly, and waited, his breath lodged in his throat, for her reply.

Isabelle's heart was pounding now, because this was something she didn't do. Never. She felt she was on the brink of a precipice—or at the gateway to a whole new era.

'I don't do this,' she said in a whisper, but he heard and he laughed under his breath.

'Nor do I.'

'I—I can't get involved.'

'That's OK.'

'So—just tonight?'

He nodded slowly. '*Si*. Just tonight, *cara*. If that's what you want.'

Why not? she thought. It had been years now. She was too fussy to sleep with anyone just for the sake of it, not desperate enough to settle for mediocrity, and she was alone by choice.

But Luca—Luca did something to her that no man had ever done. He made her heart race, her blood heat, her body throb with need. There was absolutely nothing mediocre about him.

If she walked away from him now, she'd never know what it would have been like to make love with the most interesting and attractive man she'd ever met in her life. A man she could so easily, under other circumstances, have come to love.

And maybe it was time to let herself live again—if only for one night. Taking her courage in both hands, she met his eyes. 'Your place or mine?' she asked.

He let out his breath in a rough, choppy sigh, then his lips twisted into a wry little smile. 'Yours is closer.'

Her heart nearly stopped, then started again with a vengeance as he took her hand and led her into the hotel. She picked up her key at the desk, her heart pounding, and they went up to her room in a taut, breathless silence, their fingers tightly meshed.

They'd hardly made it through the door before he reached for her, his mouth finding hers in a kiss she felt she'd been waiting for all her life. She dropped her bag on the floor, and somehow he peeled away her coat and his scarf that she was still wearing, and then his hands slid up and cradled her breasts and he gave a deep, guttural groan that turned her legs to jelly.

She whimpered, and as if it was what he'd been waiting for, he stripped the sweater off over her head, muttering incoherently as he pressed her back against the wall, his mouth on hers, his hands moulding her breasts again. His chest was heaving as she grabbed the front of his shirt and dragged it open, pinging buttons off in all directions and whimpering in frustration because she couldn't get it down over his shoulders with his arms bent and his hands doing such incredible things to her nipples.

She gave up with the shirt, her hands moving to his waistband, and then he dragged his mouth away and dropped his forehead against hers, his hands catching hers and stopping their frenzied fumbling. 'Wait,' he growled, his breath sawing in and out of his lungs. 'This is crazy. It's too fast.'

Crazy? Too fast? Maybe, but when he stepped away and released her, she felt a huge sense of loss. She didn't want to be away from him, not for a moment—but apparently that wasn't what he had in mind.

He stared at her, his eyes on fire, and shook his head slowly, his hand coming up to cradle her cheek with incredible tenderness, and she could feel that it was shaking. 'If we go on like this, it'll all be over in seconds,' he murmured roughly, 'and I don't want seconds, *Isabella*. I want hours. I want to take my time—savour every moment of this night. Touch you all over. Taste you.'

Her knees nearly buckled. *Relax,* bella. *I won't eat you.*

'Oh, Luca, please,' she whimpered, and he closed his eyes and muttered something that sounded halfway between an oath and a prayer.

'I need a shower first—come,' he said, pushing open the bathroom door and leading her in before turning on the water, then he held out his hands out to her and drew her closer.

Gentle now, and garment by garment, he slowly stripped away the rest of her clothes, his knuckles grazing softly over her skin. She closed her eyes, suddenly shy, but he touched her cheek, tipping her face up to his so she could see the heat in his eyes, so close to hers.

'You're beautiful, *cara,*' he said gruffly, his thumb dragging slowly over her lips. 'Don't be shy with me.'

She swallowed and flicked her tongue out to moisten her lips, and the tip caught his thumb. He paused, and she grew bolder, stroking it back and forth across the pad, then sucking it gently, nipping it between her teeth—just lightly, but it was enough to make him groan.

'You're going to drive me crazy,' he whispered unsteadily, and stepping back a fraction, he shed his clothes in record time then stepped into the shower, holding out his hand for her.

Her heart hammered against her ribs, and she let her eyes absorb him—the sheer potent masculine beauty of his body, so beautifully sculpted, so taut, so exquisite that he could have been one of Michelangelo's models—except this man would surely have shocked the matrons and terrified the virgins, she thought, stifling a bubble of slightly hysterical laughter, but the only thing that shocked and terrified her was her own reaction.

She wanted him—wanted to touch him—no, *needed* to

touch him, to feel him, test the texture of that hot, wet skin beneath her palms, and so she took his hand and followed him into the shower, under the streaming water that pounded over them like a tropical storm, and let her roaming fingers explore him, investigating the stark contrast between the rough texture of his body hair and the wet silk of his skin, following the streaming water from his shoulders, over his deep, solid chest to the arrow of hair that her downwards.

She moved lower, her fingers trailing over the taut muscles of his abdomen, and his teeth clenched and he sucked in his breath with a hiss.

'*Cara,* slowly,' he groaned, and, easing away from her, he squirted shower gel onto his hands and started to wash her, his hands firm and almost impersonal as they touched her everywhere. If it hadn't been for the blazing heat in his eyes she might have thought he was washing a child, but there was nothing of the nurturer in this man now, and when she filled her palms with shower gel and smoothed her hands over his body he gave a shuddering sigh, his breath hot against her face as he cupped her bottom and eased her against him. She felt the urgent pressure of his knee between her thighs and opened for him as his hand slid round and cradled the terrible, yearning ache that was building in her body.

'Luca?' she whispered, and as the water streamed over them his mouth found hers in a kiss so searing she thought she'd go up in flames. She felt the hot, sensual slide of his tongue, its probing so erotic, so explicit that she could scarcely breathe. And it wasn't just his mouth. His hand was moving against her, freeing a wanton woman she hadn't even known existed until this moment.

A woman who wanted him, this man she'd never met

before tonight but would have trusted with her soul, because already, in some obscure way, it belonged to him.

She felt fevered. She thought she'd die if she didn't have him, and then he hit the shower control, grabbed a towel and rubbed her roughly dry, then hauled it over his skin and threw it aside as he led her back into the bedroom.

His mouth found hers again, and then his thigh was between hers and he pressed her backwards until her legs hit the bed and he toppled her over, falling with her in a tangle of limbs into the centre of the mattress.

'Isabella,' he groaned, lifting his head to stare down at her, his hands shaking as they touched her. She was gorgeous. So beautiful. So perfect. So much woman. He wanted to go slowly but he couldn't. He needed her, and his control was in tatters.

Slowly, he told himself. *Slowly. Make it last.* He lifted a damp strand of hair from her face and pressed a tender, lingering kiss to her lips, then turned his attention to those soft, generous breasts, first one, then the other, kneading them gently and rolling her tightly budded nipples between his fingers until she whimpered and arched up to him, and then using his knee to ease her thighs apart, he turned his head and stared down at where the soft nest of curls hid her from his sight.

Dio, he wanted her. Wanted to taste her, to touch her, to bury himself inside her...

His mouth closed over one nipple as his hand sought her again, found the hot, sleek moisture of her delicate folds, felt the tremble in her body as his thumb found the swollen bud and stroked it gently, probing her warmth, testing her.

'Luca!' she sobbed, bucking under him, and he hushed her softly and moved on, his tongue taking over where his thumb had left off, and she cried out and trembled, her shaking fingers knotting in his hair. 'Oh, God, Luca, now, please!'

He couldn't wait any longer. He felt as if he'd been waiting for her all his life, and he couldn't wait any more. She was begging him, her voice cracking, and he moved over her, settling against her, feeling her body yield to him as he entered her with a long, slow thrust that nearly pushed him over the edge.

She gasped his name again, and he kissed her softly, trying to take it slowly, trying to give her time to adjust to him as he withdrew and thrust into her again, deeper this time, harder, bringing a tiny scream to her lips. He felt her hands clawing at him, her nails digging into his shoulders as she urged him on breathlessly, her body striving beneath him.

He needed no urging. He was on the brink, hanging on for her with the last shreds of his control, and then he couldn't wait any more.

'Now, *cara,* please, now,' he grated, his body shaking with desperate restraint, and then he felt the first contraction, the convulsions deep within her body closing around him and drawing him ever deeper, and locking his mouth to hers in a desperate kiss, he drove into her again and again, until the waves came up and claimed him and he followed her into the boiling maelstrom of their release.

She couldn't move.

He was sprawled across her, his head against her shoulder, his chest heaving, and she could feel the wild pounding of his heart gradually slowing until finally he lifted his head and stared down into her eyes.

'Oh, Isabella,' he whispered, and, wrapping her tenderly against his chest, he rolled onto his back, taking her with him so she lay draped across his body, her legs tangled with his, his hard, muscled thigh pressed against her tender flesh, still pulsing with the aftermath of the most incredible experience of her life.

She felt tears sting her eyes and blinked them away, but they still fell, and there was a stupid sob rising in her throat. She bit it down, but it escaped, and he tightened his arms and rocked her.

'Hush, *tesoro*. It's all right. I've got you.'

It was as if he knew how she felt, as if he felt it too, the amazing, incredible, tumultuous emotions that were cascading through her, and his hand stroked gently over her hair and soothed her, and gradually her limbs relaxed and she sank slowly into sleep.

Luca didn't sleep. The street light filtered through the shutters and brought with it disturbing and intrusive thoughts—thoughts that he dismissed for now. He'd deal with the consequences later. For now—for now he had Isabella, and nothing else mattered.

He turned his head and gazed wonderingly at the sleeping woman by his side. He'd never known it was possible to feel such a powerful storm of emotions. It was as if he'd come out of a coma. Everything felt—hell, it just *felt,* and so much *more* than it ever had.

He reached out a hand, then stopped before he touched her, because although he wanted her again, he also wanted to watch her, to lie there beside her and absorb her while she slept so peacefully at his side. And if he touched her, the fire would start again. He'd never known a fire like it, he thought, and he wondered how he could have felt so much for a woman he didn't know. Because he *didn't* know her. He knew hardly anything about her. She might be a real fruit-cake, a neurotic, clinging vine—or, worse, a money-grub-bing little witch out for all she could get. He'd had it with that sort, big time.

But she wasn't any of those things. She was a good, decent woman who didn't do this. He knew that, from the straight-forward honesty of her response to him. He was just trying to talk himself out of something that scared the living daylights out of him, because if this was what it felt like, his life would never be the same again.

'Luca?'

He realised she was looking at him, and he put away his dark thoughts and dredged up a smile. 'Hi,' he murmured, and, leaning over, he brushed her lips with his. 'Did you sleep well?'

'Mmm. Fabulous. What about you? Are you OK?'

'Great. Fantastic,' he told her, realising that it was true. He felt better than he had for months—years—and it was all down to her. He kissed her again, then dropped his head against hers and sighed softly. She'd been so responsive, so passionate and tender and honest, and it had blown him away.

Made him forget all sorts of things he had no business for-getting—including one rather vital and critical thing that he just couldn't believe he'd overlooked.

He lifted his head and met her soft, sleep-hazed eyes. 'Mind if I ask you a personal question?'

'No,' she said slowly, as if she wasn't too sure.

'Are you, by a miracle, on the Pill?'

Isabelle's eyes widened, and she stared at him in conster-nation. She was—only to regulate her cycle, but it worked just the same. Which was as well, since she'd forgotten about contraception completely. Forgotten everything, even how to breathe at some points. And the Pill would only protect her from pregnancy. Oh, what an idiot.

'Yes, I am,' she said, and his eyes drifted shut, his relief obvious. He muttered something in Italian, then opened them again and grinned a little wryly, making her heart flutter.

'Sorry. I just—forgot about things like that, last night, which is crazy, because I never forget, but—it was amazing.' His voice softened and he reached out for her with his hand. 'You were amazing. Incredible.'

'So were you,' she said, feeling colour mount her cheeks and the now-familiar heat invade her body, but she ignored it, her brain, brought to its senses now, suddenly remembering all the other things she'd forgotten in addition to the pill she really must remember to take later on. 'Um—I don't really know how to say this, but—well, you don't need to worry about getting anything from me.'

'Oh, Isabella.' His fingers touched her cheek gently. 'Don't worry, you're safe, *cara*. I wouldn't do that to you.'

She felt a wave of relief, then common sense dawned again. 'Luca, what's the time?'

'Nearly four.'

No! She swallowed hard. 'I have to go soon.'

'I know. My car's not far away. I'll get it while you pack.'

He gave her a tender, lingering kiss, and then got out of bed. She watched as he pulled on his clothes—the shirt with no buttons, the crumpled suit, damp from the bathroom floor, and she wanted to cry. 'I'll see you outside in fifteen minutes,' he said, kissing her again, and closed the door softly.

He drove her to Pisa airport, and as they turned in he said, 'I'll park and come in with you—get a coffee or something.'

'No. I couldn't bear to say goodbye in public,' she said, wondering how she'd even do it in private, and so he pulled into the drop-off zone, cut the engine and turned to her, his eyes shadowed by the streetlights.

'Hey, don't look like that,' he murmured.

'I can't help it. I don't want it to end,' she said, unable to lie to him. 'It's been so special, Luca. Thank you.'

'Don't thank me—and it doesn't have to end,' he said softly, as if he'd read her mind, and she shrugged.

'Of course it does—and, anyway, we said just one night.'

'Can't I change your mind?'

She shook her head. 'It's silly getting involved. Long-distance relationships never work.' Relationships, full stop. And it might be better to let it go than to ruin the memories with reality. At least this way she could treasure them unsullied.

'There are ways,' he said, oddly reluctant to let her go without some means of contacting her. 'Tell me your number, *cara.* I'll call you when I'm next in London.'

She shook her head. 'No, Luca. That wasn't the deal—and I need to go now, or I'll miss my check-in.'

Oh, lord. She didn't want to go, whatever she'd said about long-distance relationships. She didn't want to leave him—couldn't bear to—and, crazily, she thought she was going to cry. She tried to smile, but her mouth wouldn't cooperate and she felt her eyes welling. 'Look—I have to go.'

'I know.'

He took her case from the boot and stood staring down at her, his eyes brooding and unreadable, and she flung her arms round him and hugged him, the tears welling once more. 'Thank you, again, Luca. Thank you for everything,' she said, and he shook his head.

'Hush, *cara*,' he murmured, and, lifting his hands, he cupped her cheek and brushed the tears from her face, then leaned in and touched his lips to hers.

It was a gentle kiss, tender and comforting, but then something shifted, and he threaded his fingers through her hair and anchored her head and kissed her with all the passion, all the incredible sensuality that he'd shown her last night.

Then finally he lifted his head, his breathing harsh, his face taut, but his fingers on her cheek were gentle. 'Give me your number—your address. I'll come and see you.'

'No—it's silly, Luca. We live too far apart—you're going to be working in Florence.'

'Maybe not. Isabelle—take my card. Call me, even if it's just to tell me you're home safe. Please. And if you change your mind...'

She hesitated, then took it and stuffed it into her pocket. 'Oh—your scarf!' she said, reaching for it, but he stilled her hands.

'Keep it. You'll be cold on the plane.'

She nodded, her eyes filling. 'Thank you.' She blinked away the tears. 'I have to go,' she said, choked. 'Goodbye, Luca.'

'Goodbye, *Isabella*,' he said softly, and his hand fell to his side, leaving her desolate. Grabbing her case, she ran into the airport without a backward glance before she made a fool of herself and started to cry again.

Luca watched her go, shocked at the emotion that ripped through him. He had to hold himself back, force himself not to follow her into the terminal and make her stay. He didn't know what had happened to him, but for some reason, everything felt different. Real. And he couldn't bear to let her go.

He waited until she was out of sight. Gave her time to come back, to call him.

Then he got back into his car and drove slowly out of the airport, his mind still full of the woman who'd blown his world apart…

CHAPTER TWO

HER JOURNEY WAS awful.

The flight was delayed, then they hit turbulence over the Alps and just about everyone was ill—including her—and by the time she got home she felt wrung out. She groped for her house keys, and found his card in her pocket where he'd tucked it as she was leaving him.

Luca Valtieri, she read, and a mobile number. She hadn't known his surname. It hadn't really mattered, not then. Not now, really. She wasn't going to see him again.

But she missed him.

Ridiculously so, with an ache that was almost physical.

Just a quick call, she promised herself—just long enough to hear his voice and tell him she was safe. And she could withhold her number so he wouldn't be able to call her back. That way she'd have control of the relationship—

No! It wasn't a relationship. She wouldn't let it be! But she was desperate to hear his voice, to have some kind of contact with the man who'd stolen her heart so suddenly.

So she rang him, and after a few moments she got his voicemail. She rang it again, just to hear his message, to hear the low rumble of his voice, the crisp message at odds with the man she'd spent last night with, and finally she spoke.

'Hi, Luca, it's Isabelle, I'm sorry I've missed you. I'm back. And thank you—for everything.'

Then she hung up, resisting the urge to give him her number. She could always call him again. Next week, perhaps. Or tomorrow.

No! Not tomorrow. Not next week, either. She was being ridiculous. She didn't want a relationship. Last time was enough for a lifetime.

She swallowed hard and then on impulse she turned on her computer and typed 'Luca Valtieri' into a search engine, expecting nothing, really, maybe a paper or two, some medical reference—and got a whole bunch of stuff.

Exstracts from articles in medical journals, research material, awards—but nothing personal, nothing to tell her more about the man himself except the fact that he was clearly very active and involved with his field of medicine, and he'd worked with a lot of English consultants whose names she recognised.

Silly her. She'd fallen—and how!—for a truly gorgeous man with a devastating smile and a kiss that had wiped out all the common sense she'd been born with, and not only that, he was funny and intelligent and dedicated. Thank God she'd refused to see him again. He was much too dangerous to her peace of mind but, oh, she missed him.

Oh, well. She'd get over it. She had before. It wasn't the first time her heart had been broken, although that time, of course, she'd been betrayed. Idly she wondered how she would have felt about Luca if she'd been able to trust him with her heart, but she couldn't turn the clock back and she had no idea how it would feel to have that much faith in a man.

Impossible. And if she'd allowed herself to fall for Luca, how much more would it have hurt when it all went wrong?

She swallowed hard. At least she'd had the sense to withhold her number, so he wouldn't be able to contact her.

And, besides, there wasn't time in her life to mope. Until her hospital's maternity unit refurb was completed she was working in another unit not nearly so easy to get to, so it was just as well Luca was out of her life because, frankly, with the extra travelling, she wouldn't have time for a relationship at the moment.

And if she told herself that often enough, maybe she'd believe it…

He'd missed her call.

He swore softly and dropped into a chair, resting his head in his hands. Damn. Of all the stupid, stupid things, to forget to put his phone on charge when he'd got back to the flat. But maybe…

He scrolled through to his incoming calls, and the hope died. 'Withheld. Damn.'

'Maybe she'll ring again,' his brother suggested.

He shook his head and swallowed hard. 'No—no, she won't. It doesn't matter. She didn't want to see me again anyway. I just wanted to—'

'Talk to her?' Gio finished softly for him when he broke off, and he nodded, his throat curiously tight. 'So are you going to go and find her?'

He shook his head. 'No. We agreed it was only for one night. I'll just have to live with it.' But hell, he didn't want to. He hadn't realised how much he was looking forward to speaking to her again—maybe talking her into letting him see her when he was back in London.

'So—what next?'

He let the air out of his lungs on a long, slow breath and met his brother's eyes. 'I don't know. Maybe I'll go back to London and finish off my research.'

'You could look her up—it's time you had a bit of fun. Where does she live?'

'Herne Hill, but I have no idea where or I'd go and try to talk her into seeing me again.'

'You must be slipping. It's not like you to have to chase after a woman. Did you disappoint her last night?'

He met his brother's mocking eyes with disgust. 'No, I did not—not that it's your damn business.'

Gio shrugged. 'So—what about the job? Mama will be disappointed if you go back to London. She was looking forward to having you closer to home.'

'She'd cope.'

'Of course—and who knows? You may even bring home a bride. Now, that *would* make her happy.'

He grunted and stifled the little leap in his chest that felt remarkably like hope. 'Unlikely. I have to convince her first—and, anyway, aren't you jumping the gun a bit? It was only one night.'

'Of course it was,' Gio said soothingly, and smiled. 'Just promise me one thing—let me draw up the pre-nup. And don't even contemplate getting hitched without one.'

He laughed. 'Relax, Gio. I'm not going to marry her. It's not on my agenda.'

'We'll see. Coffee?'

Luca gave his phone one last regretful look and slid it into his pocket. 'Why not?'

* * *

'What's going on?'

The group of women around the central nursing station didn't take their eyes off the office door.

'Richard Crossland's got someone with him. And he's a *hunk,*' her friend Sarah said in a stage whisper. 'He's been in there ages—they must be about to come out. I swear he's the most beautiful man I've ever seen.'

'Really.'

'Really. Really really really. Even you'd think so, Little Miss Fussy-Pants.'

Not fussy enough, apparently, or she wouldn't be moping about now with a broken heart six weeks down the line, Isabelle thought, and walked away towards the staff room to dump her bag. The Tube had been delayed and she didn't even have time for a cup of tea now. She certainly didn't have time to stand and ogle some stud who the girls thought was so damn marvelous.

There was a little commotion behind her, a sudden burst of activity that could only mean the office door had opened and they'd been caught staring. Well, serve them right, she thought, and glanced over her shoulder.

And stopped dead in her tracks.

'Luca?'

The word was soundless, hardly even a breath, but he turned his head and met her eyes, and the bottom dropped out of her world.

'Isabella.'

He crossed the ward in two strides, his warm hands cupping her shoulders, sending a shock wave through her body. She eased herself away from his grasp, horribly conscious of their rapt audience, her heart drumming against her ribs like a wild thing.

'What are you doing here?' she asked, choked by a flood of emotion that was threatening to unravel her.

'I could ask you the same thing. Your hospital's miles away.'

'Not nearly as far as Florence. Anyway, the unit's—'

'Shut for a refurb. I know that, you told me. They wouldn't tell me where you'd been relocated to, though. They were— well, let's say they were profoundly unhelpful. It didn't make it any easier to find you. So—how are you?'

She ignored that, her heart pounding as she took in his words. 'You were looking for me?'

'*Si*—for the last six weeks. I'd given up.'

Six weeks? Ever since…

'We weren't going to see each other again,' she pointed out, trying to sound composed while her heart was busy breaking all over again just at the sight of him.

'No. You didn't want me.' His mouth twisted into a wry smile, and her heart flip-flopped again and then contracted. Want him? She'd never stopped wanting him, not for a moment.

Whatever, it didn't alter the facts.

'It doesn't matter anyway, does it?' she said quietly, conscious of the stares of the other midwives still clustered round the nursing station with their mouths hanging open. 'What I want. I mean, you're here anyway, regardless of my feelings.'

'What?' He gave a startled cough of laughter and shook his head. 'Of course it matters. I'm not here to see you—I didn't know you worked here.'

'So why are you here?'

'I'm an old friend of Richard's. He heard I was back in London and asked me if I could help out. I owed him a favour—so I'm here. I swear, I had no idea you'd be here or I would have spoken to you first. Is it going to be a problem?'

She shook her head, feeling incredibly foolish and naïve. 'No. Of course not. Sorry, I misunderstood.' Of course he wasn't here for her. She was being ridiculous. Neurotic.

'So—why are you in London anyway?'

He smiled wryly. 'Finishing off some research—and I wanted to see you again if I could find you.'

No. She felt a flicker of panic. She didn't want this—didn't want to see him again. It was too much.

Her body was calling her a liar, and her heart was racing, but her mind was in panic mode and she shook her head and backed away.

'Luca, I can't talk about this here. I have to work.'

'So do I, now. But later—'

'No, Luca,' she said firmly, shaking her head and hanging on to the last shreds of her dignity. 'I told you I didn't want to see you again, and I meant it. I'm sorry, I don't want to talk to you, either now or later. Please—just leave me alone.'

'Isabelle, please, give me a few minutes—'

'No. Go away, Luca. Please.'

Turning on her heel, she ignored his protest, walked into the staff room, closed the door behind her and burst into tears.

'Izzie?'

'Go away, Sarah,' she mumbled, her hands pressed hard over her mouth to keep in the sobs that were tearing her apart.

'No. Oh, sweetheart, what's happened? Who is he? What did he say to you?'

She dragged herself together, sniffing hard and lifting her chin firmly. 'Nothing. Really—please—I'll be fine. I have to go to handover. I—I can't—'

'Rubbish. Here, you need a tissue and a cup of tea.'

'No. Well, yes, the tissue,' she said with a fractured laugh, 'but I haven't got time for tea. I've just got to get on.'

'So who is he?'

'Luca? He's a guy I met in Florence.'

Sarah's eyes widened. 'Really? Oh, my God—why ever did you come back?'

She laughed a little crazily. 'Because it was just one day? Because I have a life here, and he lives in Italy?'

'Well, it doesn't look like it. He's Richard's new locum, covering the maternity leave post.'

'What?' Shock nearly took the legs out from under her, and Sarah hugged her hard and steered her to a chair. 'Sarah, you're joking. He said he was doing Richard a favour, helping him out. I assumed he meant some research or something.'

Sarah shook her head. 'Sorry, Izzie, he's here, and he's working in the unit, and you're going to have to see him every day.'

'Every…' She dragged in a lungful of air. 'Oh, God, no! I'm going on holiday. How long's he here for?'

'I don't know. Weeks, I suppose. Months, maybe.'

Months?

'Will you be OK with that? Can you do it? Because I don't think you've got that much holiday,' Sarah said with a vain attempt at a smile.

Probably not, but—work with him? For *months?* Oh, lord. Maybe she could get a transfer? Or maybe she should just get a grip.

'Of course I can,' she lied, straightening her spine and blowing her nose hard. 'I'll have to. Just keep him away from me, and I'll be fine.'

And without giving Luca another thought—well, that was

a lie, but she had to pretend—she threw herself into her work. Which would have been fine, of course, if it hadn't been for the first labouring woman she checked.

Superficially, there was nothing wrong, but it was her third baby and third babies could often be a bit different. The notes contained no special warnings, the last ultrasound scan had been fine and there was technically nothing to worry about. Certainly nothing had been mentioned at handover, but the moment she went into the woman's room, she just felt a little tingle of suspicion.

'Hi, Julie, I'm Isabelle, I'm going to be looking after you now during your labour,' she said with a smile as she ran her eyes over her patient and skimmed the notes. 'How are you feeling?'

'Oh, I love the epidural,' she said with a heartfelt chuckle. 'It's marvellous. Just like going to the dentist, only I'm going to have a baby, not a filling!'

Isabelle smiled and checked her over, listening to the baby's heart with the foetal stethoscope. Was that a little hitch?

'Can I just turn you on your side, Julie? I can't quite hear.' She helped the woman adjust her position, checked again, then shook her head. 'I still can't hear enough. I'd like to put the monitor on you to get a better feel for what's going on.'

'Sure. It does seem awfully slow, this labour.'

'Well, that can be the epidural. Because you're lying down, you aren't getting any help from gravity, but I think it's just as well to check, don't you?'

She was setting up the machine as she worked, explaining to Julie how the cardiotocograph would give her the baby's heart rate and the pressure of the uterus, and also, most importantly, the correlation of the heart rate to the contractions.

And, sure enough, every time Julie had a contraction, the baby's heart rate dipped.

'So is there a problem?' she asked, looking more worried now.

'I'm not sure. Probably not, but it is dragging on a bit and I don't think your baby's very happy at the moment, so I'll get a doctor to take a look at you to be on the safe side,' she said with a reassuring smile. 'We might need to hurry things along a little.'

She stuck her head out of the door and looked around, just as Sarah came out of the sluice. 'You couldn't page the on-call register for me, could you? I've got a query with Mrs Marchant.'

'Sure—oh, there he is. Luca, Izzie wants you.'

Oh, perfect. Luca—of course, looking more gorgeous than a man had any right to look in shapeless scrubs. And Sarah's phrasing left a lot to be desired, as well! Oh, hell.

She straightened her shoulders and tried to find a professional face. She could do this. She could…

Luca walked towards her, wishing he hadn't taken this locum job to help his old friend out, wishing he'd just found Isabelle and spoken to her, but when he'd walked out of Richard's office this morning and seen her again, it had seemed like the answer to his prayers.

Now he wasn't at all sure. Ever since he'd set eyes on her again he'd been hoping that being forced to work together might give them a chance to get to know each other, find out if they had anything worth pursuing, but her face was closed, her lips pressed tightly together, and he realised that working with her could be a nightmare. She'd got issues of some sort. God knows what, but, given time, he was sure he'd be able to break through them. He had before—and how. He only hoped that he'd be able to remain professional until then, because all he wanted to do right now was wrap his arms around her and tell her it was all right—and if he tried it, she'd probably kill him. Thank God there was a patient in the way!

'Problems?' he mouthed as he reached her, and she nodded.

'Maybe,' she murmured quietly, and he realised with relief that she was going to behave as if nothing had happened— for now, at least. 'Julie Marchant, third pregnancy, straight-forward previous history, admitted late last night in early labour. She had an epidural at five a.m.—so that's three hours ago, she's had two top-ups, but progress has slowed right down even though she's virtually fully dilated, and there's a dipping foetal heart rate—nothing much, but I'm just…'

She ground to a halt with a little shrug and bit her lip, and he dragged his eyes off it and made himself concentrate.

'Is the head high?' he asked.

'A little. It's probably nothing, just the mother's position…'

But she looked troubled, and he knew better than to ignore a troubled midwife. He gave a terse nod. 'Give me ten seconds, I have to make a note of something and I'll be with you.'

Isabelle went back to her patient, and moments later he joined her, squirting gel onto his hands and rubbing it in as he smiled at their patient and tried to focus on her.

'Hi, Mrs Marchant, I'm Luca. May I call you Julie? Tell me, how are you feeling?' he asked, but as she talked and he probed gently with his questions, he was checking the CTG, watching their patient carefully, his eyes flicking to Isabelle's from time to time for confirmation of Julie's words.

And then, as much to hear her voice as for the information she'd give him, he said, 'Isabelle, could you run over the notes with me?'

Isabelle, she thought with a stupid tinge of regret, not *Isabella,* with that wonderful, slow roll of her name over his tongue, tasting every syllable. Damn. And she needed to concentrate.

So she filled him in again, showed him the charts and pointed out her concerns without alarming the patient, although there was nothing much to alarm her, anyway—nothing very untoward, nothing drastic, really, at all, and as she was telling him about it she thought, Oh, lord, he thinks I'm overreacting, because the baby's heart rate was only dropping a tiny bit—but…

'She's contracting,' she said, forgetting the charts for a moment, and he looked back at their patient with a smile that should have melted her bones, murmured, 'May I?' and laid his hands over her abdomen, the fingers of one splayed over the baby's head to feel for its descent, watching the monitor as the contraction progressed. This time, she was both pleased and concerned to see that the dip in heart rate was more noticeable. So she hadn't imagined it—and it *was* a worry.

He made a small, thoughtful sound and his eyes flicked to Isabelle's. 'She's fully dilated?'

'Yes, except for an anterior lip,' she told him, hoping that he was going to believe her and not give Julie an unnecessary internal examination, 'and she's been in established labour for four hours.' So the head should be lower, and coming down with every contraction, not staying stubbornly high as if something—the cord?—was preventing its descent.

'Hmm,' he said again, then looked back at Julie. 'I think your baby might be a bit of an acrobat,' he said with another of those smiles. 'The cord could be a bit tangled, and if that's the case, we need to untangle it for him. Unfortunately this means a C-section, but it's nothing to worry about and you have an epidural already, so you're all set. We'll take you up now, there's a theatre free. Is there anyone here with you?'

'No, my husband's taking the children to school and getting some food in. I was taking so long—oh, damn! Can we wait for him?'

He shook his head, busily disconnecting her from the machines and kicking the brakes off the bed. 'No, your baby's not comfy so I'm not happy to wait, but we'll look after you, you don't need to be afraid. Isabelle will stay with you. I'll get someone to contact your husband—do we have a mobile number for him?'

'Um—I think so.'

'OK. Don't worry, we'll deal with it. Isabelle, could you come to Theatre with Mrs Marchant?'

'Sure. I'll just hand over my other patients to Sarah—'

'She'll understand. Come on, let's go—we can't miss the theatre slot!' he said with a grin at their patient, but Isabelle picked up the hidden meaning and pulled the bed out from the wall, relieved not only for Julie but for herself that he'd taken her concern so seriously.

Sarah must have seen them go, because they were ready and waiting in Theatre, and Julie was on the table and draped in moments.

'OK, time to meet your baby,' he said the second he was scrubbed, and Isabelle ran in after him, her gown still trailing, and watched him do the fastest section she'd ever seen.

'Good call,' he murmured to Isabelle, clamping and cutting the cord which was wrapped several times round the baby's neck, and with a smile for the mother, he eased the tiny girl out and handed her instantly to the waiting neonatal team while Isabelle wondered what it was about him that his praise could mean quite so much to her. But then she stopped thinking about that, because the baby was silent, and in the normally noisy theatre they could have heard a pin drop.

'You have a beautiful little girl, Mrs Marchant,' Luca said in a calm voice, his eyes smiling. 'Well done.'

Julie's hand tightened on Isabelle's. 'Can I see her?'

'Not just yet,' Isabelle said, squeezing back reassuringly while her ears strained for a sound of life. 'They need to clear her airway.' Luca was still busy, but she could see that like all of them he was acutely aware of the deafening silence in the room, and his eyes kept flicking to the neonatal team.

'What's taking so long?' Mrs Marchant said, her eyes filled with tears. 'Why isn't she crying?'

'It only seems a long time,' Luca lied, but one eye was on the clock and it was ticking. One minute—two...

They were all holding their breath, because if they couldn't, then the baby couldn't—and then, when they had all but given up, there was a small, mewling cry, then a shuddering breath and a full-blown bellow of rage, and they all laughed with relief and carried on, because at that moment the sound of a baby crying was the sweetest sound in the world.

'Nice work, Mr Valtieri,' Isabelle murmured while Julie met her baby daughter, fairness making her give him his due, and his eyes met hers over the mask and softened in a smile that turned her heart to pulp.

'Ditto,' he said quietly. 'What made you get me when you did?'

She lifted a shoulder. 'Gut instinct?'

'I like your instincts, *cara*,' he said, and turned back to their patient, still smiling under his mask.

Maybe working with her would be OK after all—and given time...

* * *

'What time do you finish?'

She looked up from the notes she was writing at the nursing station in the centre of the ward and contemplated telling him it was none of his business, but apart from the fact that it would have been petty, it would take him ten seconds to check the rota.

'Nine-thirty,' she told him, and he frowned.

'So late?'

'I work a thirty-seven-and-a-half-hour week. So if I do three fourteen-hour days with an hour-and-a-half break, I've done my hours. And I get four days off.'

'But you haven't had a break yet.'

She met his scowl with a dry laugh. 'That's right. I usually don't.'

'But that's not good for you—and it's not fair.'

She couldn't disagree, so she just shrugged and carried on with her notes. Until a large hand arrived in the centre of the page, the fingers splayed across it so she couldn't see. The fingers which had touched her with so much skill, making her body sing...

'Come and have a coffee, at least. We need to talk.'

'I don't think so. I told you that earlier. We're working together, by an unhappy coincidence, but that's all. Our relationship is professional only, Mr Valtieri, and that's the way it's staying.'

'Has anyone ever told you you're stubborn?'

'It's one of my more endearing qualities—but it's nothing to do with being stubborn. I just don't like my wishes being ignored.'

'I didn't ignore them!'

'So what are you doing here?'

He closed his eyes, growling in frustration. 'It was coincidence, as you said.'

'You were looking for me,' she reminded him, and a flash of dark colour swept over his cheekbones.

'I had been. I just wanted a chance to see you.'

'Well, you should have checked if I wanted to see you before you wasted your time, Luca.'

'Maybe I should. Maybe I would have, if you'd given me your number, but this is nothing to do with that. This is just chance, and I'm sorry if you don't like it, *Isabella,* but since I'm here…'

Isabella. With at least two more syllables, and a rolling purr that made her heart hitch. Well, it wouldn't work. Her heart could hitch all it liked, but she wasn't going to let herself get drawn into a relationship with him by that flagrant Italian charm.

Except professionally, and only then because she had no choice. And she couldn't do that if she allowed him to creep under her guard.

He sighed. 'Isabella, we do need to talk about this,' he said quietly. 'Maybe not now, but soon. At the very least, you owe me the chance to—'

'I owe you nothing,' she said bluntly.

He leant over the desk so his face was mere inches from hers. 'Then at least do me the decency of hearing me out.'

Isabelle swallowed. He was so close that she could smell him, smell the combination of spice and citrus and man that had trashed her defences so thoroughly in Florence, so that even now the evocative scent brought it all back and left her weak and wanting.

She shut her eyes and stifled the whimper. 'Luca, I don't want to. You've come and found me, I didn't want to see you, that's the end of it.'

'Not for me.'

'Well, tough. It is for me, and it takes two. Go and talk to Richard if you want someone to talk to. I'm not opening myself up to hurt all over again just to give you closure.'

'All over again? Is that what this is about, some man who hurt you? Who was it, Isabelle? Who hurt you so much you're afraid to try again?'

She met his eyes in desperation. 'Luca! Go away!'

He sighed softly under his breath. 'OK—for now. But I'm not finished, and we need to do this somewhere a little more private.'

She contemplated saying no, but he wasn't going to give up, so she agreed, grudgingly. 'Oh, for God's sake, all right. I'll have coffee with you later, when I've finished this, but not now. Now, please move your hand,' she said calmly, although her heart was pounding, but as he opened his mouth to say something his pager bleeped.

He gave a low growl of frustration, muttered, 'Later—and don't forget,' and stalked off down the ward, muttering something in Italian.

'Oh, that man is so-o-o sexy!' one of the midwives murmured as she walked past, and Isabelle closed her eyes.

He might be sexy—she could testify to that—but she wasn't going to be influenced by it. She'd been stupid enough already and she wasn't letting him any further into her life. She completed the labour report she was writing up for Julie Marchant, slapped the file onto the heap and reached for the next one.

She'd hear him out, over coffee, as she'd agreed, but that was all. She wasn't going to let him get to her. No way.

CHAPTER THREE

'WHAT ARE YOU doing?'

'Taking you home.'

She turned up her coat collar against the February chill and sighed shortly. 'I thought we were going for coffee? I don't need to be taken home.'

'I disagree. It's dark, it's late and you've worked fifteen hours without a proper break. You can't go home alone and unaccompanied, especially not by the time we've had coffee, it's not safe.'

She glared at him in exasperation. 'Luca, I'm twenty-eight! I've lived in London all my life, and I've been doing this journey for weeks now. It's perfectly safe!'

'But it's a long way to Herne Hill—that is where you said you live, isn't it? Unless you've moved house, as well, during the refurb?'

She contemplated lying, but it went against the grain, and, anyway, he only had to check the HR files. Probably had already. 'No—no, I haven't moved house,' she told him, amazed that he'd remembered where she lived from her fleeting mention of it weeks ago, 'but the journey's perfectly straightforward.'

'Straightforward?'

She rolled her eyes. 'I walk to the Tube, get the train to Victoria, get the bus to the end of the road next to mine and walk home.'

'In the dark? That's *not* safe.'

'It's *perfectly* safe. There are lots of streetlights.' Although it wasn't great. There were too many trees shading the lights, and there were several dark spots where she often felt a little nervous, but there was no way on God's green earth she was telling Luca that.

'And how long does this whole *straightforward* journey take you?'

She shrugged. 'Forty-five minutes?'

He swore—in English, so she could understand this time, his accent heavier as he became frustrated with her—and went on, 'I'm taking you home. Get used to it.'

'Only if I tell you the address—which I have no intention of doing. It's bad enough that you know where I work.'

'Oh, for God's sake, Isabelle! If I wanted to know your address, I'd ask Human Resources,' he pointed out. 'I'm sure I could come up with some plausible reason for needing it.'

She was sure he could.

She gave up, frustrated to bits but too tired to argue any longer.

'All right,' she snapped, 'you can take me home, if your crazy Latin sense of honour demands it, but that's it. You're not coming in. I don't want this, Luca.'

His shoulders dropped, and he stabbed a hand through his hair and gave a tired sigh that pulled at her reluctant heart-strings. 'This? What this? I just want to talk to you, Isabelle. I *need* to talk to you.'

'Why? There's nothing to say.'

'Because I've been looking for you for weeks,' he said quietly, 'and now I've found you, by a miracle, I would appreciate a chance to talk to you—even if it's only so you can tell me to go to hell. You still owe me that coffee, since you managed to avoid taking a break all day.'

She hesitated, but he was right, she had promised, and she didn't go back on her word. 'OK,' she said flatly. 'You can take me home, if you absolutely have to, and you can have a coffee and get all this off your chest so you have closure, and then you can leave.'

'I don't want closure.'

'Well, it's all you're going to get, so take your pick.'

His smile was cynical. 'You're all heart, you know that?'

'Or maybe I'll just go home on the Tube on my own.'

She turned and walked off, and after a second she heard his firm, solid footfall behind her. And for some crazy, stupid reason, her heart did a happy little jiggle. She squashed the smile and kept walking, then she felt his hand on her arm.

'Isabelle, stop. I intend to take you home whether I drive you in my car or follow you on foot, so why don't you just choose the car and make it easier for both of us?'

'Some choice,' she grumbled, but in truth she was exhausted, and the very thought of walking to the Tube, sitting in the smelly, busy carriage with all the revellers out for the night, then waiting for a bus and walking for another ten minutes at the other end was too depressing to contemplate.

'Of course, if you come in my car, we have the heater, we won't get wet in the rain and I don't have to make the same ridiculous journey back. But it's up to you.'

Stupidly—because it was his idea to take her home and

nothing at all to do with what she wanted—she felt guilty at the thought of him having to make the return journey the hard way. After all, his day had been just as long as hers. And the car did sound *awfully* tempting. Then a dribble off the edge of the canopy ran down the back of her neck and made up her mind.

'Have it your way, then,' she said grudgingly, and immediately felt rude and ungrateful and mean. And she hated that, because she wasn't naturally rude or mean, and if it hadn't been for the strings attached to it, she'd be grateful. She *was* grateful. She just didn't want to encourage him or make him feel that just because they'd spent one incredible night together they could have any more than that.

And she was still angry with him, still not entirely convinced that his turning up at her hospital was just coincidence, and still very, very vulnerable to his potent charm. Scarily so.

But she let him lead her to his car—not his Italian sports car, she noticed, but a sensible little Alfa Romeo—and she sank down into the soft leather seat and rested her head back, and in seconds she was asleep.

'Wake up, sleepyhead,' Luca said softly, reluctant to disturb her when she was clearly exhausted. 'I need directions.'

'Oh.' She struggled up from the depths of her seat and looked around. 'OK, you're nearly there. Turn left just past that pub.'

'Here?'

'Yes—down here, and turn left there and pull up. This is it.'

He parked outside a pretty little terraced house in a tree-lined street tucked away off the main road, and cut the engine, relieved to see that it was in a very respectable neighbourhood.

'So are you coming in for that coffee?' she asked, but she

sounded grudging and he realised that he still had a very long way to go.

'Am I welcome?'

She sighed. 'You've brought me home. Even I'm not that churlish. Anyway, you said you wanted to talk,' she said, reaching for the doorhandle.

He hesitated. 'When do you work again?'

'Tomorrow, seven-thirty,' she said.

'That's crazy. I can't come in now, it's far too late, we'll talk tomorrow. You need to get to bed.'

Oh, why had he said that word? Something dark and dangerous unravelled inside him, and he wished she'd just get out of the car and go into the house and shut her front door before he carried her through it and onto the nearest flat surface. He gripped the wheel tightly.

'Come on, Isabelle, get out. I'll see you in the morning,' he said, wishing she would open the door, but she hesitated and then turned to him.

'Oh, this is ridiculous, you're here now, and, anyway, I won't sleep for ages after that nap.'

She reached for the handle and got out, and after a fractional hesitation he followed her, going through her front door and into a narrow but well-kept entrance hall, his hands rammed firmly into his pockets. 'I'll make coffee,' she said, heading for the kitchen.

'Can you make that tea?' he said, starting to follow her. 'I've had so much coffee today to keep me awake that I won't sleep. And is there any chance of some toast? I'm starving.'

'Of course. Stay here.'

Stay here. An order, Isabelle setting the limits, taking control of a situation she was unhappy with, he thought, but he stayed, giving himself a little breathing space and taking the opportunity to learn a little about her and her home.

It was small, neat and full of homely touches, but a little tired round the edges. A typical rented house, like so many others, but at least she'd made an effort to make it home. But it was a ludicrous distance from her work, and he was sure she could have found something closer if this new post was going to last any length of time.

But it wasn't his business, of course, and Isabelle would be the first to tell him that, and however frustrating he found it, he was beginning to realise that he couldn't just order her about and take over her life and look after her, because she just wasn't going to let him.

However much he wanted to.

He grunted with frustration. Given the choice—which was never going to happen!—he'd take her home to his house, literally round the corner from the hospital, and install her there with him—in the spare room if she insisted—for the duration of the refurb in her own hospital. And maybe by then he would have enough time to convince her that he wasn't a bad person, and that what had happened when they'd met, that tidal wave of emotion and reaction, had been bigger than both of them.

And maybe, just maybe, they'd find they had a future.

But not yet. It was too soon. She had issues to deal with, and until he could talk her into giving them a chance, they weren't going to move this thing forward at all. So he ignored his frustration and looked around.

There was a photograph on the mantelpiece of a younger Isabelle with a woman who looked as if she could be her mother. They had their arms around each other and they were laughing, and it made him smile. It could have been a photo from his own family, bossy and interfering, but loving and supportive, too.

There had been times when he'd needed that so much. He turned away from the photograph with a sigh, and lowered himself onto the sofa cautiously. He'd sat on plenty of rented sofas in the past, and they were almost without fail too hard, too soft or just plain wrong.

This one was all of them. Shifting to avoid a spring, he leaned back cautiously, rested his head against the cushion and closed his eyes.

It was a good job it was so uncomfortable, or he might just stay here forever…

'Oh!'

She put the tray down and stared at him in frustration. He was asleep, for heaven's sake! So much for a five-minute chat and booting him out of the door. She sat down opposite him in the chair and left him to it while she sipped her tea, telling herself it was out of kindness but secretly grateful for the chance to study him.

He looked tired. His eyes were shadowed, his lashes dark against his olive skin, and he was dead to the world. No wonder pagers were so horribly aggressive and hard to ignore. Nothing else would have got through to him, she was sure, and she wondered how she'd failed to notice just how tired he was.

Probably because she'd either been too busy avoiding him or so busy with a delivery that all her attention had been on her patient. Whatever, she hadn't looked at him properly—had never had the chance to look at him really closely without him looking back, and she felt a little voyeuristic.

It didn't stop her, though. Nothing short of him waking

would have stopped her, and she let her eyes linger on his jaw, with its shadow of stubble that gave him a morning-after look reminding her so strongly of Florence. His nose was strong and straight, but there was a little bump in it where it had been broken at some time. A sporting accident? Or fighting over a girl? She could imagine him doing that, in his teens. And he would have won, of course.

His lips were slightly parted, full and soft and beautifully sculpted, like one of Michelangelo's exquisite pieces; his eyes sat deep in their sockets, his brows a clean, strong arch over them, crafted by a master's hand. She wanted to reach out and touch his face, run her fingers over the warm, silken skin, feel again the rough scrape of his stubble, the flesh and bone beneath. Feel that glossy hair, so dark it was almost black, and with a texture like raw silk.

She could remember the feel of it between her fingers, the soft, thick strands teasing her body as he moved over it, driving her mad with his wicked, clever mouth.

She swallowed and shut her eyes, letting her breath out on a whimpering sigh, and after a moment, when she opened them, he was watching her.

'Are you all right, *cara?*'

'I'm fine. You were asleep—I started without you,' she said, indicating his mug and the pile of buttered toast on the table between them.

His smile was wry. 'We didn't all have the benefit of a catnap on the journey,' he said easily, and sat forward to pick up his tea and a slice of toast.

She curled up, hitching her feet up under her bottom and wriggling back in the chair to give herself a little more personal space. Not that it helped. He was still far too close

for comfort, and her thoughts were still recovering from the
memory of his mouth trailing over her. She could move away
from him physically, she realised, but she couldn't escape so
easily from her own head.

'OK—you wanted to talk, so you'd better do it, starting with
why you were looking for me,' she said, not allowing either of
them to get sidetracked now he was awake, and he leaned
back with his tea and regarded her steadily over the top of it.

'I wanted to see you again,' he said simply. 'One night left
me with more questions than answers. I felt...' he shrugged,
'unresolved.'

Oh, she knew all about that. She'd tried so hard to resolve
it in her mind, to put him out of it, even, but her mind wasn't
having any. Unresolved? Oh, yes.

'So you thought you'd come and find me?'

He inclined his head a fraction. 'I had to come to London
anyway, to finish off my research. I had a starting point in that
I knew the name of your hospital, so I thought I'd try there.'

'So you just—what? Contacted them and asked for me?'

'Yes—and I drew a blank. I didn't know your last name,
and so I couldn't give them enough information to be convincing. And I don't know any of the clinic staff there, so I couldn't
pull strings. So I asked around a few friends without success,
and then I gave up. I told myself you had my number, you
could call me again if you wanted to, and you hadn't, so I
assumed—but if I'd needed to, believe me, I would have found
you,' he said in a voice that left her in no doubt it was true.

'How?' she asked, half-joking. 'By hiring an investigator?'

He shrugged, and she stared at him, seeing in his eyes that
it had been a possibility, and shocked by the very idea, but
suddenly it seemed to make a lot of sense. 'Is that what you did?'

she asked slowly, a cold chill creeping over her as she realised she knew nothing about him, but he gave a grunt of laughter.

'No. Why would I do that? You wouldn't give me your phone number, you didn't give me your address, and when you rang, you withheld your number. You obviously didn't want me to find you. Even I can take a hint—so, no, I didn't hire an investigator. It was purely coincidence. Richard and I have been friends for years, and he heard I was around and we met for a drink, and I told him I was taking time out and working on my research, so he offered me the job. I'd all but given up any hope of finding you, and I had no idea you worked there until I saw you.'

He sounded sincere, but she still wasn't sure. 'I thought you were working in Florence—in that job they offered you. I never expected you to turn up like that in London and shock the living daylights out of me.'

He frowned at the distrust in her eyes, and the fact that she could think those things of him. 'I'm sorry. I didn't mean to upset you and it really wasn't planned. I just wanted a chance to see you again, to talk to you—maybe spend some time together. Take you out for dinner.'

Take you to bed.

He sighed and scrubbed his hand through his hair, trying not to think about that. 'Look, I promise you, us meeting up again was just coincidence, although there aren't that many maternity units in London so maybe it was inevitable that some point I might run into you, but I've never chased a woman in my life—I've never had to. And I wouldn't contemplate chasing someone who wasn't interested. It's happened to me too damned often.'

She gave a choked splutter of laughter. 'Modesty's not one of your failings, is it?' she retorted, and he just rolled his eyes.

'It's nothing to do with modesty. It's just the truth. I'm a doctor, and I'm not exactly hideous, I'm realistic enough to know that, nor am I on the breadline. It's a pretty potent combination, so I'm told. Frankly I could do without it. And if you really don't want to see me again, I'll accept that and I'll tell Richard I can't take the job. I don't want you to feel you have to hide from me or lie to me or feel threatened, and I'm sorry if I've made you feel like that. I didn't mean to make you uncomfortable.'

She felt a pang of guilt. 'I didn't deliberately conceal anything from you,' she said quietly. 'And we'd agreed we wouldn't see each other again, so I was really shocked when you turned up. I didn't expect you to come looking for me.'

'I didn't expect to want to. I really wasn't going to, but then I couldn't seem to get you out of my head. But you didn't tell me where you were going when your department was being closed down for refurbishment, and you must have known, so you weren't being completely open with me.'

She shook her head. 'I didn't know where I was being moved to and, anyway, it didn't seem relevant. I had other things on my mind.' Things like him. Things like his smile, and the scent of his body close to hers, and the feel of his lips on hers.

She yanked her thoughts back in line. 'But, anyway, that's all beside the point, Luca. I had reasons for not wanting to see you again, that's why I didn't give you my number.'

'What reasons? Is there another man in your life? This guy that hurt you? Or is it all in the past?'

'Is it any of your business?' she asked a little desperately, and he shrugged.

'I don't know. Maybe. If it affects the way you relate to me—

and certainly if there's someone else. I don't poach from another man's territory, and I don't do infidelity, mine or anyone else's. Ever—at least, not knowingly, so if there *is* someone…'

'There isn't. Well, at least, not for me. I told you, I don't—'

'—do relationships. I know. I don't either, not recently. But you—you got under my skin, Isabelle. I've had affairs, but they don't last. They leave me cold—well, not cold, but certainly not hot,' he added, his voice dropping sensually, his accent more pronounced, 'not so hot I thought my clothes would catch fire, so hot I thought I'd die if I didn't have you right then, right there on the walkway above the Duomo in front of the entire city. Not so hot I could hardly get you through the bedroom door before I tore your clothes off so I could feel your skin against mine.'

'Stop! Stop it!' she begged, her hands shaking so much she slopped her tea over her legs. 'It was just craziness.'

'*Si,* I know. But I've never felt like that before. It was the first time in my life I'd lost control, and the first time in my life I felt really, truly alive. And I realised that, after feeling like that, despite whatever might or might not happen with us in the future, I could never settle for less. That's why I wanted to find you—to know if it was real, because it felt real, *cara.* It felt more real than anything ever has before, and I wasn't ready to let it go.'

She didn't know what to say, so she said nothing for a while, just stared into her tea while he ate toast and sipped his tea and his words went round and round in her head.

'Isabella?'

She looked up at him, shocked by his honesty and the strength of his reaction. And her own. 'Luca, I don't know what you want me to say.'

'I don't want you to say anything particularly. I want you to keep an open mind. I have no idea if this could last, but I want to find out. I want to get to know you, give you a chance to get to know me. Give us a chance.'

'You want to have an affair?'

He gave a soft grunt. 'Perhaps? Maybe not, not yet. But I feel as if I've lost my mind, having a crazy, white-hot fling with a beautiful Englishwoman who's bewitched me and turned my brain to mush. That why I tried to find you, and why I decided to come stay in London for a while longer.'

She frowned and ignored the crazy white-hot nonsense because she didn't dare think about it, and focussed instead on the one fact she hadn't registered. 'Longer? What do you mean, stay longer?'

'I've worked here off and on for years. I was doing some research here from October, then I went home for Christmas and someone told me about the job in Florence. I'd nearly finished my research, I was ready for the next step in my career, and I went for an interview. They offered me the job, I walked out of the hospital—and then I met you.'

'So—what happened with the job? Didn't they mind delaying your start?' she asked, irrationally disappointed at the thought that he'd be going back to Italy soon, but he shook his head.

'It's irrelevant. I turned it down. I wanted to find you.'

'But—why, Luca?' she asked, stunned. 'Why throw away your job in Florence for someone you didn't even know? It was only one night. How could you have let it change your whole life?'

He laughed softly. 'Because it did. Because I can't get you out of my head, *cara.* You've bewitched me. I had to find you, but I couldn't bring myself to have you hunted down by an investigator—or maybe it was that I was too proud to admit that you'd walked away from me, so I left it to the gods. I thought maybe if I hung around long enough, I might run into you. Which I did.'

By accident, if she could believe that. She still wasn't sure she could. Whatever, he was now working alongside her—potentially for months, she realised—with nothing to stop them from exploring this relationship. Except her fear and lack of trust—and she still wasn't really sure she could believe his story about how he'd found her. It all sounded too innocent to be plausible.

'So—having found me, what do you think happens next?' she asked, her heart pounding with a mixture of anticipation and dread, and he shrugged, his eyes curiously veiled.

'We see where it goes.'

Her heart stalled. 'Where what goes?'

His voice was soft and low, teasing her senses and sending a shiver through her. 'Whatever it is, this feeling between us that won't seem to go away.'

Her heart started again, and she swallowed hard, refusing to allow herself to be tempted by the serpent, no matter how sweet and juicy the apple.

'Why, Luca?' she asked with a touch of desperation. 'Why me?'

'I don't know,' he said softly. 'Why me? I have no idea why it happened, but it did—and we both felt it that night. I wasn't alone, Isabella. You felt it, too, and I won't let you deny it.'

She couldn't, but she didn't want to think about that night. She sucked in a breath. 'I acted out of character. I don't do that—don't have relationships and certainly not one-night stands.'

'Perhaps because there's never before been that much temptation,' he suggested quietly, and she swallowed hard.

'God, you've got some ego there, Luca.'

'It's not ego. It's the truth. We couldn't help ourselves, *cara.* Either of us. It was meant to be.'

Was it? She didn't want to think so, but at the time, every look, every touch had been enough to make her forget her own name.

'That still doesn't mean we've got a future,' she said, and his mouth twisted into a wry, humourless smile.

'Maybe not. But it wasn't only me. I knew it was crazy, but I couldn't let you go without knowing how it would be between us.'

'You didn't have to come and find me, though. I told you I didn't want a relationship. It was just one night.'

'No. It was more than that, Isabella, and you know it.'

Oh, God. *Isabella.*

'No. We agreed. That was all it was meant to be. I didn't want to see you again,' she lied, 'didn't want a relationship, and I still don't.

'I told you at the time, I don't do relationships.'

'So how come you're on the Pill?'

She coloured softly. 'To regulate my cycle,' she told him frankly, holding his eyes even though she clearly wanted to look away. 'Nothing more.'

'Why not? You're a beautiful woman, Isabella. You should be living your life, not just going through the motions.'

'I *am* living. I don't need a man in my life to do that. We don't all have to indulge in indiscriminate sex to validate us as human beings!'

'There was nothing indiscriminate about that night. It was incredible—every moment of it. It was wonderful.' His voice sounded rough to his ears, and he swallowed. 'You were wonderful—and you deserve to be with a man who can appreciate you.'

'Not if I don't want it.'

He sighed softly. 'But you did—and it moved you to tears. When was the last time you cried when you made love, Isabelle? When was the last time it made you weep?'

Her eyes filled, and she looked away. 'I was tired. It was just—'

'That it reached something inside your heart that hasn't been reached for years? If ever?'

A tear slid down her cheek, and he reached across the table to her, cupping her chin in his hand and tilting her head back so he could see her tortured eyes. 'Who was he, this man who hurt you, *cara?* What did he do to you that you're so afraid to love again?'

He felt her flinch slightly, and she swallowed. She looked cornered, but she wasn't telling him why. Not yet. Not now. But he would find out, in the end. She'd tell him when she was ready.

His touch was so gentle, his thumb grazing slowly back and forth over her chin, his eyes concerned, and it made her want to cry. She didn't do that. Couldn't allow it.

She stood up and went to the door and opened it. 'I think it's time you went home,' she said unevenly, and waited while he put down his mug, got to his feet and brushed past her, turning on the step to stare down into her eyes.

'I'm sorry,' he said quietly. 'I didn't mean to upset you. Whoever he was, he's hurt you badly, but don't judge us the same. Give me a chance, Isabelle. Let me prove myself to you.'

'Luca, I can't. I wish you hadn't found me.'

'I know. I'm sorry it upset you, but I'm not sorry I found you again, and I'll never be sorry that I met you, that we shared that time together, and I know you feel it too.'

'No.'

'Don't lie to me, *cara*,' he murmured gently. 'And especially don't lie to yourself. You deserve better than that.'

And because he couldn't help it, because she was just inches from him, her chest rising and falling and her eyes wide with a nameless emotion that made his chest ache to comfort her, he leaned in and kissed her.

For a moment she softened, but then she dragged her mouth away and pressed her hands against his chest, right over the ache.

'Luca, please, just *go!*' she pleaded, and with a sad smile, he stepped back and moved away from her.

'*Buonanotte, Isabelle.* Sleep well. I'll see you tomorrow.'

And turning on his heel, he strode down her path, closed the gate gently behind him and got into his car.

Her lips still tingling from his kiss, she shut the door, leant back against it and listened to the sound of him driving away into the cold, wet night, and then she closed her eyes, wrapped her arms around her waist and cried, because she still wanted him just as much as she ever had but she was too afraid to dare to love him, and no amount of reasoning was going to change that.

CHAPTER FOUR

SHE WAS DREADING seeing Luca the next day, but she needn't have worried because by the time she arrived he was already in Theatre with an emergency C-section, and so after handover she went to meet the patient she was taking over.

Jodie Kembroke was a woman who had been due to deliver at the other hospital and, like Isabelle, had been transferred. She'd met her two years before when she'd delivered her first baby, and the only reason she was in the consultant unit here now was because this baby was breech.

'It only turned last week and they say I have to have a section. I'm so cross,' she confessed. 'I really wanted to try and deliver naturally, but they won't let me. Hospital policy or something. It's dangerous. And now I've gone into labour early, so Rob's trying to find a babysitter, and I want him here.'

And with a sinking heart she realised that she was going to have to involve Luca in this one, regardless of her urge to avoid him.

'Well, it's certainly safer for the baby to deliver it with a section,' Isabelle told her honestly, 'because coming this way the head doesn't get a chance to mould to your pelvis, but you've only just had a few twinges and you're not dilating fast, so we'll watch you for a while and get Mr Valtieri to come and see you as soon as he's out of Theatre. He shouldn't be many minutes. You can discuss it with him. It's his call really.'

And with any luck, she thought, trying to ignore the little flutter in the region of her heart, he'd let her deliver the baby vaginally. She'd never seen a breech delivery, and everyone these days was so risk-averse they didn't dare to let the mothers try.

But Luca didn't strike her as someone frightened of anything, and most particularly not authority. And hadn't one of those papers she'd seen from him on the internet been about breech births?

She wished now she'd paid it more attention, but she'd been so busy missing him she hadn't really read it. There was a glimmer of a memory, though, and she had a feeling he was pro rather than con. Well, they'd soon find out, she told herself, and felt another little flutter around her heart.

So stupid. So, so stupid, after their conversation last night. He'd come too close, seen too much, and there was no way she was going to let him any closer, but on the professional side, if he'd let Jodie deliver naturally, she'd be ecstatic.

Assuming the hospital authorities would allow it, of course.

She left a message for him at the central workstation to contact her as soon as he was out of Theatre and then collected a jug of ice chips for Jodie because she was on nil by mouth pending her C-section, but by the time she went back into the room things had moved on. A lot.

'I can feel his bottom,' Jodie said, and the fact that she said 'his' made Isabelle fairly sure she knew what she was talking about. A quick glance confirmed it. And that meant it would almost certainly be too late for a C-section by the time they'd moved her to Theatre, so she was going to have her baby there on the ward, with only Isabelle to look after her, because everyone else was running flat out.

And Isabelle had never done this before.

She hit the button, opened the door and was about to call for help when Luca turned the corner.

'What's up?' he asked, following her back in and assessing the situation instantly. She filled him in fast as he turned off the call button, reached for the hand gel, then the gloves, his quiet calm filling her with confidence. 'OK, I'm Luca, Jodie, I'm going to have a quick look at you—what's the history, Isabelle?'

'Second baby, scheduled for elective C-section—I delivered the first two years ago with no problems, but things have just speeded up in the last few minutes,' Isabelle told him, wondering now about the old saying of not wishing for something lest you get it.

Well, it looked like she was getting her breech delivery, right now, and she just hoped Luca wasn't cross that she hadn't called for him sooner, but he was showing no signs of it, just smoothly, quietly taking over.

'OK, I don't want to move you to Theatre, Jodie,' he said calmly. 'I don't think it's necessary and you're doing this beautifully, so we'll just carry on here. Now, I want the baby's back facing the ceiling, so I'd like to get you onto all fours, if you can, so his back is upwards and his bottom will hang down and curl his spine nicely as he comes out, which means his head is in the best possible position for delivery. And we'll just let nature take care of it for us—OK?'

'OK,' Jodie panted, and with their help she turned over onto her hands and knees. 'Oh, my God, it's coming!' she screamed, and Luca placed a firm, gentle hand on her back and rubbed it slowly, his palm moving in rhythmic, soothing circles over her sacrum, relaxing her pelvis. Just as Isabelle would have done.

'It's all right, just let go and breathe with it. Let the baby's weight do the work. You're doing really well. Good girl. We don't touch anything,' he added softly to Isabelle, 'we just watch and catch. He's a good colour, so I'm not worried at all at the moment.'

And just like that, under his own weight and with Jodie pushing valiantly on command, little baby Kembroke was born, yelling his head off, just as his father was ushered into the room.

'Oh, Jodie,' he said softly, and tears coursed down his cheeks. 'You did it! Oh, you clever girl!'

'Let me hold him,' she said, rolling onto her back and reaching for her baby, safe in Luca's big, gentle hands.

'He's beautiful. You did really well.'

'And I didn't need a stupid section,' she murmured, lifting her son to her breast, and Isabelle met Luca's eyes and surprised a wistful, yearning look that she'd never expected to see there.

'Gets me every time,' he said under his breath to her, his grin a little off kilter, and she gave a ragged little laugh.

'Me, too,' she confessed. 'That's why I do it.'

'Me too.' He smiled at the couple and stripped off his gloves. 'I can leave you to finish, can I?' he said, watching her inject the Syntocinon, and she nodded, but in truth she would have liked him there a little longer.

'Can we talk through it later? Over coffee?'

'Sure, come and find me when you're done here,' he said, and left her to it.

* * *

'I've never seen a breech delivery before—it was amazing,' Isabelle told him, her eyes shining, and he was stunned.

'I think that's shocking. You should know how to, at least. It isn't necessary all the time to do a section—it's just being over-cautious, and then when you have to go with it because of an emergency or a precipitate labour or because the lift gets stuck, nobody knows what to do.'

'I knew the theory, but—'

'—it's not the same as the hands-on,' he said with a smile, getting into his stride because breech delivery was a bit of a hobby-horse for him. 'We're too quick to intervene, and sometimes we need to go back to basics. Look at the treatment for club foot. From the 1950s we've been using casting and stretching in combination to correct the deformity slowly, with good results, then they discovered surgery and the outcome isn't nearly as good in the long run. And now— eureka!—we're going back to casting and it's all got much more sensible again.'

'But breeches are different. If you get it wrong with club foot, nobody dies.'

'Nobody dies with breech if you're on the ball and don't take stupid risks. Everybody wants to fiddle with it, and sometimes if it's a bit slow you need to hook the legs and arms down gently, but usually it happens by itself, and it's just wonderful to watch.'

'Do you ever need forceps?'

He shrugged. 'Some people use them. I hate them, but there are times when there's no choice. Late babies are more of a problem because of the size of the head, but Jodie's baby was a little early, not too big and it went fine. And her recovery will be much faster.'

'So do you ever do a C-section for breech?'

'Oh, yes, of course I do. There are some breech presentations you just can't deliver, and I'd rather do that than end up using forceps, but I don't have a blanket ban on vaginal breech deliveries, because I think it's ridiculous.'

'It's hospital policy here.'

He grinned. 'I'll pretend I didn't hear that,' he murmured, and she felt her heart flip over.

He bent his head forwards, fiddling with his coffee, chasing a bubble round on the surface. Then he looked up and his eyes met hers. 'Have dinner with me tonight after work.'

She shook her head, so tempted it was ludicrous but too vulnerable to dare to allow it. 'No, Luca. Please. Don't start this again.'

'Lunch in the canteen?'

She gave a rueful laugh. 'I won't get a lunch break. It's a miracle I've got a coffee-break.'

'You work too hard.'

'No. I work three days a week—and it suits me. And now I have to go back. Thanks for talking it through. It was really interesting. I'm glad you didn't rush her to Theatre.'

'Why? No point. And it's a pleasure. Think about lunch.'

'I can't.'

'Rubbish. I'll come and find you.'

She was right, of course. There was no time for a lunch break, so she was glad Luca had fed her a pastry with her coffee. She stole time for a cup of tea and a bar of chocolate in the ward kitchen at five, but apart from that she'd had nothing all day.

That didn't mean she hadn't seen Luca. Far from it. He'd been haunting the ward, and now Sarah had a patient who had been in established labour for ages and was getting nowhere fast, and she was assisting her.

'I'm going to have to call Luca,' she said eventually, and Isabelle nodded.

'I agree. Want me to page him?'

'Could you?'

'Sure.'

She went out to the workstation and dialled his number, and he walked out of Richard's office and cocked an eyebrow at her. 'Are you calling me?'

'Yes—Sarah's got a problem that needs you. She's in three. I'll be back in a second, I've got to get something. I won't be long.'

He nodded and went into the delivery room and found the other midwife there with a woman and her husband. 'Right— we have a problem?' he murmured, and Sarah nodded.

'Yes—she's just exhausted. I'm sorry to call you but we've tried everything and the baby's beginning to struggle.'

He nodded. 'OK. Let's see if we can't give her a hand.'

Isabelle walked in just in time to see the slickest Ventouse delivery she'd ever seen, and in seven years she'd seen a few. And Sarah, of course, was all over him. Well, she was welcome, she told herself, and tried not to feel jealous when he smiled at her friend.

It was nothing personal. He smiled like that at everyone, but it had the same effect on them all. Us all, she thought, wishing she was unmoved by it, but she wasn't, not even slightly.

Then he lifted his head and smiled at her, and her heart skidded into hyperdrive. He was checking the baby, chatting to the mother and father, and he excused himself, stripped off his gloves and came over to her.

'I love the Ventouse. It's my party trick,' he said with a grin. 'Like pulling a rabbit from a hat.'

'The Great Valtieri? Maybe you should get your own magic show—not that you're blowing your own trumpet or anything...'

'Of course not,' he said, managing to look mischievous and affronted all at once, and so sexy that her tongue dried instantly and stuck to the roof of her mouth. She swallowed hard to free it and wiped her hands down the sides of her scrubs.

'Right, I need to get on,' she said to break the silence, and then Sarah came over to them.

'Um—we usually leave the proud parents alone and have a cup of tea at this point,' she said. 'Want to join us?'

'Thank you,' he murmured, and his grin turned to a smile that brought colour to Sarah's cheeks and made Isabelle's heart flutter. 'I could murder a cup of tea—and any chance of some toast?'

'I'm sure there will be, we can't have our resident magician fading away,' Isabelle said briskly. 'I'll just finish off in here and make sure everything's OK. You two go ahead, I'll join you in a minute,' she said, and, turning on her heel, she went to check on the mother and baby, and all the time that smile of Luca's was still echoing through the far reaches of Isabelle's body and making her heart pitter-patter.

So stupid. So many if onlys. She wished for the millionth time that she could dare to trust him, but his charm came so easily to him she wasn't sure she could. And there was still the problem of her own reluctance to commit...

'That man is incredible!'

Tell me about it, she thought, and rolled her eyes. 'If you say so. Where is he?'

'Oh, he had something to do, he'll be here in a minute. But

he is just—that was so slick. You know, that baby's head was just tipped back the tiniest bit, and she was so tired she just couldn't get it to shift—and as you know, we'd tried *everything,* Izzie. Then he just strolled in, grinned at her, attached the cup and pop! Out it came. He hardly even lifted it. He made it look so damned easy!'

She picked up a slice of toast that Sarah had just buttered and bit into it. 'It's all in the wrist action,' she mumbled round the toast. 'I expect it's from twirling all that spaghetti,'

Sarah chuckled. 'And he's so gentle with them. I've never seen a doctor treat a woman more carefully, with so much—I don't know, respect, I suppose. Almost reverence.'

And then she looked at Isabelle, and her eyes widened in distress. 'Oh, God, I can't believe I'm being so tactless. I'd completely forgotten—'

'Sarah, it's fine,' Isabelle lied, trying not to think about those reverent hands and how they'd touched her with tenderness and respect as well as passion. 'I met him, we spent the day together—it was nothing.' Except it hadn't just been the day, it had been the night, too, and that was so much harder to forget. 'Really,' she repeated, forcing her voice to sound casual, 'it was nothing—nothing out of the ordinary at all.'

And then she looked up and saw Luca standing there in the doorway. His face was like stone, and without a word he turned on his heel and walked away, and for some inexplicable reason she wanted to cry.

Nothing out of the ordinary.

Dio! He wanted to put his fist through the wall, slam doors, hurl something good and heavy through the nearest sheet of glass.

Instead he went into the office, shut the door with exaggerated care and threw himself down in the chair.

Nothing out of the ordinary.

He closed his eyes and made himself breathe slowly and deeply. She didn't mean it, of course. She was just being defensive, because of whatever it was in her past that she wouldn't give him access to. And she was angry with him for finding her. But she wasn't indifferent. He knew that, knew it in his bones, and slowly the anger dissipated.

She was just saying those things to Sarah. She didn't mean it, didn't believe it. It *had* been out of the ordinary—so out of the ordinary that it had made him throw away all his plans for the future and fly back to London on a wild goose chase to find her.

Nothing out of the ordinary?

No. Isabelle was trying to ignore her reaction to him, but she was very, very far from indifferent—and that gave him hope. Oh, it wouldn't be easy, he was under no illusions about that. But he'd get there. Especially if he could ever get her to tell him her story.

And now he had that out of the way, he was suddenly starving. Maybe there was some toast left in the kitchen...

'Right, time to go home.'

She sighed and glared at him. 'Are we going to have this fiasco every single night?' she asked crossly, but he just gave her that lazy smile and shrugged.

'I don't know. Are we? I hope not. You've had a long, busy day and you're late, which I suspect is not unusual. And I know you haven't eaten anything remotely like a vegetable all day, so I've made you supper, and then afterwards I'll run you home.'

'You've—I said no!' she protested, but he wasn't listening, just tucked his hand into her elbow and steered her to the lift.

'No arguments. You're no use to anyone hungry and exhausted, and besides, I've gone to a lot of effort.'

'Well, I could have saved you all of that. All you had to do was listen to me a little harder.'

He grinned. 'I have problems with my hearing sometimes.'

'Evidently. You need to learn to lip-read. I—said—no!' she mouthed, but he just laughed and shut his eyes, and she found herself smiling.

Not that it mattered, because his eyes were shut—or so she thought. But then she caught the gleam of an eye through his lashes, and realised he was laughing at her.

'Crazy woman,' he murmured, his hand tightening on her arm in an affectionate squeeze. 'Come on, it'll be overcooked.'

'What is it?'

'Pasta with chicken and roasted Mediterranean vegetables in tomato sauce.'

'Bottled?'

He looked shocked. 'Shh! Not so loud. My mother would be appalled. And you need to know I'm frightened of my mother.'

That made her laugh. The very idea of Luca being frightened of anyone, not least his mother, was ludicrous. And she was absolutely starving.

'Where's your car?' she asked, looking round as they emerged through the door.

'At my house. It's just round the corner. It's quicker to walk.'

'Oh! You live really close,' she said as he stopped just two streets away and opened a garden gate in front of a tall modern townhouse.

'Yes—it's handy. I hate commuting, so I bought it.'

She stared at him blankly. 'For a few weeks?'

He gave a short laugh and explained. 'No. I bought it four years ago, when I worked here, and I've used it as a base ever since. Come on in.'

And, opening the door, he ushered her inside.

Isabelle looked around, taking in the soft earth tones and the sense of light and space, conscious of a sense of order and quietness that pervaded the house. 'It's very tranquil.'

'It is. I love it. It's my favourite place. Well, except my family home in Tuscany. That'll always be top of the list, but this is mine, and that makes it special. Can I get you a drink? Coffee? Tea? Wine?'

'Have you got any juice?'

'Sure. Apple and mango?'

'Lovely.'

She followed him through to the kitchen and sniffed appreciatively. 'Oh, it smells really good.'

'Of course. Did you really think I'd be allowed out into the world without knowing how to fend for myself? Even if it is out of a bottle,' he added in a stage whisper.

She tried not to smile, but not well enough because he winked at her, took a bowl of salad from the fridge and pulled a dish from the oven, bubbling with cheese and tomato sauce and smelling utterly fabulous.

Her stomach rumbled, and he pointed to the breakfast bar, a thick, sleek glass shelf on shiny chrome supports with tall chrome and leather stools tucked in underneath. 'I thought we could be uncouth and eat in here,' he said, and she looked around at the kitchen, with its sleek granite worktops and high-gloss cupboards, thought of her house and how utterly uncouth it was in comparison to this undoubtedly extremely expensive kitchen, and her heart sank.

She'd not given a moment's thought to his financial status, but one serious look at this kitchen brought it all home to her with a vengeance.

He was so completely out of her league, so overwhelmingly different, and there was no way he would ever be interested in her except as a passing fancy. The only reason he was interested in her at all was because she was playing hard to get. Treat 'em mean, keep 'em keen—wasn't that the saying? Except she wasn't trying to be mean, and she didn't want him to be keen, she wanted him to leave her alone, because he was going to break her heart all over again and this time, she knew, it would be so very much worse.

'What's wrong?'

'Nothing. I'm just really hungry,' she said, and turned her attention to the food. It wasn't that hard. She was ravenous, she discovered after the first mouthful, and his cooking, bottled sauce or not, was sheer genius. So she ate, and he talked about breech presentations and cases he'd seen and the research he was doing, and gradually she forgot about his money and remembered only that he was a brilliant doctor, kind and gentle and yet persuasive when he needed to be, and brave enough to take a risk if he felt it was justified.

There were all too few like him, she mused. Far too few. But that didn't mean she was going to let him lure her into a relationship, and she realised she was getting dangerously close to that. Sitting in his kitchen eating food he'd cooked for her while she finished her shift was all too cosy, and she had to be mad to do it.

She pushed her plate away, nothing left on it but a touch of the rich tomato sauce, and smiled at him. 'That was really lovely. Thank you. And now I hate to be rude but I ought to be getting home.'

'No dessert?'

'Did you make one?'

He chuckled. 'No. But I have gelato—proper Italian ice cream, made by my cousin's family, that will make your toes curl.'

'What flavour?' she asked, hating herself for weakening, and as if he knew that, he leant closer and murmured in her ear.

'Ripe, juicy strawberry with fresh cream, or deep, dark chocolate—irresistible…'

Oh, lord. It was only ice cream!

'Chocolate,' she said, but then hesitated.

'You can have both,' he said, luring her with a double whammy, and she weakened.

'A little of each—not too much. And then I really must go.'

It was, as he'd promised, enough to make her toes curl. And she had a sudden picture of him feeding it to her in bed, a sensual image that made her want to whimper. She pushed the bowl away before she actually licked it, and braced her hands on the edge of the glass shelf.

'Luca, I have to go now.'

'Of course. Leave this lot, I'll sort it later. Come on.'

And he ushered her out of the door to his car and drove her home through the hubbub of London at night, until at last they turned into her quiet little street and he pulled up outside her house and cut the engine.

'I think you owe me coffee,' he said, a teasing smile playing round his mouth, and she thought, Damn him, he's going to be charming and he's hard enough to resist under normal circumstances!

'I gave you coffee last night.'

'So you did. It must be a tradition, then, and you can't mess with tradition.'

He was irrepressible, but she wasn't falling for it.

'I need my sleep. I didn't get enough last night.'

She saw the brow twitch, and tried to glare at him but he wasn't impressed. Instead he just grinned, and she ignored him and opened the car door.

He was there almost before she'd got out of the car, shutting the door behind her and escorting her down her little path. 'Just seeing you safely home,' he murmured as she turned to protest, and she caught the scent of his cologne overlying the raw, male essence that was so much more intoxicating.

'I'm safe. You can go now. Thank you for my supper.'

'You're welcome. When will I see you again?'

Her heart hiccuped, and she reminded herself that he wasn't asking her for a date and she wasn't going even if he was asking. 'I'm back in on Friday,' she told him, but his nearness was getting to her and she swallowed, and his eyes flicked to her mouth.

'I want to kiss you,' he murmured, and she shook her head. 'No.'

'You didn't say no in Florence.'

'Perhaps I should have done, then we wouldn't be in this crazy position now.'

'You think? I don't agree. We were destined to happen, *cara*.'

She shook her head. 'No. It was just sex, Luca,' she said, her heart pounding because of his nearness, because of the scent of his body drifting over her in the cold night air. 'That was all.'

Nothing out of the ordinary.

Her earlier words came back to taunt him, echoing in his head as they had been all day, and his mouth twisted in a fleeting smile. 'I don't think so,' he murmured. 'I don't think there was anything *just* about it. I think it was exceptional.'

'No.'

'Yes,' he said softly, and because he couldn't resist it, because she looked delectable and there was a trace of chocolate ice cream in the corner of her mouth, he leant in towards her and let his lips brush over hers.

His hands were rammed in his trouser pockets, hers hung by her sides. There was nothing holding them together but the touch of their lips, and as he stroked his tongue against her mouth, her lips parted for him and he was lost.

He freed his hands, tunnelled them through her hair and cradled her head to steady her, and with a tiny whimper she fisted her hands in his shirt and hung on while his mouth plundered hers, the silky glide of her tongue against his driving him wild.

For a second—for one crazy, heat-filled second—he contemplated pushing her inside, kicking the door shut and carrying her upstairs to her bedroom. He could do it. She wouldn't protest. But she would hate him tomorrow, and that wasn't part of his plan, so instead he just kissed her until his control was stretched so thin he couldn't trust himself another moment, and then he lifted his head and stared down into her feverish eyes, his chest heaving.

For a moment she said nothing, but then she stepped back, her hand coming up to cover her glistening, parted mouth, and he could see it was trembling.

'Why did you do that?' she whispered.

'What? That goodnight kiss?' He smiled a little tightly, his anger coming back now, fuelled by frustration. 'It was just a kiss—nothing out of the ordinary. Isn't that what you said to Sarah?'

She swallowed hard, her eyes filling as his words registered. 'Oh, Luca—I'm so sorry. I didn't mean it—not like that. And I wasn't talking about us—about that night. I hadn't told Sarah anything, just that I'd met you. I wasn't gossiping, I promise. I was trying to stop her getting the wrong idea about us.'

He laughed softly. 'Don't you mean the right idea? The idea that we couldn't leave each other alone in Florence and it's no better here? Because it isn't, *bella,* you know that. Even though you want me to go, you couldn't stop yourself from kissing me back.'

'That's not true.'

'Don't lie,' he murmured. 'You were with me all the way.'

'That isn't the point!'

'I would have said it was very much the point,' he argued softly, but she closed her eyes and made a tiny sound of frustration that just inflamed him further.

'Please—just go,' she said, wondering if she would be destined to say this to him every night until either she gave in or he left the country.

Except she wasn't giving in, even if her legs were like jelly and her heart was thundering against her ribs and her body was aching for him.

And then at last, when she was ready to scream, he took a step back, and then another, and finally he turned without a word, got back into his car and drove away, leaving her standing on the doorstep wondering how on earth she was going to survive working with him for the next however many weeks.

Luca spent the next few days contemplating his tactics.

If she really meant it, and she wouldn't see him, he'd have to find some other way to win her round, because he fully intended to do so.

He could easily tell himself that whatever they'd had between them on that mad, crazy night had been a little touch of magic and nothing more, and he could set it aside if necessary and work with her without compromising his professional integrity.

But he didn't want to, and it wasn't an option. So what if she said she didn't want him? He knew she did—he just had to convince her to try it. He'd had a taste of the wild, all-encompassing passion that could exist between a man and a woman, and he would settle for nothing less now. And that meant winning Isabelle.

She'd done him a favour, kick-starting his life again, saving him from a lonely and tedious life when there was so much more out there, and he wasn't going to walk away from it now, when he'd only just found her again. He'd spent six weeks convincing himself he was over her, and it had been a lie. He wasn't, and he didn't want to be.

He wanted Isabelle, and he'd have her. Somehow.

Then she walked onto the ward on Friday morning, her auburn hair swinging round her shoulders, her cheeks rosy from the cold, those beautiful amethyst eyes challenging his, and he felt a kick in his gut that told him more clearly than anything else how important this was to him.

He wasn't ready to give up on her—not even slightly. He

hadn't moved on, he couldn't forget the night they'd spent together. He wanted her as much as ever—not the wild and generous lover, curiously, although his need for her was never far away, but her, this beautiful, principled and wounded woman—and he was going to convince her to give them another chance.

'Isabelle,' he said as casually and professionally as he could manage, 'I have a patient I'd like your help with.'

'And good morning to you, too,' she retorted.

He gave a wry laugh and started again. 'Good morning. How were your days off?'

'Lovely, thank you. Peaceful. You were saying?'

'I have a patient. It's her third pregnancy, she was admitted about an hour ago with intermittent contractions, and she needs a little TLC. Her first delivery was textbook normal, then she had a C-section for a placenta previa, and she's going to try for another normal delivery, but she's scared. I've squared it with your ward manager, and I'd like you to manage her delivery.'

She met his eyes challengingly. 'Why me?'

'Because you're good.'

'Sarah's good,' she said bluntly.

'Sarah's off today.'

'Well, Helen, then. Any of them. They're all good.'

'I want you. You're the best.'

'That's rubbish.' She turned away, heading into the staff-room. 'I'll see you in a minute,' she muttered, and shut the door in his face.

He shrugged. Well, she was reluctant, but she hadn't told him to take a hike. And he could wait for her to come round.

Just so long as she didn't take too long, because he was an

impatient man, he was discovering, and the clingy little sweater she'd been wearing under her coat was enough to push him over the brink.

He went into the ward kitchen and made himself a cup of coffee. He'd been in the hospital since six, waiting for Isabelle and trying to convince himself that she would be fine if he didn't go and fetch her, and so far today he hadn't had time for a drink. And if he didn't get some caffeine down himself soon he was going to be ripping heads off.

'Right—where's this woman?' Isabelle said, appearing in the doorway in scrubs, and he offered her his mug.

'She'll keep for a moment. I'll fill you in. Want this?'

She shook her head. 'No, I'll pass. It's a bit early for coffee and I haven't really got time to make tea. I'll have a glass of water. So, tell me, how frequent are her contractions?'

'Every three minutes. It could be quite quick.'

Great. Isabelle swallowed and put the glass down, trying to psych herself up. She could do with a slow start today. She'd been feeling a bit iffy when she'd woken—edgy about seeing him again, of course—and she'd had to struggle with the bus and the Tube. She'd even been frustrated that he hadn't turned up to give her a lift, of all the contrary things...

'OK, I'll go and get handover on her and introduce myself. I take it you're happy to leave me to it?'

'Of course.'

'Right. I'll keep you posted.'

'Thank you.'

Good grief, so formal, so civilised, and yet under it all, the memory of that kiss was seething and simmering like a wild thing. She walked away, deeply conscious of his eyes on her back, trying to halt the sway of her hips as she walked. The last thing she wanted was for him to feel encouraged. She was still furious with him for kissing her, but not nearly as furious as she was with herself for responding.

Oh, damn it!

She went and found her patient.

'I hate you! Don't you dare come near me! This is all your fault!'

'Well, excuse me, but it wasn't me who forgot to take the pills regularly.'

'Hey, guys, come on, now. Lindsey, calm down, nice slow breaths. That's it. Good girl.' She shot a smile over her shoulder at the husband, standing at the foot of the bed ramming his hands through his hair and looking helpless. 'It's OK. It's not personal,' she said softly as Lindsey breathed her way through a nasty contraction. 'You'll have your baby very soon.'

'Is she all right?'

'Yes, she's just in transition. Everything looks lovely.'

His shoulders dropped, and he closed his eyes and gave a soft laugh. 'You know, once we got over the shock we were really pleased about the baby. It was just a bit unexpected, hearing her talking to me like that.'

'Ignore it. She'll be all smiles in a few minutes.'

'I won't. I hate him,' Lindsey muttered between breaths.

'Of course you do,' Isabelle said soothingly, rubbing her back and eliciting a deep groan of relief. 'Mike, why don't you do this for her?' she suggested, and then Lindsey's eyes flew wide open and she stared at Isabelle wildly.

'I have to push!'

'OK, that's fine, you're ready now. Nice and steady, you can remember how to do it.'

Behind her she heard the door open quietly, and she knew without looking round that it was Luca, and she was relieved, because one of the team was off sick and she was on her own again today and if anything went wrong...

'OK?' he murmured softly so as not to distract Lindsey, and she nodded.

'She's just gone into second stage.'

'May I stay?'

'Please do.'

'You can defend me,' Mike said, smiling at him and maybe a bit relieved to have his support. 'Apparently this is my fault.'

Luca chuckled softly. 'Isn't it always? The man can never win.'

'Well, it is his fault, so don't you join in and gang up on me—oh, hell, I want to kneel,' Lindsey said, dragging herself up the bed and hanging on to the headboard, her body draped over the pillows. And moments later, with very little fuss, their daughter was born, and Isabelle felt the familiar wave of emotion sweep over her.

'Congratulations,' she said warmly, settling the tearful, smiling Lindsey back against her pillows and putting the baby to her breast. 'She's absolutely beautiful, aren't you, sweetheart?'

Luca patted Mike on the back. 'Well done, guys. I thought you'd be fine. I'll leave you in Isabelle's capable hands. I'll get you a nursery nurse to help.'

'No hurry,' she said, because she enjoyed this moment, and once she was happy that everything was as it should be, she'd leave them alone for a while to get to know their baby.

'Aren't you glad now that I've got a lousy memory and kept

taking my pill late?' Lindsey was saying with a huge smile on her face, and Isabelle laughed.

'See? I told you you'd be forgiven,' she said to Mike.

'Oh, of course he's forgiven,' Lindsey said with a smile, 'but it's a good job we lead a fairly sober life, because I had no idea I was pregnant for months. I was still taking the Pill but I was feeling iffy, and I just thought I must have a virus and then I got over it and started to eat like a horse and put on weight. And then I looked at myself one day in the mirror and the penny dropped. All those late pills, and look where it got me, little one,' she said, her voice softening as she turned her attention to the baby again. 'In here with you! And you're just gorgeous.'

In the middle of checking the placenta, Isabelle froze. Late pills? A virus? Feeling iffy? And her last period had been really light...

Oh, dear God, no!

She felt a wave of panic and disbelief, and having checked that the placenta was intact and that Lindsey and the baby were both looking well, she left them to it for a moment, heading for the staffroom.

'I've just put the kettle on—fancy a coffee now?' Luca said as she approached the kitchen.

'Not really,' she said, unable to look at him. 'I'll get something in a minute, there's something I have to do.'

And diverting to the supplies, she took a box off the shelf, slipped it into her pocket and walked off the ward.

'Luca?'

'Isabelle? What's the matter?'

'Nothing, but—I need to see you.'

He sat up, turning off the television, his heart starting to pound slowly, his mind in freefall trying to imagine why she was calling. 'When did you have in mind?'

'Are you free now? I've just finished work. I could come to you.'

'Sure, I'm here. Can you remember the way or do you want me to come and get you?'

'No, stay there, I'll come,' she said, and headed for the exit.

Luca tidied the sitting room and put his empty mug into the dishwasher while he waited. He couldn't imagine what she wanted. He could dream, he could fantasise, but he had no real idea, and her distant greeting this morning—her distance all day, really—hadn't given him much fuel for the fantasy.

The bell rang and he let her in, taking in her pallor and the tight line of her lips. It didn't look like she was about to give in to him, he thought with regret, and hung her coat on the end of the banisters. Maybe she just wanted to talk—perhaps to tell him whatever it was that was getting in the way of them having a relationship. Hallelujah! And then maybe they could make some progress.

'What can I get you to drink?'

'Um—have you got any fruit juice?' she asked, part of her wanting to stall and the other part wanting to get it over with quick before she lost her courage.

'Sure. Apple and mango again?'

'Lovely,' she said, following him and hugging her elbows.

He poured her a glass, made himself a coffee then led her into the sitting room, gesturing to the pair of leather sofas that sat at right angles to each other. She perched on the edge of one, and he sat on the other, and silence settled over them.

'So why did you want to see me?' he said eventually, and

she swallowed hard. There was no easy way to do this, so she might just as well get it over with. Taking a deep breath, she looked up and met his eyes.

'I think I might be pregnant.'

CHAPTER FIVE

LUCA FELT THE blood drain from his face. 'Pregnant?'

'I—I think so.'

His heart thudded hard against his ribs, her words so unexpected they'd caught him completely off guard. 'And it's mine?' he asked, his voice rough even to his ears.

She stared at him, her eyes blank. 'Well—of course it's yours.'

'There hasn't been anybody else?'

'No. No! Not for years. You know I don't do relationships, and I certainly don't do one-night stands.'

'But you're on the Pill,' he challenged, pushing her, while the blood roared in his ears and the sense of déjà vu threatened to swamp him.

'To control my cycle. Nothing else. Luca, if I am pregnant, it's definitely yours.' And he could tell from her eyes that it was the truth.

He felt the shockwave go through him, and closed his eyes briefly, setting his coffee down with a little clatter into the saucer before looking up at her.

But her eyes were on the cup, and she swallowed hard. 'Bathroom,' she muttered, and, crashing her glass down onto the table, she fled into the hall.

'On the right,' he yelled, following her, but she'd found it, slamming the door behind her and leaving him in limbo. Did he follow her? Hold her hair? Or give her her dignity? He waited, while the emotions roiled through him, his heart pounding, until he heard the loo flush and water running.

Then he tapped on the door and met her wary eyes as she opened it, his heart beating heavily in his chest as they stood looking at each other in silence. Action and reaction, he thought, and asked the question that had been burning a hole in him for the past few minutes.

'Isabelle, when you say you *think*…'

'I did a test.'

Hell. 'And?'

'It was a bit inconclusive.'

Well, the last few minutes wasn't, he thought drily, and felt a skitter of nerves. 'When was your last period?' he asked, his voice deadly soft as he tried to stay calm.

She gave a tiny, defensive shrug. 'Last week. But it was light,' she added. 'So was the one before.'

'So—it's nearly seven weeks since Florence, which would make you…'

She swallowed. 'Nearly nine weeks pregnant—if I am.'

Oh, she was. He could see it a mile away, but he had to know. He took a slow, deep breath. 'Do you have another test with you?'

She nodded numbly. 'In my bag. Luca, I'm on the Pill,' she said, her voice a little desperate.

'And did you take it punctually?'

She nodded her head slowly. 'Pretty much, but it's only to regulate my periods, so I'm not religious about it. And that morning, I took it just before we boarded the flight and then

I was airsick in the turbulence and I felt so dreadful I just didn't think about it until now—'

She broke off, and he stabbed his hand through his hair. 'And I—' He'd been so inflamed with passion that he'd forgotten his own name. Damn. He picked up her bag from the floor and held it out to her. 'Just do the test, *cara,* please. We need to know this. *I* need to know it.'

She took it, her fingers shaking, and rummaged for a box— a pregnancy test kit from the ward. He recognised it instantly. She handed the bag back and shut the door, and he waited. And waited. What seemed like hours later, when he was about to tear the door down and go in and find her, she opened it and walked out, her face ashen.

'Well?' he asked, his voice tight.

She handed him the little white stick.

'Congratulations, Luca,' she said unsteadily. 'You're going to be a father.' And then she burst into tears.

He didn't even look down. One glance at her face had been enough to tell him the answer, but he'd needed to hear her say it. And his reaction was not at all what he'd expected. In the midst of the shock, somewhere buried down there amongst a whole plethora of emotions and complications and sheer, blind terror, a tiny flicker of joy burst into life.

He was going to be a father. He felt his eyes fill, and blinked hard, scarcely daring to hope, but he *knew* Isabelle was pregnant. He was an obstetrician. He knew the signs, knew it wasn't possible to fake the chalk-white skin with the faint sheen of sweat, the nausea and its inevitable result—and sure, she could have produced a positive pregnancy test stick but he'd seen her go into the loo with an unopened packet and break the seal.

He *knew.*

And now he had to think of the future.

'We need to talk.'

Talk? She nearly laughed out loud, but it would have been more than a little hysterical, so she just clamped her mouth shut and headed out of the hall, walking into the sitting room and standing there staring unseeing through the window, arms wrapped tight around her waist, while the emotions crashed through her like a tidal wave.

'Go on, then, talk.'

He laughed, an odd, fractured sound that scraped on her nerves. '*Cara,* we *have* to talk. This is going to happen, and we have to face it. What alternative is there?'

Shooting myself? Ringing my mother and telling her I've been as stupid as she was? Scrolling back through all the drugs and chemicals and foodstuffs I've been exposed to in the past few weeks?

'Going home to bed,' she said, suddenly feeling incredibly tired and tearful and wishing Luca would go away so she could curl up in the corner and howl.

She got her wish. His pager went off, and muttering something Italian and no doubt rude, he put a gentle hand on her shoulder. 'Later. I have to go back to the hospital, but you can stay here,' he said. 'Go and rest now, I'll come home as soon as I can. Use my bed.'

'I can't. I have to go home.'

'No, you can't do that awful journey in this state—or work the hours you've been working. It's ridiculous when you're sick.'

'No, Luca,' she said, turning to face him and meeting his eyes with defiance. 'I'm not sick. I'm pregnant. There's a difference, and I have no intention of being treated like an invalid—and before you even think about it, don't you *dare* go and tell my colleagues to get them to take my workload off me, or I swear to God, I'll kill you with my bare hands.'

He felt a reluctant smile tugging at his mouth. 'I'm terrified.'

'You should be.'

Their eyes locked, and then he gave a little shrug and sighed. 'OK, I won't say anything, for now—but only on condition you're sensible. And that means lying down now and waiting for me to get back, at the very least. Is that clear?'

He could see the struggle in her eyes, but finally she nodded. 'All right, I'll wait. But here. I don't need to go to bed.'

He hesitated, but then his mouth firmed and with a curt nod he turned on his heel and walked back into the hall. She turned back to the window and watched him walking down the street until he disappeared into the night. It was raining now, fat drops hitting the window and streaming down it like rivers of tears, and resting her head against the cool glass, she closed her eyes again and pressed her lips together.

Pregnant. Just like her mother, pregnant, single and alone.

Self-pity washed over her, and she firmed her spine and told herself not to be melodramatic and ridiculous. Her mother had been much younger and she'd had no training, but Isabelle had a good career, in a field where working part time was perfectly possible, her maternity leave would be assured and there was a crèche available to solve her childcare needs.

OK, it wasn't the future she'd hoped for, but it would be a good future, and at least she had the house. She'd told her mother it wasn't necessary to put it in her name, but now she was grateful, because in the end it would be the thing that above all else gave her security.

She—*they*—would be all right. And that was all that mattered.

Pushing herself away from the window, she lay down on the sofa under a lovely snuggly throw and tried to sleep, but her mind was whirling. She sat up again and noticed a newspaper on the coffee table, opened at the puzzle page. He'd started the crossword, filled in a few numbers on the Sudoku, but she could finish them off. It would keep her mind occupied till he got back…

She was asleep, her eyes shadowed, the long, thick lashes dark crescents against her pale cheeks. Her mouth was closed but her jaw was relaxed, and her lips looked soft and full and kissable.

Resisting the urge, he put the bowls down and sat beside her, his hip brushing against her abdomen as the cushion sank under his weight and she rolled towards him. His child was in there, he thought, feeling the warmth of her body against his hip, cradled in the bowl of her pelvis, a tiny baby, slowly growing in the shelter of her body, and it was suddenly real to him. Please, God, let everything be all right. He couldn't bear it if it wasn't.

He rested his hand on her hip and stared at her, the woman who was carrying his child, and a fierce wave of protective tenderness washed over him, catching him by surprise, because this was for her, not for the child. His feelings for the child were a given. His feelings for the mother were much less ordered and would take time to sort out. But for now, he had to feed her.

'Isabella?' he murmured. 'Wake up. I've cooked for you.'

'No,' she moaned, and buried her face in a little cushion.

He took it away from her. 'Yes. Come on, you need to eat. Sit up—here, it's just boiled rice and vegetables. Nothing too flavoured, but you must eat. You've had nothing all day.'

She struggled upright. 'I'm not hungry,' she grumbled, but she shoved the hair out of her eyes and took the bowl and ate, reluctantly at first and then more eagerly as it became obvious it wasn't going to be instantly rejected by her body.

'Better?' he asked, searching her face for clues, and she smiled a little wanly and nodded.

'Yes. Thank you. I was getting a bit shaky.'

'You mustn't let yourself get hungry. That's the worst thing. Low blood sugar's a killer. And don't have coffee, or cola, or strong tea or even dark chocolate. Caffeine can increase the risk of miscarriage significantly—and it's probably why it and many other potentially harmful or potentially bacteria-laden foods can trigger nausea in early pregnancy—'

He cut himself off, realising he was lecturing her, telling himself not to get over-protective, but she just gave a funny little smile.

'Luca, I do know this. I'm well aware that we're programmed to avoid the dangerous things when the foetus is most vulnerable.' She rolled her eyes. 'Don't worry, it's very effective. I won't be drinking coffee ever again, I don't think. Just the smell is enough to kill me.'

'Was it my coffee today?' he asked, suddenly realising that when she'd run away, he'd been drinking it, and she nodded. He let out a harsh sigh and shook his head.

'*Bella,* I'm sorry. You should have said.'

'I didn't know until it happened.'

'Well, it won't happen again,' he said with a twisted smile. 'Come on, you need to go to bed now, you look exhausted. And I will review your rota, whatever you say. These long days are no good for you, and I don't want you working nights.'

'The nights are fine, Luca. I like working nights. They're quiet and peaceful.'

'But you need a regular routine, so you can eat properly and your body can settle into pregnancy without constant disturbance.'

'Luca, it's my body! I'll decide.'

She had that mulish look about her chin again, and he let it go. For now. There was plenty of time to fight with her. Years and years and years, if he had his way.

'Come on, let me put you to bed, and then I've got to go shopping for things that are good for you, and in the morning we'll talk.'

'I'm not staying here,' she said, looking panicked.

'Don't be silly. It's really late, and I'm on call. I can't take you home and the Tube's about to shut. Please, *cara*. Don't try and go. I'm only trying to help you.'

She hesitated, reluctant to give up too much independence but too tired in the end to argue, so she nodded. 'OK, if you insist—but I'm not sleeping with you. I'll sleep here.'

'Don't be silly. I've got two spare rooms, the beds are made. Why don't you have a bath while I'm shopping?'

A bath. That sounded so tempting. She nodded. 'OK.'

'Not too hot, though. It'll make you sick.'

She shut her eyes. 'Luca,' she said warningly, and he got up off the sofa so that the warmth of his body was removed from her thigh. And, stupidly, she missed it.

'I'll run the bath for you,' he said, ignoring her warning, and disappeared upstairs. A few minutes later he came back down. 'It's ready for you now,' he said, and then he held out a hand and eased her to her feet.

'I've put you out a T-shirt in the bedroom at the top of the stairs, and the bathroom's just opposite. I won't be long,' he promised, and headed for the door, tossing his keys in the air and leaving her alone with her thoughts.

Or not quite alone.

Her hand slid down until it lay over the baby, curled protectively around her tiny, defenceless child, conceived in an unpremeditated and ill-considered moment of wild passion and now destined for the sort of childhood she herself had had.

Oh, well, it hadn't done her any harm, and she'd always known she was loved, but she felt a flicker of fear for the future of her child. What if something should happen to her? What would happen to her baby then?

Exhausted with emotion, longing for the oblivion of sleep and promising herself that she'd phone her mother in the morning and talk to her, she went upstairs, undressed in the bedroom he'd got ready for her and went into the bathroom.

And stopped dead.

He'd run her a bath, she'd known that, but he'd also lit candles on the side, and put a few drops of lavender oil in it from the bottle on the window sill. She bent and tested the water with her fingers, and sighed. Tepid. Well, not quite, but certainly not a long, hot soak. But it would do—and he was quite right, a hot bath would only make her feel sick. And it smelled lovely.

She eased herself into it, lay back and sighed with relief.

Five minutes, she promised herself. Even Luca couldn't shop that quickly…

The house was in silence.

He went into the kitchen, put away all the shopping and then crept upstairs to check on her. Her bedroom was empty, her clothes dropped where she'd taken them off, and so he walked across the landing to the bathroom and eased open the door.

She was asleep, lying with her knees rested to one side and her hands curled over her abdomen, and just the sight of her brought a lump to his throat.

Not the surge of lust he'd expected, but another wave of tenderness. He wanted to wake her, to lift her from the water and dry her and put her to bed, but he knew she'd only get mad at him, so he pulled the door to and tapped on it gently.

'Isabelle? Are you in there?'

There was a little gasp and a splash, and he could picture her sitting up and clutching her arms across her breasts. 'Um—yes. I'm not decent—hang on.'

'It's OK. I'm going back downstairs. I was just letting you know I'm back.'

'Oh. Thanks, Luca. Goodnight.'

Goodnight?

Stifling a strange disappointment, he went downstairs, made himself a drink and sat in front of the television, trying to focus on the news and failing. He picked up the paper that was lying on the table and finished the Sudoku he'd started. Except there were some numbers that weren't in his writing, and he realised she'd been doing it. Which was why it was wrong, he thought, and corrected it with a smile. Then he finished the crossword, filling in the last two words just as she appeared in the doorway.

'Hi,' she said, tugging at the hem of the T-shirt and triggering the surge of lust he'd expected earlier. He wanted to tug at the hem of it, too, but he'd tug it the other way.

He dragged his eyes up to her face. 'Kettle's hot. I bought some herbal teabags—I thought you might like them. There's

a selection on the side. Choose one and I'll make it for you
and bring it up.'

'I'll do it. I was going to take the paper up—I wanted to
finish the crossword.'

'Ah.'

Her eyes flew up to his and she snatched it out of his
hand. 'Have you done it? You have, haven't you? You rat—
and the sudoku!'

'It is my paper—and I'd started it,' he pointed out fairly,
but she wasn't pacified.

'That's not the point—I'd spent *ages* working out the last
clue!' she retorted, then threw the paper down again with an
exasperated sigh and spun on her heel, giving him a flash of
thigh and the peep of a warm, pink buttock scantily covered
by lavender lace as the hem flicked up and then dropped back
into place, and he felt a surge of desire that nearly took his
legs out from under him.

'I think I'll go to bed,' she said from the doorway, her chin
up in the way he was beginning to find rather endearing.

'You could sit here and talk for a minute,' he suggested,
but as he'd expected she shook her head.

'No way,' she said briskly. 'I'm going to get my tea and
then I'm going to bed. And don't go getting any ideas. I might
be having your baby, but that doesn't mean we're together.
Nothing's changed.'

He gave a soft snort. Funny, that. He hadn't doubted it for
a moment. Unfortunately…

She woke to the sound of movement in the kitchen, and a wave
of nausea that took her by surprise. She got cautiously out of
bed, but just the act of standing had her running to the

bathroom, and when she lifted her head it was to see Luca's legs in view, his hand extended with a handful of tissue for her to blow her nose and wipe her eyes.

Her teeth were chattering with reaction, and he sighed and bent to help her up.

'I'm sorry, *cara*,' he murmured, guiding her back to bed. 'I meant to come to you in time.'

'In time?'

'*Si*—with breakfast.'

'Oh, God, don't,' she said, feeling her throat close at the very suggestion, but he just tucked her into bed like a child and handed her a glass of fizzy water.

'Sip it slowly.'

She tasted it, tried a little, then put it down. 'OK. What's that?' she asked, eying the plate on the bedside table suspiciously.

'Apple. Chilled apple slices. And watermelon. Just nibble them. They'll give you some sugar and settle you, and the clean flavour is good, according to my sister.'

She sat up abruptly—not wise. 'You've told your sister?'

He gave her a crooked smile and shook his head. 'No. But because I'm an obstetrician, I discussed it with her when she was pregnant. I have a mental note of things that help and things that definitely don't.' His smile twisted. 'All caffeine products are banned from my life now,' he said wryly, 'so forgive me if my temper gets a bit ragged. It's not personal.'

She wasn't looking forward to his ragged temper, but it knocked spots off the smell of coffee. She took a proffered apple slice and nibbled it cautiously, and after a moment the rebellious churning in her stomach subsided a little and she tried another bit, then more, the watermelon this time.

'OK?'

She nodded. 'Yes—thanks.'

'I'll fetch you some dry toast and herbal tea, and then we'll talk.'

He left her with the plate of apple and watermelon slices and went away, and she lay there and wondered what he wanted to say. A long, almost sleepless night hadn't helped refine her thoughts, except to reinforce her initial fiercely protective reaction. Would he share it? Or would he try to talk her into—no! Her mind recoiled from the thought, but she realised he hadn't mentioned the baby again, and she had no idea how he'd feel about her keeping it. How would she see his future involvement in her child's life—or wouldn't he?

She had no idea, but there was only one way to find out, and the sooner the better. She threw back the bedclothes and went to wash.

Luca shut the kitchen door, opened the back door and made some toast, then once the smell had gone, he made a cup of ginger and lemon tea, because ginger root was supposed to suppress nausea, and put a scrape of sugarless fruit compote on the toast and took it upstairs, tapping on the bedroom door as he pushed it open.

He should have waited. Clearly he should have waited, because she was naked, in the act of threading her second foot into the pair of ridiculously lacy French knickers he'd glimpsed last night that had sent his blood pressure through the roof, and as she shrieked and straightened up to cover herself, he was treated to the gentle sway and bounce of her breasts, the nipples a glorious dark rose, darker than they had been before and bigger, pebbling in the cold and making his lips ache to suckle them.

She glared at him. 'You're supposed to wait when you knock,' she told him crossly, and he swallowed and tried not to choke on his tongue.

'You were supposed to stay in the bed until I brought you breakfast,' he reminded her, his self-control falling apart under the strain of standing there with her all but naked just feet away from him.

'Well, you can go now,' she snapped, whirling round and reaching for the bra she'd placed on the bed.

Lace, to match the knickers, in the same pale lavender as her eyes, and he thought, *Dio,* I'll never be able to look at her eyes again without thinking of the underwear. Swallowing hard, he turned on his heel and headed back downstairs to wait for her, her breakfast tray still clutched in his hands, forgotten.

And he'd imagined all those weeks that he was over her? Not in his wildest dreams.

She came down a few moments later, looking fragile and wary but with her head held high, and he'd never wanted a woman more in all his life.

She perched on a stool at the breakfast bar and he pushed the tray towards her. 'Eat. And drink the tea. It's lemon and ginger. It'll soothe your stomach.'

She sipped it, pulled a face and nibbled the toast. 'Did you sleep?' he asked, and she nodded.

'Yes—a bit. Not much. I was thinking.'

'Me, too. I was thinking that I want you out of that awful rented house with the hideously uncomfortable furniture, and into my house where at least I'll be able to look after you. It's only sensible—it's right next to the hospital, and you can't do that journey while you're pregnant, it's much too long and dangerous.'

She was staring at him, her eyes flashing fire, and she set the cup down with a wobbling hand and met his eyes. *'That awful rented house,'* she said in a measured tone that made him realise he'd overstepped the mark, 'happens to belong to me. And I will not move out of it. I know the journey's difficult, but I can get a cab—at least for the end of the day.'

It was *her house?* He could have kicked himself. 'I'm sorry. I didn't realise the house was yours. I just assumed—'

'Well, don't,' she said crisply. 'I don't need your assumptions, or your instructions on how to live my life. In fact, I need nothing from you at all, except one thing,' she went on, her chin lifting. 'In case you're worried about it, I've decided to keep the baby,' she told him, throwing up a subject that hadn't even crossed his mind, 'and I don't want anything from you, so don't even think about getting all macho and insisting we get married, because the answer's no. I just want your name on the birth certificate.'

CHAPTER SIX

LUCA FELT HIS jaw drop.

Of all the things she could have said, that was absolutely the last he was expecting.

Sucking in a lungful of air, he shut his mouth and tipped his head on one side.

'Is that all?' he said softly, wondering how something that should have been amazing and incredible and a source of celebration could have been reduced to something as technical as a name on a piece of paper. 'You want my name on the baby's birth certificate?'

'Yes. For the baby's sake. My father died when I was two, and because my mother wasn't married to him, she had no protection in law, no legal status as a widow, no right to his estate. She'd been buying our house—that *awful* house—for some while, though, so we weren't homeless, but his wife's family were dreadful to her.'

He was still wincing over awful, but that got his attention. 'Wife?'

'He was married—to someone so emotionally unstable he couldn't tell Mum about her. And then he died and his wife found out, and it was horrendous for my mother. I didn't know anything about it, of course, I was only a few years old, but I gather it was dreadful. And I don't want that happening to my child.'

No wonder she was so wary. It was enough to make any woman suspicious of men. But he wasn't her father, and there was no wife waiting to take revenge.

'Well, if it's any consolation there's no wife and I have no intention of dying.'

She glared at him. 'Will you please be serious?'

'I'm being totally serious. I've never been more serious about anything. But you have to know, Isabella, that I intend to be very much more to my child than a name on a birth certificate, whether I'm married to you or not.'

'Well, I won't marry you, so don't even think of asking me.'

'I won't—not yet. I think getting married just because you've made a baby between you is a very shaky way to start a marriage, but I would ask you not to rule it out for the future.'

The glare changed, softening into confusion. 'Luca, I can't—' She bit her lip, her eyes filled with pain. 'I don't want to get married. I don't want that sort of relationship.'

'Well, you should have thought about that before you had unprotected sex, shouldn't you, *cara?*'

'I didn't.'

'Yes, you did. You told me you were on the Pill, but you weren't, not reliably—not religiously taking it on time, because you weren't taking it for that reason, and if I'd known that I would have made sure you took the morning-after pill.'

'I was taking it—I was airsick.' she said drily. 'Not even you could have altered the turbulence.'

He gave a brittle laugh. 'Possibly not, but now I'm facing the reality of becoming a father to a baby whose mother won't contemplate forming a stable, loving relationship with me.'

'Luca, you can't love me!'

'Why? Why can't I?' he demanded.

'Because you don't know me,' she said, her voice distressed, 'and I don't know you. I *can't* love you.'

There was something in her voice that troubled him, and he reached out a hand to cover hers.

'Why can't you love me, *cara?*' he asked softly. 'If you give yourself time, then maybe...'

'It isn't time,' she admitted, her eyes fraught with emotion. 'And it's not that I can't love you, Luca—it's that I can't trust you. I can't trust any man.'

'Because of your father?'

'Partly.'

'And?' he coaxed. 'The other part?'

She shook her head, and he sighed softly and lifted her hand into his, cradling it between his palms, willing her to talk to him, to let him in. 'Who was he, Isabelle? What did he do to you? Tell me, *tesoro*. Talk to me.'

She swallowed hard and tilted her chin in that endearing way, and he saw her eyes were clouded with tears. For a long time he thought she wouldn't tell him, but then she turned and met his eyes defiantly.

'He was my fiancé. He changed his mind, just before the wedding, and went back to his old girlfriend. They got married, and the last I heard they had two children and they'd split up. Now you tell me, why should I trust a man after my father and my fiancé have both proved that they can't stay faithful?'

And that was why, of course, she was wary—not only because of her father, but because of her fiancé, and Luca wanted to find the man and kill him for hurting her so badly.

'Oh, Isabella,' he said softly, and without waiting for an invitation, he swung round on the bar stool and drew her into his arms. For a moment she sank against him, then she straightened up and turned away.

'Luca, stop it! I don't want to lean on you. I don't want to need you.'

'Why? What's so wrong with needing me? You can't do everything alone.'

'Why? My mother did.'

'And did it make her happy?'

She sucked in a fraught little breath and turned her head away. 'Luca, I can do this.'

'Of course you can. But you don't have to, and I don't want to be shut out, Isabella. This is my baby, too. I need to be part of its life, on a daily basis—starting now. And you're going to have to learn to trust me.'

'How? How on earth am I supposed to do that? Luca, I *can't!* I don't know you.'

'So get to know me. Spend time with me, *cara.* Come to Italy with me and meet my family, see my home, have a bit of fun. We'll start today—we'll go out for a walk, get some fresh air, feed the ducks—anything you like.'

She hesitated. It seemed like a lovely idea—and if nothing else, she had to get to know the man who was the father of her child. He couldn't remain a stranger to her. So she nodded, and said, 'Yes. All right. But—just that. Just spending time together, no—'

She broke off, and he smiled wryly. 'No reruns of Florence?' She nodded. 'OK. That's fine. It's better. Sex is too distracting. We'll stick to other fun stuff.'

So they did. They went out, via her house so she could change into jeans and trainers and a thick fleece, and they went for a walk on the park near her house and fed the ducks and he made her eat lunch—nothing elaborate, just a simple sandwich in the sunshine outside the pub.

While he was in the pub paying the bill his phone rang, and she stared at it dubiously. 'Gio,' she read, and bit her lip. His brother—or one of them.

'Hello?'

'Well, that's not Luca.'

'No. He's in the pub, he won't be a moment. Can I get him to call you?'

'In a minute. Who's that?'

'Isabelle.'

'So he found you.'

She blinked. He knew about her? 'Um—yes. We're working together.'

His brother laughed softly. 'I knew it. So how much do you know about my brother, Isabelle?'

'Not much,' she confessed. 'Not enough, really.'

'Well, don't hurt him. He's been through enough, and he hasn't had a relationship that I know of for years. Many, many years. Well, not one that's lasted more than a few weeks. But he's a good man, and you seem to have got right under his skin. I've never seen him like he was that morning, when he'd left you at the airport. And when he realised he'd missed your call—well, he was pretty mad with himself. He wanted to talk to you.'

'It wouldn't have made any difference, I didn't want to see him.'

'So—what's different? What's changed?'

Oh, lord. She couldn't tell him. 'Um—we're working together,' she said, flannelling desperately.

'Not today, if you're at the pub. So I assume you're seeing each other.'

'Sort of,' she admitted, wondering how much of this she should be sharing with his brother and when Luca was coming back.

'Well, don't worry. He's a good guy, and he's free—and personally I'd be only too delighted if you got together. He needs a good woman to save him from himself.'

'But you haven't met me.'

'I don't need to. I've only got to hear his voice when he talks about you. I think you might be what he's been waiting for all his life.'

Luca appeared at her side and arched a brow questioningly, and she turned away, filled with confusion.

'You can't—he can't know that.'

'I don't agree. I think he can. And I really hope you'll give him a chance, because of all the people I know, he's the best, most decent, honest, reliable man—and the kindest.' He hesitated, then went on, 'You have to know he's been hurt in the past. I don't want to see that happen again. But just a word of advice—if you hurt him deliberately, or cheat on him or trick him in any way, you'll have me to deal with—and I don't lose in a court of law. Get him to call me, can you?'

'Um—he's here. Luca, it's your brother.'

She handed the phone over and stared at him, trying to read his face. When had he been hurt? And how? Who had hurt him? Some woman. *I don't want to see that happen again.* Her eyes filled with tears and she turned and blinked them hastily away.

'Luca?'

'Yes, Gio. I hope you didn't scare her to death.'

'I don't know. If she scares that easily, she's no good for you. But if you're getting into this as deep as I think you are, you'd better let me get you a pre-nup organised—and I'm serious about this. We need to talk about it. After what happened—'

'Sure. If it's relevant—which it's not at the moment, I'll call you. *Ciao.*'

He hung up and met her eyes again. 'Well? What did he say?'

'Nothing much. I'm sorry I answered your phone, but I didn't know if it was important.'

'That's fine, but I know Gio, he never says nothing. So what did he say?'

'He seems to think the sun rises and sets on you,' she said, and he laughed a little roughly and sat down beside her, slipping the phone back into his pocket.

'I'm sure he didn't say any such thing.'

No, he'd said that he thought Luca had been looking for her all his life. Was it possible? Could it be true? And could she trust him?

'He was very protective.'

He laughed at that, too, but there was something guarded in his eyes. 'Protective? Just what *did* he say?'

'Only that you'd been hurt.'

His mouth tightened. 'He talks too much. Anyway, it's irrelevant and it was years ago.'

'How many?'

'Ten? It doesn't matter. He had no business discussing it with you.'

'He didn't,' she corrected. 'He just...'

'What?'

'Warned me off, I think,' she said thoughtfully. 'But only if I meant you harm. He must love you very much. I can't imagine what it's like to have a brother.'

'Suffocating,' he said frankly, 'and I have two brothers and three sisters, so you can multiply that by five,' but then he smiled and touched her cheek gently with his hand. 'Ignore him. He's just a lawyer. He spends his life immersed in the criminal mind. It distorts his vision.'

She smiled, as she was meant to, and then shook her head. 'Luca, I can't just marry you because of the baby.'

'Of course not. I realise that. And I'm not offering marriage yet. I wouldn't do that until I was sure of my feelings, and yours. But give us a chance—please. We're having a good day today. Let's do it again, see if we have what it takes to make a stable home life for our baby. See if we can fall in love.'

She gave him a sad little smile that twisted something inside him. 'Oh, falling in love with you isn't the problem, Luca,' she said softly. 'I fell in love with you that first night. It's trusting I have difficulty with. Trusting any man. And that won't come easily just because I want it to.'

He felt a surge of hope, then, that they might come out of this with something good, something honest and decent and lasting—because she did want it to, if only he could persuade her to take that leap of faith. And she loved him.

'Come to Italy with me, meet my family. Ask them all about me. They'll tell you the truth—especially my brothers. They won't hold back. You'll get chapter and verse on every time I borrowed their bikes or stole their girlfriends, and my father will tell you how I used to take his car and return it with an empty fuel tank so he'd run out on the way to the petrol station. You want the truth about me, warts and all, ask my family.'

'That's very brave,' she said, wondering if she'd be so honest or daring, and he just gave a crooked grin and shrugged.

'There's a lot at stake, *cara*. It's going to take some courage, from both of us, but the rewards—' He broke off and swallowed, and she could see the emotion in his eyes. 'I want to be a good father, Isabelle. Please don't deny me the chance.'

It was that which swayed her. The sincerity in his eyes, the genuine wholehearted endorsement from his brother. The not-even-thinly veiled threat.

'All right,' she said softly. 'But I'm scared, Luca. I don't trust easily, and it's so long since I've had a relationship I'm not sure I know how.'

'Then we'll find out together.' He smiled tenderly and held out his arms, and she moved into them, resting her head on his shoulder and feeling instantly at home. How could she? How was it possible to feel so much at ease with him when her life was in such chaos?

Or maybe it wasn't in chaos at all. Maybe, for the first time in her whole life, it was actually on the right track...

She spent the rest of Saturday with him, but she wanted to go home in the evening.

'Stay with me. Let me look after you,' he said, but she refused, and so he drove her home, picking up some food for her on the way.

He put it in the fridge, closed the door and shook his head. 'There—that should last you a day or two, you stubborn girl. I wish you'd stay with me.'

'I'm fine, Luca. Really. I'll make sure I've got a flask of iced water by the bed, and some crackers and an apple. I'll be fine.'

'Well, let me stay here, then.'

'No. Really, I'll be fine.'

'I'll come and see you before you get up.'

'You don't need to.'

'*Si,* I do. I want to. It's the least I can do. This is my fault.'

'How can it be your fault?' she asked, remembering her patient Lindsey telling her husband Mike that it was his fault and him reminding her that she'd been the one to forget her pills.

'I should have taken care of you,' he said gruffly, 'not been so wrapped up in my own needs that I forgot something so basic and simple as protecting you when we made love.'

His words curled round her heart, and she felt a fissure open up in her defences. 'Luca, I was there, too. It wasn't just your fault.'

His hand came up and cradled her cheek, and his eyes were sombre. 'Nevertheless, I should have been the one to take control of that part of it, and I'm sorry to have put you in this situation, but I *will* stand by you, Isabella. I will be here, and if and when we marry, it will be for ever. I will never leave you, or divorce you, or let you down intentionally, and I will absolutely, categorically, never be unfaithful. It isn't the man I am.'

His words nearly reduced her to tears, but he had such faith in their ability to make this work, and she wasn't sure she could share it. Not yet.

'Can we just take one step at a time?' she asked with a fragile little laugh, and he smiled and cupped her cheeks in his hands.

'Good idea,' he murmured, and, bending his head, he feathered a kiss over her mouth, teasing her lips apart with a soft stroke of his tongue so that she opened to him with a tiny sob of need. How could she want him so badly? Need him so damned much, after so short a time?

She didn't know. She just knew that his kiss, his touch, his arms were what she'd been waiting for her entire life, and nothing had ever felt so right.

'*Isabella,*' he groaned, his fingertips shaking as they traced her jaw, his eyes on fire. 'I have to go.'

'No,' she said, her hands holding him against her, and after a breathless moment, he gave an untidy sigh and wrapped her hard against his chest.

'I *have* to go. You aren't ready for this. We already know we're good in bed. You need to get to know me, *bella,* know if you can share your life with me, and this is just a beautiful distraction. Come on, let me go. We agreed.'

He squeezed her gently, then let her go, and she could have cried.

'I'll come back tomorrow,' he promised. 'We'll go shopping for you.'

'Shopping?' she said, dazed. 'What kind of shopping?'

He shrugged. 'Clothes for our holiday? We could go to Harvey Nichols or Harrods.'

She felt her jaw sag. 'I've never been there in my life!' she said. 'And besides, why do I need clothes? I have clothes.'

'Enough clothes? No woman has enough clothes.'

She ignored the teasing smile. 'I have plenty. Why would I need more?'

'To take to Italy?' he said softly. 'To meet my family? We—well, no, we don't exactly dress for dinner, but we change into something a little smarter. And if we're there a week or so…'

Oh, lord, he was serious! She'd thought he was joking, but clearly not. 'I don't know how much holiday I've got,' she flannelled. 'When are you thinking of going?'

He shrugged. 'Soon? A week? Two? We'll have to take a look at the rota.'

Her eyes widened. 'Two weeks? What about booking?'

'Booking what? We'll stay in Tuscany with the family.'

'But—we have to get there.'

He just smiled. 'I'm sure we'll find a flight,' he murmured. 'I'll see you tomorrow. Sleep well.'

And with a gentle, lingering kiss, he left her, feeling just a teeny bit like Alice falling down the rabbit hole…

'So—what do you need?'

Isabelle shrugged and laughed a little wildly. 'I have no idea. You tell me. I'm quite happy to go with what I've got.'

'What have you got?'

She shrugged again, running a mental eye over her wardrobe. Not that she needed to, it was sparse enough to see with one quick glance. 'I've got a nice dress that I feel good in. And a couple of pairs of trousers that are quite smart, and some pretty tops. How cold is it in your parents' house?'

'Not cold, but it can get draughty. You'll need jumpers, perhaps a couple of little jackets? And more than one dress. We may be invited out, and we'll go for lunch, maybe go out for dinner. You'll need quite a few changes for all that.'

She thought of her lovely little dress, and sighed. 'Luca, I really don't see the point. I am what I am.'

'Of course you are, and I don't want anybody to think anything else, but I don't want you feeling under pressure because you haven't got anything to wear. And if you have only one dress…'

'I won't feel under pressure. But I don't want to go today. I'll get something next week on my days off.'

'No. This was my idea.'

'Then I'm not going to Italy.'

She'd folded her arms, and she had that mulish look on her face again, the chin tilted up, the eyes flashing a challenge that did nothing except give him an overwhelming desire to take her straight to bed.

'OK. We'll do something else today,' he suggested, saving the shopping trip for another day when she was feeling less combative. Maybe in Florence, if she agreed.

She hesitated, then nodded. 'All right. Can we go out into the country and take a walk by the Thames? I love walking in the countryside and to be honest fresh air is much more appealing than trailing round stuffy shops. And yesterday was such fun.'

He gave in, knowing when he was beaten. For now. 'Come on, then, let's go, and we'll have lunch somewhere in a pub by the water. Happy now?'

She smiled, her eyes softening. 'Happy,' she said, and his heart melted. Tucking her coat round her shoulders, he ushered her out to his car, buckled her in and set off.

They had a wonderful day. The sun shone on them, the water sparkled and they found a lovely pub right on the river for lunch.

And Luca was like he'd been in Florence, flirting with her, attentive, funny and just plain gorgeous, and she found herself falling headlong even further in love, despite her best efforts.

Would marriage to him be so bad? She didn't know, but it was irrelevant, she told herself, because he hadn't asked her, anyway.

Until they got back to her house, and he made her a drink and sat down beside her on the sofa and took her hand in his. 'So, *cara,* have you enjoyed the weekend?'

'You know I have. It's been lovely.'

'And could you see yourself spending other days like that with me? All of them?'

Her heart speeded up, and she searched his eyes. 'What are you saying, Luca?' she asked softly, confused and stupidly, ridiculously hopeful.

His mouth twisted into a wry smile. 'I believe I'm asking you to marry me,' he said gruffly. 'Only I'm not doing it very well, if you can't work it out. So—do you think you could? Marry me, and spend your life with me, bringing up our child? There would be all sorts of advantages—a huge family, for both of you, for a start. I know that's something you lack, and something I could provide with bells on. There would be lots of little cousins for the baby, and devoted uncles and aunts and grandparents—have you told your mother yet, by the way?'

She shook her head, still wondering if he was proposing that she marry him or his family, and wondering if there was actually a difference or if it might be one and the same thing.

'You should. She needs to know. And so do my parents, but I'd like something a little more concrete to tell them— preferably that we're going to be married. But that's your call.'

She swallowed. It was such a huge step, and she wasn't at all sure she was ready for it, but it would give her baby security, and love, and she would know that if anything happened to her, God forbid, the child wouldn't be alone. And she knew that was something that had worried her mother a great deal.

'If I said yes—there would have to be conditions,' she warned, and he raised a brow.

'Conditions?'

She nodded. 'I want a pre-nuptial agreement, so that my house is protected for the baby. I know that probably seems silly to you, since your house is worth much more than mine, but I need that security, in case anything happens in the future.

And I'm not interested in your house. That's not what this is about. My childhood was so uncertain, and I just want to protect my baby's future.'

She wanted a pre-nup? He nearly laughed out loud. If she'd had the slightest idea how rich he was, just how much family money was behind him, she would have been mortified. But clearly she didn't, or she wouldn't have suggested it for an instant. She'd be mad to.

'Well?'

He smiled slightly. 'OK—but there are conditions on my side, too. At some point, we'll probably end up moving back to Italy. Can you do that? Would you?'

Her eyes widened. 'Move there? To live?'

'*Si*. It's my home. It's where I live, where I want my child brought up, ideally, surrounded by his family, so that he knows who he is and understands my place in his life, but we'll make sure the house will remain cared for so you can stay in it when we come back to England to visit your friends and family, if you don't want to stay in mine.'

'Luca, I can't!'

He lifted a brow. 'Can't? Can't what?'

'Live in Italy,' she said, panic starting to choke her. 'I can't speak a word of Italian, Luca! I struggled to order a coffee.'

'You can learn, *cara,*' he said, his voice softening persuasively. 'It's not so hard. And all my family speak perfect English. Think of the advantages—beautiful countryside, a warm, loving family…'

'Suffocating, you said,' she reminded him, the panic invading every part of her, and he smiled gently.

'They can be, but mostly it's wonderful. And the weather is fantastic. You'll love it.'

He let his words hang for a moment, then lifted his shoulders. 'So that's my choice for us, anyway. I marry you, we live in Italy, at least at some point in the future, and we bring up our child—our children—together. The choice is yours, *cara*. You don't have to marry me, of course you don't, but there are huge advantages for all of us, and I know it'll mean compromises for you, but we can't just think about ourselves any more. Let me know when you've decided—but you need to know that this will be a proper marriage, one that we work on together. I'll give you and our child the protection of my name, but you won't have affairs and neither will I, you and the child will live with me and there will be no divorce, Isabelle. When I marry, it will be for life. I won't betray you, and I'll give it everything I have, but I won't give up on us, and I don't expect you to. So don't say yes unless you're absolutely sure.'

She stared into his eyes, her mind reeling. Live in Italy, with Luca—or here, without him, with the child dragged from pillar to post, shared custody, rows about access, the trauma and drama of holidays and birthdays and Christmas? And in Italy there'd be a family, a great, huge suffocating family to love their baby to pieces.

If she didn't marry him, there was the possibility that she could face the future alone and without support. She had friends and family, but would they pay her bills when she was sick, or look after the baby if she died?

She felt her jaw sag, and snapped it up and turned away hastily. She hadn't given that possibility serious thought, but what if she *did* die? Accidents happened. Would he have her baby? And if so, would he know their child, or would it be a stranger to him? Would the baby know him, if they lived in different countries? Or even be able to speak the same language as its new-found family?

'Difficult, isn't it, *cara?*' he murmured, and she closed her eyes and took a steadying breath. Emotion was another thing, she'd discovered, that pushed her nausea over the edge, and she could feel her throat closing with the prospect of all that uncertainty.

If her mother had been the one to die and not her father, would she have gone to him? And would he have loved her? What if she didn't marry Luca and he married someone else who had his children? Would her child be welcomed by them if she died, any more than she would have been welcomed by her father's other family? She doubted it.

At a time when his or her world had already fallen apart, her baby could be lonely and isolated and afraid. Without any emotional security.

And that, above all, was the thing that mattered. Luca and his family represented security, a safety net for all of them, and that was something she'd never had and always yearned for.

There was no contest, really. She found a rather wobbly smile and took a deep breath.

'Yes,' she said softly. 'I will marry you, Luca. And we'll make it work.'

He closed his eyes briefly, and when he opened them again, he was smiling. 'Thank you. I'll tell my mother—she can start planning.'

'Planning what?' she asked, a horrible suspicion suddenly entering her mind. 'I don't want a big wedding.'

He laughed. 'Neither do I, but I have a huge family.'

'No. I'm not joking, Luca. I won't marry you if it has to be a big wedding. I was going to do that last time, and it was all planned and bought and organised, right down to the name cards for the tables. I don't want that again. I just want to marry you.'

He studied her thoughtfully for a moment, then nodded slowly and to her surprise he backed down. 'OK—but I want to do this surrounded by my close family, at least, and some old friends. And your mother should be with you, *tesoro*. We could get married in the local church?'

She shook her head. 'No. Can't we get married in a registry office? I just—I want a really simple ceremony, no fuss. Just a couple of witnesses. Please, Luca. I can't face all that razzamatazz.'

'We must have family.'

She shrugged. 'Really? It hardly seems worth it—it's not like it's a proper wedding. It'll be over in half an hour.'

Luca opened his mouth, shut it again and said nothing. She was asking him to marry without his family, in a civil ceremony—because it wasn't a *proper wedding?*

'It will be a proper wedding,' he told her firmly. 'It will just be quiet. Please, *cara*. Do this for me. Marry me in Tuscany— we can have a quiet wedding there.'

'Very quiet,' she insisted.

'Of course. Just our families and maybe a few close friends.'

She nodded. 'I'm sorry—I know it's probably not at all what you had in mind.'

'*Tesoro,* none of this is what I had in mind, but it's all negotiable, and if this is what you would like, then it's what we'll have. We can have a civil wedding in the town hall followed by a church blessing and a small reception. OK?'

'Won't your mother mind?'

He laughed softly. 'It's not up to my mother. It's our

wedding, we'll have what we want. I won't tell them yet, though. I'll save it until we get there. And now I'm going to leave you to rest. I'll see you tomorrow.'

He stood up, drew her into his arms and kissed her tenderly, then wrapped her firmly against his chest. 'Just a few more weeks, *cara*,' he murmured, and eased away from her, kissing her fleetingly once more before letting himself out of the house and closing the door, leaving her alone to wonder what on earth she'd talked herself into.

'You're doing *what?*'

'Going to Italy with Luca to meet his family, and to plan our wedding.'

'Ohmigod, you jammy thing!' Sarah exclaimed, her eyes filling. 'Oh, that's fantastic!'

Was it? Fantastic, to be planning a wedding when she was pregnant with his child?

Yes, actually, she realised, it was—not that Sarah knew about that, because they'd agreed not to tell anyone yet, but the baby was getting more real with every hour that passed, and Luca was spoiling her rotten. She still wouldn't yield on the clothes, though, and so she enlisted Sarah's help. 'I need your advice. I'm going to need lots more clothes for when I go to meet them, and I want decent ones, but I won't let him buy them for me.'

'You must be mad. I'd let him. Hell, any man that wants to take me shopping can have me. The only place I get to go these days with a man is the supermarket, and that's only to make sure I buy him enough meat! For heaven's sake, Izzie, he's going to be your husband!'

'Shh!' Isabelle chuckled and shook her head. 'Not too

loud, we're not broadcasting it. Anyway, I'm not letting him do it, so what can I do on a shoestring?'

'Charity shops. I know just the one,' Sarah said, her eyes alight. 'There's a woman who brings the most gorgeous things in, and they're too tall and too tight for me, but they'd fit you perfectly, and they're fabulous. Some of them still have tags on. We'll go tomorrow.'

So they did, and by a stroke of luck they arrived just a few minutes after another consignment from the mystery lady.

And they were a perfect fit. Half an hour later, Isabelle emerged with three dresses, four tops, a jacket, another pair of trousers—and there were even a pair of Jimmy Choos in her size that looked unworn, and the prices were ridiculous. Even so, she'd still spent part of her re-roofing budget, but not nearly as much as if she'd gone to the designers directly—and the charity would benefit, which was an added bonus.

'Oh, you're so lucky, I love those shoes,' Sarah said wistfully. 'Oh, you're going to look fabulous.'

'I hope so. I really don't want to let him down.'

'Don't be absurd! How on earth could you let him down? Who the hell *is* he? Anyway, you're wonderful. He should consider himself lucky to have you.'

Isabelle didn't bother to explain. She wasn't sure she really knew, anyway, and she just hoped that yesterday's fashion would be good enough.

He was waiting on her doorstep when she arrived home with a carrier bag in each hand emblazoned with the name of the charity.

'Where have you been?' he asked curiously.

'Shopping,' she said, cursing her luck that he should have been there so she couldn't smuggle the things into her house without him knowing.

He frowned at the bags. 'In a charity shop?'

'Why not? If I'm having to buy clothes for Italy, I can't afford to do everything in the high street shops,' she said, aware of how distinctly frugal she was being with the truth, but he just frowned.

'You went to a charity shop for clothes to wear to meet my family?' he said, looking appalled, and she met his eyes defiantly.

'It's called recycling. Very environmentally sound.' And cheaper by miles.

'But I offered—'

'I know. And I declined. Besides, it's pointless spending a fortune because they won't fit me for long, and I hate waste. Do you have a problem with that?'

His mouth opened, then snapped shut. 'No. No problem,' he said through clenched teeth, and she suppressed a smile.

'Good. Just so we both know where we stand. Don't worry, it's all really good stuff, I won't disgrace you.'

'I didn't think you would for a moment.'

'Good. What's in your shopping bag?'

'Food. Some of it could do with going in the freezer. Luckily it's not warm out here.'

She felt a pang of guilt and quickly suppressed it. She hadn't been expecting him, hadn't asked him to shop for her, and it was in no way her fault that he was there mid-way through the afternoon. Then she remembered he'd been on call last night and this was his afternoon off, and then she did feel guilty, because he was probably exhausted.

'You should have rung me.'

'I did. You weren't answering your phone.'

Just then it let out a series of beeps, and she pulled it out and found several messages about missed calls from him. 'Sorry. I must have been on the Tube. Come on in. I'll put the kettle on.'

'I'll do it. Go and hang up your things.'

He went into the kitchen, inwardly seething, and listened to her pottering upstairs with her charity shop finds—charity shop, of all things!—while he put the shopping away and made them tea, dropping the tea bag in the bin just as she ran back downstairs.

'Perfect timing. Here—it's ginger and lemon.'

'Thanks. So—have you had a nice afternoon?' she asked brightly.

'Busy. I've booked the flights for Friday morning. We need to be at the airport at six-thirty. I take it your passport's valid?'

She nodded numbly.

'Good. We're going via Pisa because my car's in Firenze. I'll get it delivered to the airport ready for us.'

She caught her jaw in time. Get it delivered? It was slowly beginning to dawn on her what she was getting herself into, and she felt a shiver of apprehension. Maybe she should have let him take her to Harrods—or not.

This way, at least, her pride would be intact, and she was reasonably confident she wouldn't disgrace him, but— Friday? Dear heaven.

CHAPTER SEVEN

THEY TOUCHED DOWN late in the morning on a gloriously sunny day, and Isabelle was never more glad to be back on land in her life.

Her legs were wobbly, her heart was pounding and she'd struggled with nausea for the entire flight. And now they were standing outside the airport in the brilliant early March sunshine, and all she wanted was to go somewhere still and quiet and lie down for a while until the vibrations had gone from her body and her heart had slowed.

Not that that was likely to happen in a hurry. She was on a knife-edge, filled with apprehension over meeting Luca's family, no matter how wonderful and welcoming and marvellous he said they were.

'Come on, let's get you home,' he said, and she nearly laughed hysterically. Home? Her safe, cosy little house in Herne Hill with its shabby décor and tired furniture that she couldn't afford to update, with its roof in need of attention and its tiny courtyard garden filled with pots that she would plant up later in the year—that was home.

'*Isabella?* Are you all right, *cara?*'

'I'll be fine.'

'We'll take the main road, it's quicker. They're expecting us for a late lunch.'

Her stomach turned over at the thought, but she didn't know if it was lunch or the family which worried her more. She fell into step beside him as he towed the luggage across to the short-stay car park and unlocked his car—the outrageously sexy Italian sports job she'd last been in when he'd brought her here all those weeks before, after the night that had changed both their lives forever.

'So how did you get your car here?' she asked, still amazed by that ridiculous detail and trying to focus on something other than the upcoming meeting.

'I had it dropped off by the garage where I store it if I'm out of the country,' he said, and stashed their cases in the boot before settling her into the seat. The leather was warm, and she relaxed back against it with a little sigh.

'All right, *cara?*'

'I will be. The turbulence was a bit much.'

There had hardly been any, he thought, but she'd looked doggedly out of the window for the entire journey, her face chalk white, and he wondered if it had been the turbulence or if she was just nervous. Not that she normally seemed a nervous person. Rather the opposite, but he guessed there was a lot going on today and he already knew she wasn't a good flyer. Still, the flight was over now, and there was only the drive left. With a quick glance into his mirror, he pulled out into the traffic and set off for home.

His parents were expecting them, but he hadn't told them anything about Isabelle because he didn't want them making a great fuss and putting on some massive welcoming committee that would scare her off. He was just happy that she was here, that he'd got her here at all. She was tense enough as it was without any added fuss.

He put his hand on her leg and gave it a quick squeeze, and she glanced across at him and smiled fleetingly.

It was all she could manage. Her stomach was in knots, and the nearer they got to his home, the worse it became. Thank God the main A1 Rome road was smooth, although it twisted and turned and plunged from time to time into long, dark tunnels as it wove through the Tuscan hills.

Then they turned off onto the twisting little minor road that wriggled its way through the beautiful rolling countryside, the picture-postcard landscape of Tuscany unfolding in front of her, with the avenues of cypress trees like sentries along the roads, the little hilltop towns sprinkled along the way keeping guard against the Florentine invasion.

'It's beautiful,' she said softly, staring out at the scene so familiar from postcards and paintings that it was almost a cliché now, and yet in the flesh she found she loved it, and the tension started to leave her, taking the nausea with it.

'It's my favourite place in the world,' he told her. 'And not just because it's home. It's also very beautiful in a stark, rather severe way, but there are problems here, of course, which the tourists don't see. It's hard to keep the young people here in the old towns. There's nothing for them. Agriculture is dependent on the weather, and not everyone wants to make wine or olive oil or cheese, or act as a guide for the tourists. So they go to the cities—to Siena, to Firenze, to Pisa—or further, maybe, to Roma or Milano, and so the elderly lose their support and the schools lack children.'

'But your family are still here, and you keep coming back.'

'We belong here,' he said simply, and with a sudden shock

she realised it was true, that this was his home, and if she'd imagined that when they got married she could talk him into living a cosy little life in London away from his family, she was almost certainly deluded.

And beautiful though the landscape was, she couldn't imagine it feeling like home, and she wasn't sure how she felt about that.

He decided to go straight to the lodge so she could rest and freshen up before going to meet the family, but when he turned onto the drive he could see cars over there clustered in front of the building. Several cars—or vans. Workmen?

Damn. That meant it was out of action, and of course the alternative to being in the lodge was to be in his usual room in the house, with her in the adjoining room. Damn. At least in the lodge they'd have had a bit more privacy, which was why he'd suggested it, and he much preferred the simplicity of the lodge.

Not that the privacy was an issue, and maybe it would be easier in the house to maintain a little more distance. It had been an unwritten rule that whatever any of them did, they would be discreet and not subject the family to their romantic entanglements until they were married. And so far, only Massimo and his sister Carla had tied the knot. The rest of them—Gio, Anna and Serena—were still single. And him, of course, at the moment. But not for much longer.

Beside him, Isabelle sat up a little straighter. 'Are we nearly there?'

'Yes, but we can't stay at the lodge. There are vans outside—it must be being decorated or something.'

She turned her head towards him. 'So where will we stay?'

'In my parents' house.'

She looked ahead along the curving drive lined by an avenue of trademark cypress trees, but the only buildings she could see were a village in the distance and a huge stone edifice, more like a castle than a house. A fortress? Or a fortified hill town, but so small it only had this gravel road to it? That was what it looked like. A little fortified hill town. But of course his parents' house was also a farm, so perhaps that was the house and the farm buildings and all the offices and workers' accommodation. That would make sense.

And maybe it would be smaller close up. She'd find out soon enough, she told herself as they drove along the gravel track and up the hill.

'Massimo will be here—he runs the family business and lives here with his children. He's a single parent—he lost his wife shortly after their third child was born—she had a brain haemorrhage.'

'Oh, how dreadful! How old are the children?'

'Eight, five and three, or something like that. I don't know. They grow up so fast. They live in a wing of the house.'

A wing? So maybe it wouldn't be smaller…

'Gio's here, too,' he said, as they went through a great archway into an area at the front of the huge building and pulled up beside a black Ferrari. 'I thought he might come to check you out. Come on. Let's go in.'

She opened the door and got out, transfixed by the size of the building. So much for her idea that it might be smaller than it appeared. It was truly huge, even larger close up, great sweeping steps climbing to the huge double doors on the first floor, and as she stared at the forbidding and impressive entrance, the door opened and an elderly man hobbled down the steps towards them, holding out his hands in welcome.

'*Signore!*' he cried, and she realised in shock that this man must be the archetypal ancient retainer, and this enormous edifice, this monumental building, was Luca's family home.

Luca turned towards him with a smile and took his outstretched hands, touched as ever by the warmth of the old man's greeting.

'Roberto! It's good to see you again. How are you?'

'I am well, *Signore.* And you?'

'Very well, thank you. Is my mother inside?'

'*Si, Signore.* And your father. They're expecting you, and your brothers are with them. Carlotta said to tell you lunch will keep until you're ready.'

'Good. Thank you.' He switched to English for Isabelle's benefit. 'Roberto, let me introduce you to a friend of mine, Isabelle Thompson. She'll be a guest with us for a few days.'

Roberto's eyes swivelled to her, standing very still a little behind Luca, and he hauled himself up straighter and beamed a welcome. '*Signorina,*' he said gravely, bowing low, 'Welcome to the Palazzo Valtieri.' And then he turned back to Luca, and embraced him. 'It's good to see you again,' he said, reverting to Italian. 'You've been gone too long. Carlotta is very excited. She's busy cooking for you.'

Luca laughed softly. 'Thank you.'

'Now I will take your luggage upstairs.'

'No. I'll do it. I'll take Isabelle up and let her change and freshen up, and then we'll go and meet my parents. Just tell Carlotta we're here—oh, and get some Prosecco on ice. We have something to celebrate.'

'*Si, Signore.* At once!' And he scurried off, shaking his head and grinning from ear to ear.

'Right. Let's go and find my parents,' he said.

'Do you supply maps?' she asked a little drily, and he gave a tired laugh.

'It's not that big.'

'Not? Luca, don't be ridiculous! It's enormous!' Isabelle exclaimed, still reeling. 'I mean, I knew it would be big, but this is crazy! Why didn't you tell me?'

'Because it's nothing to do with anything.'

She rolled her eyes and glared at him. 'Luca, you have *servants!* You live in a *palazzo,* for heaven's sake! That is not *nothing!'*

She climbed the first few steps, staring around her and taking it all in, her heart pounding.

It was stunning. Absolutely stunning. Huge terracotta pots containing what looked like olive trees flanked the broad steps which led to the massive dark wooden doors in the centre of the house, and tall windows were arranged symmetrically in three rows across the front, taking advantage of the spectacular view. At roof level, high up over the front door, was what looked like a massive mantel clock with a fine black iron frame above it supporting a brass bell.

And then she thought of her little house that he'd been so damning about, and the pre-nuptial agreement she'd asked him to sign before their marriage, and she wanted to die of humiliation.

She didn't feel so much out of her depth as nailed to the bottom of the ocean, and she was furious with him for not warning her. Or with herself for not having worked it out. She felt so ill prepared, so stupid, so totally unready for this whole meeting that she could have wept.

But she wouldn't. She was made of sterner stuff than that. Instead she tucked her bag under her arm and went down to the back of the car where Luca had removed the cases from the boot. Thank God for Sarah and her charity shop, she thought, and reached for her case, only to receive a warning growl.

'I'll take that. You're not carrying anything except the baby,' he said firmly, and she gave in. Let him carry it, if it made him feel good. She didn't have the energy to argue. Instead she straightened her shoulders and followed him up the steps and through the great heavy entrance doors.

She wasn't going to cry, and she wasn't going to waste her energy arguing. She was busy saving it for the coming confrontation, when his parents met her and realised that their son had brought home a plain, very ordinary and slightly pregnant Englishwoman for their inspection.

Oh, well. Look on the bright side. At least the baby didn't show yet...

'They'll be in the salon overlooking the garden,' he told her. 'Would you like to take a shower and change into something fresh before we go and join them?'

She was staring around her at the frescoed walls of the colonnaded logia around the central courtyard as he led her through the villa to the main stairs, and she looked utterly overawed. 'Please,' she said quietly, and he felt a prickle of guilt for the fact that she'd had to travel when she still wasn't feeling good—but what was he to have done?

Flying at this stage wouldn't hurt her or the baby, and he was keen to introduce her to his family and let her see the home that he loved so much—the home he hoped to return to at some point in the future. And he badly wanted her to love it at least a little.

'Maybe I should let you rest—go and talk to them myself first.'

'Warn them about me, you mean?' she said drily, and he grimaced.

'That's not what I meant.'

'But it's what you'll have to do, Luca. They don't know anything about me, never mind that I'm pregnant—they'll be so upset.'

'No. They'll love you.' As I do.

The thought shocked him into immobility for a moment, but she didn't notice. She was busy studying the frescoes on the stairs, her face growing more and more serious.

'These are wonderful, Luca. This must be a really important house.'

He pulled himself together. 'It may have been one of the Medici villas. The provenance is a little uncertain, and it had a chequered history before my ancestors acquired it. It's been in my family for over three hundred years.'

She was silent then until he led her into the bedroom adjoining his, and again she stared around in shock. As well she might, he thought, because in comparison to the frescoed halls, it was almost monastic in its simplicity, and that was the way he liked it.

There were no plastered ceilings in this part of the house, just terracotta tiles between the beams to match the floors, and the walls were white.

But it was the view that held Isabelle's attention, and she stood at the window and stared out over the landscape, her face turned away from him so he couldn't read her expression.

'Is this land all yours?'

'Yes. Pretty much what you can see from here belongs to the family.'

'I thought you were farmers,' she said, her voice shocked, and he winced.

'Well, we are, in a way. Growing grapes and olives is farming.'

She gave a tiny but distinctly unladylike snort. 'How large *is* your farm, Luca?'

He shrugged. 'I don't know. You'll have to ask Massimo, he's the figures man. Several thousand hectares. I'm not sure how it's divided up. About one third each of pasture, vines and olive groves. I'll take you on a guided tour—or get him to do it. He'll be better, if you're really interested. It's his passion.'

She turned away from the window, her nerves starting to get the better of her the more she found out.

'Is there a bathroom? I'd like to wash and change, then we need to go and drop this bombshell on your parents,' she said, and he could tell from her expressionless face how much she was dreading it.

'Sure,' he said, and opened the bathroom door. 'Help yourself.'

She took her washbag from her case and paused in the bathroom doorway.

'You don't need to wait,' she told him. 'I'll come and find you when I'm ready. Where will you be?'

'My bedroom's through that door. We share the bathroom. I'll go and get changed—give me a tap when you're finished so I can shave.'

She nodded and closed the door, turning her back to it and staring round at the very modern and beautiful fittings. Marble walls, a huge walk-in shower with a head the size of a dustbin lid and a bath you could get an entire family in.

She looked at it longingly, but settled instead for a shower, which made her feel a little better, but by the time she'd dried and dressed herself in her new trousers and a soft sweater, her heart was pounding.

She went into the bathroom and tapped on the door. 'I'm finished,' she called, and the knob turned and he came through it.

'Thanks. I won't be long.'

He'd changed his trousers, but he'd taken off his shirt and the sight of that shadowed jaw above his beautifully muscled chest made her mouth dry. She backed away, shut the door to her side and walked to the window, sitting down on the padded window seat and staring out over the beautiful rolling countryside.

A few minutes later he tapped and came through, looking good enough to eat. 'Are you ready?' he asked.

'As I'll ever be,' she said, and stood up, running her hands a little nervously over the front of the trousers. 'Will I do?'

He smiled at her and nodded. 'You look lovely. Cool and fresh and composed.' His smile softened. 'They're just people, *cara.* That's what my old university professor used to say to us about patients, whether they were intimidating or from a very humble background. "We're all just people." Remember that.'

'Just so long as they do,' she murmured under her breath, and squaring her shoulders and lifting her chin, she followed him through the twisting, winding corridors, down the ornately frescoed staircase to the courtyard, and then round to the other side and into a huge room overlooking the terrace.

'Ah, they're outside, taking advantage of the sun.'

A group of people, three men and a woman, were sitting under a beautiful colonnaded pergola entwined with the stems of jasmine, just bursting into leaf, and he took her by the hand and led her towards them, their feet crunching over the gravel and alerting the dogs, who leapt up and ran towards them, tails wagging furiously as they greeted Luca and checked her out.

'Luca! *Figlio mio!*' An elegant middle-aged woman got to her feet and hurried over to him, hugging and kissing him, and then her eyes found Isabelle's and she let him go and put her head on one side, a hesitant smile touching her mouth, as if she was uncertain of her ground. As well she might be, Isabelle thought, suddenly presented with a strange woman on the arm of her son.

'And you must be Isabelle. Welcome to Italy,' his mother said, and she thought there was something a little wary about her eyes. Oh, lord, what am I doing here? she thought, but then his mother smiled and took her hand. 'I'm Elisa, and this is my husband Vittorio.'

'I'm very pleased to meet you. I'm sorry, I don't speak any Italian—I feel really rude but I will try and learn it.'

'It's no problem. We all speak English,' Vittorio said. 'It's good to meet you, too. Welcome.'

He shook her hand firmly, his eyes assessing but less wary than his wife's, and then she was being introduced to two men who were clearly related to both the others—Luca's older brother Massimo, who apparently ran the estate, and his younger brother Gio—the lawyer who'd delivered the thinly veiled threat, owner of the black Ferrari and with a distinctly speculative look in his eyes.

Then Roberto hobbled up with a tray of glasses, and someone appeared with an ice bucket and champagne, and a plump, white-haired woman who looked almost as old as Roberto bustled in with a tray of nibbles and Luca took the tray from her, set it down and swept her up into his arms.

'Carlotta!' he said, kissing her wrinkled cheek, and she laughed and coloured like a girl and said something in Italian.

'*Si.* Carlotta, this is Isabelle. *Cara,* Carlotta knows more about me than anyone in the world. She delivered me, and my father before me, and she is a very important member of the family. She is also the *cucinare*—the cook—and so even more important. Be nice to her.'

She laughed and smacked his hand, then turned to Isabelle with a beaming smile. '*Signorina,*' Carlotta said, taking her hand and clasping it in both of hers, her eyes sparkling with delight. 'Welcome.'

'Thank you.'

She rattled off something in Italian, and Luca laughed and translated.

'Carlotta's a superb cook. She says she's looking forward to cooking for you.'

Oh, lord. And she'd have to eat all sorts. Well, she was feeling a little better this week, so maybe it would be all right.

'*Si.* I look after you,' she said, patting her hand, and for a moment she wondered if Carlotta had realised she was pregnant. No. She couldn't have done. It didn't show.

'*Grazie,*' she said with a smile.

Carlotta beamed and said, '*Prego,*' and waddled away, wheezing slightly.

Prego? she thought in panic, and then remembered it meant something on the lines of 'You're welcome' and was nothing to do with pregnant.

But then she forgot Carlotta, because Luca slid his fingers through hers and held her hand firmly against his side, and said, 'We have something to tell you.'

The family snapped to attention. Luca's fingers tightened

fractionally, and, turning to her, his eyes smiling reassurance, he went on, 'Isabelle has done me the honour of agreeing to become my wife.'

He didn't get any further, because his mother gave a little cry and threw her arms around them both, then his father was moving her gently out of the way so he could kiss Isabelle on both cheeks, his eyes, so like Luca's, warm with welcome.

Then it was Massimo's turn, at first a formal handshake, then a hug and a smile, and it was down to Gio.

Gio, who'd warned her not to hurt his brother, who'd told her she'd have him to deal with and that he never lost in a court of law. He walked over to her, took her hand and bent to brush his lips against her cheek.

'Welcome to the clan, Isabelle—but remember what I said and be kind to him,' he murmured, and stepped back, the smile not really disguising the warning in his eyes.

But Luca was there, his arm round her again, holding her firmly by his side in a demonstration of possessive affection that nobody could misunderstand, and she met Gio's eyes and didn't back down. Why should she? She had no intention of hurting Luca. She just hoped he felt the same way.

'So, we have to plan the wedding!' Elisa said, clapping her hands. 'Oh, Luca, we'll get Anita tomorrow, she'll be marvellous—and, Massimo, call your sisters, tell them to come, we need to celebrate! Vittorio, open the wine!'

'Mama, slow down, we want a quiet wedding,' Luca said, laughing softly. 'A hundred people, max.'

'A hundred!'

Isabelle and Elisa spoke in unison, but she had the feeling her future mother-in-law was appalled at the small number, whereas she—

A loud pop interrupted her thoughts, and Vittorio poured the Prosecco into the glasses. 'Here, *cara,* welcome to the family,' he said kindly, handing her a glass, and she had a tiny sip before Elisa came over to her and took her hand and led her to the chairs.

'Come, sit next to me and tell me all about my new daughter-in-law. I can't tell you how much I've looked forward to this day. I was beginning to wonder if Luca would ever find a woman he could love, but he has. I can see it in his eyes, and I'm so happy for you both.'

She didn't bother to correct her. How could she? But in the warmth of her welcome, she was able to forget about Gio's warning for a while, and concentrate on getting to know her future husband's family.

They moved inside when the wind picked up, sipping wine and nibbling all sorts of tasty little treats until Roberto called them to the table, and while the conversation ebbed and flowed around her, Isabelle watched them all and wondered what it must be like to grow up in a family. Suffocating? She didn't think so...

'See? I told you they'd love you.'

'Well, some of them. Gio's a bit suspicious.'

'Ignore him. My mother thinks you're wonderful.'

'I think your mother's wonderful—a really very nice woman, but she doesn't know about the baby yet,' she pointed out, and stifled a yawn. It had been a long day, starting before six that morning with the drive to the airport, and it was almost nine at night now.

Lunch had gone on until almost four, and they'd had a light supper an hour ago. Now, they were strolling hand in hand along the terrace, snuggled up in coats and letting Carlotta's plain but delicious food settle before they went to bed.

It was nice to be alone, she thought. His family were lovely, but she was tired, and as they stood there in the cool of the evening she yawned again.

'Come, *cara,* you've had a long day. You need to go to bed,' he murmured, letting go of her, and she felt a pang of loss.

They walked back along the terrace, then up the steps to the pergola where they had all sat earlier, and he took her hand again as they went in through the doors into the lovely sitting room. His parents were there, sharing a last cup of coffee before bed, and they looked up and smiled.

'*Buonanotte,*' he murmured, and his mother blew him a kiss.

'Don't hurry in the morning,' she said, a smile in her voice. 'Breakfast can wait for you. You are on holiday now, and you both work too hard. Enjoy it.'

'Thank you,' she murmured. 'Goodnight.'

'*Buonanotte,* Isabella—and welcome.'

As they walked back through the corridors and courtyards, their footsteps echoing quietly in the night, she felt awe again that he lived here, in this spectacular house—that this was his home, his birthright. And it would be her child's.

The thought was daunting.

He opened the bedroom door for her, and she saw that the room had been prepared—the covers turned down, her case emptied and set aside, her clothes presumably hung up in the cupboard. More evidence, as if she needed it, of the gulf between them.

Her nightdress and dressing gown were laid over one side of the bed, and she turned to him in the doorway. 'What time do you want me to get up tomorrow?' she asked, and he shrugged.

'I don't. Please yourself—I'll be around. Give me a call on my mobile when you wake up and I'll get you something light to eat before you get up—and come and ask me if you need anything in the night. I'm going to find my brothers now and have a drink with them, but I won't be long. Call me if you need anything.'

Only you, she thought as he bent his head and kissed her. And then he was gone, the door closing softly behind him, leaving her alone with her tumbling thoughts and emotions.

'So what's the story, then?'

Luca dropped into the battered old leather sofa in Massimo's apartment in the house and rolled his eyes.

'Gio, shut up,' Massimo said softly. 'Luca, what can I get you? I've got a nice Pinot Grigio in the fridge, or there's a lovely Barosa open.'

'No, I've drunk enough.'

'Rubbish. Give him the Barosa, loosen his tongue a bit. I want to hear all about his *bella regazza*. I can see why you've fallen for her. She's gorgeous. I just hope it hasn't blinded you.'

'Leave her alone, Gio. She's done nothing to deserve this treatment from you.'

Gio arched a brow. 'Let's just wait and see.'

'Shut up, Gio. Where did you meet her?' Massimo asked, butting in.

'Firenze, in a café, in January.'

Massimo put a glass in his hand. 'The day of your interview? You dropped off the radar for twenty-four hours. Could this be anything to do with the lady in question?'

He gave a soft snort and nodded. *'Dio*, does nothing escape you guys? Yes. I spent the day with her.'

'And the night,' Gio prodded, and he sighed.

'Do you have to be so damn rude?'

'That's a yes, Massimo, by the way. So how come you're working with her?'

'It's just coincidence.'

'Yeah, right.'

'No, really. I'm helping a friend out with a locum job—'

'Why? You're right in the middle of your research paper,' Massimo said, getting to the heart of it. 'And what happened about the professorship in Firenze?'

'I took a rain check.'

'To follow her back to London,' Gio said, and Luca realised they were going to drag every last painful millimetre of this out of him.

'Yes, if you must know,' he confessed, to get it over with. 'I wanted to find her. And I couldn't. So I took a job with Richard, and there she was.'

'She seems a little wary,' Massimo commented, swirling his wine thoughtfully in the glass.

Luca snorted. 'Wouldn't you be? You were watching her like hawks, especially Gio.'

'Mama seems to have taken to her new daughter-in-law, anyway. Does she realise she's pregnant, I wonder?'

'Is she?' Massimo asked, looking shocked, and not for the first time that night Luca felt the urge to kill his little brother.

The silence seemed to stretch on and on, and finally he cracked and broke it. 'Yes. Yes, she is. The baby's due in September.'

He met Massimo's eyes, and after a second his brother sighed softly.

'Oh, hell, Luca. Are you OK with it? I take it she really is pregnant?'

'Yes, she really is.'

'Don't sound so indignant. It wouldn't have been the first mistake of that sort.'

Luca cut Gio a slashing look. 'I'm an obstetrician. I think I can tell by now when a woman's pregnant,' he said cuttingly.

'Oh, I don't doubt she's pregnant,' Gio said. 'But are you sure it's yours?'

'Yes,' he said tightly.

'Why?'

'Because—there are sound reasons why that I have no intention of going into with you, and I have no reason to doubt her, because I trust her,' he told them bluntly, ignoring Gio's snort of disbelief. 'As for how I am about it, that rather depends on whether you guys put her off completely before the wedding. That's why we're here—so she can learn all about me from you, and see if she feels she can trust me. We don't exactly know much about each other, but we need to. I thought this would fast-forward it a bit, but I'm relying on you.'

Gio swore softly, and Luca waited for the mockery that would follow, but there was none. Not this time.

'What do you want us to tell her?'

'That I'm not a lying, cheating bastard like her father and her ex-fiancé would be good.'

Massimo winced. 'Ouch. So it's not just you with a messy past, then. OK. Consider it done.'

He looked at Gio, who shrugged. 'OK. But I'll be watching her.'

'I never doubted it for a moment. There is one thing you'll like, though. She wants a pre-nup.'

'What?' Gio started to laugh, then shook his head in disbelief when he realised Luca was serious. 'Why?'

'She has a house—a two-bedroomed terraced house in Herne Hill. She wants it protected for the baby if anything happens to us.'

'Is that likely? I know what you feel about marriage.'

'No. No, it's not likely, but it's what she wants, so she can have it.'

Gio gave a low laugh. 'Does the woman have any idea what you're worth?'

'No—well, she didn't, not until we got here. And I thought there was something very touching about the way she wanted to protect the baby if anything went wrong.'

'Or could it be the fact that she doesn't trust you?'

'She's been hurt. Trust is hard. Anyway, my money's irrelevant. It's not who I am, Gio.'

'On the contrary, Luca. It's very much who you are, and who you are is too damn trusting. I'll make sure your interests as well as hers are protected. I'll draw you something up in the morning.'

'She gets half,' he said firmly. 'And I want a will, not a prenup. The other half goes to the baby.'

Gio went pale. 'Hell, Luca. Massimo, give him another drink. He's lost his mind.'

'No. I think, actually, he might just have found it,' Massimo said with an understanding smile, and topped up his glass.

The following day was a whirlwind.

Massimo was going to take them round the estate in his car after he'd dropped his children at school, but at the last minute something cropped up, so he lent them the off-road car and they set off as soon as they were ready.

'I'm sorry about his wife. He's a really nice man,' Isabelle said to Luca as they drove away.

'It was dreadful. I don't think he'll ever marry again. He adored her. They were childhood sweethearts. He's a nice guy. A good friend. He likes you.'

'Gio doesn't.'

'He doesn't trust you. He's got his reasons—it's not personal.'

'The woman who hurt you ten years ago? Tell me about it, Luca. What happened?' she said, but he wouldn't go into it, and then they arrived at the winery for their guided tour with the manager, and the opportunity was gone.

The rest of the morning was taken up by their tour of the estate—even larger than she'd imagined—then lunch in a trattoria some miles away before the return journey through the arable part of the land. 'That's Anita's family home over there, on the top of that hill,' Luca said as they paused on a rise. 'She's an old friend, more of a sister really, and she's a wedding planner. We'll talk to her later. No doubt Mama will be discussing things with her already. She's dying to meet you.'

Was she? Really? 'How good a friend?' she asked, and Luca shot her a wry smile.

'Not that good. I tried—she slapped my face when I was sixteen, and I haven't dared to try again. She's very nice. You'll like her.'

She hoped so. A wedding planner? It sounded a bit scary, but she needn't have worried. Anita *was* lovely, and hugged her warmly when they met at the end of the afternoon, after their tour was over.

Then, once the introductions were out of the way, she shooed Luca and his mother away and settled down in the corner of a comfy sofa with a glass of fruit juice on the table beside her, tucked her feet under her bottom and produced a notebook from her bag. 'I like to talk to the bride on her own,' she said with a grin. 'Everybody has so many opinions, but really only one person's opinion matters. So, talk to me.'

'About what?' she asked, at a loss. 'I haven't really thought about it—not the detail. I've done all this before—got right to the wire,' she admitted reluctantly, because she wanted Anita on her side. 'Then it all went wrong and it never happened. So I don't want anything remotely like what I'd planned before, because apart from anything else, none of it was my choice.'

'OK, so tell me about your dream wedding for you and Luca,' Anita said.

'Oh. Well, we're not planning my dream wedding, are we? Just something quick and quiet. I've got over the dream scenario.'

Anita tutted. 'You should never get over your dream wedding.'

'You do, believe me, when you see how easily it all turns into a nightmare.'

'So how was it, while it was still a dream in your head, when you were a little girl? Tell me about your dress—what did you want? Tulle? Satin? Lace?'

'Raw silk. I never really knew what it was, and I'm still not sure I do, but it sounds so lovely!'

Anita laughed. 'I agree. So—silk?'

'I think so. But ivory, I think. White's a bit harsh against my skin.'

'Ivory suits most people better. Or maybe even a pale dove grey, or soft coffee?'

'Coffee might be nice.'

'And what about the style?'

Isabelle shrugged, not sure quite how to deal with this one, so in her usual way, she met it head-on. 'I don't know. When I was a child, I always wanted to be a princess, but most princesses aren't pregnant when they get married.'

Anita's eyes widened, and she clapped her hand over her mouth and gasped. 'You're having a baby?'

She nodded, wondering why Anita was so shocked. And if it was anything to do with Gio's hostility. Had Luca had a baby in his past? Was that it?

'It's due in September, so I'd like to get married soon, before it shows. Another eight weeks, maximum. And we don't want a huge do.'

'But—it's your wedding! Luca's family—'

'Will do as they're told,' Luca said, coming into the room with a tray of tea and cakes. 'Here, something to keep you going while you plan. I'm going for a walk with Papa, I'll see you later. Nita, don't bully her.' And stooping down to Isabelle, he kissed her lingeringly on the lips, winked at Anita and walked out.

Anita shook her head, staring after him with a thoughtful expression. 'He'll be a wonderful father. He's brilliant with children. Have you met Massimo's tribe yet?'

She shook her head. 'No, not yet. They'd gone to school when I got up.'

'They're lovely. They adore their Uncle Luca. So, while I pour the tea, tell me all about your fairytale princess wedding...'

CHAPTER EIGHT

THE WEDDING WAS scheduled for the last Sunday in April—
ludicrously quick compared to those of her friends who'd
married recently. Their weddings had taken at least a year to
plan and cost about half a year's salary or more.

Not hers. Apart from the fact that they simply didn't *have*
a year to spend planning it if it was to happen before the baby
was born, they didn't have any planning to do. Anita was doing
it all, after asking Isabelle all sorts of questions that she couldn't
believe were actually relevant to such a small wedding.

'Leave it to me to sort out the details,' Anita said with a
smile after the date was set. 'Just talk, and I'll make sure you
have the day you want.'

She wasn't sure it was in Anita's control to give her that,
because the thing she'd want at the top of her list was a
husband who had chosen her for herself and not for the fact
that she was pregnant. And no matter what he might say, there
was no way she'd ever know the truth about that, so she put it
out of her mind and concentrated on getting through the days.

Their holiday was wonderful, his family were lovely and
once he'd told them there was a baby on the way they pulled
out all the stops to sort out the wedding as quickly as possible.

There were dress fittings—dresses in all sorts of subtle off-whites and coffee-creams, some spangled with crystals, others delicately scattered with pearls or tiny beads. Strapless, off the shoulder, high necked, halter—the choice was bewildering, but they narrowed it down to a simple dress in raw silk with a sweetheart neckline, pleats fanning from the waist on one side and a little duster train, in a delicate coffee cream sprinkled lightly with pearls. And a veil, even though she protested that it was hardly appropriate, but Anita shook her head and told her that it was a family heirloom and it would mean breaking with tradition to marry without it.

'It's probably breaking with tradition to be pregnant,' she said drily, but Elisa blushed and shook her head, so with a little laugh Isabelle agreed to the veil.

And then they were back in London, where they'd be working right up until the week before the wedding.

She was still feeling nauseous, despite Luca's intervention every morning with apple slices and dry toast and his constant nagging all day to eat little and often, tempting her with little tasty snacks. He'd moved her into his house as soon as they'd got back from Italy which slashed her journey time almost to zero, insisted she change her work pattern to something less taxing and he cooked every evening unless he was on call. Without him she had to admit she would have really been struggling.

And every night, he went into his bedroom beside hers, closed the door and kept severely to himself.

'I don't want it to change the way we feel, and if we sleep together now, it will. I don't want to cloud the issue, *cara*,' he told her. 'And I want you to feel free to change your mind right up to the last minute. I would rather you did if you weren't still absolutely sure.'

But she was more sure than ever with every day that passed. Working with him was fascinating, challenging and a source of constant debate and discussion, but in the evenings after work was over, after they'd eaten and before he sent her up to bed before him, they would sit side by side on one of the soft leather sofas and wrangle over the television remote, or he'd lean over and give her the word she was groping for in a crossword or wait for her to go to the loo and correct the mistake in her Sudoku which was holding her up.

And if she challenged him about it, he'd just grin and say nothing.

It was surprisingly easy to live with him, she was learning, and gradually her fears for their future were ebbing away. His reaction to her scan had been interesting, too. He must have seen hundreds—no, thousands—but not, of course, of his own baby, and he'd taken her hand and hung on tight, his eyes riveted to the screen as the tiny little heart had blipped away, and his eyes had been over-bright. And after that, he'd taken to touching her there, over the baby, his hand gentle, his eyes smiling.

They were lying in front of the television one evening, his hand idly resting on her tummy as his fingers caressed the tiny curve that was the only very slight evidence of her baby, when he said out of the blue, 'Have you thought about the birth?'

'Mmm. Of course.' She'd thought about little else, wondering what it would have in store, and knowing that so long as Luca was beside her, it would be all right. 'I think I'd like a water birth. I've got a lady scheduled for one just before we go away—Naomi. She's got a cervical suture—she's already lost two babies, the first at twenty-four weeks, the second at twenty-one. She has an incompetent cervix and they've been devastated, but she's been all right this time. She had the suture in nice and early, and we're hoping for a natural labour. She should be an ideal candidate, and I can't wait. I've told her to call me and I'll go in whatever, even if I'm not on. I really want to be with her.'

'Not that you're getting too involved,' he teased, and she laughed.

'Well, I am, and this time I've got a personal interest. I really want to do another water birth and it should be a good one. I have a feeling it'll be quick, so you'll just have to take the suture out nice and promptly first thing in the morning so she's delivered by the end of the day to make sure I can be there. And I'll just hang on until she has it.'

'You don't need to. You'll only be here—unless we're in Italy.'

She shook her head. 'She won't go that long. I have a feeling about her. I bet you she's admitted before the suture's scheduled to be removed.'

Luca groaned. 'Your feelings are all too accurate for my liking. Just tell me when she's there.'

'Are you busy, Isabelle?'

'No—do you need me?'

He nodded. 'There's a new admission just arriving. She's specifically asking for you. If you wouldn't mind?'

'Sure,' she said, only too grateful to get out of the staffroom before Sarah started quizzing her any more about the wedding.

'So who's this woman?' she asked, and Luca smiled wryly.

'Naomi Brown.'

'Naomi! Oh, Luca, no! She's not due yet! She's only—what—thirty-three weeks now?'

'Thirty-four and a half.'

'So why's she come in?'

'She's having contractions. We have to remove the suture.'

Isabelle felt a shiver of apprehension. 'Oh, lord. Luca, we have to make sure they keep this baby. They were devastated when they lost the others. We have to save it for them.'

He stopped and turned to her, and his smile was crooked. '*Cara,* I fully intend to save this baby whatever the mother's history, and at over thirty-four weeks, that shouldn't be an issue. Come on, let's go and see her. If her labour's not yet established, perhaps we can delay it.'

'And if not? Are you happy for her to have a water birth still, because she really wants it, Luca.'

'Probably. Let's go and see if we can stall it first.'

But they couldn't. Her cervix was fighting against the suture, and as soon as Luca had removed it, Naomi's distress eased and she sighed with relief.

'Oh, that feels so much better,' she murmured. 'Thank you.'

'My pleasure,' Luca said with a smile, getting up off the stool and moving out of the way so they could reinstate the end of the bed. 'Now we'll just keep an eye on things and see how you go. It may be fairly fast, your cervix is already thinning.'

Thinning was the understatement of the century, Isabelle thought as she examined her a short while later, the moment the huge delivery bath was filled. Her contractions were coming thick and fast, and she was starting to get distressed again.

'Do you want to go in the water?' Isabelle asked her gently, and she nodded.

'Please. I know this is a bit hurried, but—you know, we planned it, Isabelle, and I'd love to do it. I just think it's so gentle for the baby.'

'It is, for both of you. Come on, we'll get you in now. It's all ready.'

She and Ryan, Naomi's husband, steadied her as she stepped into the warm bath, and as she sank down into the welcoming water she gave a sigh of relief.

'Oh, that feels so good. Can we turn the lights down?'

'Sure.' Isabelle lowered the lights, Ryan turned on some soft instrumental music and Naomi rested her head back, moaning softly from time to time, but utterly relaxed as Ryan knelt beside her outside the pool and stroked her tummy slowly.

Then she opened her eyes and looked into Isabelle's, calm and composed. 'I want to push.'

'OK. Let me check you.' She knelt down and leant over into the water and examined her, and not surprisingly her cervix was fully effaced. 'Whenever you're ready,' she said quietly.

She heard the door open almost silently, and knew it was Luca, but she didn't look up, just held Naomi's hand as she pushed. He read her mind, though, because very slowly, so as not to startle them, he turned the lights back up so she could see what was happening.

'OK, the baby's head is crowning now, I can see lots and lots of hair. Well done. Keep going, keep pushing gently. And again. Good girl. You're nearly there.'

Another contraction gripped her, and the baby's head slipped free, followed by the rest of his body in a slithering rush.

'Oh!' Naomi breathed, reaching down to her baby, her face filled with wonder.

'Lift him up out of the water now, nice and gently—that's it,' she murmured, and as Naomi lifted the baby to her breast, he drew in a little breath and sighed.

'Is it all right? Why isn't she crying?' Naomi asked, panicking, but Isabelle just smiled.

'They often don't with a water birth, because it's so gentle. It's fine—he's breathing properly and pinking up nicely. Well done.'

Ryan sucked in a great shuddering breath, and Naomi sagged back, tears pouring down her face.

'Is she really all right?'

'He—you've got a little boy, Naomi—and he's beautiful. Congratulations.'

'Oh, Ryan! We've got a boy—a baby boy!' she sobbed, cradling him tenderly against her. 'Oh, he's so small!'

'He is small, but he's strong. We need to keep him warm,' Luca said, and covered him with a towel, tucking it in round him to protect him from draughts until the paediatric team arrived to take over.

Isabelle blinked away her tears and looked up at him as he straightened, and mouthed, 'Thank you.'

He gave a crooked smile. 'Any time,' he murmured, and as he turned his head away, she thought she saw a tear glisten on his cheek.

A man of his experience, moved to tears by a simple delivery? Except of course it wasn't simple, it was the end of years of hope and grief and heartache for this couple, culminating in the successful delivery of a live baby who would have every chance of survival.

And only a robot would fail to be moved by that.

But nevertheless…

Luca left them to it and walked out, once he was sure the mother was fine in Isabelle's hands and the baby was doing well. He was to be taken up to SCBU as a precaution, and he would have steroids to mature his lungs. There'd been no time to start Naomi on them because of the speed of her labour but, at thirty-four weeks plus, Luca was confident the baby would be fine, and so would the parents, who had gone through so much to reach this point and were now celebrating tearfully.

And Luca, who didn't even know the family, was getting carried along by the sentiment in a way he never usually did. Oh, he loved a successful outcome, and he took pride in the fact that he really cared about his patients, but he couldn't remember the last time a delivery had brought real, wholesale tears to his eyes.

He blinked hard and went into the kitchen to make himself a drink. Not coffee, still, in deference to Isabelle. In fact he was almost tempted to tip the jar into the bin. And then he thought about his own baby, growing slowly inside her, the woman who had changed the course of his life completely. He'd seen her face at the twelve-week scan just after they'd come back from Italy, and he knew that she already loved it.

And so did he.

It didn't surprise him that he felt strongly. What did surprise him was *how* strongly he felt, and he wondered how he'd feel if anything happened to it.

Gutted, he realised. Absolutely, completely gutted. Most of all for Isabelle, but also for himself. It must be worse for the mother, so close to the baby, but the thought of losing it was shocking.

He just hoped everything went smoothly, starting with the wedding. He wondered briefly what he would do if Isabelle changed her mind and refused to marry him after all, but dismissed the negative thought. She wouldn't do that.

Would she?

Well, he'd soon find out. Three more weeks to go. Only two weeks until they flew back to Italy, and three weeks to the wedding, and another twenty-four to the baby's birth.

He realised he could hardly wait.

They flew back to Italy the week before the wedding, and this time she hadn't argued about buying clothes.

Luca had taken her to a boutique in London, and she'd been dressed and undressed a hundred times while he'd sat there and made all the right noises. The price tags were eye watering, but she didn't argue, she just refused to have too many. 'I'll outgrow them in weeks, Luca,' she pointed out. 'We can get something over there if necessary.'

'Of course, but you'll need things for this week.'

'Won't these do? I'm tired,' she protested, and it wasn't really a lie, but she felt guilty about so much wanton extravagance. After all, it wasn't as if he wanted to spoil her. He was doing it out of necessity, but all she really wanted was a few things to wear—and a ring. An engagement ring, a symbol of his love—but of course, although they were getting on well now, he *didn't* love her, and with the wedding coming up so fast, it hardly seemed worth bothering with anything other than a wedding ring.

And Luca hadn't mentioned it.

He was talking to the sales assistant now as she dressed. 'Could you wrap them please and have them delivered to this address?' he said, and as she came out of the changing room he was putting his wallet away, and he turned to her with a smile.

'Lunch?'

Curiously deflated suddenly, she shook her head. 'No, I don't think so. Can we just go home?'

'Of course.'

The following day while she was sorting out their washing ready for Italy, the clothes arrived. Plus some others she'd turned down, and it made her want to cry. It all seemed so unnecessary, she thought, but she packed them anyway.

Two days later, they flew to Tuscany, amid a hail of good wishes from their colleagues and friends at the hospital and promises to throw them a party when they got back.

They arrived at the *palazzo* in the early afternoon, to be greeted with a frenzy of activity.

'Heavens, what on earth is going on?' she asked Luca, but he just gave her a wry smile.

'There's going to be a wedding—remember?'

'But only a small one.'

He snorted, and she felt a wave of panic. 'Luca, you promised!'

'It will be small,' he assured her. 'That doesn't necessarily mean it will be low key. Anita will have organised it all—don't worry. It looks like a lot of fuss, but when they all go away, it'll be just us. Trust me, *cara*. It will be a lovely day.'

Could she trust him? There seemed to be an army of vans and trucks, and when they went through the house to the salon overlooking the terrace, she could see why. The terrace was smothered in white canvas, and as they watched it was hauled upright.

'Good grief! I've never seen a marquee that size!' she said, stunned, and he laughed.

'Come on, let's go and find the family. They'll be in the library, I suspect, overseeing operations from the control centre.'

It sounded terrifying, and clearly everything she'd said had been ignored. It was just like last time, everything taken away from her, planned to death by others to give them the day they were expecting.

But she'd reckoned without Anita.

As they went into the library, she got to her feet and came over and hugged her. 'Hi. How are you?'

'Worried. That marquee's huge.'

'Oh, no, it's a very moderate one. Don't worry. It's for afterwards—the wedding feast is set up at one end, and the dancing will be at the other, and that way we don't have to move the tables. There are more people coming for the evening, as well, but you can slip away then and leave them to it. I expect you'll be tired anyway, and I should think Luca will want you to himself.'

Luca would. Luca wanted her to himself now, and he could see the worry on her face and wanted to take her away from it all, but there was no way they could have got married without a certain amount of fuss, and he trusted Anita.

'Right. We need to freshen up and have some lunch, and then we'll come and see you. No doubt you've got lots of questions.'

'No, not really. Luca, you need a suit fitting this afternoon, and, Isabelle, the designer is here with your dress. She's going to do the first fitting today and then another tomorrow, if necessary, to give them time. I'm sorry to land it on you when you've just arrived, but she'll wait until you've rested.'

'I hope it fits,' she said softly to Luca as they walked up to their rooms. 'I really have no idea if it will, but lots of my things don't now.'

'It doesn't show yet to the casual eye.'

'But there won't be a casual eye, will there?' she said drily. 'They'll all be watching me like hawks, and something like that will be top of their list, with the speed of the wedding.'

'Does that bother you?' he asked. 'Because it doesn't bother me, in the least. I'm not ashamed that you're carrying my child, Isabelle—quite the opposite, and I'm more than proud to show you off.'

His softly spoken words brought a lump to her throat, and with a sigh he opened her bedroom door, took her in and drew her into his arms. 'Hush, *tesoro*. It will be all right. They'll all love you.'

Do you, though? Luca, tell me—!

'Right, I'm going to have a quick shower and go and sort this suit out. I suggest you rest for a while, then come down when you're ready.'

The next few days were a whirlwind of activity, but very little of it seemed to involve Isabelle, and she had little to do but fret.

The guests had started to arrive—his sisters, Carla with her husband Roberto and their three children, and Anna and Serena, unmarried but both with boyfriends in tow, and of course Giovanni, who finally seemed to have decided that she was all right. Massimo of course was already there with his children, and then there was Luca's grandparents too, who'd she'd already met, adding to the numbers, but the result of the influx was that every meal was a feast.

'I'm really not going to be able to get into the dress if I keep on like this,' she said to Anita, who chuckled and told her not to be silly.

'You'll worry it all off—I can see it in your face. Have faith in me, Isabelle. It will be a beautiful day.'

'You have a hotline to the weatherman?' she said with a smile, and Anita laughed.

'Of course! All part of the service. But the long-range forecast is superb. It's going to be a fabulous day.'

'I hope so,' she murmured, but the weather was the least of her worries, and the man who was to become her husband was so involved with his family that she had hardly had any time with him for the last couple of days, and she missed him. Missed working with him, missed spending the evenings alone with him, missed all of it.

She went out onto the terrace and found a seat tucked away in a quiet spot, and then she saw Luca down below her, walking along a path towards his brother Massimo. They greeted each other, and she watched them, her heart wistful. Massimo had loved his wife deeply, and she'd been torn from him, but at least they'd shared that love while she was alive.

She loved Luca desperately, but she couldn't tell him, unless she was sure he loved her too.

'Luca?'

'Hi, Massimo. How are you doing?'

'OK.'

Luca searched his brother's face, and saw sadness in his eyes. 'I'm sorry, this must be hard for you.'

'Don't worry about it. I have something for you.' And he slipped his hand into his pocket and pulled out a little box.

Luca felt a lump in his throat. 'No, Massimo.'

'Yes. Please. I'll never give it to another woman, and she hasn't got a ring.'

'I didn't think of it,' he said, shocked at his lapse. 'I've been more concerned about her and the baby—the ring didn't seem—I've ordered a wedding ring set with diamonds, it's here somewhere, Anita said it arrived today, but—I didn't think—damn. Massimo, I can't take Angelina's ring.'

'Of course you can. It's no use to her, and, anyway, it's a family ring. It belongs in the family, and Isabelle is family now. According to Anita it's even the right size. Please—take it. It should be worn, and I'd be overjoyed to see it on your wife's hand.'

'Oh, hell…'

He took the little box, slipped it into his pocket and hugged his brother hard. 'Thank you.'

'My pleasure.' He stepped back, his face stiff with emotion, and with a brisk nod he walked away. Luca watched him go, then pulled the box from his pocket and stared down at the ring. Would Isabelle accept it from him?

He slipped it back into his pocket, strode up the steps and found her sitting on a seat in the gloom, looking out over the valley.

'Are you all right?'

'Yes. I was watching the swallows. They're amazing—there's a sort of shift change, have you noticed? Just before nine, when the swallows go to bed and the bats come out. It's incredible. Fascinating. I could watch them for hours. And the lights are really pretty. I've been watching them come on in all the little villages. It's beautiful—peaceful.'

'It is peaceful. That's why I love it so much.'

He sat down beside her and took her hand. 'Isabelle, I have something for you. I don't know whether you'll want to accept it, but I hope you will, because it would mean a great deal to all of us.' He hesitated, then went on, 'It's been passed down in the family for generations, and I hadn't even thought of it, because it was Angelina's—Massimo's wife's—but he's just given it to me to give to you, and I know it's a bit late, and the wedding's happening anyway, and it's not what either of us had planned, but—'

He broke off, put his hand in his pocket and knelt down on the gravel in front of her. 'Isabelle, I love you. You once said that loving me wasn't the problem, it was trusting me. And I don't want you to marry me on Sunday unless you feel you can trust me. So—will you marry me? Will you wear this ring for me, to show the world that you love me, too, and that you trust me with your heart?'

Her eyes filled, and she pressed her fingers to her lips and held back a tiny sob. 'Oh, Luca—I never thought I'd hear you say that. Of course I'll marry you.'

'But can you trust me?'

'Yes,' she said, and then, realising she hadn't even thought about it for days, maybe weeks, she said it again, more firmly this time. 'Yes, Luca, I trust you—and I'm so sorry it's taken me so long.'

'Don't be sorry. I've had trust issues, too. The girl in my past—she told me she was pregnant, and I asked her to marry me, doing the decent thing, of course, and then three weeks before the wedding I found out she was on the Pill, and she had been all along.'

'Oh, no—so when I told you I was pregnant...'

'I knew you were. You were very obviously pregnant. But my faith had been shaken, and I wasn't absolutely sure it was mine. But she only wanted me for my money, and when you asked for a pre-nup to protect our baby, I knew then that the baby was ours. Apart from anything else, you didn't know anything about me, so if you wanted me, it was for myself and not for my money. But you didn't.'

'Oh, I did, Luca. I did—but I was so afraid of being hurt, and I knew that if you walked away, it would hurt me so much more than I'd been hurt before, and I'd have to see you over and over again for the next twenty or so years as our child grew up, and it would tear me apart. But you aren't going to walk away, are you? You're not that sort of man, and I realise that now. And I'd be honoured to wear your ring.'

He let his breath out on a sigh, and, opening the box, he took the ring out and slipped it onto her finger.

'Oh, Luca, it's beautiful,' she said, and felt her eyes fill with tears. 'Poor Angelina—will Massimo be all right with this?'

'He said so. He said he'd be overjoyed to see it on my wife's hand.'

He stood up and drew her up into his arms. 'I love you— *te amo, Isabella,*' he murmured, and then he kissed her, his lips gentle on hers. Then he drew reluctantly away with a ragged sigh. 'Only three more days,' he said, and, threading his fingers through hers, he led her up to her room, kissed her again and then walked away.

CHAPTER NINE

THE DAY OF the wedding dawned bright and clear, just as Anita had promised, and Isabelle couldn't wait.

Her mother had arrived two days before with her husband, and she'd been stunned at Luca's family's obvious wealth. Stunned and wary, but the moment she met Luca, she was smitten. 'He's lovely—such a nice man, darling,' she'd said, misty-eyed. 'I'm so happy for you. He's just exactly right for you.'

'I think so,' Isabella had replied, and now, on the morning of her wedding, she just wanted all the hoopla to be over so she could be with him, but of course there was so much to do.

The hair, the nails, the dress, the make-up, the veil—and then finally it was time to go, and she walked down the beautiful stone staircase to the central courtyard with its exquisite frescoes, and Luca, looking more handsome than she'd ever seen him, was standing there waiting.

Luca, who she loved with all her heart.

Luca who, if the expression on his face was anything to go by, loved her every bit as much. He took her hands in his and stared wordlessly down at her, his heart in his eyes, and then, tucking her hand into the crook of his arm, he led her out to the beautiful vintage car smothered in ribbons and flowers, and they set off together for the little hill town nearby.

They were cheered along the way by the estate workers, the villagers and then all the townspeople, and she felt near to tears. 'They really love you,' she said, and he just smiled and waved back.

'They love a wedding. Italians are all deeply romantic.'

'Except Gio.'

'Oh, he's romantic. He's just disillusioned. I was the same, but then I met you, and everything changed. Wave to them, *cara*. This is as much for you as it is for me.'

They pulled up outside the town hall, and amongst the cheers she heard the word *'bellissima'*. Beautiful. Her? Her eyes filled, and she smiled at them, and they cheered again.

The town hall, when they managed to get inside, was packed. 'I thought it was going to be small?' she murmured spotting her friend Sarah and Richard Crossland in the crowd, and he laughed softly and squeezed her hand.

'This is small,' he assured her, and then paused, staring deep into her eyes. 'Last chance to change your mind,' he murmured.

'No,' she said firmly. 'I love you, Luca. *Te amo*. Let's get married.'

It was nearly midnight before they got away.

They'd been wined and dined, there had been speeches, and everything had been punctuated by cries of 'Kiss, Kiss!' and Luca, laughing, had dutifully kissed her, again and again and again, until by the time they'd been dancing for a while she could feel the tension radiating off him.

Then another cry went up, and he stopped dancing, cupped her face in his hands and plundered her mouth with his, while everyone cheered and catcalled all around them. Then he lifted his head, his eyes glittering, scooped her up in his arms and carried her inside in a hail of confetti and sugared almonds.

'Where are we going?'

'To our new quarters. We've got the two big rooms on the end overlooking the terrace.'

'Two rooms?'

He gave a lazy, sexy smile. 'Only one bedroom. The other one's a sitting room.'

'They'll see the lights,' she said as he carried her in and turned them on, and he laughed.

'They know what we're doing, *tesoro,*' he murmured. 'It's not a secret. Does it worry you?'

She thought of all the people outside, people she'd never met, but others whom she'd grown to love, and she shook her head. 'No. I'm not ashamed to be in love with you. I'm proud to be your wife, Luca, and it's been a very long wait. But you could close the curtains.'

They slept late the next day—and the day after, and the day after that.

After all the hustle of the wedding, it was wonderful to relax and do nothing, and now, in the middle of her pregnancy, Isabelle felt really well.

They went sightseeing around some of the little hill towns, and walked through the pretty streets while he told her the history of each one, and they walked through the forests and sat under olive trees in the shade and ate impromptu picnics of bread and cheese and ham with ripe, juicy tomatoes which dribbled down their chins, and then they had to kiss the juice away, of course, so that on most days they came home early and went back to bed, using her pregnancy as an excuse, but nobody believed them and neither of them cared.

They were deeply in love, blissfully happy, and life was wonderful.

And then at the end of the week, he took her to a friend's private clinic for her routine twenty-week scan to check for problems, and it all fell apart.

'Are you sure about the dates?'

'Absolutely,' she said. 'It could only have been one occasion. Why?'

'Because the baby seems a little small. I would say it was eighteen, maybe nineteen weeks from the skull measurements.'

Beside her, Luca went very still, and Isabelle felt her heart start to pound as she began to flick the pages of a mental midwifery textbook. 'Is there anything else?' he asked, and his friend shrugged.

'Not that I can see. It's hard—the baby's position isn't the best, I can't get a good view of the heart, but the spine's OK and the skull's a good shape. It's not anencephalic, if that's what you're thinking, and the placenta looks OK.'

'The heart,' Luca said. 'Why can't you get a good view?'

'It's a bit shadowed. I don't know. We'll have to give it two weeks and check again, to see if we can get a better look and to make sure the baby's growing, but I think the most likely thing is that you've got the wrong dates.'

'But we can't. We haven't.' She was feeling sick, fear for her baby beginning to swamp her, and she reached for Luca's hand, but it wasn't there. He was standing staring at the screen, his hands rammed deep in his pockets, and he didn't say a word.

'Luca?'

'We'll come back,' he said, and helped her wipe the gel off her tummy with curious detachment. 'Two weeks?'

His friend nodded. 'That should be long enough. I'm sure it's nothing to worry about.'

Maybe not for him, but for them it was going to be an eternity, Isabelle thought as she sat in the car beside a silent Luca all the way back to his home.

'Luca, why?' she asked, worrying. 'What can it be?'

'There's no sense speculating,' he said, and so she sat there and speculated and worried and panicked on her own, while he maintained a stony silence.

They pulled up at the bottom of the steps, and he helped her out of the car and in through the door. 'Go and rest. I've got things to do,' he said, and disappeared without another word.

'Luca?'

But he didn't hear her, because she'd only mouthed the word, and she stared after him, a horrible suspicion dawning.

Surely he didn't believe that the dates were wrong, did he? Because that would mean that he thought the baby wasn't his.

'No!'

She bit her lip, and then, turning away from the cloistered courtyard, she ran upstairs to their room and threw herself sobbing down on the bed. He couldn't believe that! After all they'd been through, the journey they'd made to reach this point of trust, to have it all wiped away so easily was devastating.

So devastating, in fact, that the only thing she could think of was getting away. She didn't even care about her luggage. Her own clothes, ones bought with her own money, were at home—her real home, the one her mother had struggled for so many years to buy. Her mother was there now. She'd go home to her, go and see Richard Crossland and ask him what could be wrong with her baby, and then she'd deal with whatever fate threw at her alone.

Her passport was in her handbag, and her mobile phone. She'd learned enough Italian to get herself to the airport. All she needed was a lift down the drive—and Roberto would take her.

But, first, she needed to see Massimo.

She found him in the office at the back of the house, and he got to his feet with a startled exclamation when he saw her.

'Isabelle, *cara,* whatever's wrong? You look dreadful—come, sit down, what is it?'

She shook her head, and with shaking fingers she tried to pull the ring from her finger—the ring he had given Luca to give her barely a week ago—but it wouldn't come off, and she started to cry again, and he pulled her gently into his arms and hugged her while she wept. 'Oh, Isabelle, no—what is it? Talk to me.'

'I had my scan—and there's something wrong, the baby's small, and Luca doesn't believe me now—he thinks it isn't his.'

'No. No, I don't believe that. He was so sure, he had such trust in you.'

'Well, not any more. He thinks I've lied, and I haven't, there must be something wrong with my baby, and I can't bear it, Massimo. I can't bear it if anything happens to my baby.'

'Hush, *cara,* hush, this is wrong. Let me ring him.'

'No! I just wanted to give you this back, and I'm leaving.'

'No!'

'Yes. I can't stay. I have to get away— Here.' She tugged it off, scraping her finger and making it bleed, and she dropped it in his hand and turned away, heading blindly for the door and a life without another man who'd let her down…

* * *

He thought he'd felt pain before, but it was nothing compared to this, this pain like a knife through his heart.

He'd gone over and over it, but there were so many things it could be, and none of them were good. The heart? *Dio,* not that, he thought, his mind searching the vast number of things that could cause a baby to fail to grow.

And he'd let her fly—let her work ludicrous hours, when he should have told her to sit at home with her feet up and rest—should have brought her back here right at the beginning and made her take it easy instead of working fifteen hours at a time and then flying back and forth.

He jackknifed out of the chair and strode out onto the terrace, but the sun was too bright and his mood was too black. And then he saw her, a distant figure stumbling down the drive, hurrying away.

'No!'

His phone rang, but he ignored it and ran for the car, just as Massimo came out. 'Luca! Isabelle's gone.'

'I know! Why didn't you stop her?' he raged, but he didn't wait for the answer, just threw himself into the car and shot off down the drive after her, his heart in his mouth. What the hell was she doing in the full heat of the sun, running along the uneven road? And why?

He skidded to a halt just in front of her and leapt out, running back and grabbing her arms. He just stopped himself from shaking her, but he wanted to, to shake some sense into her.

'What are you doing?'

She jerked herself upright and glared at him, her face ravaged with tears. 'I'm leaving. What does it look like?'

'But why?'

'Because you don't believe me. Because you think I've lied to you about the baby being yours.'

'No! *Tesoro,* no! Never!'

'Then why wouldn't you talk to me?' she screamed, tears coursing down her dusty cheeks and leaving muddy trails in their wake. She scrubbed them away, biting her lip and fighting for control, and he felt another crushing wave of guilt.

'Oh, Isabelle, my love—I couldn't talk,' he said unsteadily. 'I was going through all the things it could be, wondering what was wrong with our child, if it would live or die—'

His voice cracked, and he let go of her and turned away, his shoulders heaving, and she stared at him, taking in his words, letting them sink in and make some sense of this sad and senseless day, and then tentatively she reached out her hand and laid it on his shoulder.

'Luca? Please hold me.'

He turned, his face contorted, and dragged her hard up against him, and together they stood on the long, winding drive and wept.

Finally he lifted his head and led her into the shade of a cypress tree, and they sat down side by side, his arm around her shoulders, and he spoke softly to her, her hand wrapped firmly in his.

'I was so busy blaming myself and feeling guilty for letting you work so hard and making you fly, and not letting you have your quiet little wedding, and all the time you thought I didn't believe it was mine? Oh, Isabelle, I thought we'd got past this.'

'I thought we had. I thought you would have talked to me, shared your fears.'

'I wanted to protect you from it.'

'How?' she asked. 'By refusing to discuss it? I'm a midwife, Luca—I know all the things it could be. How did you think not talking it through would help me?'

He shook his head. 'I'm sorry. Of course it wouldn't, but I was afraid to put too much into your head. I should have realised it was already there from the first suspicion that everything wasn't right. I'm so sorry. I can't believe you were running away.'

'I thought you didn't trust me. I couldn't bear that.'

'I'm sorry. Of course I trust you. You're far too honest to lie about a thing like that. That's one of the things I love most about you.'

He pressed a gentle kiss to her forehead, and she leant against him with a sigh, taking comfort from him and at the same time offering it.

'Luca, what are we going to do?'

'Wait,' he said quietly. 'What else can we do? We wait, and when we have the next scan, we'll hopefully have more answers.'

'And if there's something wrong? I mean, there might not be. It could just be a little baby. I was working too hard, and I should have stopped, and I wasn't eating properly, and I was so busy being stubborn I didn't do the best thing for the baby, but what if—'

'Hush,' he murmured, pulling her closer. 'It's not your fault, and working hard and flying and the wedding are not responsible. If we're logical, we both know that, but we're doing what people do when things go wrong and blaming something or someone instead of just accepting fate. And if there *is* something wrong,' he said, 'then we'll face it together, and somehow we'll find the strength to do that, and to work through it together and support each other and our child.

Whatever it is, however great or small, we can deal with it, *cara*. It *will* be all right. Come on, let's go home.'

And getting to his feet, he held out his hand to her and pulled her up beside him. Then he saw her hand and lifted it questioningly, frowning at the little scrape on her finger where her nails had scratched it.

'Where's your ring?'

'I gave it back to Massimo,' she told him, and he tutted and smiled gently.

'Then we'll go and get it, and put it back where it belongs,' he said, and putting his arm round her shoulders, he steered her carefully back to the car.

The next two weeks were agony, but they spent them together, for the most part. On the last day, though, he disappeared, and she found him eventually in the little chapel at the side of the house, sitting quietly.

'Luca?'

He looked up and smiled, and held out his arm and she snuggled under it, glad to have found him.

'I lit a candle for our baby,' he said. 'I do it every day. It's funny, I haven't prayed for years, but I've prayed more these last two weeks than I have in my life.'

'Asking for miracles?' she asked, moved by his simple words but unsure about the power of even that much prayer, and he laughed softly.

'No. Not miracles. Just strength, for both of us.'

'It's nice in here—tranquil. It reminds me of your house in London in a way.'

'Do you want to go back there?'

'Why?'

He shrugged. 'I don't know. I just wondered. If there is something wrong, then I'd like to come home, really. The family would give us so much support, but I don't want you to be unhappy, and I know you have reservations.'

'Not any more,' she said truthfully. 'They've been so wonderful the past two weeks—well, all the time, really, but especially recently—and I've grown to love it here. London was always my home, but only because it was where I lived. But this—this could be home, too, in a different way. But you'll have to help me with my Italian, and I'd like my mother to come often—will you help with the air fares, Luca?'

'Of course. Don't be absurd, they can come as often as you like. And maybe we'll need a house of our own.'

He left his thoughts hanging, but she could read his mind, and only the scan would answer that question. If then.

He looked at his watch. 'It's time. Shall we go?'

'Well, there's the heart—and it looks good. The flow's excellent, the vessels all look fine—and the baby's grown. Have you been resting?'

She laughed a little, and squeezed Luca's hand. 'Yes, I've been resting,' she told him.

'Well, it must have just had a slow start, because it's caught up now—I would say it's just a few days behind, maybe three or four, and that could be simply that it's a small baby—a girl, probably, but I'm not sure without looking. Do you want to know?'

'No.'

They spoke in unison, and Luca went on, 'It doesn't matter. All we have to do now is sit back and wait. Oh, and find a job here in Tuscany, at some point, before I forget how to deliver babies.'

His friend laughed. 'How about the professorship? It's still up for grabs.'

'Professorship?' Isabelle said, stunned, and he gave a wry grin.

'Mmm—in Firenze. That was the job I turned down.'

'For me?' she said, even more stunned. 'You turned down a professorship *for me?*'

'*Si.* Because I loved you—from the first moment I saw you through the café window.'

'Oh, Luca,' she said, and started to laugh, but the laughter turned to tears of joy and relief, and as he gathered her up into his arms, his friend went quietly out and closed the door behind him...

EPILOGUE

ISABELLE STRAIGHTENED UP and arched her back, exhausted.

Heavens, the house had been dirty, she thought, and then the backache grew and spread, and she rested her hand over the baby and felt the contraction ease.

She glanced at her watch, and went into the kitchen to make a drink. It was probably just a Braxton-Hicks, she'd been having lots of them.

'Ahh!'

She sagged against the worktop, hanging on and staring out over the valley at the Palazzo in the distance. It was mid-September, and they were harvesting the wheat, and Elisa was visiting Carla and the children, snatching the chance before Luca's baby arrived.

She was alone, and she was having contractions every three minutes. That wasn't good.

She went into out onto the veranda of the old shooting lodge and uncovered the birthing pool again. She'd just scrubbed it out and rinsed it thoroughly in preparation— because she'd known? Maybe.

She turned on the taps, all plumbed in in readiness, and started to fill it. It had to be at exactly the right temperature, thirty-seven degrees, and as it filled she would need to adjust it to keep it right.

Well, it would give her something to think about till Luca got home, she thought, and then another contraction took her breath away. The moment it was past, she phoned the hospital and said, in halting Italian, 'Could you please page Professor Valtieri and tell him his wife's in labour and he's needed at home? Yes, that's right. Now, please. Thank you.'

Then she put the phone down within reach, turned on a soothing CD, peeled off her clothes and stepped into the water. Bliss. The music soothed her, the water was perfect, and the next contraction washed over her.

She tuned into it, feeling the power of it sweep through her body, and as she rested her head back, she relaxed her muscles and allowed them to do their work.

'She's *what?*'

'In labour—I'm sorry, *Dottore,* I tried to page you but they said you were in Theatre, and I had to find you to tell you…'

His secretary's words faded into the distance as he sprinted for his office to grab his car keys and phone. As he headed for the car park, he stabbed the speed dial for Isabelle and fumed impatiently until she answered.

'Are you all right?'

'I'm fine. I'm in the pool.'

'Who's with you?'

'No one, but I'm fine, Luca. I'm propped up, I can't slip, I'm really comfortable and don't even contemplate suggesting I get out. Just get home carefully.'

'I'm on my way,' he said. 'Ring me—any change, ring me. How close are your contractions?'

'Two minutes.'

He swore, fluently and succinctly, and gunned the car out of the car park into the stream of traffic heading out of the city. He hit the A1 in record time, drove faster than was sensible but slower than he wanted to, and skidded onto the drive a little over an hour later.

'Isabelle!'

He ran out to the veranda and found her lying in the water, panting softly, her eyes closed and her legs drawn up. And he could see that the baby's head was crowning.

Dear God.

He tore off his shirt, knelt down beside her and kissed her gently on the shoulder. 'I'm here, *tesoro*. I've got you.'

'Mmm,' she sighed, and then made a little pushing noise and the baby's head was delivered. She put her hand down and stroked it, and a smile drifted over her face, and he felt a huge lump in his throat. He'd so nearly missed this.

'You're doing really well,' he murmured, holding her, and then with the next contraction, their baby was born and she lifted it, silent and peaceful, up to her breast.

He reached out, blinking away the tears, and laid his hand on the soft, soft skin of his child. It was pale, as babies born underwater so often were, and as it took its first shuddering little breath, its face went pink, then its body, then its arms and legs.

'Hello, baby,' she murmured, turning it so it could reach her nipple, and he got his first clear look at his baby.

'She's a girl,' he said, his voice cracking. 'She's a girl, Isabella. She's beautiful.'

'Can you check her? Please? Make sure everything's all right?'

'Sì.' He took his tiny daughter from her, his hands sure and confident, and wrapped her in a towel. It wasn't cold—the weather was beautiful—but he didn't want her to be chilled. He dealt with the cord, then laid her down on the towel beside Isabelle's pool so she could watch and he checked her thoroughly.

Eyes, nose, mouth, ears, head, neck, hands, fingers, feet, toes, hips, bottom—perfect. And indignant now, wanting her mum, angry at being disturbed when she'd been so peaceful, and he smiled and lifted her to his shoulder.

'Hush, baby. I need to look after your mama. You rest now.'

And putting her down in the waiting crib and wrapping her up gently, he turned back to his wife.

'That was amazing. I'm so glad I was able to have a water birth, it was just wonderful.'

'I can't believe you did it without me—if I'd been any later—'

'Shh,' she said, smiling at her frowning, panicking husband. 'You weren't, so it's all right, but maybe next time you'd better book a good chunk of time off and be a little closer.'

'Next time?' he said, smiling quizzically, and she smiled back, then looked down at their little daughter, asleep at her breast.

'Oh, yes. And the time after, and the time after that.'

He laughed, then hugged her. 'How can you even talk about it so soon? Crazy woman.'

'Crazy about you,' she murmured, and his smile faded as a dozen emotions chased across his familiar and beloved features.

'Oh, *tesoro*.' He closed his eyes briefly, and when he opened them, they were bright with tears. 'I love you,' he said gruffly. 'You and our beautiful little daughter. I can't believe how much light and joy you've brought into my life.'

Unbearably moved, she reached up a gentle hand and cradled his cheek. 'I feel the same. My life was empty without you, Luca, and now I've got so much—you, our daughter, your family—but most of all, you. I love you. *Te amo,* Luca.'

'Te amo, Isabella,' he murmured, and, bending his head, he touched his lips to hers in a kiss filled with tenderness and promise—the promise of a future rich with warmth and love and laughter, fiery with passion and with a deep, enduring trust to underlie it all.

He would be there for her, his kiss said; so long as there was breath in his body, he would be there for her, as she would for him. Forever…

THE ITALIAN
DOCTOR'S BRIDE

BY
MARGARET McDONAGH

Margaret McDonagh says of herself: "I began losing myself in the magical world of books from a very young age, and I always knew that I had to write, pursuing the dream for over twenty years, often with cussed stubbornness in the face of rejection letters! Despite having numerous romance novellas, short stories and serials published, the news that my first "proper book" had been accepted by Mills & Boon for their Medical™ romance line brought indescribable joy! Having a passion for learning makes researching an involving pleasure, and I love developing new characters, getting to know them, setting them challenges to overcome. The hardest part is saying goodbye to them, because they become so real to me. And I always fall in love with my heroes! Writing and reading books, keeping in touch with friends, watching sport and meeting the demands of my four-legged companions keeps me well occupied. I hope you enjoy reading this book as much as I loved writing it."

You can contact Margaret at http://margaretmcdonagh. bravehost.com

The Italian Doctor's Bride was **Margaret's emotional, heart-rending debut novel for Mills & Boon® Medical™ romance!**

With special thanks…

To: John Morton, Mr Lamont and Professor Hannay
for helping with my research.

To: Christina Jones, Sue Haasler, Liz Young,
Kate Hardy, Hilary Johnson, Wendy Wootton,
Victoria Connelly, Lorraine, Anne & Richard, Hsin-Yi,
Gwen, Gill and Heather for their friendship and
for believing in me.

And to Joanne and all at M&B for making
a dream come true.

CHAPTER ONE

'SOMETHING *has* to be done.'

Dr Hannah Frost did not do panic, but the chaotic Monday morning surgery pushed her as close to it as she ever hoped to come. Being one doctor down meant that her staff were harassed and overworked. More importantly, from a safety point of view, she could not continue to give her best to her patients under such exhausting circumstances. She had to find an answer to their current predicament…and soon.

For now it was a question of maintaining focus and dealing with the heavy workload. The waiting room was already filling with patients but the problem of a replacement locum nagged at her throughout the morning until her consultations, overrunning as usual, drew to an end nearly three hours later.

'You're a grand lassie, Dr Frost.' Old Mr Ferguson balanced unsteadily, both walking sticks clasped in one gnarled hand as he reached out with the other to pat her arm. 'It was a lucky day for us all when you chose to come back to Lochanrig to be our doctor.'

'Thank you. This is my home and I'm happy to be here.' Hannah smiled, touched by her elderly patient's words.

She could never imagine living and working anywhere else. The responsibility of taking over the running of the practice from her father weighed heavily upon her because she cared so much, both for her patients and the family tradition. These were her people. The rugged beauty of this part of south-west Scotland was her home. She felt safe here. Her challenges were professional, not personal. Hannah suppressed an inner shiver. She didn't do personal. Not any more.

Conscious of Mr Ferguson's frailty, and aware of his fierce independence, she pushed her thoughts away and moved slowly by his side as he shuffled from her consulting room towards the reception area where Jim Henderson, the local taxi driver, was waiting.

'All ready now?' Jim placed a protective hand under Mr Ferguson's arm. 'Don't you worry, Doc, I'll make sure he arrives home safely.'

'Thanks, Jim. I'll see you next week, Mr Ferguson, but ring any time if you need me.'

'Aye, lass, thank you.'

Hannah held the door open for them, then turned to survey the empty waiting room with weary satisfaction before smiling ruefully at Kirsty Gordon, her practice manager and chief receptionist.

'I know, I'm running hideously late…again.'

Kirsty, in her early fifties, small in stature if not in personality and famous for speaking her mind, gave a wry grimace. 'I thought Mr Ferguson was here for the day.'

'He's lonely since his wife died two months ago. He needs a bit of time at the moment.'

'Poor man,' Kirsty allowed, her dark brows puckering in a frown. 'But it's not surprising you're exhausted the way you devote so much of yourself to everyone, Hannah. You're taking on too much alone.'

'Which is why we're trying so hard to find a new locum.'

'Let's hope they'll be better than the last one.'

Kirsty's tone was derisive and Hannah had a sneaking suspicion that an 'I told you so' lurked unspoken, hovering between them. Her practice manager had advised against Dr Lane's appointment and Hannah silently admitted that she had made a mistake. To say the young locum had been unsatisfactory was an understatement. Now they were in this mess.

'It's not easy, attracting people to an overstretched, rural Scottish practice at the best of times,' she reflected, setting the tray of patient notes from morning surgery on the counter, ready for filing. 'But with there being such a shortage of doctors willing to work in general practice at the moment, it's proving harder than usual.'

'Maybe I have some good news for you, then!'

Hannah's green eyes widened at Kirsty's grin. 'You've heard from the agency?'

'About an hour ago.'

'And?'

'Your plan to look further afield may have paid off. They think they've found our perfect doctor. An Italian—Nicola some-one—who is interested in a six-month contract and who speaks fluent English, has excellent references and an impressive CV. The agency are faxing the information through to me.'

'Fantastic!' Hannah sighed with relief, grateful for Kirsty's efficiency. 'If all the paper work is in order, we can have a chat on the phone, and the sooner she can start the better.'

'Why don't you leave it all to me? I'll do the ground work and you can check over the information and make a decision. That would save you some time.'

'Are you sure, Kirsty? It isn't as if you have nothing to do yourself.'

'It will be fine. According to the agency, Nicola is on holiday this week so may not be easy to reach. I'll see to everything, Hannah, don't worry.'

Thankful that the locum problem might soon be resolved, she felt confident about handing the initial responsibility over to her manager. 'Thanks, Kirsty, that would be a big help. Any queries, let me know. Right,' she added, checking her watch and stifling a groan, 'I'd better be away for the house calls if I'm ever to start afternoon surgery on time.'

'Speaking of house calls, Mary McFee rang. She sounded shaky and her chest was rough.'

'OK.' Hannah frowned, concerned for the elderly lady who insisted on living alone in her isolated home. 'I'm heading out that way to see Joe MacLean, aren't I? I'll pop in and check on Mary at the same time.'

'As if you aren't busy enough,' Kirsty tutted with disapproval. 'Hopefully we'll have some help around here soon.'

Gathering the notes for the patients she had to visit, Hannah left the surgery, heartily seconding Kirsty's final statement.

Dr Nicola di Angelis's CV was certainly impressive, Hannah acknowledged later, grabbing a hasty late lunch at her desk and looking over the papers Kirsty had prepared for her. Two years younger than her own age of thirty-three, the Italian had experience in trauma and general practice, having worked in Italy, Canada and the UK. The latter included six months in a busy London A and E department eighteen months ago, followed by three months' GP work in Sussex. The letters of recommendation were glowing.

'I thought you might want to speak with the department head at the hospital in Milan where Nicola last worked,' Kirsty suggested, setting a cup of coffee down on Hannah's desk. 'I checked out the UK references and everything is fine.'

Hannah smiled, sipping the welcome drink. 'Thanks, Kirsty. Yes, I'll ring now. Everything looks to be in order. You feel happy about the appointment?'

'Indeed. From all I have heard, Nicola di Angelis is professionally respected and personally admired.'

Hannah glanced up, puzzled by the inflection in the older woman's voice. 'Let's hope she is.'

'I'll leave you to it.' Kirsty rose to her feet. 'If this last reference is good, you'll offer Nicola the job?'

'Definitely. Let's just hope she is willing to come here.'

'Good, I'm sure it's the best thing. Say if I can do anything else.'

'I appreciate all your help, Kirsty.'

After her practice manager had gone, Hannah reached for the
phone and dialled the number of the Milan hospital, hoping this
verbal reference would be as encouraging as the written ones.

'*Buongiorno. Pronto Soccorso*,' an efficient-sounding man announced when Hannah was connected to Accident and Emergency.

'Hello, do you speak English?' she enquired.

'*Sì*. I help you, yes?'

'Thank you. My name is Dr Hannah Frost and I'm calling from
Scotland. May I speak with Francesca Simone about a reference?'

'A moment please.'

As Hannah waited, she glanced through the paperwork on
Nicola di Angelis, reviewing the impressive CV once more.

'Dr Frost? I am Francesca Simone,' a voice introduced in
halting English. 'What help can I be for you?'

Hannah exchanged pleasantries and explained the reason for
her call. 'I understand Dr Nicola di Angelis worked for you in
Trauma. Are you able to provide a reference?'

'But, yes. Trauma and general clinics. A wonderful doctor. We
were sorry to say goodbye. The patients, they love Dr di Angelis.
The staff also.'

The woman gave a throaty chuckle, but before Hannah
could question her further, she heard an alarm sounding in the
background.

'*Scusi*, Dr Frost. I am needed. An emergency.'

'Of course. Thank you, you've been very helpful.'

'*Prego*. Dr di Angelis will not disappoint you.'

Hanging up, Hannah had to admit that, given all the evidence,
it looked as if Nicola di Angelis might indeed be their perfect
doctor. Glancing at her watch with a grimace, she decided there

was just time to email the Italian before surgery began. She outlined the job offer, explained a little about the practice and clicked on 'Send'. Hopefully it would not be too long before a reply came back. Satisfied, Hannah updated Kirsty on progress, then turned her attention to the full patient list she had for the afternoon.

Despite a disturbed night, during which she had been called out twice, Hannah was at her desk early the next morning. With luck she would have nearly an hour before morning surgery to tackle the mountain of paperwork that increasingly plagued a GP's life. Switching on her computer, she sipped her first coffee of the day and, stifling a yawn, logged on, to find several emails waiting in her inbox.

Aside from some unwanted adverts and offers from medical supply and drug companies, she discovered a personal message from her friend Lauren, a doctor with whom she had trained and who was now working in paediatrics at a hospital in Edinburgh. But it was another message that claimed her attention. A reply from Nicola di Angelis.

Dear Dr Frost,
    Thank you for your email and your offer of a contract to work alongside you in your practice for six months. The information you provided was most interesting to me. I would be happy to accept the position and will be in touch so we can make further arrangements.
    I am presently in France, nearing the end of a short holiday. Depending on your needs, I would be free to start work any time from next week onwards. I have all the necessary paperwork and permits to allow this.
    Kind regards,
    Nicola di Angelis

Relief flooded through her as she read the message a second time. Kirsty would be delighted, as would all the practice staff who, together, worked so hard, serving their rural community. Her promise to tackle the outstanding paperwork forgotten, Hannah composed a reply straight away.

Dear Nicola,

Thank you for your swift reply and acceptance of the position. All of us here are glad that you will be joining us. We would be grateful if you could begin work as soon as possible. Next week would suit us perfectly, unless you need more time.

Please contact me or my practice manager, Kirsty Gordon, to confirm the details and ask if there is any further information you require.

Best wishes,
Hannah Frost

Her task completed, Hannah left her consulting room and, hearing chatter coming from the staffroom, went to pass on the news.

'Dr di Angelis has accepted the locum contract.'

'Excellent!' Kirsty grinned. 'Any start date given?'

'Maybe as early as next week. I've asked her to contact you, Kirsty, if I'm unavailable. I've sent you copies of the emails.'

Kirsty nodded. 'No problem.'

'This is wonderful,' Morag, the efficient and maternal practice nurse, agreed. 'We've all been worried about you, Hannah. You've taken the brunt of everything since Dr Lane departed.'

Shona, one of the district nurses, snorted in derision. 'Not that Dr Lane did much when she was here. I hope this new one is more dedicated to our patients.'

A series of locums had come their way since her father's untimely death three years previously had left her in sole charge of the practice. Some had been good, some not so good, but none had been persuaded to stay in the locality for very long. The swift departure of Dr Lane barely two weeks into a six-month contract had been a severe blow and had plunged the whole practice into chaos.

'Let's hope Nicola di Angelis proves as perfect as her qualifications and references suggest,' she murmured now.

A speculative gleam brightened Kirsty's eyes. 'You may even discover a life outside the surgery, Hannah.'

'I'm a doctor, I don't have a social life.' And she didn't want one, she added silently. Disconcerted, Hannah turned her attention to the district nurse on duty. 'Shona, I was out at Mary McFee's yesterday and her chest is sounding grim again. She's adamant she won't be moved, but her place is terribly damp. The dry, warm summer seems to have made little difference and I'm worried about her being there for another winter.'

Brown eyes thoughtful, Shona nodded. 'I'll talk to Debbie and we'll keep a check on her.'

'Thanks.' Hannah was relieved. She knew how dedicated and reliable the two district nurses were. 'Right, I expect there's a full list again this morning so I had better press on. Send the first one through when you're ready, Kirsty.'

She had been right—it *was* another busy surgery. Amongst other things her case load included a suspected stomach ulcer, a woman with unexplained pelvic pain, a few colds and coughs, a ten-year-old with probable appendicitis, who had to be despatched to hospital, a toddler with eczema, confirmation of a pregnancy for a young couple delighted to be expecting their first baby and, lastly, Allan Pollock, who ran the local garage.

'What can I do for you today, Allan?' she greeted him, trying to hide her weariness as the stocky, middle-aged man sat down at her desk.

'It's my knee,' he explained. 'I've been taking the paracetamol or ibuprofen when I had a painful spell, like you said last time, but it's more swollen now and is annoying me most of the time.'

Hannah nodded sympathetically and rose to her feet. 'OK,

let's have you sitting on the table so I can have a look at you. Can you roll your trouser legs up, please—and don't be telling me you only washed one knee!'

'As if I'd kid you, Doc,' he protested with mock innocence, blue eyes twinkling.

'Mmm!' Smiling, Hannah began her examination, gently assessing Allan's joint. 'The left knee is very inflamed. Do you find the damp, cool weather affects it at all?'

He nodded in agreement. 'It is worse then. And when I've been sitting a while, it's hard to get moving again.'

'It's important to keep up some gentle exercise,' Hannah encouraged, probing the joint carefully. 'I'll prescribe you some non-steroidal anti-inflammatory tablets, which should help with the swelling and the discomfort. I'd also like you to see Murray McGiven, the physiotherapist, as he should be able to give you a programme to help maintain movement. The next step is to arrange an X-ray so we can see what's going on, then we can adjust your medication as necessary.'

'You think it's arthritis?'

As Allan lowered his trouser legs and slipped down from the table, Hannah returned to her desk, aware of his concern. 'With your history, it is most likely. I'll refer you for the X-ray and you'll get an appointment through the post,' she told him, turning for a moment to tap out a prescription for the NSAIDS, waiting as the printer delivered it before signing her name. 'You should be fine with these, Allan, but if you have any side-effects or stomach pains, let me know and we'll change you to something else.'

'Thanks, Doc.' He folded the prescription and put it in his pocket. 'Kirsty was telling me you might have a new locum starting soon?'

'Yes, hopefully.'

'Anything I can do to help?'

Hannah smiled. 'I was going to come and see you. I'll need to sort out a vehicle for her—a four-by-four like mine to cope with the terrain and whatever the winter weather throws at us.'

'Not like that sporty piece the last doctor arrived in!' he joked.

'Indeed.'

'You leave it with me, Doc, I'll see you right. You know Dorothy and I will never forget what you did for our Barrie.'

Hannah remembered two summers ago when the boy, then eight, had suffered bee stings. The allergic reaction had been frightening and she had been worried at the outcome of his anaphylaxis. It had needed several doses of adrenalin, followed by antihistamine and intravenous hydrocortisone, before things had been brought under control and Barrie had been stabilised for transfer to hospital.

'How's he doing?'

'He's grand, Doc.' Allan beamed. 'Always up to mischief.'

'Takes after his father, does he?'

Allan laughed and stood up. 'I'll let you know about the vehicle, Doc.'

'Thank you. And no special favours. You have a living to make for your family. Promise me.'

'I'll take care of it, Doc,' was as far as he would go.

At the end of another frantically busy day, Hannah felt out on her feet. Thank goodness the rota system with the next nearest practices meant she did not have to be on call that night. Munching an apple, she wandered round the house, her memories flooding back as she recalled her childhood in this rambling old building, her parents working all hours, caring for their widespread community. Unlike some other medical facilities, they had survived changes, closures and financial cuts, and the opportunity to build the modern new surgery a decade ago had been a real bonus.

Hannah had gladly returned to work in Lochanrig. It had suited her just fine, being professionally challenging and personally safe. But losing both her parents so soon had been devastating. First her mother in a hit-and-run accident. Then, swamped with grief and working too hard, her father had driven himself to an early grave a year later. Literally. She shivered, wrapping her arms around herself, recalling that terrible day. When the call had come in for her to attend the accident on the mountain road, she had set out, not knowing the victim was her own father, that he had suffered a heart attack at the wheel and crashed, that it had already been too late to save him.

Battling her own grief, Hannah had summoned a strength she had not known she possessed to keep the practice running. A quiet determination not to fail her patients, or her family tradition, had kept her going. The one major headache had been keeping another doctor. Maybe this time it would be different.

'ETA on the air ambulance is ten minutes.'

'Thanks.' Hannah nodded towards the police constable who had slithered down the slope to deliver the information. She shook her head, looking at the tangled wreckage of the vehicle, which had run off the hill road and crashed in a gully. 'Let's hope we have this boy out of the car by then.'

'They never learn, do they? A night out in the city, too much to drink and they think they are invincible.'

Hannah nodded again. Being called out in the early hours of Sunday morning in her role as BASICS emergency doctor on call had been the last thing she had needed after an unusually hectic week. A week during which Kirsty had talked with Dr di Angelis on the telephone. Hannah would rather have spoken to the new locum herself but she had been out on house visits when the call had come in. Kirsty had been taken with their new doctor and foresaw no problems. Given the predicament the practice was in, Hannah had been content to delegate responsibility to her knowledgeable manager.

Dragging her thoughts back to the current situation, Hannah addressed the young policeman. 'At least we got the other two out quickly and away to hospital.'

'Were they badly injured?' he asked, watching as the firefighters fought to cut the driver free.

'A few broken bones, nothing that won't heal. It's this one I'm worried about.'

'Foolish bloke wasn't wearing a seat belt, I hear,' the constable remarked.

'That's right. He has a very nasty head injury.'

'Should—? I mean, don't you need to be with him?'

Hannah glanced at the young policeman and saw alarm mixed with curiosity in his eyes. 'I've done what I can to stabilise him and have fitted a neck brace. One of the paramedics is in the car, keeping his head still while they cut him out. No room for all of us while the fire crew are working.'

'I see. Thanks, Doc. I've not been to many of these.'

'They are never pleasant, I'm afraid.'

The sound of the helicopter alerted them to the arrival of the specialist medical team. Hovering for several moments, searching for a safe place to land, the yellow aircraft finally dropped out of sight round a bend in the road above them, just as the early October dawn was breaking over the eastern hills.

Hannah breathed a sigh of relief when she recognised the experienced Dr Stewart scrambling down the gully towards her, a paramedic behind him.

'Morning, Archie,' she greeted with a brief smile. 'Sorry to bring you out.'

'What have we got, Hannah?'

'Male driver, early twenties. Serious head trauma. He's been unconscious since I arrived. No seat belt worn. Suspected high alcohol intake. I've stabilised him as best I can. His airway has been secured, he's having oxygen and I fitted a neck brace. There's a paramedic with him, monitoring his head while he's being cut out. There is not much outward blood loss but some seepage of fluid and blood from the nose and ears, which may mean he has a basal skull fracture. He also has facial fractures. We've put a line in and are giving saline and analgesia. Pupils are even but slow to react. Glasgow coma scale about 5 or 6. No sign of thoracic or abdominal injury but he's trapped by his lower legs—there will likely be trauma there when he's free and can be assessed,' she summed up, adding details of pulse and blood pressure.

'Good work,' Archie Stewart praised. 'We'll get a muscle blockade into him before he's moved. How long until they have him out of there?'

'Only a few more moments, I hope. It's been a struggle.'

His experienced blue gaze scanned the tangled wreckage. 'I can see that. Anyone else hurt?'

'Two other young males. Broken bones and cuts only. They've gone to hospital by road ambulance.'

'And how are things with you? Heard you were looking for a locum again.'

Hannah raised an eyebrow. 'Word certainly gets around. We have a new doctor due this coming week.'

'There's always a place for you in trauma if you get fed up with the hassles of general practice.'

Hannah shook her head. 'Thanks, but I enjoy what I do.'

A flurry of activity near the wreck and a call from a fire-fighter told them the casualty was ready to be moved and cur-tailed further conversation. Hannah followed as Archie scrambled to the wreckage to assess what was now his patient and supervise the extraction. It took several minutes more before he was happy, then agonising moments as the patient was carefully transferred, his head and neck immobilised with tapes and sandbags, and he was safely secured for the danger-ous trip ahead.

'Right, we're away to Glasgow,' Archie announced, as they finally scrambled out of the gully and reached the road. 'Good job, Hannah.'

'Thanks.'

She lingered with the rescue workers as the group bearing the young man disappeared round the bend in the road. They heard the helicopter start up and after a few moments it lifted above the stone outcrop and into the sky, before heading north.

'Do you think the guy will make it?' The fire officer in charge grimaced as his team gathered up their equipment.

'Hard to tell. He's very poorly. But you've all done a terrific job as usual, and given him the best chance,' Hannah smiled, her praise including the road paramedics and the young policeman who also lingered nearby. 'Thanks for your help.'

The firefighters grinned. 'You too, Doc.'

'Fancy a coffee back at base?' one of the paramedics asked.

Hannah craved lashings of strong, hot coffee, but at home. Alone. 'Thanks, but I'd best get back to Lochanrig. I need a clean-up and some breakfast.'

It was a relief to turn in between the old stone pillars that marked the entrance to the house half an hour later, but as she headed up the gravel drive, she groaned at the sight of a motorbike parked to one side.

'Oh, no. What now?'

Still wearing the grubby coveralls and BASICS jacket she had donned to work at the crash site, she climbed out of her car and looked around for the owner of the motorbike. Although a helmet was propped on the seat and a bag rested on the ground, no one was in sight. Sighing, she went round to the boot and took out her medical case. Feeling tired and dishevelled after hours of crawling around the twisted wreckage of the car, she walked towards the house. As she fumbled for her key, she heard footsteps in the gravel behind her. Heart sinking, she turned round, hoping there was not some other emergency requiring her attention.

Her eyes widened as she saw a man approaching. His gait loose-limbed, he exuded an easy confidence and self-assurance. She felt distinctly on edge. As he came closer, she could see he was incredibly good-looking in a rugged and dangerous kind of way, his raven-black hair short but thick, his dark eyes watchful as his disturbing gaze raked over her. Tense, Hannah instinctively stepped back towards the door, tamping down a rush of deep-seated anxiety.

Her breath lodging in her throat, Hannah faced the dark stranger. An inch or so under six feet, he cut an imposing figure, athletically built and wearing faded, figure-hugging jeans and a battered dark brown leather jacket. His face was classically sculpted, with the merest hint of a cleft in his determined chin. Smouldering dark eyes watched her intently.

'What do you want?' she challenged, the uncharacteristic snap in her voice evidence of the reawakening of her inner fears at this unexpected and unwanted confrontation.

His sensuous mouth curved at her feisty reaction. 'Dr Frost?'

Hannah faced him warily, flicking back strands of wayward chestnut hair which had escaped her hurried braid. 'You need medical attention?' she queried doubtfully, seldom having seen anyone in better health.

'No!' He unleashed a killer smile, his voice huskily accented as he continued, 'It is good to meet you at last, Hannah. I am Dr Nicola di Angelis.'

CHAPTER TWO

DEAR God, no! Hannah stared at him in horrified disbelief, uncharacteristic panic forming a heavy knot in her stomach. 'But you can't be.'

'There is a problem?'

'You're supposed to be a woman.'

He raised one dark eyebrow, quizzical amusement glittering in his eyes at her accusatory tone. 'I can assure you, Hannah, I am very much a man.'

'Look,' she began, flustered by the huskiness of his accented voice, disturbed by his presence and his blatant masculinity, 'there's obviously been some mistake.'

'It is necessary to discuss this in the driveway?'

Hannah didn't want to discuss it at all. She just wanted him to get on his bike and go back where he had come from. How could she have been so stupid? Had Kirsty deliberately allowed her to believe their new locum was a woman? The practice manager had spoken to him, for goodness' sake, and hadn't corrected her when she had referred to Nicola as 'she'. But what could she have done if she had realised? She pressed her hand to her temple. She had just never considered this possibility. The fact that he was so...so *male* made it worse.

'I do not understand. Why is this such a difficulty?' he probed, clearly perplexed by her reaction. 'You desperately need a doctor, do you not?'

'Yes, but—'

'But?'

'Nicola is a girl's name,' Hannah rallied, her insides churning at the disaster unfolding before her. 'You must have realised I would think that.'

His good humour undaunted by her coldness, he smiled. 'In Italy this is not so. And it never occurred to me that gender was an issue. You gave no indication of only requiring a woman doctor and Kirsty made no such comment when I telephoned and we discussed me working here. But, please, Hannah, call me Nic if it makes you feel better.'

It didn't make her feel better at all. Not one jot. Dear God, she needed to think, but he was right, this wasn't the place. How could she go on with this as if nothing had happened? How could she cope with him living in her house? It just wouldn't work. And just wait until she saw Kirsty!

'A doctor is wanted. I am here. Please, can we carry on now we have this misunderstanding out of the way? I have rushed to get here, knowing you needed me. I am tired and I have had a long journey. We can go inside, yes?'

'Yes. No. I mean…'

Why did he have to be so reasonable, so right? Why did she have to start behaving like some flustered teenager rather than the mature and controlled adult she was? This muddle would be sorted out, but for now there was little to do but invite him in. A shiver of alarm ran through her. Calm down, she told herself. Nothing is going to happen. Unable to meet his gaze, she turned back to fumble with the key, her fingers trembling as she tried to insert it in the lock.

Nic collected his helmet and bag before following as Hannah stalked briskly inside the impressive, stone-built house, tension and distress evident in her bearing. Whatever was wrong?

OK, there had been an amusing mistake over his gender, but so what? Given the dire need she claimed the practice was in, what difference did it make if he was male or female? He did not understand, but clearly it mattered to his new employer. Frost by name, frosty by nature? That was his first impression on meeting her. But her emails had been warm, open…when she had thought he was a woman. Frowning, he wondered why Kirsty had kept the information to herself.

He watched as Hannah left her medical bag on a chair in the wide, slate-floored hallway and tossed her protective jacket on top. It was a beautiful house from the little he had seen, but it felt…what? Lonely, empty? A bit like Hannah, he decided, noting the way she held herself, remote and guarded. She gestured him to follow her to the kitchen and, as she set about thoroughly washing her hands and gathering things to make coffee, he stood back and observed her.

Dr Hannah Frost was younger than he had expected, around his own age, he estimated, and she was a very attractive woman in an understated way. Three or four inches shorter than himself, she moved with supple grace, and even in her coveralls he could tell her body was pleasingly curvy. A riot of long, chestnut tresses were barely restrained and tendrils had escaped a loose plait to frame an interesting and intelligent face. Her skin was creamy smooth, free of make-up, and an intriguing line of pale freckles trailed across her cheekbones and over the bridge of her nose.

It was her eyes, however, that had arrested his attention from the first. An unusual, intense green, they had a smattering of golden flecks that sparkled with her mood. And they spoke volumes, reflecting every passing emotion. In the space of their brief acquaintance she had been worried, annoyed, confused, shocked and, unless he was very much mistaken, frightened. It was the latter that troubled him the most.

At the moment she also looked dishevelled and he judged

from her rumpled outfit and smudges of dirt that she had been out on a difficult call. 'Bad night?'

'You could say that.' Her tone brisk and to the point, she filled him in on the car accident she had attended. 'Whether the young man will pull through remains to be seen.'

'Let us hope so. You must be tired.'

She shrugged, keeping her gaze averted. 'I'm certainly grubby. I must go and change. Please, help yourself to coffee when it's ready and something to eat.'

Nic watched her leave the room, her back ramrod straight. He didn't understand her at all. Friendly in her emails, obviously in need of help in the practice, but now he had arrived she appeared cold and unwelcoming. Something didn't fit. A frown of consideration on his face, he examined the contents of the fridge and set about preparing breakfast.

When she returned to the kitchen half an hour later, he was unsurprised by her altered appearance. Clearly she had needed fortifying. The hair was tamed and scraped back in a severe knot. It was a shame. He had looked forward to seeing it in all its glory. Disturbed at the sudden tightening in his gut, he ruthlessly banished wayward and unwanted thoughts, the stab of desire he had not felt for two long years since... Again, he tamped down painful, dangerous thoughts and continued his assessment.

Hannah obviously thought this image made her more unapproachable while in reality it highlighted the perfection of her bone structure and the beauty of her face, the small, straight nose, the curve of pleasingly full lips, the classic jaw line. She was dressed in a smart but demure navy trouser suit, one which was well cut but neutralised her shape. He had the feeling it was a costume, her work persona, something she wore for protection, to maintain a front.

'Sit.' He smiled. 'You are hungry, no?'

It looked as if she wanted to say something, to argue, but he turned away to dish up the food, and after a moment he heard a chair scrape on the slate floor as she sat at the table. Her wary green gaze skittered from his as he crossed the room and set a plate of bacon, scrambled eggs and grilled tomatoes in front of her.

'You did this?'

Her surprise amused him. 'I am quite domesticated.' He smiled, pouring two mugs of coffee. 'Milk and sugar?'

'Just milk. Thank you.' He watched a frown crease the smoothness of her brow when she realised there was only one plate. 'Aren't you eating?'

'I had breakfast on the way.'

When she began her meal, Nic drew out a chair across from her, sensing she would be more comfortable if he did not sit too close.

'I had expected you to let us know your travel plans.'

The cool, accusing tone was back in her voice. 'I came straight from France. It seemed easier than going back to Italy and starting again. I made better time than I anticipated.'

'And your things?'

'I've organised for them to be sent on. My medical kit and essentials always travel with me. Including my papers,' he added, pushing them across the table for her to examine and confirm his identity.

He leaned back in the chair, his cup of coffee cradled in his hands as he watched her sift through the documents, smiling when, with a small sigh, clearly unable to find anything wrong, she pushed them back to him. 'Thanks.'

'So how long have you been managing alone here?'

'Nearly three weeks.'

'It's a lot to take on for one person,' he allowed, noting the dark circles under her eyes. 'You are exhausted, no?'

She glanced towards him warily, failing to meet his gaze. 'I was more worried for my staff and patients, but it has been a difficult few weeks. It's not always like this. We were badly let down by someone, hence the urgent search for a new locum.'

'Not easy to find.'

'Indeed.'

'Then it is silly to worry whether I am male or female, no? You need help. I am here to do a job.'

'But—'

'You have a queue of other people waiting to fill the position?'

'No. No, I don't.'

Nic watched as she briefly closed her eyes. When she opened them again he caught her gaze and held it, seeing resignation and annoyance in those expressive green eyes, but a latent fear still lurked within their depths, puzzling him anew. Something was wrong. He didn't know what...not yet. But before his time here was over, he intended to find out what demons haunted this woman and what lay beneath her frosty exterior.

Hannah finished her food in silence, unwilling to admit she had been touched by his thoughtfulness preparing her a meal. She felt worn out—physically exhausted from working such long hours and mentally worn down by Nic's arguments. The hell of it was, he was right. He would have to stay. But the thought of sharing her house with him brought an ache of doubt and alarm to her stomach.

There was no way out. She could hardly ask him to make other living arrangements. Accommodation in the main house was part of the deal. Everyone knew it was how things had always been done, ever since her father's day, and both the staff and the community would find her overreaction to Nic's identity inexplicable. Given she had no intention of explaining to anyone, she would have to cope with the situation. Somehow. Either that or draw unwelcome attention to her own anxiety. And that was out of the question.

It had never been a problem before. In fact, she had enjoyed the extra company, but most of the visiting locums had been female, or married with spouses. It was true there had been a couple of single men early on, but they had not been attracted to her, or she to them, and she had seen little of them.

She reined her thoughts in with a jerk. Where had that come from? What had attraction to do with anything? Of course she wasn't attracted to Nic. She had no intention of being attracted to anyone. Not now, not ever. And why would he be attracted to her? He barely knew her and probably had a string of girlfriends at home or left behind at his various ports of call over the last couple of years. She had been anything but welcoming and friendly so far, so all she had to do was maintain a distance, keep up her guard, and she could see this through.

'Thank you for breakfast,' she said with cool politeness. 'Perhaps I should show you to your room—if you plan to stay.'

'Oh, I'm definitely staying, *cara*.'

Hannah tried to ignore the shiver that ran through her at the knowing amusement in his reply. Conscious of him following as she led the way up the wide, curving staircase, she was glad the guest rooms were at the other end of the house to her own, and that she had thought to prepare everything in advance.

'You'll be in here,' she informed briskly, nodding across the room. 'There's an *en suite* bathroom through that door. I'll give you a set of keys for the house and surgery. And there's a file of useful local information on the dressing-table about shops, services, local attractions, that kind of thing. And maps.'

'Thank you, Hannah, I'm sure I shall be very comfortable.'

She saw his gaze take in every detail of the room. 'Good. Let me know if there is anything you need.'

'I will, believe me.'

His throaty promise, accompanied by the glint of laughter in those dark, watchful eyes had her backing towards the door. 'I'll leave you to settle in.'

'Are you on call today?' he queried, detaining her.

'No, why?'

He dropped his bag on the bed and turned to face her. 'I need a shower and a change of clothes but I thought it might be a good day for you to show me round the surgery. It will be quiet, yes?'

'Yes.' The rest of the day stretched ahead in terrifying fashion. What on earth was she going to do about him? A visit to the surgery would certainly fill in some of the time with official activities. 'A good idea.'

'Then shall I meet you downstairs in an hour or so?'

'Fine.'

Hannah felt anything but fine as, having spent an hour in the sanctuary of her room, fretting over the turn of events, she now found herself walking briskly down the road with Nic towards the surgery a mile from the house. Set in a gentle valley and surrounded by wooded hills, Lochanrig was an attractive and well-equipped village. The main street curved gently and buildings lined both sides—houses, shops, the pub, chemist, post office, Allan Pollock's garage, and at the far end from the surgery was the village school. Sheltered by the hills, it was an idyllic setting with its loch, rolling farmland, woods and the small river that flowed south, down from the hills.

'This is a very beautiful area.'

She glanced at Nic and saw he was looking around with interest. 'Yes, we are very lucky. The community might be quite scattered, but it is very friendly and close-knit.'

'I shall look forward to meeting everyone.' His dark gaze turned to her and he smiled. 'So, tell me more about how you came to be here in Lochanrig.'

'It's very much a family concern,' she explained, grateful to have something neutral to discuss. 'The practice was started by my grandfather nearly seventy years ago. My father was born here and he became a doctor, working with my grandfather and then taking over the practice. My mother was a practice nurse and worked with my father for many years. I was born here, too. The new purpose-built surgery was built ten years ago and provides a good range of facilities. After I finished my training, and with the retirement of my father's partner in the practice, I came home to take my place here.'

'You must have enjoyed working together.'

Hannah looked steadfastly ahead. 'We did. Unfortunately it was not to be for very long.'

'What happened, Hannah?' he queried after a few moments of silence, his voice soft with concern, something about the way he pronounced her name sending a disturbing shiver along her spine.

'My mother was killed in a hit-and-run accident four years ago and, sadly, my father suffered a fatal heart attack in his car a year later,' she informed him, giving the bare details but divulging nothing of the horror of events.

'I am so sorry.'

'Thank you.'

His sympathy sounded genuine, but his accompanying gesture, placing a consoling hand on her back, had her mental alarm bells clanging. Her defence mechanism springing unconsciously into action, she stepped hastily away from his touch.

She sensed his hesitation, knew he was aware of her rejection. 'And you've been running things since then?' he finally asked.

'Yes. With locum cover. And an excellent staff.'

'Do—?'

'This is the surgery,' she interrupted, thankful for an excuse to forestall further conversation. 'I'll show you the alarm system. It's key-operated but we have a code number which we change regularly.'

'You keep medications on site?'

'The usual. Patient prescriptions are obtained from the local pharmacy.'

Once inside, Nic stopped to inspect the board in the spacious reception area that displayed photos of the team of staff. 'This will help me until I remember who everyone is.'

Hannah waited while he examined the pictures, realising that the photograph of her looked severe and she was the only person not smiling. The annoying grin on his face as he turned to her raised her irritation and made her wonder if he had noticed, too.

'As you can see, we have two receptionists, including Kirsty who doubles as my practice manager. There are two district nurses, a practice nurse and a midwife.'

Nic nodded, looking back at the photographs. 'You also have support staff?'

'Yes, we can outsource anything that is needed. The physiotherapist runs a clinic here once a week and we have a counsellor who comes in two days a month,' Hannah confirmed, before moving on.

Nic's examination of the surgery was equally thorough. Appointment system, patients' records, staffroom, small kitchen, nurses' and visiting practitioner rooms, a quiet room sometimes needed for troubled patients, small play area for children, treatment room and, finally, the consulting rooms.

'You'll be in here,' Hannah said, opening the door to what had once been her father's domain. She hadn't been able to move in herself, but it no longer troubled her to have others use it.

'You have excellent facilities here,' Nic praised, walking across the room and widening the slats of the blind at the window with the fingers of one hand. 'Great views also!'

'I doubt you'll get much time to appreciate that with the patient workload we have at the moment.'

Hannah regretted her asperity when she saw one eyebrow rise and his lips quirk in a smile. 'I won't shirk my duties, I promise you.'

'Fine.' Feeling foolish, she watched as he sat at the desk, already looking as if he belonged there, damn him! 'There will be some night and weekend calls on a rota basis, otherwise it is customary general practice work—daily surgeries, clinics and home visits. I'm arranging a car for you.'

'Thank you, Hannah.'

Ignoring the disturbing smile, she concentrated on matters at hand. 'Perhaps I should show you the computer system.'

'OK.'

Was he always so good-natured and equable? she wondered

sourly, realising this had not been her best idea as she had to stand far too close to him while she ran through the standard practice procedures for recording patient details, follow-ups, requesting tests and consultations with hospitals or specialists, writing prescriptions and so on. Surely it was imagination that she could feel his body heat across the distance that separated them? She could certainly detect the sensual and disturbing aroma of his aftershave. Sandalwood, she thought. Not that she was a connoisseur of men's fragrances. This was ridiculous, she had to be losing her mind. He leaned forward, brushing against her as he experimented with some of her directions. Uncomfortable, she drew back, alarmed at how breathless she suddenly felt.

'That all seems fine,' Nic confirmed, and if he had noticed her reaction he thankfully chose to make no comment. 'I can always shout, if I get stuck.'

'Of course.'

He swivelled round in the chair, watching her. 'So, did you always want to be a GP?'

Hannah shrugged. 'I toyed with the idea of trauma once but…'

'What happened?'

'How do you mean?'

She saw Nic frown and told herself not to be so jumpy, or to imagine ulterior motives where none existed.

'I just wondered why you had come back here to be a GP.'

'Mum and Dad needed me. The practice needed me.'

'And what did you need?'

To be safe, she admitted to herself, but no way was she telling him that. 'I just need to do my job.'

'You are not what I expected.'

'Excuse me?' Hannah bristled.

'I imagined someone in sole charge of running a practice like this would be older.'

'I'm a good doctor.'

'I don't doubt your abilities, Hannah,' he replied, a thread of chastisement in his voice. 'I meant simply that the responsibility must have been hard for you, especially in the circumstances, when your loss was so raw.'

Hannah swallowed down a prickle of emotion at his sympathetic understanding. 'I just did what was necessary in order to carry on. That's all any of us can do, isn't it?'

'Yes. It is.'

His words were soft, laced with unexpected emotion. Hannah's gaze met his and she nearly gasped at the anguish that bruised his dark eyes before he blinked and looked away from her. What had happened in his own life to cause him such pain? Questions hovered but remained unasked. Aside from the fact that she hated people questioning her about her personal life, she had no wish to come to know Nic more closely, or to find more common ground with him than their shared profession.

'Is there anything else you wish to see here?' she asked instead, determined to draw things back to a more comfortable level.

'No.' He rose to his feet with the sinuous grace of a jungle cat. 'Let's go.'

'What made you interested in spending time in a small rural practice in Scotland?' Hannah queried as they walked back to the house.

'My mama's father was a Scot and I have always wanted to spend some time in his country. The remoteness does not concern me,' he reassured her with a smile, looking towards the hills with an expression of contentment on his face. 'I feel sure my stay in Lochanrig will provide me with all the challenges I need, both in my working life and whatever leisure time is available to me. I love to walk, cycle, climb...' His dark gaze met hers. 'There will be plenty here to hold my attention.'

Hannah hoped he didn't for a moment imagine turning any of his attention onto her. She mulled over his words with a frown, thankful that she saw little of Nic for the rest of the afternoon. He went for a walk, familiarising himself with the village, and then spent time in his room, apparently looking at the local maps and other information she had left for him. It was only when he came downstairs and joined her in the kitchen that she realised with alarm that the whole evening still stretched ahead of them.

'If you have plans to go out, don't let me being here stop you,' he remarked, as if reading her mind.

'Pardon?'

'A date or anything.'

'No, no, I—'

She snapped off her words. There was no way she was going to tell him that she didn't do dates, that she had no real social life to speak of. But now she was stuck here. Why on earth hadn't she just agreed and used the excuse to escape for a while? And go where, to do what? she taunted herself. Sit in the car in the dark?

Instead, she found herself preparing bowls of home-made soup, which they ate at the kitchen table with fresh, chunky bread and then fresh fruit to follow. Several times she was aware of him watching her and felt her tension and awareness increase. Unable to prevent it, her gaze strayed to him. He sat with his head resting on one hand, his fingers sunk in the thickness of his hair. For a crazy moment she had the compelling urge to run her own fingers through it. What would it feel like against her skin? She looked away hastily, getting herself under control. What on earth was the matter with her? And why did he keep looking at her like that? The rest of the evening was going to be torture at this rate.

Uncomfortable, Hannah cleared her throat. 'How come you speak English so fluently?' she asked, searching for some safe subject to break the difficult silence.

'My grandpapa encouraged my mama to speak English from childhood and she did the same for me.'

They chatted for a while about the village and Hannah filled him in on the staff and information on some of their regular patients and more tricky cases. But all the while she felt on edge, unsettled, far too aware of her unwelcome new house guest and colleague. She was relieved when the telephone rang and she rose to her feet.

'Excuse me.'

His meal finished, Nic watched as Hannah moved to the phone in the hall. What flustered her so much? She had been on edge all day, had never relaxed or lost that flicker of fear that shadowed her eyes.

'Anything wrong?' he asked when she returned to the kitchen, a frown on her face.

'I have to go out after all.'

'I thought you weren't on call.'

'I'm not, officially, but that was Dr Robert MacKenzie, who is cover for tonight. He's stuck with a difficult birth about fifteen miles away and now there's an urgent call to a sick child just down the road,' she explained, pulling on her coat. 'It's easier if I go.'

Nic rose to his feet. 'I'll come with you.'

'But—'

'I have to start work some time.'

He could see she wasn't pleased but she wasted no more time arguing. Grabbing his bag and his jacket, he joined her at the car.

'These are patients of yours?' he questioned once they were on their way.

'Yes. Claire Carlyle is a single mum in her early twenties. She doesn't call us out for nothing. She has two children, Tom, who is six, and Faye, who is two. It's the little girl we're going to see.'

'And Claire, has she anyone to help?'

'No. Her parents threw her out when she was expecting Tom.'

Nic heard the frustration and disapproval in her voice. 'And the boyfriend?'

'Took off with someone else about six months ago.'

'Charming.' Nic scowled, sharing the anger and sympathy Hannah betrayed. 'It sounds as if she's had a hard time.'

'Indeed. We're here.'

Nic followed as Hannah led the way up a grubby flight of

stairs in a grey, bleak building to a flat on the second floor. The door stood ajar and she pushed it open and went in, calling Claire's name. A harassed, anxious-looking girl greeted them. She looked anaemic and in need of a good meal, Nic assessed, concerned at her thinness and her pallor.

'Oh, Dr Frost, I'm so sorry to trouble you,' the girl cried, wringing her hands in agitation. 'Faye's been poorly all afternoon and I just got scared.'

'It's all right, Claire, you did the right thing,' Hannah soothed, surprising Nic with her complete change in manner.

'She's through here. I didn't know what to do. A neighbour has had Tom in to play with her kids.'

They followed the worried mother through the untidy flat to a tiny back bedroom where the young child grizzled in a cot. Hannah set down her bag and took off her coat, glancing towards him.

'Claire, this is Dr di Angelis, he's going to be working with the practice for a while.'

Frightened blue eyes met his. 'Oh, OK.'

'Hello, Claire.' He smiled, stepping forward. 'I know you must be scared but we'll do our best to help your little one. May I take a look at her?'

He sensed Hannah's surprise, but his focus was on the young mother. When she nodded, he smiled again and, opening his bag, took out his stethoscope and digital thermometer, asking a few questions as he readied himself.

'Faye has had a fever?'

'Yes,' Claire confirmed. 'And she's been crying and crying.'

'Has she vomited at all? Got a rash?'

Claire nodded. 'She's been sick a couple of times. But she hasn't got an actual rash. I just didn't know what to do.'

'You were right to call us,' Hannah reassured again.

'Poor *bambina*.' Nic soothed the fractious child, frowning as he made a thorough assessment. The skin was blotchy, although there was no sign of the purpura rash often associated with meningitis. The child's breathing was rapid, though, and she exhibited some joint stiffness, along with photophobia, resistance to light. Concerned, he looked up and met Hannah's gaze, his voice soft. 'Call an ambulance, please.'

'Do you think it is meningitis?' Claire fretted as Hannah took out her mobile phone and made the call without question.

'It is better to be safe than sorry.' Nic spoke softly, trying not to alarm the young woman unduly. 'The signs are worrying and I would feel happier if Faye is properly checked out. OK? Is your daughter allergic to penicillin?'

Claire shook her head, seeming uncertain. 'I don't think so. No.'

'Good. We will give her an injection now and then she will be transferred to hospital.'

'Can I go with her?'

'Yes, of course.'

'The ambulance is on its way,' Hannah announced, turning to Claire with a smile. 'Would you like me to help you pack a few things you might need to take with you? Dr di Angelis will look after Faye.'

Tears escaping down her pale cheeks, Claire nodded. As Hannah ushered her out, Nic returned his attention to the sick child, administering the injection of penicillin, hoping they had caught things in time.

Twenty minutes later they returned home, Faye safely on her way to hospital, a frightened Claire accompanying her in the ambulance, and the neighbour promising to care for Tom.

'Poor girl,' Nic sighed as he followed Hannah indoors.

'You were very good with her.'

Nic smiled at Hannah's unexpected praise, even if it had been delivered in those cool, controlled tones. 'Thank you.'

'Coffee?'

'Please. Shall I make it?' he volunteered, moving towards her.

'It's OK.'

She stepped quickly away from him and busied herself with

the task, keeping her back to him. He had learned something this evening, Nic reflected, a frown of consideration on his face as he leant against the counter and watched her. Doctor Hannah and private Hannah appeared to be two very different personalities. She had been softer, warmer with her patients. And it was the first time he had seen her smile. It had been as if someone had switched a light on inside her, transforming her whole face, and it had brought a flicker of awareness inside him. As soon as the ambulance had left, though, she had gone back to her serious, prickly self. Now she seemed paralysed by discomfort. Was it just him, or was she like this with other people? Intrigued, he vowed to unravel the mysteries of this woman in the days and weeks ahead.

He accepted the coffee she handed him and smiled as he gently chinked their mugs together. 'Here's to our new partnership.'

Varied emotions chased each other across those expressive eyes. Doubt, annoyance, resignation...but always that underlying shadow of fear that troubled him.

'Drink up,' he instructed, keeping his tone light and teasing. 'It looks as if you are stuck with me, Hannah!'

'So it would seem—for now,' she allowed, her voice cool, her reluctance and disapproval evident. 'Welcome to Lochanrig, Dr di Angelis.'

A slow smile curved his mouth. 'Thank you, Dr Frost. I'm sure my stay here with you is going to be a very interesting one indeed. For both of us.'

CHAPTER THREE

'KIRSTY, this is our new doctor, Nic di Angelis,' Hannah announced brusquely as she walked towards the reception desk at the surgery on Monday morning, Nic close behind her.

She had the satisfaction of seeing the surprise and chagrin on her practice manager's face as Kirsty's gaze slid guiltily from hers and towards Nic. Clearing her throat, the older woman smiled.

'Hello, Nic, nice to have you join us.' Kirsty's welcome was accompanied by a rare broad smile. 'We didn't expect you so soon.'

'So I have discovered.' Hannah bristled as Nic flicked her a grin before returning his attention to Kirsty and shaking hands. 'It is a pleasure to meet you, also.'

Hannah looked on with a scowl as her usually straight-talking manager, wary of new people, simpered over their new doctor. 'Kirsty, I'm sure Nic doesn't need babysitting, so I suggest we divide up the morning surgery and you pass some consultations over to him. Is that all right with you, Nic?' she added as politely as she could.

'Fine, *cara*,' he replied, amusement glittering in his eyes. 'It is nice to know you have confidence in my skills.'

'I don't think your competence as a doctor has ever been in doubt.'

Looking from one to the other, clearly aware of the tension, Kirsty's eyebrows rose. 'Is everything all right?'

'Fine,' Hannah stated before Nic could speak, planning to take her manager to task in private. 'It will be a week or two before we have a car for you, so I suggest you accompany me on some house calls to learn the lie of the land.'

'I shall be delighted, Hannah,' Nic agreed with a mock-solicitousness that set her teeth on edge.

'It would also be a good idea if you went out with the district nurses sometimes.' The more often the better, she added silently, welcoming the prospect of getting rid of him. 'Kirsty, perhaps you could arrange that? And assisting with some of the clinics?'

'Of course. What about a staff meeting?'

Hannah frowned. 'A staff meeting?'

'To introduce Nic to everyone,' Kirsty tutted.

'I see. Well…' Hannah floundered, uncomfortably aware of Nic's amused gaze on her and of her own desperate need to put some distance between them. 'Yes, I suppose that would be a good idea,' she allowed grudgingly. 'Perhaps you could see to it?'

'My pleasure.' Kirsty grinned.

Hannah was relieved to have matters settled. 'Fine. Now, can we check the patient list and see who can go where?'

With Nic standing far too close, Hannah inched away and tried to concentrate on the task at hand, dividing up the morning appointments. She glanced at his profile while he was occupied talking with Kirsty. He had the kind of eyelashes many women paid good money to fake. They were long and lustrous, fringing eyes the colour of rich, melted chocolate, warm and tempting… Dear God! Whatever had come over her?

'Hannah?'

She blinked and realised both Kirsty and Nic were staring at her. 'I'm sorry, I was thinking about something,' she excused herself, warmth washing her face as she avoided Nic's gaze.

'I asked if you were happy with the assignment of the morning list,' Kirsty repeated, a quizzical expression on her face.

'Yes, of course,' Hannah said. She hadn't been following the discussion at all. What had happened to her in the last twenty-four hours? Why had Nic's arrival addled her brain? Pulling herself together, she picked up her box of notes and stepped back. 'Shall we get on, then?'

Smiling at Kirsty, Nic collected his own pile of notes and turned to follow her. 'We set to work, Hannah.'

'Let me know if you have any problems.'

'Don't worry,' he chided softly as they paused outside the door of her consulting room. Holding her gaze for a long moment, his own expression intense, he touched one finger to the tip of her nose before walking on towards his own door. 'Everything will be fine.'

Escaping to the privacy of her room, she closed the door and leant back against it for a moment, wondering what Nic had meant. She sensed there was much more behind his words than the success of morning surgery. Her legs unusually shaky, Hannah crossed to her desk and sat down. Disturbed at the way her skin still tingled, she rubbed her hand over her nose, wanting to erase the unexpected and unwanted feel of his touch. Why had he done that? Why did he appear so in control while her whole world had suddenly spun horribly out of kilter?

Picking up the telephone, she called through to Reception. 'Kirsty, I'd like a word in my room, please.'

A rap on the door announced Kirsty's arrival a few moments later. Hannah glanced up and beckoned her in.

'I've introduced Nic to Morag,' Kirsty informed her before Hannah could begin her inquisition. 'As practice nurse, she's going to be available should he need a chaperone for any consultations.'

Hannah frowned, knowing she should have thought of that herself. 'Thank you, Kirsty. Sit down, please,' she invited, tension roiling within her.

'Hannah—'

Unprepared to be mollified before she had even had her say, Hannah held up her hand. 'Why did you continue to allow me to believe our new locum was female even after you had spoken to Nic on the telephone? When exactly did you plan to tell me? It was very embarrassing, being confronted on my own doorstep and having no idea who he was.'

'I planned to tell you before he arrived. I wasn't expecting him to be here until today or tomorrow. I'm sorry if that caused you any difficulties—that wasn't my intention,' Kirsty said, not looking as contrite as Hannah would have wished.

'So what was your intention?'

'To obtain an excellent locum doctor for the practice.'

Hannah's eyebrows rose. 'And you think I don't want the same thing?' she challenged, her annoyance growing.

'Listen, Hannah. We were in a desperate situation and having you working beyond endurance alone was impacting not only on your own health but also on your patients and all the rest of the staff,' Kirsty explained, not mincing her words. 'You have to admit that you find all manner of excuses to avoid employing men, and if I had told you last week that Nicola di Angelis was a man, you would have done the same thing, holding out who knows how long in the hope of finding another woman locum. Well, I'm sorry, but we didn't have the luxury of going through all that,' she continued mercilessly. 'Locums are hard to find, good ones are like gold dust. I don't know what the issue is, it isn't my business unless it affects work, but my duty is to the well-being of the whole practice, has been so for the twenty years I worked for your parents and now for you. I did what I thought was right for everyone, for the sake of the patients and the rest of us, and I suggest that whatever your problem is, you put it aside once and for all and appreciate what an excellent doctor we have for the next six months.'

Shocked, Hannah closed her eyes, feeling both furious and chastened, unable to deal with the underlying issues to which Kirsty referred, scared her practice manager had struck too close to the bone, that she had allowed her own personal prejudices to adversely affect her professional judgement.

'Hannah?' Kirsty sounded concerned, her voice softer. 'I'm sorry.'

'I appreciate you were acting out of concern for the practice but I would be grateful if you would not keep things from me in future,' she managed, stiff with tension, unable to meet her manager's all-seeing gaze.

'Of course.'

Clasping her hands together on her lap, Hannah took a deep breath. 'That will be all. Please, send the first patient in when you are ready.'

'Sure,' Kirsty agreed, but it was clear from her tone her feathers had been ruffled by the terse dismissal.

'If you get a minute, could you phone the hospital and see if there is any news on little Faye Carlyle? She was admitted last night with suspected meningitis.'

'Oh, no, poor Claire,' Kirsty sympathised with concern, her strop forgotten. 'She's had a lot to deal with, that girl. I'll let you know if there's any news.'

'Thanks.'

Trying to set her confrontation with Kirsty and her jumbled thoughts about Nic aside, Hannah switched on her computer, straightened her desk and prepared for her first patient.

Morning surgery was finished in half the usual time and, as far as Hannah knew, Nic had not experienced any problems. Relieved, she lingered in her consulting room far longer than was necessary, unaccountably nervous about joining the others. Eventually, unable to delay any longer, she slipped into the staffroom as surreptitiously as possible, but as she poured herself a cup of coffee, the hairs on the back of her neck prickled and she knew Nic was looking at her.

'What part of Italy are you from, Nic?' Shona Brown, one of the district nurses, asked him.

'The region of Umbria. A small village between Assisi and the Le Marche border,' he informed.

'But you've been working in various places, haven't you?' Kirsty questioned. 'You were in Canada, as well as the UK?'

'Yes, I have enjoyed my travels and new experiences.'

His response was friendly, but Hannah sensed his discomfort answering questions about himself. Maybe she recognised it because she shared it? Either way, she found herself stepping in, assuring herself it was because she was impatient to return to work.

'Are you ready for house calls, Nic?'

'I need just a moment to collect my things,' he replied, rising to his feet and washing his mug at the sink. 'I'll meet you outside.'

'Fine.'

As he left the room, Hannah finished her coffee and washed her own mug, uncomfortable at the excited chat around her.

'Wow! He's amazing,' Debbie enthused.

'And very good with the patients,' Morag said approvingly. 'I went in to help on a couple of occasions and was very impressed.'

'We've certainly hit the jackpot this time,' Kirsty declared with satisfaction, her tone raising Hannah's hackles again, but everyone else chorused their agreement on Nic's virtues.

Irritated, Hannah tossed down the teatowel she had used to dry her mug and turned to leave. She certainly didn't want to keep hearing how wonderful Nic was, or join some unofficial fan club for the man!

'Don't you like him, Hannah?' Jane asked. 'He seems so lovely.'

The young receptionist's soft enquiry startled her. She hadn't realised her antipathy was so apparent. Aware they were all waiting for her answer, Hannah shrugged. 'I've not really thought about it,' she fibbed. 'As long as he's a good doctor, that's all that matters.'

Disgruntled, she left the room to collect her coat, bag and the notes she needed for the home visits. It seemed Nic had charmed everyone in the short time he had been there. And it was genuine, not just an act. He was simply a nice man. Which made it even more important for her to keep up her guard, she decided, afraid that she could be in danger of liking him far too much.

* * *

Nic leant against the car, waiting for Hannah to join him. He suspected she had understood his discomfort with talking about himself back there. But he sensed they were two of a kind, not that she would ever admit that, he knew. He had no idea why she had buried herself in her work, what she was hiding from, but he recognised it because he had done the same these past two years.

He straightened as Hannah left the surgery and walked briskly towards him, dressed in a sober dark grey trouser suit, her hair restrained as usual in a tight plait. There was a grim expression on her face that didn't bode well for an easing of the atmosphere between them. He wondered if she had any idea how expressive those amazing eyes were. It was doubtful. She would hate to know he could tell pretty much everything she was thinking. He chuckled.

'Is something funny?'

Realising his chuckle must have been audible, he glanced at her and saw her fiery expression. 'No, Hannah, I was just thinking of something.'

She looked at him suspiciously for a moment. 'I thought you would like to know that Kirsty has been in touch with the hospital and Faye Carlyle does have meningitis but is responding to treatment.'

'That's great.' Nic smiled with relief. 'I hope she comes through without any lasting problems.'

'Indeed.'

As Hannah drove out of the car park and headed away from the village, Nic tried to stop thinking about her and turn his attention to the work ahead. 'Where are we going?'

'To see Joanne McStay and her mother,' Hannah informed him. 'Mrs McStay has been poorly for a long time with Alzheimer's disease. She's quite frail now and difficult at times. Joanne gave up an option to go to university to get a job and stay at home to care for her mother. This last year she's had to give up the job as well.'

'And there's no other family to help?'

'No.'

Nic thought quietly for a moment. 'So are we going to see Joanne, Mrs McStay or both?'

'Both,' she agreed, and he noticed her flicker of surprise. 'Why?'

'You seem rightly as concerned for Joanne as for her mama. It must be very hard for her.'

'It is. She's very isolated and I don't have as much time to give her as I would like.'

'Why don't you let me have a chat with Joanne while you see her mama?'

He saw her frown as she considered his suggestion. 'What do you have in mind?'

'I'll talk to her about things we can do to help. What options are available here? Is there help at home? How about respite care?'

'Believe me, I've tried,' Hannah assured him, frustration in her voice as she explained what was available locally and the choices she had already discussed. 'Joanne won't hear of it.'

Nic said no more as they arrived at the small cottage on the outskirts of a nearby village. As they waited at the front door, he heard bolts being undone before it was finally opened and they were being shown inside by a tall, thin girl who looked on the point of exhaustion.

'Joanne, this is Dr di Angelis.' Hannah introduced them with a smile for the girl. 'He's just joined the practice for a short while.'

'Hello.'

Joanne's voice was listless but Nic smiled and shook her hand, finding her skin cool and dry to the touch. 'Nice to meet you, Joanne.'

'How have things been?' Hannah asked, taking off her coat and draping it over a chair.

'A bit grim,' the girl allowed, her voice flat. 'We had a bad night. Mum was up a lot, trying to get out, and she wouldn't settle. She's been asleep this morning, though.'

'You look as if you could do with a good sleep yourself, Joanne.' Hannah smiled sympathetically.

The girl gave a mirthless laugh. 'Not much chance of that, Doctor.'

Nic met Hannah's concerned gaze. 'Joanne, Dr Frost is going to see your mama, and we'll sit here and have a chat about things—is that all right?'

Joanne looked puzzled and awkward as she gazed from one to the other. 'Well, I suppose so…'

'I won't be long. I know the way.' Hannah smiled, picked up her bag and left the room.

Encouraging the girl to sit down, Nic took a place on the shabby sofa next to her. 'Things must be very hard for you. It's not easy, is it, caring for someone?'

'No.' Joanne's chin wobbled. 'But she's my mum. I can't just leave her.'

'I understand and I think you are doing a great job, but there are things we can do to help make it easier for you.'

'She doesn't want strangers coming in to her. I ought to be able to manage,' she cried, tears slipping between her lashes.

Nic handed her a tissue. 'It's not wrong to need help, Joanne. Neither is it wrong to feel resentful or angry at your mama and the situation you are in. It all seems very unfair sometimes, no?'

'I feel so selfish and guilty,' she admitted, crying openly now.

'That is normal,' Nic soothed, holding her hand. 'It is a very difficult thing you are doing and it doesn't mean you care less.' He looked up as Hannah came quietly back into the room and sat down, a look of amazement on her face. 'Dr Frost has told me you've been coping so well in desperately difficult circumstances.'

'I just don't know what to do. Sometimes I don't think I can cope any more,' the girl sobbed, accepting a fresh tissue.

'You don't have to cope on your own. But if you don't take care of yourself, of your own health, you are not going to be able to help either your mama or yourself, no?'

'I suppose not.' She looked up at them. 'Sometimes I think it would be better if Mum went into care, but I promised her I wouldn't let that happen.'

'We don't have to do that, Joanne, not for a while anyway, but the choices are getting fewer, you know that,' Hannah told her softly.

Joanne nodded, her hazel eyes sad. 'What can I do, then?'

'You need to think about yourself, for a little while at least,' Nic advised. 'If you allowed us to arrange some respite care, just for a week or two, your mama would be well cared for and you could have a break, even go away for a holiday. You would feel so much better and more able to cope when you came back.'

'Do you think so?' Joanne asked, a flicker of hope on her face.

Hannah smiled at her. 'I'm sure of it. And when you come back we can make sure you have some daily help and more regular breaks. How does that sound?'

'Amazing!' she admitted, laughing and sniffing at the same time.

'And you don't have to be alone,' Nic advised, glancing at Hannah for confirmation. 'There is a support group where you can be in touch with other carers coping with Alzheimer's, who will understand what you are going through, is that not right, Dr Frost?'

'It is. A local group would help, Joanne, and there are national ones, too.'

'Thanks.' Joanne wiped her eyes and gave a watery smile. 'OK. Will you see what's available? I thought I could cope, but it is getting so much harder.'

'We'll do all we can to help you, Joanne,' Hannah promised.

Nic rose to his feet, assisting Hannah with her coat, noting how swiftly she moved away from him. Filing the moment away for another time, he turned to smile again at Joanne. 'You can always ring the surgery if you need anything or you just want to talk.'

'Thank you both. I feel much better.'

Holding her bag in front of her, like a shield, Nic thought, Hannah walked towards the front door. 'Your mum's still sleeping, Joanne, so I've not disturbed her. You have a rest while you can and we'll be in touch soon with some proposals for you, and someone will pop back in a day or two to see your mum.'

Back in the car, Hannah was quiet for a while as she drove them away from the McStays' cottage. They had covered a couple of miles before she threw him a brief glance, curiosity and puzzlement in her eyes.

'I don't know what you did, but thank you for bringing Joanne round.'

'Let's hope it works for her.'

They had several other routine house calls and Nic used the time not only to begin to know more of his new patient base but also to observe Hannah at work, impressed with her professionalism, her skills as a doctor and her rapport with her patients. As they returned to the surgery in time for lunch, he wondered again at the two very different sides to her character.

'Feel free to go home and eat if you want to,' Hannah offered, turning her car into its parking place. 'The village has a good bakery or a pub if you prefer.'

He undid his seat belt and turned to look at her. 'And what do you do?'

'I usually just have a sandwich at my desk. Plenty of paperwork to do,' she added, sounding as if she was trying to be casual.

'Hannah?'

'What?'

He waited in silence until she reluctantly turned her head and met his gaze, her green eyes anxious.

'Why are you afraid?'

'I'm not,' she refuted, her eyes betraying her words. 'I don't know what you mean.'

'I think you do. I've known you a little more than twenty-four hours but I can see what a good doctor you are, that you give yourself to your patients and care deeply about people. But you don't let anyone close to you, do you? Not to the private Hannah.'

Her hands tightened on the steering-wheel, her knuckles whitening. 'I have a busy and fulfilling career, security. I don't need anything or anyone else in my life.'

'Why?'

'It's just the way I am.'

'Or the way you have become?'

He knew he had touched a raw nerve by the flash of temper that momentarily replaced the fear in her eyes. 'You are not here to psychoanalyse me, Dr di Angelis,' she snapped, gathering her things together and reaching for the doorhandle.

'I don't want to be your therapist, Hannah.'

She glanced back at him, confused, troubled. 'Then what do you want?'

'To be your friend.'

'Well, you can't.' If anything, his words served only to increase her alarm. Dragging her startled gaze from his, she flung open the door and all but scrambled out. 'Excuse me, I have work to do.'

He walked beside her towards the building, sensing her tension and discomfort. 'Of course. It's always work, isn't it? Especially when the going gets tough. But believe me, Hannah, it doesn't make things better or take the pain away.'

'Just do the job you came here for, Nic, and leave me alone.'

He watched her go, concerned at the suspicion of moisture in her eyes, the constant battle she had to keep up the coldness and the front. Her inner pain and loneliness were almost palpable to him and, whatever her protests, there was no way he was going to turn his back on that. Pain was something he was all too familiar with. He closed his eyes, fighting down his own memories, his own nightmare. The sting of pain was mellowing, he realised, but he would never forget.

Two years was a long time, and he'd moved about since then, afraid to put down roots again. He hadn't been involved with a woman in all that time, he hadn't been interested. But meeting

Hannah had brought back emotions and desires he'd thought lost for ever. Now, for the first time, he was attracted to another woman. Not just attracted, he admitted with a self-mocking smile. From the moment he had first seen her, Hannah had stirred his senses and brought desire stabbing back to him.

Perhaps he had pushed too hard too soon today, but he could tell that Hannah was special, and she was hurting. Slowly but surely, he was going to use this time here to help them both to heal.

Still smarting and unsettled after her confrontation with Nic in the car on Monday, Hannah did her best to stay out of his way as much as possible, both at the surgery and at home, as the week progressed. The times he had been out to house calls with her, or when he had insisted on accompanying her on any night calls until he could do them alone, he had been polite and friendly, and there had been no more probing questions. She should have been relieved, but Nic didn't have to say anything to make her feel uncomfortable and out of sorts. He accomplished that just by existing. It was silly, but she couldn't help feeling a bit miffed at how swiftly he had fitted in, how popular he had become with both staff and patients. Kirsty, usually cautious about people until they had proved themselves, had taken to Nic from the beginning, clearly feeling justified by her own role in securing his employment.

'We've had people making appointments who've not seen a doctor for years,' she said, beaming when Hannah returned to the surgery late on Friday morning.

Hannah frowned. 'I don't understand.'

'Nic. Having a male doctor again. Some people prefer it.'

'No one said anything to me.'

'Well, they wouldn't, Hannah,' the other woman pointed out gently, making her think again of their confrontation on Monday. 'They all like and respect you so much.'

Disturbed, Hannah collected her patient notes and messages

before seeking the privacy of her consulting room. Was Kirsty right? And what was it about Nic that made people trust him so rapidly, to feel they could unburden themselves? He wasn't just a pretty face, he was also an exceedingly good doctor, an asset to the practice.

She started when a tap on her door drew her from her reverie and she sat back nervously as Nic came into her room. How could she have forgotten he was already here, taking early surgery?

'Have you got a minute?' he asked, his expression thoughtful.

'I have now,' she replied briskly, trying to get her wayward thoughts back under control, 'but I have the health board meeting this afternoon.'

'I hadn't forgotten.'

He smiled, one of those half amused, half knowing smiles that brought a knot of unfamiliar awareness to her stomach. Unbidden, her gaze lingered on his mouth. The breath locked in her throat as she helplessly studied the sensual curve of his lips. That mouth was sinful.

'What can I do for you?' she managed, her voice more fractured than usual.

'Do we have access to sex therapy?'

Momentarily startled, her mind completely on the wrong path, Hannah bristled. 'Are you trying to be funny?'

'Excuse me?' A rare flash of annoyance glinted in his eyes. 'Far from it, Hannah. I am trying my best to help a troubled patient who is waiting in my consulting room as we speak.'

She blushed, chastened and embarrassed, and turned to search for a card in her desk drawer. 'Sarah Baxter is our visiting counsellor. She'll know of a specialist and can either refer your patient on or you can discuss it with her at her clinic next week'

'Thank you.'

His tone was cool, the look her gave her so penetrating that it made her cringe. She hated it when he looked at her like that, as if he could see right inside her soul. And she feared he saw too damn much. Tense, expecting him to make some further comment, she was surprised when he took the card from her and turned away without another word, quietly closing the door behind him.

Hannah buried her head in her hands. Why did she keep doing and saying all the wrong things around him? Something about Nic made her act out of character and feel things, think things she had never wanted or expected to feel or think about. Things she had suppressed for a long, long time, ever since… No! She was *not* going there. Had she learned none of the lessons of the past? She had moved on, found her niche, made her choices. So why was her body now letting her down? Why was she starting to feel things for Nic which she knew to be a lie?

Trying to concentrate on her patients over her lunchtime surgery was difficult, but Hannah was determined not to allow Nic to invade every area of her existence. She was soon involved with a list of usual complaints from stomach upsets to skin problems, worries about a mystery lump for which she arranged an emergency referral, and then an elderly lady with a persistent leg ulcer.

She was relieved when her final consultation came to an end. 'Come and see me again next week, Moira, and we'll see how things are looking then.'

'I will, Dr Frost, and thank you.'

Hannah opened the door to show the patient out just as Nic walked by.

'Is that the new doctor?' Moira asked, after Nic had smiled at them and closed the door of his room.

'Yes, that's right.'

'Italian, I understand. I've heard he's very good. He certainly looks a picture, doesn't he?' She grinned. 'If that's what eating spaghetti and lasagne does for a man, my Ray will be having a rapid change of diet!'

Hannah forced a smile, hiding her irritation as Moira hurried back to Reception to make another appointment and no doubt have a good gossip, she thought with a grimace. What was wrong with everyone in this place? The man had been there a week and all the female population were falling over him. Feeling grumpy and unwilling to acknowledge her own confused feelings where Nic was concerned, she returned to her desk. She had time to mark up her notes and check her emails before it was time to leave for her meeting.

Opening her inbox a while later, she was surprised to find an email waiting for her from Nic. She imagined him sitting in the nearby room, writing to her, and a warm tingle ran through her. Did he know how uncomfortable she was feeling around him? Of course he did. She frowned. He seemed sensitive to everything she was thinking, and it troubled her. Anxious this was going to be about their embarrassing misunderstanding earlier, Hannah tentatively opened the message.

'Do you like pasta?'

A half-smile on her face, she emailed back. *'Yes.'*

Seconds later, a new message arrived. *'Mushrooms?'*

'Not keen. Why?'

'Wait and see!'

She was perversely disappointed there were no further messages but, pressed for time, she dealt with a couple of other emails then logged off and, after briefly stopping at Reception to leave some notes and correspondence with Jane, Hannah set off for her appointment, leaving Nic to handle the last surgery of the day.

The meeting ran on longer than expected and it was after seven when she arrived home, tired and cold. She opened the front door, hearing soft music coming from the kitchen and a delicious aroma filling the air. Frowning, she left her case on the hall chair, hung up her coat and walked to the kitchen door. Dressed in jeans and a jumper, Nic was relaxing at the table, reading a medical journal. He glanced up when she hesitated in the doorway and, closing the magazine, he smiled.

'Hi.'

'You've cooked?' Belatedly, she realised what the emails had been for.

'My speciality. Hungry?'

She was about to deny it, but her stomach betrayed her, giving an audible rumble. Embarrassed, she glanced at Nic and saw his eyes crinkle at the corners as he laughed.

'I think that was a yes,' he said, the intensity of his gaze making her feel both shy and wary.

'Have I got time to change?'

'Of course. How long?'

'Ten minutes?'

'No problem.'

As he rose effortlessly to his feet, Hannah backed out of the door and ran up the stairs. By the time she walked more slowly back down, after a hurried wash and change of clothes, Nic was dishing up the pasta. The table had been laid. He'd even found a candle and lit it, she noticed, suddenly nervous about why he had gone to so much trouble. As he turned to place a dish on the table he stopped and stared at her.

Heat washed through her under the scrutiny of his dark gaze and she shifted anxiously. 'What's wrong?' she queried uneasily.

'Nothing.' She saw him swallow before he looked away from her to set the dish down then he turned back to face her, his slow smile tightening her stomach. 'Nothing, *cara*. I wondered how many days it would be before you relaxed a bit and gave up the power suit morning, noon and night.'

Hannah glanced down in surprise, shocked to discover she had pulled on jeans and a russet-coloured fleece top without thinking, the kind of things she wore off duty when she was alone, although her hair was still held back in its braid.

'I—'

'Don't,' he interrupted. 'It suits you. Sit, yes? The food is ready.'

Uncertain, Hannah sat at the table, sipping a glass of water.

She felt ridiculously panicky. What did Nic want of her? she fretted. He was an excellent doctor, seemed to be a compassionate and thoughtful man…but he was a dangerous one. She would do well to remember that and not let her guard down.

'This is delicious, thank you,' she murmured politely once Nic had sat down across from her and they had started their meal.

'My pleasure.'

Was it her imagination, or did his voice sound even more husky and intimate than usual? Studiously keeping her gaze averted, she searched for something safe to talk about, filling him in on some details from the health meeting, realising she was chattering nervously.

She took another hasty swallow of water. 'Everything OK at afternoon surgery?'

'Yes, fine. Hannah, let's not—'

'I'm sorry about this morning,' she rushed on, without thinking. Out of the corner of her eye she saw Nic frown. 'This morning?'

'Yes, your patient. It's just we don't get much call for that sort of thing.'

'What sort of thing?'

Dear God, what had she done now? 'Um…relationship counselling. I mean…' The words trailed off when she discovered she now had Nic's full attention. Oh, damnation!

'Sex sort of things?'

'Well, yes.' Her heart started thudding uncomfortably against her ribs. Please, please, let the floor open up and swallow her. 'We've not had much demand for that sort of therapy in Lochanrig.'

'I see.'

Did he? She hoped to God he didn't. 'Well, it's just a mechanical act of procreation after all. Nothing to get so bothered about,' she dismissed, her voice heavy with cynicism. She'd never believed all that rubbish about the earth moving and stars exploding. After all, she had experienced how wrong all that nonsense was. Just lies and— Hannah suddenly realised that Nic was staring at her with a look of astonishment on his face, the fork in his hand suspended part way to his mouth. 'What's the matter?'

With careful deliberation he lowered the fork back to his plate, puffing out his cheeks as he released a long, unsteady breath. '*Madre del Dio*,' he muttered, his shocked gaze sliding away from hers.

'Nic?'

'Hannah, I—' He cleared his throat, the fingers of one hand running across his forehead as if he was trying to get his thoughts straight. '*Cara*, are you ser—?'

Whatever he had been about to say was interrupted by the telephone. Shaking his head, he seemed pleased to get away from her as he hurried from the table, and Hannah listened as he talked briefly to the caller, before coming back to the kitchen holding his medical bag.

'I have to go.'

'Do you want me to drive you?'

'No!' he refused, rather too hurriedly, she thought. 'It's a man from an outlying farm bringing someone in with a bad cut. Sounds like stitching is needed. I'm meeting them at the surgery.'

Grateful for the reprieve, she smiled. 'OK. Well, thanks for dinner. It's lovely.'

'Hannah.'

Her tentative smile faded as he walked towards her. 'What?' she murmured, wishing she didn't sound so shaky.

He stopped beside her, his dark gaze burning into hers, and she clenched her hands together in her lap to stop them trembling. 'We'll talk about this another time.'

Over her dead body, she thought, but he silenced any further words and trapped the breath inside her as he reached out and ran a finger across her cheek before turning away and leaving the house.

Hannah swallowed the uncomfortable restriction in her throat, managing to breathe again now she had been freed from his mesmerising presence. Her skin burned from his touch. She raised a hand to her face, covering the spot where his finger had laid its trail of fire. She closed her eyes, scared and confused. If the merest brush of one finger had this effect on her, what on earth would it be like if he really touched her?

No! Her eyes snapped open. No, that was never going to happen. She wouldn't let it happen. She couldn't. Not ever.

CHAPTER FOUR

'IS NIC OK?'

Stifling a sigh, Hannah glanced up from the paperwork she was going through during her lunch-break and noted the concern on Kirsty's face. 'I assume so. Why do you ask?'

'Well, he's just come back from his rounds and he looks odd.'

'What do you mean, odd?'

Kirsty frowned again, glancing down the corridor before closing the door and crossing to stand by the desk. 'I don't know. Kind of...furtive.'

'Furtive?'

'Yes. And now he's shut himself in the treatment room,' the older woman said, clearly puzzled.

'Is anyone else in there with him?'

'Well, no,' Kirsty admitted. 'He just didn't seem himself. I thought you should check.'

Sighing again, Hannah closed her file and put her sandwich back in its wrapper. 'I'll see what I can find out,' she agreed with reluctance.

Apparently satisfied, Kirsty returned to her own work. Disgruntled, Hannah walked slowly towards the treatment room. The last thing she needed was to be in Nic's presence more than absolutely necessary. She'd managed to avoid him fairly well since their disastrous supper the week before but every time she did see him, she was on tenterhooks, thinking he was going to refer back to their embarrassing conversation at any moment. So far he hadn't, but she wasn't about to push her luck. She had the uncomfortable feeling he was biding his time.

Fortunately, not only had his belongings arrived from Italy at the weekend, keeping him occupied sorting things out in his room, but Allan Pollock had come up with a car. Hannah had scarcely been able to hide her relief. Mobile, Nic had taken on home visits and out-of-hours calls on his own, cutting down the time she had to spend with him.

Now she paused outside the treatment room, wondering what had happened to make Kirsty suspicious. She listened, but there were no sounds from within. Frowning, she hesitated, but as she closed her fingers on the doorhandle, she heard muffled curses from within.

'Come on, *gattino. Lotta*—fight, little one. No, no, *maledizione! Non sto lasciandoli morire!* I'm not letting you die.'

Kirsty had been certain no one else was in the treatment room, so who on earth was Nic talking to? Unable to bear another moment of suspense, Hannah quietly opened the door and stepped inside, speechless at the scene that greeted her.

'Nic?'

He looked up, an endearingly guilty look on his face, like a child caught with its hand in the cake tin. 'Hannah!'

'What on earth is going on?' she demanded, finding her voice at last, unable to take her eyes from the minuscule scrap of fur on the treatment table, supported with exquisite gentleness by one of Nic's olive-toned hands.

'I was coming back from calls, *cara*, and there was this sack beside the road. It moved, so I stopped, yes, to look? I found some kittens,' he added, anger and disgust at the cruelty evident in his emotional tone. 'The rest were dead, but this little man, he has a chance.'

Hannah's stomach tightened at the hopeless waste. 'What did you do?'

'He was more dead than alive, frightened and cold and dehydrated, so I put him inside my jumper, put the sack in the boot and came back here.'

'But—'

He looked up at her, his eyes determined. 'I'm not letting him die, Hannah.'

'No. No, of course not.' She was incredibly touched by his compassion and sensitivity. 'What can I do to help?'

'You're not mad at me?'

His eyes twinkled, drawing a reluctant smile from her. 'I should be, it is a bit unconventional. Goodness knows what anyone would think.'

'It will be our secret. Yes?'

'OK.'

What was it about this man that made her go against her better judgement? She met his gaze and he smiled, a slow, warm, intimate smile that seemed to suck all the breath from her lungs and turn her insides to jelly. Dear God, what was happening to her?

'I put a hot pack to warm. Could you fetch it for me, *cara*?'

Thankful to have something to do, Hannah crossed the room and tested the temperature of the pack to make sure it wasn't too hot. Wrapping it in a towel, she handed it to Nic, who set the little kitten on top.

'Do you think it will be all right?' she asked, watching as he worked, carefully drying the little scrap and urging it back to life.

'I hope so. But he's very young.'

'What age do you think?'

Nic shrugged. 'About three weeks, maybe four. His eyes are open, but they have not yet changed colour.'

'You seem to know a lot about it. Have you done this before?'

'Sadly, yes.'

Moved by the look of remembered hurt in his eyes, Hannah

bent to get a better view of their tiny patient, who stared back myopically and let out a plaintive mew.

'See, he is a fighter!' Nic grinned.

Unexpected tears pricked Hannah's eyes at Nic's obvious care for anything that needed him. He had healing hands, she decided, watching the gentleness with which he touched the kitten. A pale ginger colour, the little animal had a white tip to his skinny tail and an untidy scruff of hair around his scrawny neck, like a mane. Tiny white claws peeped out from the tips of minuscule paws, the pads underneath pink, Hannah noted. She straightened, trying to pull herself together. This was a busy doctor's surgery, not a home for waifs and strays.

'Shona's husband is a vet. He has a practice in Rigtownbrae, about eight miles away. You're off this afternoon so why don't you take the kitten there and let Alistair look him over and make some suggestions?'

'I will. Thank you.'

'You'll have to get past Kirsty, though. She sent me in here. Said you looked furtive when you came back.'

'Did she?' His dark eyes shone with laughter. 'Maybe I doubted how she would feel if she knew what I was up to.'

'And you knew how I'd react?' she queried, regretting too late that she was stepping on dangerous ground.

His gaze held hers, sending a shiver of fearful awareness down her spine. 'I think I'm coming to know you very well, Hannah,' he replied huskily, unnerving her.

'Then you'll know it's past time I got back to work,' she retorted, stepping away.

'I know that's what you think,' he said with an enigmatic smile, concentrating on wrapping the little kitten up for the journey to the vet. 'I'll see you later.'

Discomfited, Hannah watched him walk away, hearing the oohs and ahs as he paused in Reception to show Kirsty and Jane the kitten, before leaving on his mercy mission.

Back in her consulting room, Hannah disposed of the remains of her sandwich, her appetite having deserted her. All she seemed to be able to think about was Nic and the havoc he was playing with her life and her peace of mind. He had upset everything, disturbing her, pressuring her, questioning her…tempting her. She had started to think of things long forgotten and discarded. Things she had no wish to start up again. Perhaps because she had never met anyone to whom she had been attracted in the past, she had never been tested, never had any cause to question her chosen path. It had been so easy to stick to her decision to focus solely on the career she loved to the exclusion of all else. In a short time Nic had upset her equilibrium and she was frightened where it could lead.

Nic was relaxing in the living room when he heard the front door open and Hannah return home. Funny how he, who had become so scared of putting down any kind of roots in the last two years, thought of this as home after just two weeks. Maybe it was better not to go there. He frowned, tossing his book aside. He glanced up as Hannah hesitated in the doorway, her gaze sweeping round the room.

'Have you cleared up?'

'Hello to you, also.' Nic smiled, amused at her surprise. 'I vacuumed and did a few things. Is that wrong?'

'Not exactly.'

'So?'

She shifted uncomfortably. 'I didn't expect you to be doing chores around the house and cleaning up after me.'

'Why should you clean up after me?' he challenged softly. 'I don't know what kind of men you have lived with in the past, Hannah, but we are not all…what do you call them? Couch potatoes? I certainly do not expect to be waited on.'

He heard her soft intake of breath as she stared at him, clearly uneasy.

'What's wrong?'

'Nothing.'

Her rebuttal was unconvincing. 'Which part of that remark has upset you?' he mused, watching the play of emotions across her face.

'How did you get on with the vet?'

Nic raised an eyebrow at her unsubtle change of subject. He waited a moment, wondering whether to let her get away with it or not, but she looked so anxious he gave in. Again. But only for now. He already had a whole list of interesting things he planned to discuss with her…when the time was right. He had learned, however, not to push her too far too soon.

'Alistair was very helpful.'

'Good.' Relief washed across her face and he knew it wasn't because of the kitten. 'Is he going to find it a new home?'

'Not exactly.'

His evasive statement had Hannah pausing as she turned to leave the room. Her eyes narrowed. 'You've brought him home, haven't you?'

'The vet or the cat?' he teased, earning himself another fiery glare.

'Nic!'

'OK,' he relented. 'Yes, I have. Did you really think I wouldn't?'

'I suppose not. Where is he?'

Nic rose to his feet and walked with her to the kitchen. 'Alistair lent me a kitten pen and I bought some other things we need.'

'We?'

He smiled as her gaze softened when she looked at the kitten asleep in his pen, cuddled up to a soft toy on top of a covered hot-water bottle.

'His name is Wallace.'

'Wallace? After William?'

'No! Did you never hear of Wallace the lion?' he asked, but

she shook her head. 'My mama and grandpapa used to read me the comic poem "The Lion and Albert" when I was a child. This little one just looks like a lion, no?'

'Nic, he's nothing like a lion!'

Delighted to hear her laugh, Nic grinned. 'He has a little mane like a lion, no? And he certainly has the fight and courage of one.'

She sobered and glanced at him. 'What about the others?'

'They are buried, *cara*,' he confirmed softly.

Looking sad, she turned back to Wallace. 'It's madness to keep him,' she sighed, looking again at the little ball of fur.

'Don't you ever do mad things now and again?'

'No.'

'Maybe it's time you started.'

She straightened, avoiding his gaze. 'And what is supposed to happen to him when you leave?'

'Wallace can keep you company and look after you for me.'

He could see his words had rattled her, made her back off again, as if things were getting too heavy for her to handle. 'I don't need looking after,' she refuted, her voice cool and distant.

'Don't you?' He watched her knot her fingers together in anxiety. 'And I suppose you don't need company, either?'

Bruised green eyes looked at him. 'Why are you doing this?'

'What do you think I'm doing?'

'I don't know.' She pushed back some wayward strands of hair. 'I—'

Temptation bettered him as a curl of desire licked through his gut. He reached out, ignoring her protesting gasp as he pulled out the pins and watched her hair cascade down around her shoulders.

'Nic?'

'I've wanted to do this since the moment I first met you,' he whispered, running his fingers through the lustrous chestnut thickness. 'You have such beautiful hair, Hannah, you shouldn't hide it.'

Trembling, she pushed his hands away. 'Stop it!'

'Does it upset you that I find you attractive?'

'You can't.' Green eyes widened in shocked alarm. 'You mustn't.'

'Why?'

'Leave me alone, Nic.'

He allowed her retreat, wondering how he was going to break through the barriers she had placed between herself and the rest of the world. What had happened to make her so sad, so alone, so scared? A lost love? He didn't yet know but, despite her protests, her eyes sent out mixed messages and he wasn't going to give up on her.

Wallace mewed plaintively and Nic sighed, gently lifting the warm little body out of the pen, holding him close while he prepared his food. 'Looks like it's just me and you for now, *uomo piccolo*.'

As the days went by, Hannah felt on edge. Nic seemed to be chipping away a bit at a time at her defences, fortifications she had once assured herself were impenetrable. That he had admitted he was attracted to her shocked her to the core. It frightened her but also made her feel an unwanted and alarming tingle of awareness, which confused her even more. She'd given him no encouragement, had tried to be cool and distant from the first. He must have countless women falling over him, so how could he be interested in her?

'You're away with the fairies today, girl!'

The joking admonishment jerked Hannah from her reverie. 'Jimmy, I'm sorry,' she apologised, her cheeks warming.

'Aye, well, I reckon it's not surprising the way you've been working of late,' he stated with concern. 'And you look far too tired. You need a holiday now you have the new locum.'

'I'm fine, Jimmy.'

'Settling in all right, is he?'

'Who?' she fudged, stalling for time.

'The angel doctor.' Jimmy laughed at the look on her face.

'Aye, that's what they're calling him, girl. You did a good job, finding him.'

Hannah busied herself taking Jimmy McCall's blood pressure, disturbed by his words. The angel doctor with the healing touch. Concentrating on her task, she removed her stethoscope and unwound the band from Jimmy's arm. She sat back and looked at him, wrapped in a blanket in his chair by the fire.

'Are your sister and nephew still visiting every week?'

'Aye, lot of fuss the pair of them make. She does like to tidy does Alice. But she makes a good casserole. Not that I can eat much now. What with the family and the home help, plus you and the nurses, I'm not for want of company. And I have the odd surprise guest now and then,' he added, tapping the side of his nose.

Hannah smiled, moved by his spirit. 'So, how are you feeling, really?'

'Oh, you know, not too bad.' The sixty-eight-year-old widower shrugged with a sad smile. 'For a dying man.'

'Don't talk like that, Jimmy.'

'I'm not daft, girl.'

She leaned forward, holding his bony hand, knowing that his cancer was advanced and untreatable, that at best they could keep him comfortable and at home, as he wished, for his last days or weeks. 'Is there anything you need?'

'I've made peace with most people.' He smiled. 'But there is one thing that's bothering me.'

'Can I help?'

'You could,' he allowed mysteriously.

Hannah frowned at him. 'Come on, Jimmy, you're my favourite patient,' she whispered, keeping up their familiar banter, trying to hide her emotions and concern for this man.

'Aye, and you were always my favourite pupil, girl. I mean that. You had so much promise to go with that kind heart of yours. It was a pleasure watching you grow all through your school days. My Jean and I were as proud as anything when you became a doctor. Same as your mum and dad were. You've done us all proud here,' he finished, his voice hoarse, bringing tears to Hannah's eyes.

'Jimmy,' she murmured, but he forestalled her.

'What happened, girl?'

The question surprised her and, tensing, she released his hand and sat back. 'What do you mean?'

'When you came home to us you were so different.' He broke off as a coughing fit caught him and Hannah helped him take a drink of water as it passed. 'Something happened, didn't it, in the city?'

'I just grew up, Jimmy,' she insisted, busying herself packing her things away in her medical bag.

'It was more than that, girl.'

'Jimmy—'

'You never see anyone, have no social life.'

'I'm busy, you know that.'

He regarded her for a moment. 'I hear Sandy Douglas still carries a torch for you.'

'Don't be silly,' she dismissed. 'We went out a couple of times when we were sixteen. There was never anything between us and there never will be.'

'What about the new doctor? He's a nice young man and you get a glint in your eyes when you talk about him!'

'I do not,' she protested in alarm.

'Hannah?'

She rose to her feet, snapping the bag closed and pulling on her coat. 'I know you mean well, Jimmy, but Nic is only here for a few months. Besides, I'm fine as I am. I don't want Sandy Douglas, Nic or anyone else in my life.'

'You asked what you could do for me,' he reminded her, his voice gruff. 'We all love you here in Lochanrig. You are the best of doctors, but you've lost yourself somewhere along the way. That's my last wish, girl, for you to be happy, to bring the old Hannah back.'

Jimmy's words plagued her as she drove back to the surgery, her eyes blurred. At least it was Saturday lunchtime and everyone would have gone, she thought, blinking away fresh tears. Her relief was short-lived and she groaned when she saw Nic's car in the parking space next to hers. This was all she needed, now of all times. Flipping down the sun visor, she checked her appearance in the mirror, wiping away any signs of her tears.

She unlocked the surgery door and walked in, planning to head quietly to her consulting room undetected, but Nic was standing behind the reception desk, checking a patient's notes and talking on the phone. He looked up, the beginnings of a smile dying on his face as he looked at her.

Oh, God! How could she have imagined he wouldn't notice? Hannah felt nervous tension coil through her. Dragging her gaze away, she headed for her room, hearing him return his attention to his telephone conversation.

'Sorry,' he said to the caller. 'I'm still here. Paracetamol and plenty of water and fruit juice to drink. That's right. Call again if you are worried, yes?'

She barely had time to set her bag down and take off her coat before there was a tap on her door and Nic came in.

'Hannah?'

'Yes?' she said, concentrating far more than necessary on the task of hanging up her coat.

'What's wrong?'

She closed her eyes. His voice was closer. Too close. 'Nothing,' she refuted as lightly as she could. She tried to step away, but his hand on her arm made her freeze.

'Why do you do that?' he demanded, sounding frustrated, turning her to face him. 'Why do you deny your own hurt?'

'I don't.'

'You do it all the time,' he corrected her, his voice more gentle, concern in his compelling dark eyes.

Alarmed, she freed her arm from his hold, taking a step back, uncomfortable at the physical contact. 'I'm fine. I was just…concerned about a patient.' Nic stood there, arms folded across his chest, blocking her retreat. 'I've been out to see Jimmy McCall.'

'We've met.'

'Have you?' She glanced up at him in surprise. 'I didn't know that.'

'You've known him a long time.'

It was a statement, not a question, and Hannah nodded, fighting for control, pushing the memories of Jimmy's last words away. 'All my life. I hate that I can't do anything more for him,' she admitted, cursing the wobble in her voice.

'You're allowed to care, *innamorata*, to hurt, to be human.'

She sucked in a breath and bit her lip, unable to say anything, desperate not to cry in front of him.

'You give everything to others but never take anything for yourself,' he whispered, his hands taking her reluctant ones in his. 'It's not a crime to need someone, to let someone help you.'

'Nic…'

He let go of her hands and opened his arms. 'A hug, yes?'

She couldn't. He waited patiently, unthreatening, letting her make up her mind. Confused, she met his dark gaze, seeing nothing but kindness. She didn't do this sort of thing, shouldn't even be tempted, but something about Nic made her act out of character. A tiny step nearer him and she hesitated, uncertain. He took a step to meet her, his arms gently closing round her.

'Nic, I—'

Her whispered words were muffled against the hard wall of his chest and she held herself stiffly in his arms, her hands lifting to his sides, clenching in the fabric of his jacket, unsure whether she was trying to push him away or hold him close—too scared to find out.

'Relax,' he soothed, one hand moving lightly on her back. 'You don't like to be hugged?'

Fresh tears pricked her eyes as she shook her head. 'No,' she whispered. She hated being touched at all. It made her skin crawl when she thought about… With a desperate effort she pushed the unwanted memories away, but the remembered panic had made her tense and she could feel a tremor run through her.

'Everything's OK, *cara*.'

Nic's soft reassurances confused her and she wondered how she could feel so scared and so safe at the same time. Warmth seemed to permeate her whole body from the top of her head to the tips of her toes, and every time she breathed in she absorbed Nic's scent, his sandalwood aftershave mixed with something elementally him.

She had no idea how long they stood there, but when Nic finally eased away, she looked up at him in confusion, alarmed at the way his eyes darkened, his gaze intent as he stared back at her. When he bent his head so that his lips brushed hers with gentle softness, Hannah thought she would expire with shock. She was desperate to pull away but she couldn't move, held captive by his sheer magnetism. The caress was almost chaste, yet held the promise—or the threat—of so much more. The thought permeated and she jerked her head back from him.

A small smile played around his mouth as he stepped back a pace, taking hold of her hands again. 'Come on, we're getting out of here.'

'What?'

'It's a free Saturday afternoon for us both. We're going to have some fun.'

Hannah stared at him. 'Fun?'

'Have you not heard of it?' he teased.

'Of course, but—'

'Are you always so controlled?'

'Aren't we all?'

'I don't feel in control when I'm with you,' he confided, shocking her. 'Not at all.'

'Nic—'

'It's scary but exciting.'

She didn't want to think about these things, didn't want to listen to him. 'Don't.'

'We make a deal. Come with me now, or…'

'Or?' she whispered as he paused, hardly daring to hear the answer as she saw the intent expression in his eyes.

'Or I kiss you again—properly this time.'

Renewed panic set in and she looked back at him, wide-eyed. 'I'll get my coat and bag.'

Laughing, Nic let go of her hands and she tried to regroup as she picked up her things and followed him out of the surgery.

'Where are we going?'

'You'll see. I'll meet you back at the house.'

Puzzled, Hannah followed him home. 'Nic—'

'Go and change,' he instructed her as they faced each other in the hall. 'Jeans, jumper, boots, gloves and something warm, OK?'

'But—'

'Go, or I might forget our deal!'

Filled with nervous apprehension, Hannah met him back downstairs ten minutes later to discover he had also changed and was seeing to Wallace, settling the little kitten back in his pen. He turned and smiled, nodding his approval of her outfit as she pulled on a thick jacket. Taking her hesitant hand in his, he led her out of the house.

'No way!' she protested when she realised he was heading towards his motorbike.

'Have you been on one?'

'Of course not! And I'm not going to now.'

He set two helmets on the seat and faced her. 'Don't you ever take risks? Feel alive?'

'No.'

'You do now.'

Ignoring her mumbled protests, he helped her on with a helmet, double-checking that it fitted. Then made sure her gloves were on and she was well buttoned up for the cold before he

swung onto the bike with effortless ease and started the engine.
As it throbbed in the stillness of the afternoon, Nic gave her a
few instructions.

'Sit up close to me. You can either hold the bar behind you,
or you can hold me,' he added with a smile, daring her, tempting
her. 'Whichever you find more comfortable. Watch what I'm
doing and how I lean. Move gently with me, and keep your feet
on the pegs. OK?'

Hannah stared at him. 'Nic…?'

'Trust me, *innamorata*.'

He held his hand out to her and waited. She really didn't want
to do this but something about Nic made her behave in the most
foolish of ways. Placing her hand in his, she allowed him to
steady her as she climbed on behind him. Closing her eyes as Nic
pulled on his own helmet and gloves, Hannah clasped the little
handle thing behind her as instructed and held on. He kicked up
the rest and eased slowly down the drive.

It was a beautiful late October day, the sun low in the sky, the
trees and hedgerows turning golden browns and russet reds. Her
fear subsiding, Hannah found herself relaxing, although she
didn't feel so comfortable holding onto the grip behind her seat.
When they stopped at a crossroad, he glanced back to see if she
was OK. Hesitantly she released her hold and forced herself to
inch forward and slide her arms around his waist. Despite it being
windy and cold in the breeze from the bike, she found she was
enjoying herself. As Nic headed up into the hills, her confidence
in him was growing, he was in charge and would keep her safe.

They stopped a few times to absorb the views of hillsides and
hidden lochs, the heather almost over now but the bracken turning.
The southern uplands were so beautiful that she sighed, flipping
up her visor to breathe in the crisp autumn air. When they stopped
by St Mary's Loch, she wished she had the free time to come out
here more often, to lose herself in the tranquil, unpopulated remoteness of her home landscape. They moved on again, stopping

for Nic to see the Grey Mare's Tail waterfall before heading on towards the pretty town of Moffat. The landscape was incredible, and she felt more at ease, both on the bike and with Nic. It was the most exhilarating afternoon of her life! She grinned, surprising herself, sorry when they headed back towards Lochanrig and Nic finally drew the bike to a halt outside the house.

Hannah released her hold on him, pulling off her gloves to fumble with the strap of her helmet, her nerves returning as Nic's hands moved to help her, his fingers brushing against hers. She slid off the bike, her legs shaky, and handed him the helmet.

His dark gaze slid over her. 'OK?'

Hannah nodded, feeling shy and uneasy again.

'Did you enjoy it?' he asked with a smile, stepping off the bike.

'Yes,' she was forced to admit. 'Thank you.'

Nic took her hand, silken lashes fanning his cheeks as he closed his eyes and pressed a kiss to her palm, making her skin tingle. His eyes opened, warm and disturbing, his voice husky with promise. 'Any time, Hannah. Any time.'

Trembling, she watched as Nic walked away from her towards the house, very much afraid that his promise offered her more than just another trip on his bike.

CHAPTER FIVE

THE crisp, sunny days of October were replaced with rain and wind as November arrived. Nothing else had happened between Nic and herself since the ride on his bike, but Hannah felt as if she was living in a tinderbox that would flare up at the slightest provocation. She felt more jumpy than ever, conscious of Nic's dark gaze on her whenever they were together, knowing that he watched her and that he saw too much. Pushing her concerns away, Hannah concentrated on her task.

'You must get Gavin to Casualty now, Mrs Miller,' she stressed, making sure the boy who had tumbled from his bike was as comfortable as possible. 'I'm sure it is just a simple fracture but it will need an X-ray and cast. And I imagine they will check to make sure he didn't knock his head. Do you need me to call an ambulance for you?'

'No, Doctor, don't you worry none. My husband's on his way home from work and he'll drive us down.'

'All right. Just let me know if there is anything I can do.'

'Long-term sedation would be appealing,' she admitted with a harassed smile. 'You need eyes in the back of your head with this boy.'

Smiling back, Hannah packed her bag and ruffled young Gavin's blond curls. 'Take care, young man.'

'Thanks for coming, Doctor,' Mrs Miller sighed, seeing her out.

'No problem.'

Glancing at her watch and seeing how late she was, having had this emergency call added at the end of her home visits, Hannah drove back to the surgery.

'I'm glad you're here,' Jane greeted her.

'What's wrong?'

'Nic. He's not very well. Kirsty and Morag are in his room trying to persuade him to go home.'

More concerned than she wanted to admit, Hannah left the patient notes with Jane to file away and walked along to Nic's consulting room.

'Ah, Hannah.' Kirsty smiled grimly, hands on hips, a determined glint in her eye. 'Perhaps you can talk some sense into the man.'

Morag moved from her place beside Nic and gestured Hannah forward. 'I'll go and get my car so I can run him home and get him settled.'

'You're all fussing about nothing,' Nic protested, but he didn't sound his usual energetic and mischievous self.

'I'll start moving appointments,' Kirsty insisted firmly, bustling from the room.

Hannah looked at Nic for a moment, seeing the pallor beneath the unnatural flush on his cheeks, the slightly glazed look in his eyes. She walked round the desk, a frown on her face.

'How are you feeling?' she asked him.

'I probably just ate something that disagreed with me.'

'You look funny.'

'Is that a professional medical term?' he queried, his eyes crinkling at the corners as he managed a weak smile, before leaning back in the chair with a smothered groan, his eyes closing.

'I'm serious, Nic.' The man was impossible. She laid her hand on his forehead. 'You're burning up! This is silly. You've obviously picked up some bug or other. Let Morag give you a lift home and get some rest. You are not to come back in today, that's an order. I can manage surgery and you can ring down if you need anything. We'll see how things are tomorrow.'

'OK.' He gave in with obvious reluctance. '*Dio*, you can be bossy, Dr Frost.'

'Just remember it and do as you're told,' she chided, noting how shaky he was when he got to his feet.

Concerned, she walked with him to Reception and allowed Morag to take over as she rushed into mother-hen mode and ushered Nic out to her car. 'Don't worry, I'll see he has fluids to hand and is warm,' the kindly nurse reassured Hannah.

It was late by the time Hannah was free to go back to the house, surgery having overrun because she had taken Nic's patients as well as her own. She let herself into the house, her concern increasing when she found him flaked out on the settee, where Morag had left him, looking decidedly peaky. She'd told the silly man he wasn't well. Not that it gave her any satisfaction to be proved right.

'Nic?' Hannah frowned, seeing how shivery he was, his skin clammy to the touch. 'Come on, let's get you up to bed. You're going to have to help me.'

He mumbled something but did as she told him, although it took a ridiculous amount of time before he was safely up the stairs and they were edging along to his room. Once there, he tumbled rather unceremoniously onto the bed, and Hannah found herself sprawled haphazardly beside him, her arm wedged underneath his shoulders. She freed herself and sat up, breathless from the effort.

'Nic, can you get undressed?'

He groaned, eyes closed, breathing laboured. It seemed the last of his energy had been sapped reaching his room, so she steeled herself to do the job, trying not to be rough but having a bit of a struggle as he was too weak and out of it to be of much help. She finally managed to peel off his jumper, shoes and socks, then hesitated, a lump in her throat, before her fingers fumbled with the belt and fastening of his trousers.

The task done, she fetched an extra sheet and blankets and covered him with them before putting the duvet back on top, telling herself she really hadn't been unprofessional and had not allowed herself any lingering appraisal of his well-defined torso, with its dusting of dark hair arrowing down his abdomen, his intriguing muscles and textures, olive-toned skin and long legs. Uncomfortable, she checked his temperature, concerned how his fever was raging, and went to get her medical bag and some fluids for him.

When he was sleeping fitfully, she hurried around, doing the chores, seeing to Wallace and locking up, then made herself a sandwich and coffee and took them back to Nic's room, along with something to read. Feeling pooped herself, she settled down in a cosy chair for her vigil.

'Wally, your food smells revolting,' Hannah complained two days later, shaking her head as the kitten received it joyfully and then seemed to get more all over himself than he ate, each little foot paddling in the shallow bowl.

Lifting him out when he had finished, she gently wiped him over, a smile curving her mouth as she admitted how cute he was. 'At least you're an easier patient to look after than your master,' she murmured, a frown replacing her smile.

Nic's fever and sickness had run for over twenty-four hours and either Debbie, Shona or Morag had covered for her during the day, checking on him while she herself had managed the surgery and house calls.

'There you go, little man,' she murmured to Wallace, unconsciously mirroring Nic's nickname for the kitten as she settled him back in his pen. 'I'd better go and check on him, see if he's ready for some supper.'

She was going mad now, talking to a cat. Smiling, she went up the stairs and peeped round Nic's door, relieved the nurses had managed to persuade him into pyjama bottoms and a T-shirt. At least he'd been too ill to know anything when she'd had to care for him herself that first night, but now he was on the mend and getting more difficult, as well as bored with staying in bed.

'How are you feeling?'

'Better, but pathetically weak,' he allowed, shifting further up in the bed and propping himself on the pillows.

Hannah's gaze skittered away from him. He looked like a rogue with a couple of days' stubble darkening his jaw. As ever her insides tied themselves into knots when she was anywhere near him.

'Do you feel like anything to eat?' she asked now, fussing with the bed clothes. 'I was going to make omelettes.'

'That sounds great. I'll come down.'

'Not until tomorrow, you won't.'

She jumped when his fingers curled round her wrist. 'Your bedside manner could do with some working on, Dr Frost. You can be a hard woman,' he teased.

'As I remember it, you are supposed to be here as an extra doctor, not an extra patient,' she pointed out, hoping to distract attention from the way her pulse had started racing from his touch.

'I'm sorry about that, *cara*,' he apologised, immediately contrite. His gaze scanned her face. 'You look tired. Give me tomorrow to recover and I'll be back at work on Monday.'

'Don't worry about it.'

'Hannah—'

She managed to free her arm and stepped out of reach. 'I'll bring your omelette up shortly.'

'Bring yours, too, I'd enjoy your company.'

Hannah had no intention whatsoever of sitting on his bed, eating her supper! The sooner he was up and about again, the better.

'So tell me all the news,' Nic suggested a while later as they finished their omelettes and Hannah sat awkwardly on his bed, wondering how she had ended up in this situation after all.

She busied herself peeling and coring an apple to share with him. 'There hasn't been anything very exciting happening—

except the little boy who managed to get his fingers stuck in his toy train!'

'You're kidding?' He laughed, dropping weakly back against the pillows.

'Nope.' Her stomach turned over just looking at him. 'His fingers had swollen so much we had to send him down to Casualty. Come on, now, you get some rest.'

'I'm fine,' he protested.

Hannah couldn't help but smile. 'Sure you are. That's why you've had the undivided attention of three nurses and a doctor for the last forty-eight hours, mopping your fevered brow!'

'I'll have to remember your expert diagnosis, *innamorata*,' he joked, raising his eyebrows, a smile curving that far too tempting mouth. 'What was it again? "You look funny"?'

'At the moment you look like a pirate,' she quipped sarcastically.

Nic ran a hand over his stubbled jaw, drawing her attention shamefully to his rakish good looks. 'I'll be up tomorrow and restored to respectability.'

'Just take things easy this time. Remember you nearly fell over when you tried that this morning.' Her gaze met his for another long, breath-stealing moment, then she gathered up the plates. 'I've got paperwork to do, so I'll leave you some things to read if you're bored, but try and get some more sleep. And before you ask for the hundredth time, Wallace is fine.'

'Thank you.'

'It's OK. Now, do as you're told!'

'Like I said, you're a hard woman, Dr Frost.' His smile warmed her from the inside out. 'I'll be all right, you know, if you want to join the others for the firework party this evening.'

The words caught her unawares and she froze, fumbling the plates. 'I don't want to,' she snapped, hearing the tension in her voice.

'Hannah?'

Damn him! She saw the puzzled concern at her change of

mood but could do nothing to alter it. She hated November the fifth. It had happened on Bonfire Night, with the sky ablaze and the air filled with the sound of rockets and laughter and... Fighting back the memories, she dragged her gaze from Nic's.

'I don't like fireworks. Rest now,' she mumbled, hurrying from his room.

Hannah was about to slip into bed about three hours later when she hesitated. Had Nic called her? He'd been sleeping peacefully when she had checked him a while ago. Frowning, she pulled her robe on over her pyjamas, knotting it round her waist as she padded barefoot down the landing, her concern growing as she heard Nic shouting out in distress.

Rushing into his room, she stopped, realising he was dreaming, tossing to and fro on the bed, talking in his native language, his words urgent and anguished. What demons tortured his sleep? Concerned, Hannah crossed to the bed and switched on the side light.

'Nic.' She gave him a gentle shake, repeating it more strongly as he failed to stir. 'Nic! Wake up.'

Finally her efforts had an effect and he woke with a start, staring at her in confusion, the pain in his eyes tugging at her heart.

'What happened?' he queried, clearly trying to make sense of where he was and why she was there.

'You were having a bad dream.'

'I'm sorry I disturbed you.'

Hannah shook her head, feeling at a loss, moved by the despair in his voice. 'You were talking, calling for someone, more than one person.'

'Lorenzo,' he breathed, his eyes closing.

'Yes.' Hannah bit her lip, curious despite herself but hating to intrude. 'And Federica, is it?'

His eyes opened again, reflecting some terrible inner pain. 'Federica, sì.' He draped an arm across his face as if trying to block out the memories, the hurt.

'Do you want to tell me about it?'

'The region of Italy I called home is prone to earthquakes,' he told her after long moments of silence, his voice raw. 'Just over two years ago we were hit by a big one. I was at the hospital some miles away. Everyone at home was lost. My parents, my elder brother, Lorenzo, his wife...'

'Federica?' she supplied when he paused.

'No, Sofia was Lorenzo's wife. Federica was my fiancée.'

Tears pricked Hannah's eyes and she didn't want to examine the rush of mixed emotions that assailed her at the horrible news, or at knowing Nic had loved this unknown woman, Federica.

'Nic, I'm so sorry.'

Without thinking, she sat on the edge of the bed, holding his hand in hers, aware of its strength and its gentleness and its warmth.

'I've never talked about this before.'

'Maybe it's a good thing you do now, then,' she prompted softly.

His dark gaze held hers captive. 'Do as you say and not as you do, is that right, *cara*?'

'I don't know what you mean.'

'Oh, I think you do. So we make a deal, yes?' he suggested, the fingers of the hand she held twining sinuously and disturbingly with hers, preventing her withdrawal. 'I tell you my secrets, you tell me yours. We share each other's pain.'

Alarmed, she sought an escape route. 'Nic, I—'

At that moment a firework went off at a neighbouring house and Hannah jumped out of her skin, a startled cry drawn from her.

Feeling her tremble with fear as more loud bangs sounded, Nic looked at her pale face and haunted eyes. 'You really are frightened of fireworks, aren't you?'

'Did you think I was making it up?'

'No, but...' He just wasn't sure where it fitted in with the rest of the jigsaw puzzle he was trying to piece together about her. 'Come here.'

Holding her hand, knowing she would bolt given half the chance, Nic steered her round to the other side of the bed. He flipped up the duvet only, so that the extra sheet and blanket he'd been using while ill remained between them, and encouraged her to sit down.

'I don't think this is a good idea,' she resisted.

'You're quite safe, Hannah.'

He could feel her tension and her fear as he gently encouraged her down with him, folding the duvet back over her rigid form. Lying on their sides, with her back towards him, her head was pillowed on his arm, his hand still holding hers. With his free hand, he brushed some of the loose strands of hair back from her face, revelling in being able to touch it. He closed his eyes, breathing in the scent of her shampoo mixed with the vanilla fragrance of her perfume, warm, pure and arousing.

A distant volley of fireworks exploded and he felt the shiver run through her. He stroked her hair, urging her to relax.

'I o-ought to go and check W-Wallace. He might be f-frightened.'

'He'll be fine,' Nic soothed, knowing the kitten was safe and protected. It was her fear that concerned him. 'Hannah—'

'Tell me about your family,' she whispered.

And so he did, finding that although the past still haunted him, he could talk about his parents, his brother and sister-in-law, even Federica, with warmth and love and humour, and that the pain, though always there, had lost its power to destroy him.

'Had you and Federica been together long?'

'Five years, nearly to the day." He sighed, remembering the woman with whom he had expected to spend the rest of his life. 'We had everything planned, how many children we would have, everything.'

'You wanted a family?'

Nic frowned, hearing the stiffness in Hannah's voice. 'Yes,

of course. I'm Italian!' But she didn't laugh as he had meant her to, and his frown deepened.

'So what happened?' she asked after a long silence.

'One day we all breakfasted together, happy, making plans for the weekend. A few hours later, they were all gone, in the blink of an eye.' He hesitated, finding the words difficult. 'And I was not there.'

'It wasn't your fault.'

'I should have been with them when they needed me.'

'So you could have died as well?' she protested. 'Who would that have helped?'

Her stark words made him pause. 'Perhaps it would have helped me, *cara*,' he finally whispered, his voice choked with anguish. 'Then I would not have been the only one left to identify the broken bodies of my parents, my fiancée, my brother and sister-in-law.'

He let go of her hand as she wriggled round to face him, gold-flecked green eyes shadowed in the pale glow from the lamp, reflecting her sorrow and her compassion. Tentatively, as if fighting some inner struggle, she reached out a hand and softly touched his face.

'It must have been terrible to cope with that alone.'

Nic just nodded, affected by the feel of her fingers on his skin. She was so close. If he moved a few inches he could kiss her and—

'Is that why you've travelled around so much the last couple of years?'

Her question snapped him back to his senses. 'Yes. I don't do commitment, I don't put down roots. Not any more.'

His loss had devastated him, left him homeless, searching for something unknown yet never seeming to belong. Now, for the first time in a long while, he felt settled. As much as he loved his own country, there was something captivating about this place and these people that made him feel…what? He frowned, recognising the danger of his thoughts.

'Nic?'

'There seemed nothing left for me. It was all too painful,' he explained. 'I needed to get away, to come to terms with it, to see if I could go on.'

'And you can. You have.'

'Yes, but not without the guilt that I am alive and they are not.'

Her hand retreated and she tipped her head back to look at him. 'Would any of them have wanted you to die?'

'No, of course not,' he responded in shock.

'And had you been there when it happened and any of them had been elsewhere, safe, would you have wanted them back with you, to die with you?'

'*Dio!*' The shock turned to a slow-burning anger. 'What do you think of me?'

'Nic, I'm trying to make you see that as you wouldn't have wanted any of them to die with you, neither would they have wanted you to die. Knowing that you were away, safe, probably gave them huge comfort. Not all was lost.'

He ran a hand through his hair in agitation, struggling with himself, mulling over what she had said, but the rare flash of anger was gone.

'You have nothing to feel guilty for, Nic, it was the cruelty of fate. The same for my mother being in the wrong place at the wrong time. It's not your fault you are alive. Instead, you are giving of yourself to help others, to heal them.'

He was silent for a long time but he could almost feel a new calmness seep into him.

'Thank you, *innamorata*.'

As if she heard something new in his voice, he saw alarm flicker in her eyes and she smiled dismissively, inching further away, her gaze sliding from his.

'Hannah…'

She stopped wriggling and met his gaze with obvious reluctance. 'What?'

'One day—soon—I'm going to help you heal.'

His fingers at her wrist felt the rapid flicker of her pulse and he watched as she raised her free hand unconsciously to her throat in a protective, shielding gesture. 'I'm fine,' she finally responded, but her voice was hoarse with discomfort.

Dio, she was beautiful. Complex, mysterious and enigmatic, she sent out jumbled signals, but she excited him more than any other woman had ever done—even Federica, he realised with a stab of guilt at his disloyalty. Watching the play of emotions in Hannah's eyes, he allowed the fingers of one hand to trace the line of freckles across her face. He heard the cadence of her breathing change and her lashes drifted shut, only to snap open again when he brushed the pad of his thumb across her lips.

'Nic?' she whispered, sounding uncertain and scared.

'Shush.'

His thumb under her chin, he bent his head with infinite care and touched his mouth to hers. Slowly, slowly, he told himself, fighting the rush of desire that swept through him. Don't mess this up.

The tip of his tongue teased along the line of her lips and she gasped, trembling. 'D-don't...'

'I have to,' he whispered back.

A second later she sighed, the sweetness of her breath mingling with his own as her lips parted to the pressure of his.

He had longed for this. Sinking his fingers into the hair at her nape, he slowly deepened the kiss, coaxing her through her hesitancy and into willing participation, groaning at the tentative exploration as her own tongue glided with his. She tasted exquisite, fresh and pure, and he knew right away he would never tire of kissing her, that he wanted so much more... Nic sensed the moment when Hannah's response changed and panic set in. Then she was pushing against him with a whimper of distress and he forced himself to retreat, pulling back at once.

'It's OK,' he soothed, giving her some space, gently stroking her face. 'What is it that scares you so much?'

She shook her head, withdrawing further, clearly determined

to keep her secrets. He let her turn over again, with her back to him, knowing she really wanted to leave.

'Stay,' he urged softly, holding his breath for what seemed an age as she hesitated, deliberating the wisdom of his request.

As she gradually began to relax again, his breath sighed out in relief. He slipped an arm round her, careful to make sure she didn't feel trapped. She wriggled around for a moment, getting comfortable, and he groaned, anything but relaxed when he was so hopelessly aroused. Maybe this hadn't been such a good idea!

'Are you in pain?' she asked with concern.

'Yes.' His smile was rueful as he shifted in the bed, trying to make his problem less obvious. 'But not in the way you are thinking.'

'I don't understand.'

'No, and, believe me, you wouldn't want to!'

'But—'

'Go to sleep, *cara*.'

Nic lay awake for a long time, savouring the feel of her in his arms. He had no illusions that she would still be there in the morning, but for now he could pretend she was his. It nearly killed him not to kiss her, to touch her, to make love to her, but he knew he couldn't. Not yet. For whatever reason, this was as far as she could go for now. He had to be patient, take things slowly.

As he lay listening to her breathing, he thought back to their kiss, a frown on his face. She had seemed uncertain, almost in-experienced. Maybe she was just rusty, out of practice—like him. He smiled into the darkness. If he had his way, they would enjoy plenty of practice in the weeks ahead. All he had to do was persuade Hannah it was what she wanted, too.

CHAPTER SIX

'HI.'

Hannah glanced up as Nic stepped inside her consulting room, her heart contracting, as it always seemed to, just at the sight of him. 'Hi,' she managed in reply.

He approached the desk with lazy strides. 'I thought you'd like to see this, it's just arrived.'

'What is it?'

She took the postcard he held out to her, a smile spreading across her face as she realised it was from Joanne McStay, the carer they had been so worried about. She had taken their advice for some respite care and this was the result, a glowing account of her two-week holiday in Greece.

'It's great, no?'

'Amazing!' Hannah looked up, her gaze clashing with his, one look at those slumberous dark eyes setting her pulse racing again. 'She sounds happy.'

'Let's hope we can keep her that way when she comes home.'

Nic perched on the corner of her desk, the action tightening the fabric of his dark grey trousers over the muscled length of his thigh.

'Absolutely.'

Hannah cleared her throat, dragging her gaze away. Whatever was wrong with her lately? She couldn't even seem to form a coherent sentence any more. He'd only kissed her, for goodness' sake! Two weeks ago. So why did she think she could still taste him? She sighed, her tongue running over her lips. A faint indrawn breath alerted her and she glanced up, finding his gaze fixed on her mouth, his eyes sultry. Hannah froze. Nothing had happened since that night and yet every look, every innocuous touch seemed more heated, more charged than before.

'There you are, Nic,' Kirsty announced, bustling into the room, seemingly oblivious of the tension that, to Hannah, crackled in the air. 'Mr Maxwell is on the phone, he'd like a word with you about his test results. I've left his notes on your desk.'

'Of course. Thank you, Kirsty,' he responded, although his gaze never left Hannah's face.

'Right you are. Hannah, your first appointment is here.'

'OK.'

Kirsty bustled out again as Nic slowly rose from the desk. 'I'll see you later.' He smiled, his voice more throaty than usual.

'Yes, I expect so,' she agreed, aiming for a nonchalance she was far from feeling. 'Thanks for the card.'

'No problem.'

Hannah sank back into her chair as the door closed behind him, her hands clenching on the arms. Dear God, this had to stop. Compassion for the pain of his loss had overwhelmed both her common sense and her fear of intimacy, so much so she had acted completely out of character. And look where it had led her. Into his arms. She closed her eyes, remembering the texture of his stubbled jaw under her hand, the exciting rasp of it across her skin as he'd kissed her. Heat and anxiety curled inside her in equal measure. She'd never felt anything like this before. Had never been kissed like that before, either, with a combination of such exquisite tenderness and fiery sensuality. When she had been sure Nic had fallen asleep, she had slid from his bed and returned to her room, shaken and confused. And strangely bereft. A feeling that had stayed with her, unnerving, distracting.

Nic had confided in her about the terrible loss of his family and his fiancée, the tragedy that now drove him from place to place. It sounded as if his heart had been buried with his fiancée, that no one would fill the hole she had left in his life. She knew Nic wanted her to share her secrets with him in return, but she couldn't. She had never told anyone. It had been years since she had even given the events any conscious thought, she realised now. And yet they governed her existence. Back here, in the place she loved, she had found her niche. She felt safe and comfortable and controlled. At least she had, until Nic had arrived and started to upset everything. Now all those bad memories were flowing back to the surface, unsettling her.

For the last two weeks she had tried to avoid him as much as possible, but it wasn't easy, especially at home. He made her feel vulnerable and out of control. She had to remember that she was just a project to him. Another Wallace. Something he thought he could heal while he was there. Then he would be gone and he'd forget all about her. She couldn't allow things to get out of hand, no matter the temptation, because there was no doubt Nic would go and she would be left putting the pieces of her life back together. Again.

'Hannah?'

Her intercom buzzed, making her jump. She sat forward and pressed the button. 'Yes?'

'Is something wrong?' Kirsty asked impatiently, clearly bemused at the delay. 'Are you ready for your patients now?'

'I'm sorry. Of course. Send the first one in.'

Taking the notes from her tray, Hannah drew in a deep breath, endeavouring to put thoughts of Nic, and her past, from her mind and concentrate on her morning list.

It was a long surgery. Everyone seemed to have fiddly or difficult problems, and Hannah was thankful when she showed her last patient out. She was anticipating a reviving cup of coffee when Kirsty appeared at the door, another set of notes in her hand.

'Can you see one more?'

'Of course,' Hannah sighed, smothering a yawn. 'Who is it?'

'Sally, the barmaid from the Furry Ferret,' she sniffed with disapproval, making Hannah smile, both at her tone and the use of the jocular nickname for the local inn.

'What's the problem?'

'She's asking to see Nic but he's already out on calls. Not that I'd let the floosie loose on him. They call her The Piranha, you know.'

'Kirsty!'

The plain-speaking woman sniffed again. 'It's no secret around the village that Sally has set her sights on our new doctor, not that I can see him being remotely interested in *her*! Still, I'm not having her harassing him for irrelevant appointments.'

'Send her in, then,' Hannah requested, taking the notes Kirsty handed her.

She disapproved of gossip, but the news that someone was interested in Nic on a personal level left her feeling distinctly uncomfortable. She frowned as the young woman in question tottered into the room wearing a very low-cut top, a skirt that was so short it was nearly a belt and impossibly high heels.

Hannah smothered a rush of uncharacteristic annoyance and, offering a cool smile, gestured for the young woman to sit down. 'What can I do for you today, Sally?'

'I had been hoping to see Dr di Angelis.' She pouted prettily, tossing bleached blonde curls over her shoulder.

'I'm afraid he's out at the moment. Can I help?'

Disappointment evident, Sally used a long, scarlet-painted nail to sweep her fringe from her heavily mascara'd blue eyes. 'I suppose so. There are a couple of things now I am here.'

'Of course,' Hannah allowed stiffly. 'The first?'

'My eczema is flaring up again. I wonder if there is something different I could try?' she asked, pointing to the reddened patches on her arms, some of which looked inflamed and crusty.

Hannah studied her notes, seeing she had been using Betnovate cream for some while. 'Do you have any patches elsewhere?'

'I sometimes have it behind the knees, but not at the moment.' She grimaced, wrinkling her pert little nose. 'Not very attractive, is it?'

'It can be very unpleasant. You find the Betnovate isn't working for you?'

'Not really.'

Having examined Sally's arms, Hannah tapped out a prescription request on her keyboard and turned to Sally while it printed. 'I'll give you some Dermovate ointment but make sure you use it sparingly and only once a day. You should find it more efficient than the cream you've been using,' she added, signing the prescription and handing it across.

'Thank you, Dr Frost.'

'You might also find it helps to use a cream like E45 or Diprobase to avoid irritating the skin.'

'I'll try that, thanks.'

'Good.' Hannah forced another cool smile. 'Was there something else you wanted to discuss, Sally?'

'Oh, yes, silly me!' She smirked with a tinkly giggle.

Hannah hid her irritation by looking over her notes again. 'How else can I help?' she prompted.

'Birth control.'

'Right.' Hannah felt her jaw tighten involuntarily. 'I see you were taking the Pill until recently?'

'I was, but I stopped them for a while. Now I want to start again. Just in case I get lucky!'

This time Hannah couldn't force a smile as Sally giggled suggestively. 'And did you have any problems taking them before, Sally?'

'No, none at all.'

'I'll just check your blood pressure, if I may.'

Hannah concentrated on her task, not wanting to consider with whom Sally was hoping to 'get lucky'. Something hot and insidious curled inside her. Something that felt suspiciously like jealousy. Nonsense, she berated herself. She unsnapped the cuff and hooked her stethoscope round her neck.

'That's fine,' she confirmed to Sally, writing down the blood-pressure figures in her notes. 'I'll give you a new prescription for the same brand, all right? Come and see me again if you have any problems with them.'

'Thanks.'

Hannah handed over the second prescription, eager for this tortuous consultation to be over, but the attractive blonde still lingered.

'Was there something else, Sally?'

'I wondered… Is the new doctor staying long?'

'Just temporarily,' Hannah said, barely keeping the snap from her voice.

'That's a shame. He's the dishiest man we've had round here in ages! He comes into the pub sometimes with his walking friends,' Sally confided. 'He's always so friendly.'

Hannah gritted her teeth and rose to her feet. 'Is he really?'

Nic occasionally went out in the evenings, she knew not where, but she did know he enjoyed hill walking and mountain biking at the weekends when he wasn't on call. Not that it was any of her business what he did. Or with whom he did it. She frowned. He had clearly been accepted into village life very rapidly, she thought sourly, not quite sure why she was feeling so grumpy and out of sorts.

'Well, thanks,' the girl murmured, reluctantly rising, too. 'Is Dr di Angelis, you know, attached?'

'I really have no idea, Sally. Now, I'm afraid you'll have to excuse me as I'm running late.'

She barely resisted slamming the door as Sally retreated towards Reception in those ridiculous shoes. Serve her right if she ended up in A and E with a broken ankle, Hannah fumed.

She wrote up her notes and closed the file with a thud. Stuffing the patient files back in the tray with more force than necessary, she caused the whole lot to shoot off the edge of the desk and spill across the floor. Her temper stoked, Hannah started to retrieve them, resisting the childish temptation to kick the empty plastic tray across the room.

'Bloody woman! Anyone would think I was running a bloody dating service, not a doctor's surgery!'

'Can I help?'

Hannah spun round in shock at the sound of Nic's amused query from the doorway. Bloody man! This was all his fault, anyway. She slammed the tray back on the desk and rammed the notes inside.

'I thought you were out on calls?' she snapped at him.

'I was,' he agreed equably. 'I've just come back to collect something.'

'Well, now you can go again.'

Nic leaned against the doorjamb, his arms folded across his chest, an annoying smile on his face. Well, she thought it was annoying, anyway. *He* was annoying.

'What's got you so riled?'

'None of your business,' she muttered, shoving a new prescription pad in her bag and searching crossly for her stethoscope before realising it was still around her neck. Wrenching it free, she tossed it inside before snapping her bag shut.

'Kirsty said I was to thank you.'

'Did she?'

'What am I to thank you for?'

'Why don't you ask her? The pair of you can do your own dirty work in future.'

Nic's eyes shone with laughter as she struggled to get her coat on. He crossed the room and took it from her. 'Let me help.'

'I can manage, thank you,' she said through gritted teeth, pulling it away from him and tossing it over her arm.

'Sembrate bei guando siete arrabbiati, innamorata!'

Hannah's temper flared anew. 'And stop talking to me in Italian when you know I don't bloody well understand what you are saying!'

'I said you look beautiful when you are angry, sweetheart,' Nic explained patiently, still smiling.

Face flushed, she stared up at him in confusion. 'Well, don't. Say it, I mean. In English or Italian. Now, please, get out of my way. I'm late.'

Gathering up her bag and notes, she stalked out of the room, fuming when she heard him chuckling behind her. In Reception, she slammed the tray of patient notes down on the counter, startling both Kirsty and Jane, who stared at her in amazement.

She glared at them. 'Something wrong?'

'No.' Kirsty grinned. 'Nothing at all.'

'Good. I'm going out.'

With as much dignity as she could muster, feeling stupid and not at all understanding her sudden burst of temper, Hannah hurried out to her car.

'Hannah was in earlier,' Jimmy McCall said in an increasingly rare wakeful spell, his breathing poor, his voice raspy and weak.

Nic smiled. 'She had a bit of a temper this morning.'

'Aye! Always had some fire about her. Used to, any road. Good to see.' Jimmy drew in a rasping breath and placed a gnarled, papery hand on Nic's. 'Hannah wasn't like this, not before she went away.'

'Don't try and talk now, Jimmy.'

'Must tell you. Important.'

Frowning, concerned how much Jimmy had deteriorated in the last week, Nic gently held his hand. 'OK.'

'I've known her since she was a wee one,' the dying man confided. 'So proud when she went to medical school.' He broke off to cough again, having a puff of oxygen before pushing the mask aside. 'When she came back she was different.'

'How was she different?' Nic prompted, curious but unwilling to tire Jimmy.

'She came home the first year or two, Christmas and such. Things seemed fine. She was leaning towards A and E then. Suddenly she changed. Said hospital life was not for her, she was training to be a GP and coming home.'

Nic helped him sip some water and waited as Jimmy caught his breath before he continued.

'When she first got back for good she was jumpy. Pale and thin. Sad most of all. Her father said it was like a light had been turned out inside her,' he went on, nodding his head slowly. 'It was true. These last years her life has been her work. Nothing else.'

While Jimmy paused to rest, Nic pondered on what Jimmy had said. It confirmed what he knew. Hannah had been hurt in some way. What he still didn't know was how. Did Jimmy know? But as keen as he was to learn more about Hannah's past, he was determined not to let the sick man tire himself.

'You sleep now, Jimmy.'

'No, no. Not long left,' he protested, and Nic leaned closer to hear as the man struggled to speak. 'Need to finish. Hannah like the daughter I never had. Her father was my best friend. I hate to see her so closed off. Part of her is in cold storage. Kindness itself with patients and staff, but not many could say they were close to her now. Something happened, Nic. I know it. But Hannah won't talk. She never speaks of her life away from here.'

'Why are you telling me this?'

'Hannah needs you.'

Nic was silent for a while, giving Jimmy time to rest, shaky fingers holding the oxygen mask to his face. 'What makes you think I could do anything, even if Hannah wanted me to?' he asked when the man rallied again.

'I may have only hours left, but I'm not blind. Or stupid.' Jimmy tried to smile. 'I see the way you look when you talk about her. And she's had some spark back since you came.

She's lonely. I think you are, too, inside. You need each other. And now I've said too much. We never had this conversation, you understand?'

'I understand.'

Nic managed a smile, shaken by the older man's perception. Again it confirmed his own instincts about Hannah, but the missing pieces of the puzzle remained illusive. He spent some moments making Jimmy more comfortable, checking the oxygen and the settings on the morphine pump, those same instincts telling him the kindly man didn't have too much longer.

'You rest now, Jimmy,' he soothed. 'I'll come back later.'

'Not long. It's time. Don't let Hannah come,' he rasped.

'She'll want to see you.'

'No,' he protested in distress. 'Promise.'

Feeling bad, wondering if Jimmy would wake again, Nic squeezed his hand. 'I'll do all I can.'

Apparently satisfied, Jimmy relaxed. When he was confident Jimmy was sleeping peacefully, Nic slipped out of the room, smiling at the nurse now employed by the family to stay with the ill man all night.

'He's settled now. You'll call me as soon as there's any change?'

'I will, Doctor,' she promised, heading back into Jimmy's room to sit quietly with him.

When he got home that evening, he found Hannah sitting on the living room floor in front of the log fire, playing with Wallace. The little kitten was much more mobile now, quite a handful, keen to explore and usually getting himself into trouble. Despite his tiredness and his concern, Nic smiled. She looked up, her gaze wary, but all trace of her earlier temper gone from her eyes.

'Have you had supper?' she asked.

'No. I'll get something later.'

'There's some cauliflower cheese in the oven if you'd like it.'

Nic nodded, realising how long it was since he'd eaten and

suspecting he had a long night ahead of him. 'Thanks, I think I will. Can I get you anything?'

'No, I'm fine.'

Hannah frowned as he left the room and she heard him go upstairs to change. He looked tired and worried about something. Was he thinking about his family? About Federica? The woman he'd loved, with whom he'd planned a family and a happy ever after, whose death had closed his heart? She swallowed the lump in her throat, dismissing a welter of confusing thoughts and unwanted emotions. Perhaps Nic was just wary after her strop that morning. It hadn't been fair, taking her temper out on him. She heard him moving about the kitchen a while later and was surprised when he carried his plate and a glass of water into the living room, sitting on the settee across from her to eat his meal. Hannah focused her concentration on Wallace, who pounced on the stands of wool she dangled for him. He still didn't look remotely lion-like, she mused, but Nic had been right—the little kitten was definitely a fighter.

'Thanks, Hannah, that was delicious.' Nic set his empty plate down, his smile tired.

'Can I get you some coffee?'

'Not right now.'

She watched as he sat back with a sigh, his long legs stretched out in front of him. He was very quiet tonight.

'Rough day?' she asked after a few moments of silence.

'I've had better.' He managed another smile. 'You?'

She flushed, thinking of her earlier behaviour. 'Likewise.'

'Who upset you this morning?'

'The blonde bombshell.'

'Who?'

'Sally Archibald.'

'I don't know her.'

Didn't he? Hannah looked at him with a frown. 'The barmaid at the village inn.'

'Oh.' Nic grimaced. 'I know who you mean.'

'I'm sure you've noticed her,' she muttered, with more sarcasm than she'd intended.

'Why do you say that?'

He didn't sound very pleased, she realised. 'Isn't that what most men go for? Petite, beautiful blondes?' she pressed, regretting the impulse when she saw his eyes narrow.

'I wouldn't know. I'm not most men. Don't stereotype me, Hannah, and file me away in some convenient box in your head.'

She swallowed, feeling well and truly put in her place. Out of the corner of her eye, she saw Nic get up and carry his plate and glass out to the kitchen. That hadn't been very clever of her, had it? Sitting cross-legged on the floor, she gathered Wallace onto her lap, stroking his soft, warm little body, surprised when Nic returned a couple of minutes later with two mugs of coffee.

'Thanks,' she murmured in confusion, setting hers on the table out of Wallace's reach.

Nic sat down in one of the armchairs closer to her. 'So what did she want?'

'Sally?' she queried nervously, and Nic nodded. 'You.'

'Excuse me?'

She almost smiled at the look of horrified surprise on his face. 'To quote Kirsty, Sally has "set her sights" on you.'

'Il Dio lo aiuta.' Seeing her frown, Nic smiled. 'God help me.'

'You might not need him. You've got Kirsty riding shotgun for you!'

Nic raised an eyebrow. 'Why?'

'You'll have to ask her. Sally showed up angling to see you so Kirsty shoved her on the end of my list.'

'I am sorry for that.'

Hannah shrugged, tickling Wallace under the chin, making him purr like a road drill. 'It doesn't matter.'

'I will sort things out with Kirsty and fight my own battles in future.'

'But—'

'Don't worry, *cara*, I'll deal with Sally if necessary.'

She wasn't sure whether to be relieved or not. The thought of Nic having anything to do with Sally still made her curiously disturbed and protective. Which was nonsense, of course. She took a sip of her coffee, nearly dropping the mug when she glanced at Nic and found him looking at her, interest in those watchful brown eyes. Oh, God, now what? she worried, setting her mug back down with shaky fingers.

'So,' he began, a slow, sexy smile pulling at the corners of his mouth.

Unnerved, Hannah shifted uncomfortably. 'So what?'

'What was it about Sally wanting me that had you so fired up?'

Damn the man! 'It wasn't that at all,' she denied airily, desperately trying to fabricate something plausible.

'Oh?'

'No. I'm afraid Sally's always rubbed me the wrong way. We just don't get on very well.'

'I see.'

He probably did, too, she realised, darting a hasty glance at him and seeing the glitter of amusement back in his eyes. She had another sip of coffee before returning her attention to Wallace. The little kitten seemed to have run out of steam at last and had curled up in her lap, fast asleep. Aware of Nic's gaze still on her, her own was drawn reluctantly back to him.

'I was just thinking,' he murmured, leaning back in the chair as she frowned at him.

'What about?'

'You. Why don't you have a man in your life?' Nic regarded her for a moment, and she felt the familiar curl of heat inside her under the intensity of his gaze. 'You haven't answered my question.'

She looked down at Wallace again. 'Because I don't want one.'

'Why?'

'Why does there have to be a why?' she countered stiffly. 'I'm contented with my life as it is.'

'Are you?'

He always made her think about things she didn't want to face. With a sigh, she glanced at him. 'Why are you looking at me?'

'Because I like to.' He smiled, sitting forward, his elbows resting on his knees. 'You're a very beautiful woman.'

'Don't start that again,' she protested uncomfortably.

'In English or Italian?'

She scowled at him. 'Either.'

'I'm telling the truth.' He cupped her chin and she was forced to look at him. 'You are beautiful. And you're generous and kind, smart and caring, sexy and—'

'Oh, stop! That's ridiculous.'

'Someone has done a very thorough job on you, haven't they?'

His serious expression unsettled her and she moved away, needing to escape his touch, passing Wallace to him as she stood up. 'I don't know what you mean.'

'Don't let them win, Hannah, and rob you of so much in life.'

She took the mugs out to the kitchen and washed up, her hands shaking, alarmed when Nic came through and settled Wallace down in his pen.

'I'm going to bed,' she announced, anxious to put some distance between them.

'*Desidero che potrei unirlo,*' he murmured, casting a mischievous glance at her as he told her how much he would like to join her.

Hands on hips she glared at him, infuriated again. 'What did you say?'

'I was talking to Wallace.'

'No, you weren't.' The gleam of wicked laughter in his eyes belied his innocent words. 'Nic—'

'I said, I wish you a good night.'

Hannah didn't believe him for a moment. As she climbed into

bed a while later, she was sure she wouldn't sleep. Her mind seemed to be buzzing with so many disturbing and confusing things. All of which were Nic's fault. Frowning, she thumped the pillow and turned over. Did he flatter himself or what, thinking she'd been in a temper because Sally fancied him! Which, an annoying inner voice taunted her, was precisely what had happened. There was just no way she was going to admit she wanted Nic herself. She didn't. And even if she did, it was impossible.

Dawn was breaking when she woke up. She had slept better than she'd expected, although she had half stirred in the early hours, imagining she'd heard the phone ring and the front door close.

Showered and dressed for morning surgery, she went downstairs, chatting to Wallace as she put some coffee on to percolate. She heard a car door slam and then a key in the front door. So Nic had gone out. She frowned. His bag hit the floor and there was a rustle as he hung up his leather jacket. She looked round with a smile as he came into the kitchen but her smile faded when she saw him. He looked terrible.

'Have you been out all night? I thought I heard the phone but—' She broke off at the look on his face. 'What is it?'

He came towards her, eyes full of sadness and concern. Fear curled through her as he slid his hands up her arms to her shoulders.

'Nic?'

'I'm so very sorry, *innamorata*,' he murmured hoarsely, the fingers of one hand stroking her face. 'Jimmy died a little while ago.'

She blinked back tears at the loss of the man she had known all her life and of whom she was so fond. 'I should have been there. Why didn't you call me?'

'Jimmy made me promise not to.'

'But why?' A wave of rejection swamped her. 'Why would he do that?'

'He cared for you. He didn't want you to see it at the end.'

'But it's my job… I wanted to be there for him.'

'I know, *cara*.'

Hannah was unable to prevent the tears escaping and she went, unresisting, into Nic's arms. He held her as she sobbed out her hurt and sadness, soothing her with words whose meaning she couldn't comprehend but which reached her in some elemental way, assuring her of his compassion, his own sadness.

As her first wave of tears subsided, he released her, handing her a tissue before he poured two mugs of coffee and encouraged her into the living room. Once there, he drew her down onto the settee.

'You knew, didn't you? Last night?' she accused, setting down her mug as her hands were too shaky to hold it.

'I suspected, yes.'

'I don't understand why he didn't want me there.'

He took her hand, his touch warm, both disturbing and comforting at the same time. 'Hannah, he loved you, he thought he was protecting you.'

'But I'm a doctor,' she protested.

'Yes, but you were also his friend.' Nic's thumb traced circles on her palm, distracting her. 'The daughter he never had.'

She stared at him in surprise. 'Jimmy said that?'

'He did.'

'But when? I…'

'I spent some time with him,' Nic confessed, surprising her anew. 'In the evenings, at weekends. At the beginning we'd play chess when he felt able, later we just talked, or I sat with him while he slept.'

The knowledge that Nic had done that for a man he scarcely knew touched her beyond measure. 'I didn't realise. But he shouldn't have been alone, with just a nurse,' she said, her voice unsteady.

'He wasn't alone, *cara*.'

'You were there?' She swallowed as he nodded. 'You did that for him?'

'And for you.'

Fresh tears pricked her eyes. 'For me?'

'I knew Jimmy was important to you. When I found out that he had said you were not to be called, I thought you might feel easier if you knew I'd been there instead.'

Hannah didn't know what to say. It must have been hard for Nic to take on such a promise, to accept the responsibility of being with Jimmy, especially after all he himself had been through, losing those he loved. Tears spilled down her cheeks, not just for Jimmy and his death, but because Nic had done what he had done out of genuine kindness and care...had understood what this meant to her.

Now, as he held her, stroking her hair as she cried, she struggled to make sense of all the ramifications, not least the effect this man was having on her life.

CHAPTER SEVEN

'Ouch!' Nic complained as Wallace used his leg for climbing practice, sharp little claws digging through the denim of his jeans and into his thigh. 'Play fair, *uomo piccolo*.'

Gently he lifted Wallace off his leg, amazed how much the kitten had grown since the day he had found him so bedraggled and on the point of death. Stroking him, he set him on the bed, encouraging him to play with a little ball that had a bell inside it. Wallace swiped it with his paw and then pounced, rolling on his back with his prize. Laughing, Nic tickled his tummy.

Sobering, he glanced out of the window into the darkness. Not that he could have seen much had it been daytime as November was ending as wet and windy as it had begun, the ridge of the hills masked by low, grey cloud. The only sunshine had come, symbolically, on the day of Jimmy's funeral. With a frown Nic checked his watch. After six. He'd expected Hannah back by now. He hoped she was all right but she had been so sure she wanted to go alone to Jimmy's to meet his sister and collect some books that the kindly man had left to her.

Trying to concentrate, he turned his attention back to his research. He made some notes but all the time part of him was listening out for the sound of a car in the drive and the front door closing. When it finally came, half an hour later, a sigh of relief whispered from him.

'Hannah?' he called, hearing her footsteps on the stairs a few moments later.

'Hi,' she greeted him, hesitating just inside the door, a package tucked under her arm.

He scanned her face. 'You OK, *cara*?'

'I'm fine.' She moved across towards him, a wary look back in her eyes as she approached the bed, holding out the package. 'Here.'

'From you?' he questioned in surprise, setting his medical book aside.

'No, from Jimmy. Alice said he left instructions that you were to have it.'

Nic swallowed the lump in his throat and took the package, too overwhelmed to speak when he discovered the man he had known for far too short a time had left him his precious antique chess set. He glanced up at Hannah, knowing his feelings were reflected in his eyes, seeing her sad smile of understanding.

He cleared his throat. 'I don't know what to say.'

'You don't have to say anything,' she assured softly. 'We both know why Jimmy did it, what it meant to him.'

'And to me.'

'Yes.'

Nic watched as she crossed to the window and drew the curtains, his breath catching as his gaze ran over her. He almost wished she'd kept to the power suits. The sight of her legs and the curve of her rear in those jeans that moulded themselves like a second skin was driving him mad. And she'd left her hair loose for once. His fingers itched to feel it again.

Touched by how moved Nic was to receive Jimmy's final gift, Hannah fiddled with the curtains for a few moments, giving them both time to work through their emotions. When she turned from the window, heat curled through her at the look on Nic's face. There was a hunger in his eyes that scared her. Nervous, she looked beyond him to where Wallace was sleeping on his back, his little paws dangling in the air.

'You've worn Wally out, I see.'

'He's been using me as a climbing frame.' Nic smiled, mischief replacing the intensity in his gaze. 'I'm covered in scratches. Maybe you ought to look at them, make sure I don't get an infection, yes?'

Hannah didn't want to think about touching him again. 'No.'

'Shame,' he teased.

Shameless, Hannah corrected silently, trying not to smile. Nic had been amazing since Jimmy's death, never crowding her, yet always there if she needed anything. And he'd gone with her to the funeral. She knew it had been difficult for him, that he had been moved about Jimmy but also remembered his own tragic losses, too. Throughout it all, though, the tension remained between them, the air fizzing with electricity. Her awareness of him was becoming a major problem. She closed her eyes. What was she going to do about him?

'Did you collect your books?'

'Yes.' Nic's question dragged her mind away from her disturbing thoughts. 'There are more than I was expecting. I've left the boxes downstairs for now.'

'I'll help you with them later,' he offered softly, and she knew he understood what the things Jimmy had left meant to her.

'What are you working on?' she asked, as a charged silence threatened to stretch between them.

'I'm trying to get some information for a patient I saw today.' Frowning, he picked up his medical reference book. 'Do you know anything about gynaecomastia?'

'Male breasts? Not much. I saw a case once, while I was training. You?'

Nic shook his head. 'I know more now than I did this morning when the guy came in. I asked him to come back on Monday to give me forty-eight hours to do some research so I'll know how best to advise him. Here, look at this,' he invited, patting the bed beside him.

Interested, Hannah crossed the room, thinking how rumpled and attractive he looked, sitting there with one denim-clad leg tucked under him, the other dangling off the edge of the bed, his feet bare. Conscious of his nearness, the subtle aroma of sandalwood that had become so familiar, she forced herself to concentrate on the papers he handed her.

'I found an interesting site on the internet,' he told her now. 'If my patient has online access, this would be helpful for him.'

'What did you find when you examined him?'

'No evidence of tissue attached to muscle, no lumps and no testicular tumours. But the breasts are noticeably very enlarged on both sides.'

Reading the advice from the sources he had already consulted, Hannah nodded. 'How old is he?'

'Twenty-one. The poor guy has been living with this for years, hoping it would end after puberty, too scared to ask for help,' he said, his sympathy evident in his voice.

'That's sad.' Hannah tucked some wayward strands of hair behind her ear, concentrating on the notes. 'Any reason he's come in now?'

Nic shrugged. 'It's affecting his whole life. He's too embarrassed to go out, to swim, to join in team sports, ask a girl out.'

'He's going to need a lot of emotional support, then, as well as any physical interventions.'

'I agree.'

She met Nic's gaze, warmed by the approval in his dark eyes. 'Any signs of the things it mentions here…liver disease or drug use, steroids or anything?'

'Not that I could tell on first consultation,' he replied, 'but I didn't know everything to look for this morning. My instinct says it is most likely to be hormonal.'

'So what are you going to do? Refer him to the endocrinologist?'

Nic nodded. 'If the patient will go. The question is, do we handle any counselling here, or do they deal with that at the hospital? And, if we do it, should it be before we refer him on?'

'You probably need to talk to him about that. If he's confident to go to the specialist now, that's great. If he needs more psychological support first, he can talk to Sarah,' Hannah said. 'How did he seem?'

'Scared but determined,' he assessed after some deliberation. 'It's an interesting one.'

Nic sighed, a pout of consideration on his lips. 'I might ring the endocrinologist on Monday and sound him out before I see the patient.'

'That's a good idea. Sorry I couldn't be more help.'

'You have helped.' She shivered as he took hold of her hand. 'It's good being able to discuss it. Thank you.'

'No problem,' she murmured, far too conscious of the distracting movement of his fingers on her skin.

Hannah groaned inwardly. Why did she always feel so ridiculously out of her depth with this man? If only she was more sophisticated and knew how do deal with him. Instead, Nic was two years younger than her in age but way ahead in terms of experience and being worldly wise. What she still could not understand was what he wanted with her, why he was interested.

'I was wondering,' she said, trying to inject some normality into her voice and, unsuccessfully, to extract her hand from his, 'if it was a time when you were not rostered on night calls, would you mind coping if I had a couple of days off?'

His fingers briefly stilled their caress but didn't release her. 'You want to go away?'

'Well, I just thought for a day or two,' she confirmed, disconcerted by the thread of disappointment in his voice.

'Of course, *cara*, we can manage, if you'd like a break.'

Against her better judgement, her gaze was drawn to his and a new prickle of awareness tingled down her spine as she looked into those dark, molten eyes. 'I, um, have a friend in Edinburgh and—'

'A friend?'

'Yes.' Why did she feel she had to explain everything? What business was it of his what she did and where she went? 'Lauren. Haven't I mentioned her?'

Nic's smile was more natural, almost relieved. 'No, I don't think you have.'

'We did some of our training together. She's in Paeds in Edinburgh now. I don't see her much but we email news occasionally and I go to Edinburgh once or twice a year.'

'And do you keep in touch with anyone else from your training days?' he queried lightly.

The question brought an uncomfortable lump to her throat. 'No.'

'Where was it you trained?'

'Birmingham,' she murmured, determined not to think about her time there. Or part of it, at least.

His fingers seemed to home in on the point at her wrist where her pulse had started beating erratically. 'A long way from home.'

'Mmm.' She cleared her throat. 'Anyway, I thought I'd go to Edinburgh next week, do some Christmas shopping, get my hair cut, see—'

'No! Don't you dare,' he interrupted, a horrified expression on his face.

Hannah hid a smile, some reckless streak making her tease him. 'I fancy a whole new look. Something short and chic and easier to manage.'

'You can tell your hairdresser that if he cuts off more than one centimetre he will have to answer to me,' he declared passionately, releasing her wrist but only so he could sink the fingers of both hands into her long, chestnut waves. 'Your hair is magnificent.'

Breathless, Hannah stared at him, shocked by his intense reaction and by the feel of his hands on her. She hadn't meant things to go this far. 'Nic...' she whispered.

'Tell me you are joking.'

'I am,' she managed hoarsely. 'I'm only having it trimmed.'

'Promise me.'

Hannah nodded in response to his husky demand. When had he moved closer? Nervous, she looked at him, saw his eyes darken further with sultry desire as his gaze slid to her mouth and back to her eyes again. Oh, God, no! She didn't want him to kiss her again. Did she? Why had she been so foolish as to tease him? Heat curled through her at the determined intensity of his gaze. His hands in her hair tilted her head as he bent towards her, his mouth inexorably finding hers.

She whimpered, whether in protest or longing, she was too scared to question. Her lips parted under his, fire licking through her veins as he instantly took possession of her mouth, kissing her with melting intensity. Consumed. That was the only word for it, Hannah thought dazedly. It was as if he consumed her totally and completely. She was so out of practice, but no one had ever kissed her like this.

Nic groaned, one hand gliding down her body as he lay back and drew her with him. She felt the solid breadth of his chest beneath her, felt him slide one leg between hers as his hand shaped the rounded swell of her rear before rising again, his fingers slipping under the hem of her top, caressing the hollow of her back. His touch on her bare skin made her gasp. She felt an unfamiliar ache low inside her and momentarily tried to assuage it by pressing herself more closely against him, feeling the evidence of his own arousal.

He broke the kiss, breathing heavily, pressing hot kisses to her throat as he whispered to her, his voice thick with desire. 'I want you so much.'

'No.' It was too much, too intense. Scared, she struggled against him, shocked by how quickly things had flared out of control. 'I can't! Stop it, please!'

'Hannah?' He relaxed his hold at once, eyes black with

passion and confusion as he stared at her, hands cupping her face. 'Don't cry, *cara*.'

Panicked, Hannah pushed his hands away, scrambling to her feet, her legs feeling too shaky to hold her. Her lips were swollen and fiery from the intensity of his kiss. She stared at him, wiping away the tears she had not realised she was shedding, unaware how starkly her fear was etched on her face, how bruised her eyes were.

'I'm sorry,' she whispered, hearing him say something in Italian as she fled.

Nic swore succinctly in his native language as Hannah ran from him. What tortured her so much? One moment they were making progress, he was getting close to her and she was responding eagerly and then, in a heartbeat, some inner demon panicked her. Concerned, ignoring his own discomfort, he rose to his feet and walked along the landing to Hannah's room, unable to just let her rush away.

'Hannah?' he called, tapping on the door.

There was a long moment of silence before she replied. 'What?'

'I'm worried about you, *innamorata*.'

'I'm fine.'

'We both know that's not true.' He sighed, not knowing how to reach her. 'Can I come in?'

'No.'

'I'll just sit out here, then, and talk to you,' he said, lowering himself and leaning his back against the door.

There was another long pause before she spoke again. 'I'm sorry.'

'Stop apologising. Tell me what it is, *cara*.'

'I can't,' she refuted, her voice unsteady. 'It's not you, it's me.'

He rubbed a hand along his jaw. 'Hannah—'

'Please, Nic.'

'I want to understand. Let me help you.'

Her reply was slow in coming and not what he wanted to hear. 'I'm sorry. Leave me alone now.'

'If that's what you want.' Frustrated, hurting for her, he stood up, a frown on his face. 'Call me if you need anything.'

He didn't see her the next day. He'd planned to go hill walking with a few of his new friends from the village and, while tempted to cancel, he decided to give Hannah the space she had asked for. Whatever spooked her was something deep rooted and he wasn't going to uncover it in five minutes. Or by pushing her too hard. At first he had imagined there had been some love affair gone wrong, but doubts were creeping in. Her reactions appeared too extreme for that. When he arrived back at the house after dark, there was no sign of her and no light coming from her room. But when she had left the house before him on Monday morning, his suspicions that she was avoiding him increased.

At his desk, he put a call through to the endocrinologist, pleased to secure the information and advice he needed for when he saw his troubled patient later in the morning.

Frowning, he turned to his computer. *'Are you all right?'* he emailed, waiting impatiently for Hannah to reply, knowing she was mere feet away from him. Finally a ping announced the arrival of a message in his inbox.

'Yes. How did you go with the endocrinologist?'

OK, so she wanted to ignore what was happening. At least she was talking to him. Sort of. Following her lead, he gave her a brief rundown on what the specialist had told him. *'I'll discuss the options with the patient later on,'* he finished.

'That's good, I hope all goes well. If it's OK, I think I'll go to Edinburgh today. The rota is covered for the next couple of nights so you don't need to worry,' she informed him.

'I'll worry about you,' he emailed back, frustrated that she was running away. Again.

'Don't.'

He couldn't help it. Despite being so busy covering all the surgeries, clinics and home visits, the days passed with painful slowness while she was away, the house feeling empty, even with Wallace's increasingly active companionship. Scared to look too closely at his own emotions and how involved he was becoming, Nic counted the minutes until she came home.

It was dark when Hannah drove back to Lochanrig on Wednesday, her car full of parcels. She let herself in, thankful Nic was not yet back from the surgery. The time away had done nothing to resolve things in her head, she admitted, making several trips to carry everything inside. While shopping, along Princes Street and many other nooks and crannies she knew in the city, visiting the hairdresser, and meeting up with Lauren, when they had gone for a meal at a renowned Indian restaurant on Dalry Road, and caught up on their news, thoughts of Nic had nagged constantly, and Jimmy's words had plagued her, too.

She was greeting Wallace when she heard Nic return. Her eyes closed for a moment as she steeled herself to face him again after the disastrous events of the weekend. He had every right to be angry with her. That he remained so understanding and concerned almost made her feel worse.

'Hi.'

The sound of his husky, accented voice sent a prickle of heat along her spine and she turned, not quite able to meet his gaze. 'Hi.'

'How was Edinburgh?'

'Too busy and crowded. But I did the things I wanted to do.'

'You kept your promise with your hair.'

Her gaze clashed with his and she saw the relief mixed with the amusement in his dark eyes. 'I was never going to cut it,' she murmured, a flush warming her cheeks.

'*Dio grazie.*' A smile curved that sensual mouth. 'And did you see your friend?'

Hannah struggled to drag her gaze and her thoughts away from his mouth and how it had felt on hers. 'Lauren? Yes, we had a meal last night,' she managed, her voice rough.

'Hannah—'

'I've put something on for supper,' she broke in, scared he was going to bring up anything personal again. 'How did things go with your gynaecomastia patient?'

She heard Nic sigh and he moved to pick up Wallace to make a fuss of him. 'I am going to refer him to the endocrinologist. While he's waiting for an appointment, he's going to talk with Sarah and come and see me again.'

'I'm glad.'

'I'll go and get changed,' Nic decided, handing Wallace over to her, his dark eyes serious. 'It's good to have you back, we missed you.'

It was good to be back, Hannah allowed, though she was far less willing to admit the fact that she had missed him, too. As the days passed, she felt calmer and although she knew it was a temporary respite and he would not give up, Nic respected her need for space and didn't press her for any answers to his questions.

'Doesn't it look festive?' Kirsty demanded, casting a satisfied eye over the Christmas decorations around the reception and waiting areas.

'You've all done a good job.' Hannah smiled, hiding her personal feelings about Christmas—lonely and sad since the loss of her parents.

'Nearly time for our meal out!' Jane grinned as she joined the rest gathered in the staffroom.

'You are coming, aren't you, Nic?' Shona asked.

Hannah saw him glance up from his coffee. 'If I'm invited,' he agreed, his smile making her stomach churn.

'Oh, Hannah, haven't you mentioned it?' Kirsty chastised. 'Of course you're invited, Nic! It's the one time of the year we all go out and have a meal and a drink together!'

'I'll look forward to it.'

'There's New Year as well,' Morag reminded them. 'Is everyone going to the dance?'

There was a chorus of agreement and Debbie looked at Hannah. 'You'll come, won't you?'

'No,' she refused, 'not this time.'

Morag frowned. 'You say that every year.'

'Please, come,' Jane begged.

'No, I'm afraid not.'

'You've got a special invite!' Kirsty chipped in, a mischievous glint in her eyes. 'Sandy Douglas wants you to go with him. I said I'd tell you.'

Hannah stared at her in horrified surprise. 'Well, you can thank him but the answer is no.'

'He's been sweet on you for years,' Kirsty teased, and the others laughed.

'Don't be silly, Kirsty,' Hannah responded, feeling distinctly uncomfortable. Out of the corner of her eye she saw Nic rise to his feet and wash his mug, a frown on his face. 'I'm not interested in Sandy Douglas and I never will be.'

An awkward silence followed her statement and Hannah knew they were all looking at her, all wondering, imagining. She swallowed, wishing she could make a dignified exit.

'Hannah, have you got a moment to spare before surgery? I need to ask your advice about a patient,' Nic asked, heading for the door.

A wave of relief swamped her and she all but shot out of her chair. 'Yes, of course.'

She followed him into his consulting room and he turned to face her, leaning against his desk. The scrutiny of his dark gaze made her fidget.

'You, um, wanted to ask me something?'

'No.' He smiled.

'But you said…'

He shrugged. 'I thought you wanted rescuing.'

'Oh.' Colour washed her cheeks. 'Thank you.'

'Who is this Sandy Douglas?'

Her colour deepened. 'Don't, Nic, please. He's just a guy I was at school with. We went out a couple of times when we were about sixteen, that's all. A lifetime ago. It's nothing,' she insisted, not sure why she wanted him to understand.

'So when is this meal out for all of us?'

'December the twenty-third. And I didn't deliberately not invite you—I'd forgotten all about it,' she explained, relieved he'd changed the subject.

His smile crinkled the corners of his eyes. 'Don't worry, Hannah.'

'I meant to say,' she rushed on, 'if you want some time off to go back to Italy for Christmas or anything, just ask.'

'I don't. But thank you. I already have plans for Christmas.'

'Oh, of course.' Hannah fought down a sinking feeling of disappointment. 'That's fine.'

'I'm really looking forward to it.'

Did he have to rub it in? 'That's good.'

Straightening, he stepped closer, making her nervous, then his fingers trailed down her cheek, leaving her skin burning from his touch. 'I'm planning on spending my Christmas with you and Wallace.' He smiled, moving round his desk to sit down.

Hannah returned to her own consulting room feeling ridiculously pleased. If she could just stop things getting too personal between them, maybe this Christmas would be much less lonely than usual. A curl of anticipation inside her, she forced herself to concentrate on another busy surgery.

'I've had a letter from your optician, telling me that he found some abnormalities when you had your recent eye test, Mr Scott,' Hannah explained gently, regarding the elderly man who sat across from her, his wife next to him, both anxious.

Mr Scott nodded, his voice gruff. 'Yes, he said something about the pressure?'

'That's right. It's a classic sign of chronic simple glaucoma. Increased pressure in the fluids in the eye damages the optic nerve. You may have noticed that your field of vision has been narrowing.'

'Will it get better, Doctor?' Mrs Scott asked, her hand nervously reaching for her husband's.

'I'm afraid the damage already caused is irreversible,' she told them as gently as she could. 'But we can do things to minimise and slow down any further deterioration.'

The elderly couple glanced at each other and Hannah felt sorry for them. It was always worrying when something went wrong, especially with the eyesight. She didn't want to alarm them at this stage with the knowledge that his condition could ultimately lead to blindness later in his life. She hoped it wouldn't happen.

'What I'll do,' she continued, 'is refer you to the eye clinic, Mr Scott. They will do some more detailed tests and look in your eyes to assess any damage and monitor the pressures. The specialist will likely prescribe you some drops to put in your eyes each day from now on and he'll write to me and let me know his findings. Is there anything else you want to ask me?'

'You say I'll have to have drops?' the elderly man asked worriedly.

'The condition can usually be controlled with eye drops, although you will probably have some deterioration over the years. You'll be monitored by us and the eye clinic. And if you have any children or grandchildren, do let them know about your condition. It can be congenital so it is important for close relatives to have regular eye tests.'

The couple rose to their feet, managing smiles. 'Thank you, Dr Frost, you've been very kind.'

'It's no problem,' she assured them, showing them out. 'Always get in touch if you are worried.'

Surgery over, Hannah went out to do a few house calls and she was running late when she headed back to Lochanrig.

'What on earth…?' she exclaimed, as she approached the village. The scene was chaotic. Vehicles had been abandoned in the road and up ahead a lorry, one of the loaders that carried trees away from the forestry felling operations, was at an angle across the road, its nose buried in the front of the newsagent's, the squashed remains of a car poking out from beneath it.

'Oh, my God.'

Hannah grabbed her medical bag, and ran to the scene, pushing her way determinedly through the people who milled about, telling them to move further back, away from the dangerous lorry, which rested precariously, making horrible creaking, groaning noises and threatening to shift at any moment.

'What happened here?' she demanded, seeing Jane, the surgery's young receptionist, standing nearby.

'I was g-going to the post office. The lorry was coming through and it just s-swerved out of control, hit a car, went over the pavement and p-ploughed into the shop,' she explained, visibly shaken. 'We've c-called an ambulance and everything.'

'How many hurt?'

'A few cuts and bruises. We th-think the lorry driver m-must have died at the w-wheel.'

Hannah gave Jane a quick once-over. Clearly the girl was very shocked. 'Go back to the surgery and sit down for a while with a cup of tea,' she instructed, looking around and seeing that Morag, their practice nurse, was on scene and trying to calm a hysterical young woman. 'And, Jane, ask Nic to come down with some more supplies.'

'B-but he's already here.'

The girl stared at her with frightened eyes. Something about her expression caused a knot of fear to curl through Hannah's stomach and a chill creep up her spine.

'What do you mean, Jane?'

'N-Nic,' the girl confirmed, her voice trembling. 'He's u-under the lorry.'

CHAPTER EIGHT

'*MALEDIZIONE*!'

Swearing under his breath, Nic wriggled through the tangled mess under the lorry in an attempt to reach the child in the pushchair who had been swept underneath in the carnage and was stuck fast. He stopped, holding his breath, his heart racing, as the lorry shifted above him, twisting the remains of the empty car that was now mangled beyond recognition.

Dragging his kit with him, he inched his way further in, able in the light of his torch beam to see the battered pushchair and a pair of pink-clad feet sticking out. It seemed to take for ever to crawl the rest of the way and get some kind of view of the little girl, but when he did, he could see the seriousness of the situation at once. As well as a head wound, which was bleeding profusely but seemed superficial, she appeared to have a nasty leg break and other cuts and bruises. By far the worst, he feared, was the penetrating trauma to her chest.

'*Maledizione*!' he repeated, hearing the audible sucking of air as he reached her.

It was clear the parietal pleura was broken and open, allowing the pleural cavity exposure to the outside air. He had to treat that quickly, before the lung fully collapsed. Tucking the torch awkwardly under his chin, he opened his bag and searched for a sterile occlusive dressing and some tape.

'Nic?'

Dio! What was Hannah doing here? 'Don't you dare come near this lorry,' he shouted to her.

'What have you got?'

'Open pneumothorax.'

He didn't waste time on further explanations. With no sign of any foreign bodies apparent on his examination, he worked swiftly to cover the wound, taping it down on three sides, creating a valve flap of the fourth side that prevented air getting in but allowed any excess air out. Satisfied the temporary action had improved things for the time being, he shifted uncomfortably in the cramped space to assess the girl's other injuries, concerned that she was conscious and watching him, but apparently traumatised. She seemed to be able to move but was mute with fear.

'OK, *ragazza piccola*. We'll soon have you out, little girl.'

He managed to get a line in and, after giving some analgesia, he set up some fluids for the shock and blood loss. Turning his attention to her head, he confirmed his first assessment that the scalp wound was superficial and no other serious injuries seemed to have occurred to her head or face. Straining in the confines available to him, he shone his torch in her eyes, relieved to find the pupils even and reacting normally.

Huge, tear-filled blue eyes focused on him and he smiled, gently stroking her cheek with one finger. 'My name is Nic. You're doing well, *ragazza piccola*.'

Having dressed the head wound, he shifted down to take a closer look at her lower leg. It was clearly broken below the knee, but he was thankful there was no bone showing.

'Hannah?'

'I'm here,' she responded, far too quickly.

'I told you to move away.'

'I wouldn't have heard you, then, would I?'

He let the snappy riposte go for now. 'Any sign of the fire service or the paramedics?'

There was a brief pause. 'Ambulance just pulling up and fire service ETA two minutes. What do you need?'

'A lower leg gutter or vacuum splint for a small child,' he requested. 'But don't you bring it. This lorry could shift again at any time.'

He frowned when she didn't answer, but as if he had brought about his own fears, creaking and groaning marked more movement in the wreckage. As he shuffled to try and protect the child from further harm, he tore his arm on some jagged metal from the mangled car. Swearing at the lancing pain, he had to force himself free, feeling blood flow down his arm.

'Nic, are you OK?'

'I'm fine,' he lied, gritting his teeth as he moved, hearing the anxiety in Hannah's voice.

'We're pushing the splint in now,' she called. 'Can you see it?'

'Yes.'

As he reached for the pack, ignoring the pain in his arm, there was a thud as he smacked his face on a piece of wreckage.

'Merda!'

'What happened?'

'Nothing to worry about.'

His fingers tested his cheekbone but he couldn't find anything broken. Muttering darkly in Italian, he grabbed the gutter splint and crawled back to the child, taking the vinyl-covered pad and wrapping it round the damaged leg as gently as he could, fastening the Velcro straps in place.

'The fire service is here. They're going to use air bags to make the lorry safe,' Hannah called. 'Can you come out now?'

'No.'

'Nic…I can smell petrol.'

Now she mentioned it, so could he. He could also hear how scared she was. 'We'll be all right, *cara*. You move away now, please.'

It seemed to take for ever waiting for the air bags to be inflated and the scene made safe. *Dio.* He wished Hannah hadn't told him about the petrol, he'd been anxious enough as it was. Talking softly to the little girl, he checked her injuries constantly, paying extra attention to her breathing and the temporary repair he'd made to the sucking chest wound. There was more that needed doing, but the cramped conditions made it impossible.

'Hi, Doc,' a firefighter greeted him, wriggling in beside him. 'I'm Drew. You OK?'

'I've been better.'

'What have we got?'

Nic ran swiftly through the child's injures. 'She's conscious but quiet. I can't get her out of the pushchair, the way it's pinned. It's going to need cutting out.'

'We can do that.'

'And the petrol?' Nic said.

Drew grinned. 'All in a day's work!'

'Right.' Nic smiled back. 'How long?'

'Hard to say. You want to come out now?'

Nic shook his head, looking at his small patient. 'No, I'm here to the end.'

'OK, Doc.' Drew gave him a pat on the shoulder. 'Back soon.'

It took nearly half an hour of skilful work before the child was free and able to be slid out to the waiting paramedics. By the time Nic scrambled out, she was already on a stretcher and being loaded into the ambulance, her shocked and sobbing mother being helped inside by Morag. He gave the paramedics a quick debrief on what he had done.

'You coming with us?' one of them asked, gesturing to his arm. 'That could use some attention.'

'No, I'll be OK here. Thanks.'

He watched the ambulance drive away, hoping the child would recover well. Turning, his gaze clashed with a furious green one. Hannah looked fit to burst, he realised, watching as she stalked across to him, her face deathly pale.

'What the hell did you think you were doing?' she demanded angrily.

'The same thing you would have done had you been here first.'

He saw confusion mix with the anger and fright. 'That's not the point. You could have been killed.'

'It's nice to know you care about me,' he teased, trying to lighten the situation.

'This isn't funny.'

'Hannah, I'm fine.'

'Like hell.' Her stormy gaze raked over him, a suspicion of tears glinting in her eyes. 'Go back to the house and get out of those things. You're bleeding. I'll get some stuff and take a look at you.'

He wanted to argue but his arm throbbed like hell and his clothes were wet with a combination of blood, rain and fuel. What she said made sense. After a moment's further hesitation, he collected his things and accepted a lift home from the local policeman.

'Nic?' Hannah called as she let herself into the house a short while later.

She was still shaking. She would never forget the moment when Jane had told her Nic was under the lorry. For one terrifying instant she had thought he'd been involved in the accident, that she was going to lose him, the shock bringing home how much he had come to mean to her in the last weeks. When it had become clear he had wriggled under there to get to the trapped child, she had been angry, scared, relieved and desperately confused about her own emotions. Sighing, she walked up the stairs and, hearing running water, went along the landing to his room.

'Nic?' She tapped on the open door. 'Are you OK?'

The noise of the water stopped. 'I will be just a minute.'

'Come down to the kitchen when you're ready.'

The short wait stretched like hours. She double-checked her medical bag making sure she had everything she could possibly need. When she heard his footsteps on the stairs, she sucked in a breath and braced herself, only to find she was completely unprepared for the sight of him. He'd had the sense to put a pack and waterproof dressing on his arm before he'd had a shower, she noted absently. Other than that, he had pulled on a pair of disreputable jeans…and nothing else. His feet were bare, and so was the rest of him.

'Sit down,' she instructed, her voice sounding alien to her own ears.

She turned away and closed her eyes, but even so the image of his perfectly sculpted chest and arms seemed imprinted on her brain—olive-toned skin drawn over muscle, a light dusting of dark hair tapering from his chest down his abdomen to the unfastened waistband of his jeans, broad shoulders, his dark hair still damp from the shower.

Forcing herself to turn round, she evaded his gaze as she stepped closer to examine the damage. He had some superficial cuts and grazes on his face, forearms and hands, and a nasty bruise was swelling up along one cheekbone. It was disconcerting, leaning in close to him, checking for signs of grit, glass or metal fragments in the cuts. She was too close. She could feel the warmth of him, feel the draught of his breath, scent his aroma…clean male skin and sandalwood. Then there was that mouth, temptingly close. Disconcerted, her gaze strayed to his as she stepped back, finding him watching her through dark, sultry eyes.

'The abrasions don't look too bad,' she informed him stiffly. 'I'll clean them up when I've had a look at that arm.'

Which meant she had to touch him. Briefly she closed her eyes again. She couldn't do this. For goodness' sake, she was a doctor, she berated herself. What was wrong with her? She did this sort of thing all the time, saw all kinds of people in all states of undress. Just think of Nic as any other patient, the same as when he was ill, her rational brain instructed, but the wires seemed to get crossed somewhere along the line, and she couldn't visualise him like that at all. Not now. Hannah swallowed. She was a professional, it was time she acted like one.

Pulling herself together, she gently removed the temporary dressing, her fingers gliding over the warm skin and smooth muscle of his upper arm as she examined the nasty-looking cut. She heard Nic's hiss of breath and glanced at him.

'I'm sorry, did I hurt you?'

Smouldering dark eyes looked back at her. 'No.'

'There are no fragments,' she told him briskly, withdrawing her fingers as if his flesh burned them. 'But it will need a clean before I stitch it.'

'Fine.'

She turned back to her bag and pulled on a pair of latex gloves. In case of cross-infection, she told herself, knowing it was a lie. She just didn't think she could touch that bare flesh again and stay sane. 'I'll give you a local,' she told him, her voice sounding strange.

'It's OK.'

Frowning, she turned to face him. 'Nic, that's silly—'

'Just do it,' he insisted, his voice rough.

Her gaze met his and she couldn't recognise the disturbing expression in his eyes. 'Nic?'

'Hannah. Do it.'

'Is this some stupid macho thing?' she grumbled, readying the items she needed, unable to understand him. 'What's the point of this? Haven't you been enough of a hero for one day?'

She took a deep breath. Everything was ready, but anxiety and confusion made her edgy. With infinite care she cleaned the wound, feeling him tense, knowing it must hurt. She prepared to stitch, her fingers not as steady as she would wish. And the gloves made not a scrap of difference to her awareness, either. Hesitating, she looked at him, desperate not to hurt him, but he gave no ground at all, his expression implacable.

Hannah sucked in a breath. Stupid, idiot man. She hooked a chair closer with her foot and sat down. Working as carefully and

gently as she could, she began to close the jagged wound with a
row of neat stitches, aware every time he winced, tears stinging
her eyes as she glimpsed his rigid jaw and bruised, battered face.
Her gaze strayed to his chest, the rhythmic, slightly rapid rise and
fall as he breathed. Hannah swallowed. Stop looking at his body
and concentrate on what you are doing, she berated herself,
thankful her task was nearly over. The stitches finished, she
covered the wound with a sterile dressing and held it in place with
a bandage. Pushing back her chair, she cleaned the cuts and
abrasions on his face, before peeling off her gloves and tossing
them aside.

'All done. You should have some antibiotics, though. Is your
tetanus up to date?'

'Yes' His unfathomable gaze met hers, increasing her awk-
wardness and discomfort. 'Thank you.'

'OK.'

She looked down into his dark eyes, still unsure what fired
his intense expression. Turning her back on him to tidy up, she
discovered her hands were shaking.

'Hannah—'

'I have to get back for afternoon surgery now,' she forestalled
him, keeping herself busy and avoiding looking at him again.

'I can come in and do my list,' he argued.

Annoyed, she turned to face him, finding he was back on his
feet and closing in on her. 'Don't be silly.'

'*Cara*, I'm fine, really. It's nothing some painkillers and a few
days' healing will not fix. I'm not an invalid.'

'No, you just could have been dead. It was a recklessly stupid
thing to do.'

'And you would have done the same, no?' He took her shaking
hands in his. 'I'm sorry you were frightened.'

'Don't flatter yourself.'

She blinked back a fresh sting of tears as his gaze held hers
and his voice dropped. 'You do this all the time, hide your

feelings. I can see when you're scared, when you are hurting and putting on a brave front and need someone but won't admit it.'

'I don't,' she refuted, her throat tightening under his speculation, realising this was no longer just about today's events. 'Nic…'

'You think I don't worry or get scared for you when you are out on an emergency call, crawling around some gully or a car wreck on the motorway? Why do you find it so hard to admit you have feelings, or that other people have feelings for you?'

'Don't.'

'When are you going to trust me, *innamorata*?'

She fought to resist his persuasive appeal, trying without success to free her hands from his. 'I've told you, it's not you, it's me.'

'I can't help put things right until I know what went wrong.'

'There's nothing to put right,' she insisted, unable to meet his dark and compelling gaze.

'Believe me, Hannah, there is. And before I leave here, I'm going to prove it to you.'

Nic's words stayed with her in the busy days ahead. While the local community treated him as a hero, much to his embarrassment, she still trembled when she thought of the risk he had taken, equally disturbed at how emotionally involved she was becoming.

'Come on, sleepyhead.'

A husky voice permeated her consciousness. 'Hmm?'

'Time to wake up,' the voice cajoled. 'Hurry, *cara*, or I'll be tempted to climb in there with you!'

'What?' Hannah's eyes flew open, her gaze focusing on Nic's laughing dark eyes as he leaned over her bed. She grabbed the duvet, holding it under her chin. 'What are you doing?'

'It's after ten and we have chores to do.'

'We do?'

He set a wriggling Wallace down on top of her. 'I'll leave our little friend to hassle you awake, but I'll be back if you're not downstairs in half an hour.'

Still muzzy from sleep, Hannah was too slow to react as he closed the last of the distance and dropped a lingering, toe-curling kiss on her startled lips before leaving the room. God, what was going on? She yawned, trying to remember what day it was. Christmas Eve. And they'd been to the staff dinner the night before. Oh, hell and damnation. She had the most terrible recollection that she might have kissed him!

Forcing her mind to function, she went back over her memories of the evening. They'd had a good meal, shared plenty of laughter. She'd stuck to mineral water and Nic had only had a couple of glasses of red wine, but some of the others had been a bit merry, teasing Jane about her upcoming wedding in February. She remembered going to the bar to buy a round of drinks and being hassled by some creep, then Nic had material-ised from nowhere and rescued her. When they'd got home, he'd said she could give him a goodnight kiss in payment.

'I won't touch!' he'd teased, slipping his hands in his trouser pockets.

Clearly he'd issued the challenge, never expecting her to act on it. So why the hell had she? She remembered standing on the stairs, a couple of risers above him, turning, stepping down one and pressing her lips to his. He was shocked, if his indrawn breath had been any guide. There had been no point of contact apart from their lips. Nothing to detain her. Nothing to prevent her from pulling back, as she had intended to when she had embarked on her foolish deed. But the peck she had planned had been forgotten the moment his mouth had opened under hers, hot and demanding and, oh, so seductive. Nothing had detained her but his magnetism and her weakness. Dear God, whatever had possessed her?

'Wally, don't sit on my head,' she groaned, gently lifting him off and struggling to sit up. 'I can't see.'

Setting the playful kitten on the bed, she pushed the tangled fall of hair out of her face and looked at the clock. Nic was right. It was after ten. But what chores did they have to do? She frowned, unable to remember anything outstanding from work. Still, she didn't put it past him to come back if she didn't get up, and that thought alone was enough to have her scrambling from the bed. She went to have a quick shower and then returned to dress, selecting jeans, boots and a warm, russet-coloured, hooded sweater that came halfway down her thighs. Dragging a brush through her wayward chestnut waves, she drew her hair back in a ponytail. A quick sweep of a honey stick lip balm across her lips and a squirt of perfume and she was ready.

Wallace scrambled backwards down the sheer cliff face that was the side of the bed and padded after her on stubby little legs, determined not to be left behind as she headed for the stairs. 'Not down here, little man,' she told him, scooping him up, frightened he would fall.

Nic was in the kitchen and he looked up with a smile, the bruise on his cheek slowly fading. 'Five minutes to spare, *cara*,' he teased, checking his watch.

'I need breakfast,' Hannah warned, setting Wallace on the floor.

'Coming up. Toast, honey, coffee and juice, yes?'

The warmth in his gaze made her tingle. 'Thank you.'

'Pleasure.'

'So,' she asked, trying to steer things away from dangerous territory, terrified he would refer to what had happened last night, 'what are these chores we apparently have to do?'

'Wait and see.'

Hannah frowned at Nic's mysterious smile. 'I was looking forward to my day off.'

'It's not work,' he promised.

'Is this a bike thing?'

Nic sat on a chair opposite, his presence unnerving her. 'Not today, don't worry.'

'Oh.' Hannah spread honey on her toast, secretly regretting that he'd never asked her for another outing after that one time. 'That's OK.'

'You're disappointed, aren't you?'

Her gaze skittered away from the knowing look on his face. 'Not at all.'

'We can share a ride together any time you want, *innamorata*,' he murmured huskily. 'You only have to ask.'

The breath locked in her lungs. Now she was very much afraid they were not talking about motorbikes at all. Deciding it would be much safer if she stopped verbally sparring with him, Hannah ducked her head and concentrated on finishing her breakfast.

'So where are we going?' she asked a while later, as they headed off in Nic's car.

'You'll soon find out.'

Before long he turned down a muddy track leading to a forestry plantation. 'Christmas trees?' she asked in surprise.

'Exactly!'

'I don't usually bother.'

'This year we are having a proper tree,' he decreed. 'With roots. So it can be planted afterwards in the garden.'

So she'd always have to look at it and remember the Christmas Nic was there? A lump lodged in her throat. 'But—'

'Enough. It's Wallace's first Christmas. We can't let him down.'

Laughter bubbled inside her. 'That is so ridiculous!'

She was still giggling as Nic, trying to look affronted, drew the car to a halt next to others near a wooden hut that served as a sales office. 'You are going to be in so much trouble, *cara*,' he warned, dark eyes glinting with laughter.

Very much afraid she already was, she made no further comment and trailed in his wake as he set off to examine the rows of trees. It took an inordinate amount of time to choose one.

'They all look the same,' she complained after a while, earning herself another warning look. She would have just picked the first thing and been on her way, but Nic examined one after the other and she shook her head in bemusement.

'This one.' He finally selected a freshly dug specimen, a good seven feet high with a healthy root system. 'Perfect!'

'You shouldn't be carrying it with your bad arm.'

Nic shook his head dismissively. 'My arm is nearly healed. You'll be taking the stitches out in a day or two, no?'

'No. Morag's offered to do that.'

'Coward,' he teased, a knowing smile curving his mouth.

'Anyway, that tree is much too big.'

Nic's smile widened at her unsubtle change of subject. 'Nonsense. It has a beautiful shape—like you, *innamorata*!' he added in a husky aside as he walked past her and headed for the sales office.

Disconcerted, she followed him. Slowly but surely he was wearing down her resistance and she would have to redouble her guard if she didn't want to get into further trouble. And what if she did want to? She tried to push traitorous thoughts aside as she helped Nic tie their deliciously scented tree to the roof rack before they headed back to Lochanrig. She could never deny what an excellent doctor he was, but on a personal level he disturbed and unsettled her more every day. She was scared of the things he made her think and feel. Her life might not have been exciting before he'd arrived but she had felt safe. Now Nic not only challenged her present, he was stirring up painful things from the past she did not want to face.

'If you want to fetch a tub from the garage to put the tree in, I'll go and find the decorations,' she suggested when they arrived home.

'No problem.'

Wallace was excited by the strange activity and had to be removed from the various boxes of baubles and tinsel on numerous occasions.

'You're a menace, Wally.' Hannah laughed, rescuing him for the umpteenth time and sitting back on her heels on the floor to cuddle him.

Draping a strand of lights through the tree, Nic smiled. 'He has to have his first vaccination next week.'

'I can't bear to think of him having his injections. He's so tiny.'

'I know.' Nic grinned at her. 'I feel like an anxious papa!'

'When does he have the second vaccination?'

'Three weeks after the first one, when he's twelve weeks.'

Sighing, she set Wallace down to play with a toy and handed Nic the star for the top of the tree. She watched as he climbed the steps and reached to fix it in place, swallowing at the way his jeans tightened across his muscled thighs and taut rear, his jumper riding up to reveal a brief but tantalising glimpse of olive-toned flesh. What was happening to her? She turned away, seeking to banish the thoughts and deny the simmering awareness she had no wish to feel.

Nic woke on Christmas morning sensing that something was different. Frowning, he crossed to the window and looked out on a magical snowy landscape. Everything sounded hushed and muted, while a pale sun cast a clear and shimmering light, prisms glinting off suspended flakes and icicles that hung from the bare twigs of trees and the edges of gutters and garden railings.

Hearing noises downstairs, he dressed hurriedly and went down to find Hannah busy in the kitchen. She was wearing jeans and a fleecy top and she looked good enough to eat. His hands itched to hold her, but he was still wary of overstepping her boundaries, even though temptation often got the better of him.

'Good morning.'

She turned at the sound of his voice and gave a wary smile. 'Hi.'

'It snowed!'

'It looks lovely, doesn't it?' she agreed, glancing out of the window. 'Not so good if we get a callout, though.'

'Don't even think it,' he groaned.

'Someone, somewhere is bound to fall off their new bike or get their finger stuck in some new toy,' she teased. 'It happens every Christmas.'

Nic shook his head. 'Not today.'

'We'll see!'

'You're not planning to be working in here all day, are you?' He frowned, helping himself to some coffee.

'The turkey won't cook itself.'

'Then I help, yes? And we get the chores done sooner. Tell me what I can do.'

Hannah shook her head. 'Why don't you go and occupy Wallace before he wrecks all the presents under the tree?'

'Then we can open them, yes?'

'Go away!' She laughed, reaching out to give him a push. Nic caught her hand, drawing her towards him, seeing uncertainty shadow her eyes. 'Nic?'

'Happy Christmas, *cara*.'

As her lips parted to respond to his greeting, he bent his head, unable to resist another moment. His mouth caressed hers, his tongue beginning a leisurely exploration, finding her as sweet as he remembered. As ever when he touched her, it threatened to flare out of control in an instant, and he was fighting his own need. He couldn't rely on the pain of stitches without local anaesthetic every day to stop himself giving in to temptation and reaching for her. Now there was nothing he wanted more than to back her up against the table and have her wrap her legs around him as he united them, but it wasn't going to happen, not until her ghosts had been laid to rest. He could feel it in her now, the initial spontaneous response followed by the awakening of whatever haunted her. She was pulling back, emotionally and physically. Reluctantly, his breathing as ragged as hers, he let her go, looking down at her flushed face and the confusion in her gold-flecked green eyes.

'I'm going,' he promised, his voice rough with unfulfilled need.

It would be a long day if he didn't get himself under some kind of control. He lit the fire in the living room, setting the guard round it to prevent Wallace hurting himself, then rescued the kitten from under the tree where he had been intent on ripping as much paper as possible.

'That's enough, *uomo piccolo*,' he murmured. 'Or we'll both be in Hannah's bad books.'

After encouraging Wallace away from the presents and helping Hannah in the kitchen, peeling potatoes and doing other chores, Nic persuaded her to relax by the fire and get round to opening presents.

His eyes widened when he discovered her first gift to him. 'Where did you find it?' he murmured in delight as he looked over the book containing a collection of Stanley Holloway monologues, including Marriott Edgar's comic rhyme from which Wallace had got his name.

'In a second-hand bookshop near the Castle in Edinburgh.' She smiled. 'Is it the right one?'

'Perfect! Have you read "The Lion and Albert"?'

'I have. And I still think Wally is misnamed!' She laughed, their gazes straying to where the kitten played with rolled-up balls of wrapping paper, purring contentedly.

Nic reached out and took her hand. 'Thank you, Hannah. It means a lot to me to have this. My copy was lost when the house was destroyed in the earthquake.'

'I'm glad you like it,' she whispered, her eyes reflecting her rush of emotions, from sympathy for his loss to awareness of his touch.

Resisting the urge to pull her back into his arms, he pressed a kiss to her palm before releasing her, then handed over his first present to her, a smile curving his mouth at her delighted reaction when she opened it.

'Oh, it's gorgeous!' she exclaimed, studying the hand-crafted silver brooch of a mischievous kitten caught suspended from a branch by its front paws, a comical expression on its face. She pinned it to her top. 'Thank you.'

The rest of their presents, from each other, friends, staff and the community, left them both with piles of books, CDs and chocolates, and Wallace with far too many treats and new toys. After clearing up the mess of discarded paper and packaging, they had lunch, the mood light and companionable.

'That was amazing,' Nic praised, unable to manage another mouthful of the wonderful fare Hannah had prepared. 'I should never have let you persuade me to have that second piece of pudding.'

Relaxed and flushed, she smiled. 'Perhaps you should go and walk it off while I do the washing-up.'

'No, we will wash up together and then walk together,' he decided, rising to his feet with a groan and giving his full stomach a rueful pat.

It was crisp but sunny when they left the house, walking through the woods at the end of the garden before joining the path that took them behind the village and around the side of the loch. The landscape looked beautiful with its coating of snow, the cold expanse of water backdropped by trees and hills. He stood still for a moment, enjoying the silence, watching a flotilla of wild ducks on the loch, feeling more at peace than he had for a very long time. More and more, Lochanrig was seeping into his blood, his very being.

A cold, wet snowball hit him squarely on the side of the neck, icy liquid trickling uncomfortably down inside the top of his jacket and jumper.

'Dio!'

He spun round and managed to duck as Hannah launched a second missile at him. Picking up a handful of snow, he began shaping it as he advanced towards her, smiling as her grin faded and she started stepping backwards. Another second and she turned and ran towards the woods but he caught her easily before she reached the trees and they tumbled down into a soft bank of snow, laughing and gasping for breath. As he held the neck of her jacket back, her hands grasped his arm, eyes wide with a mix of fun and disbelief.

'You wouldn't,' she challenged.

'No?' He teased her a bit longer, allowing a few icy drops to reach her skin, but having her wriggling under him was playing havoc with his self-control. As his awareness and arousal grew, so did Hannah's wary discomfort and, not wanting to spoil this special day, or the happy, relaxed mood, he relented. 'You are right. I am too much of a gentleman!'

Pushing himself off her with reluctance, he rose to his feet and helped her up, keeping hold of her hand as they made their way back to the house, wet, chilly but contented. He helped her off with her jacket, hanging it near the fire to dry.

'Thanks.' She smiled. 'I'm going to pop upstairs and put some dry jeans on.'

Before she went, he caught her to him for a moment, cupping her cool face in his hands and giving her an all too brief kiss. 'Thank you, *cara*, for making this such a special Christmas.'

CHAPTER NINE

HAVING miraculously stayed quiet on Christmas Day, the phone calls came thick and fast in the days ahead and the week sped by. The snow lingered and, while it looked pretty, it made getting to outlying patients in the hills even harder.

'*Dio*, it's cold,' Nic exclaimed as he came in after dark from a call on New Year's Eve. 'You were right about falls from new bicycles. I've dealt with two broken collar-bones and a dislocated shoulder in the last couple of days, not to mention assorted grazes, sprains and a chipped tooth!'

'It's been mad, hasn't it?'

She glanced at Nic as he lay on the settee, Wallace's little paws massaging his chest as the kitten danced up and down, playing with Nic's fingers. How had these two become so much a part of her very existence so quickly? Thanks to Nic, for the first time in many years her Christmas had not been lonely. Now nearly half his time here was over. Having been desperate to send him away the moment she had realised who he was, she now couldn't bear the thought of him leaving. But she had so many issues to resolve, things she didn't think she could face. And, by his own admission, Nic couldn't put down roots or do commitment. His heart remained with Federica, the woman he had lost his heart to and with whom he had planned a family. Her unsettling thoughts were interrupted by the ringing of the telephone and she groaned as she rose to her feet to answer it.

'Hello, Dr Frost speaking.'

She listened to the information, her nerves jangling, a knot of dread in the pit of her stomach at the summons to the police station. Hanging up the phone a few moments later, she twisted her trembling fingers together and turned to Nic, unable to meet his darkly intent gaze.

'I have to go out.'

'Hannah?' She heard the concern and puzzlement in his voice as he sat up, swinging his feet off the settee and on to the floor. 'Do you want me to do it?'

Yes, she wanted to beg, but couldn't. 'No. It's all right,' she tried to reassure him, her voice edgy.

She pulled on her coat and picked up her bag, checking she had her keys and mobile phone. Nic came to the door, Wallace cupped gently in one olive-toned hand. Hannah swallowed, her gaze skittering away when she saw the troubled expression in his eyes.

'Hannah?'

'There's a chicken casserole in the oven. You get on with your supper, I might be a while,' she said evasively, walking to the door but wishing she didn't have to face what lay ahead.

'Thanks for coming so quickly,' Sergeant Harris greeted her when she arrived at the police station.

Hannah nodded, tightening her hold on her bag to stop her hands shaking. 'What happened?'

'Young woman on holiday here. She got separated from her friends and was assaulted. She's not been able to tell us much more but she refused to go to hospital so we need you to check her over.'

'Of course. What's her name?'

'Suzanne Smyth.'

Legs like jelly, Hannah followed the gruff but kindly policeman to the small treatment room in the station. The girl was huddled in a chair, a blanket round her shoulders, her clothes torn, her face streaked with mascara from her tears. The breath lodged in Hannah's throat. She found it impossible to stay detached from the victim's distress.

'Hello, Suzanne,' she said with a smile when they were alone, setting her bag down on the desk and taking off her coat. 'I'm Dr Hannah Frost. I've come to see how you are and if there's anything I can do. I need to check you over. Is that OK?'

The tall, thin blonde looked at her through tear-filled hazel eyes. 'I suppose so. I just feel so horrible.'

'I know. Can you tell me what happened?' she asked gently, helping the girl up onto the examination table.

'One moment I was with my friends, the next they'd gone in the crowds. This man, he—'

As Suzanne broke off, sobbing, Hannah did her best to comfort her, despite the emotions churning inside her, the sick dread of fear in her stomach. Slowly the story emerged. It could have been much worse, Hannah knew, but it was bad enough to leave the poor girl bruised and shaken and very frightened.

Hannah felt shaken herself when she finally arrived home from the police station, her examination of Suzanne completed. She had done what she could to advise the girl and had promised to write to her own general practitioner, but it was understandable Suzanne had found it overwhelming. Her fingers shook as she inserted her key in the lock, went inside and closed the front door as quietly as she could, tiptoeing towards the stairs.

'Hannah?' Her heart sank as Nic appeared in the kitchen doorway. 'Is something wrong?'

'No,' she lied.

'I've saved supper for you.'

'I'm not hungry.'

A frown creased his brow. 'You need to eat, *cara*.'

'Not right now.'

'Hannah…'

Setting down her bag, she hung up her coat, aware of the tremor that refused to leave her. She manufactured a feeble smile, unable to hold on much longer. 'I'm very tired. If you'll excuse me, I'm going to have an early night.'

'But—'

'Goodnight, Nic.'

She all but ran up the stairs to her room. Closing the door, she leant back against it, raising her hands to her face and finding her cheeks wet with tears. Slipping off her clothes, she went to the shower, her tears mingling with the spray of water as she scrubbed herself clean. Poor Suzanne. Hannah shivered, struggling to push the thoughts and images away. She pulled on comforting pyjamas, then snuggled down in bed, dragging a spare pillow towards her and hugging it close. She squeezed her eyes shut against the tears, against the memories, but she couldn't banish them.

Not for the first time in her life, she felt scared and unutterably alone…

Nic hesitated outside Hannah's door. The water had run for ages, but now all was silent. He couldn't banish the disquieting feeling that something was very wrong. Softly, he tapped on the door. When there was no answer, he cautiously opened it and stepped inside. The bedside light was on, casting its pale glow across the figure in the bed. Moving forward, he looked down at Hannah, his throat tightening as he saw the way she hugged the pillow—for comfort or protection, he didn't know—her pale cheeks marked by the tracks of tears. He swallowed, his eyes closing briefly, his heart heavy with her pain.

'Hannah?' he whispered. 'Can I sit down?'

No invitation was forthcoming but neither did she reject him when, after a few moments' hesitation, he sat on the edge of the bed as close to her as he dared. The urge to hold her was overwhelming, but he forced himself to resist the temptation. What had happened this evening? Where had she been?

'Talk to me.'

She shook her head, chestnut waves falling across her face, hiding her expression. Reaching out, he gently brushed the strands away and began to stroke her hair. He felt the tremor run through her, couldn't forget the way her hands had been shaking earlier, even before she had gone out.

'Hannah, let me help, please.'

'You can't,' she whispered, her voice throaty.

'How do you know until we try?'

She wiped a hand across her face, smudging the tears. 'I can't.'

'Don't you trust me?' he murmured, moving closer, his hand leaving her hair, his fingers closing around hers.

'It's not that.' She sighed, rolling onto her back but still not meeting his gaze. 'It's not you, Nic.'

He was silent for a few moments, caressing her hand, feeling the erratic dance of her pulse as his fingers strayed over her wrist. 'Where have you been?'

'Just on a difficult call,' she said evasively.

'Who to?'

'No one we know—not a local.' Her gaze, anxious and bruised, slid to his face then away again. 'Why the inquisition?'

'You're surprised I am concerned? You are fine one moment, get a call that upsets you, go out and come home in tears… How am I meant to react, *cara*?' he questioned, unable to keep an edge of frustration from his voice.

'You don't have to worry about me.'

He saw fresh tears glisten in her eyes and slid his hand to her face, preventing her looking away. 'I can't help but worry. Why is it so hard for you to allow anyone to care or get close? What are you worried I might find out?' he asked huskily, seeing her alarm, feeling her tense.

'Nothing,' she whispered, but he knew it was a lie.

'Move over,' he instructed, releasing her and taking off his boots.

'W-what are you doing?'

Dio, she looked scared. 'I'm not leaving you alone, Hannah, but I think I am a bit warmer and more understanding to hug than a pillow,' he teased, aiming for a lightness he was far from feeling as he took it from her and tucked it behind his head as he slid, fully clothed, into bed beside her.

'But—'

'Nothing's going to happen to you,' he murmured, soothing her. 'Is that what you're frightened of?'

'No.'

He heard her indrawn breath, the rushed denial he didn't believe, and turned onto his side to look at her. 'Hannah—'

'Don't, Nic. I can't do this. Not tonight. Maybe not ever.'

Aching for the pain that was so evident in her voice, frustrated that he couldn't yet help her, Nic frowned, realising he would get nowhere by pushing further. As had been the way from the beginning with this woman, he had to tread softly and slowly.

'It's OK, *innamorata*.' He shifted on to his back, trying to get more comfortable. 'No more talking. At least have a hug, yes?'

An eternity passed before she moved. Nic found he was holding his breath, knowing how difficult she found this, hoping she wasn't going to reject even the most basic of comforts. He exhaled with a sigh of relief as she finally turned towards him and he wrapped his arms around her, feeling her hesitancy before her arm came to rest over his stomach and she tentatively settled her cheek on his chest. With one hand he brushed the hair back from her face, dropping a kiss on the top of her head.

'Sleep now. I won't let anything happen to you.'

He lay, staring into the darkness, feeling her gradually relax, hearing her breathing change, his mind busy as he wondered what was wrong and how he was going to help her.

Hannah felt confused but incredibly safe. Eyes closed, she struggled from sleep, trying to remember why things felt different, what had happened. As the memories unfolded one by one, she tensed, her lashes slowly rising to assess the situation and find out if the body to which she was pressed was real or some figment of her imagination. Oh, God, it was real!

It was very dark outside and although the bedside lamp cast a muted glow, she couldn't see the clock. What had possessed her to turn into Nic's arms? Yes, he was warmer and more understanding than the pillow she had been cuddling, but he was also infinitely more dangerous. Frightened to move in case she woke him, Hannah took stock. Somehow her legs had ended up tangled with his and, she realised absently, he must be uncomfortable sleeping in all those clothes. His arms were around her, the hand at her waist having somehow found the gap between her pyjama top and bottoms. It rested on her skin, making her burn. One of her arms was thrown across his abdomen, the other trapped underneath her and going numb. She tried unsuccessfully to move it and stifled a whimper of pain.

Carefully, she lifted her head from his chest, easing back to look at his face. Impossibly long lashes fanned lean cheeks and stubble darkened his jaw. Her gaze moved to his mouth. No one should be allowed to look like that. His mouth could tempt a saint. She studied his lips, slightly parted as he slept, remembering how they had felt when he had kissed her, the taste of him. Unconsciously, she licked her own lips. With a sigh her gaze drifted back up his face, a gasp of shock escaping as she found his eyes open, watching her, the expression in them hot and sultry.

'I promised not to touch you,' he whispered, his voice rough, the fingers on her bare back starting to move in a soft, spine-tingling caress. 'So don't look at me like that. My willpower is not infallible.'

Unable to look away, she swallowed. 'What time is it?'

'Four a.m.,' he told her after a brief glimpse at the clock.

'M-my arm's gone to sleep.'

She wriggled, freeing her arm from under her, unintention-
ally rubbing against him.

'*Arresto!*' he groaned, his hands tightening on her to hold her
still. 'Stop.'

'Sorry.'

Her gaze flew back to his face, seeing the faint flush across
his cheekbones, the warmth of desire darkening his eyes.

'Hannah,' he breathed huskily.

Oh, help! One hand locked in the hair at her nape and he drew
her head down to his. Unresisting, her eyes fluttered closed, her
lips parting to the touch of his. Dear God, the man could kiss. It
was like an art form to him, something to be savoured and
indulged in, his tongue exploring, teasing and driving her to a
delicious frenzy. His hand trailed up her side, slowly moving
round to shape the fullness of her breast through the fabric of her
top, his thumb stroking over the hardened peak, making her
moan, her body arching against him.

He wrenched away, dragging his jumper over his head before
reaching for her again, his mouth trailing a hot line of kisses
down her throat, the rasp of stubble on her skin making her
tingle. One by one, his fingers freed the buttons of her pyjama
top before sliding inside, his caresses setting her aflame.

'Nic…'

'Touch me,' he breathed, his teeth nibbling her earlobe.

Uncertain, she tentatively ran her hand across his chest,
feeling the thud of his heart beneath his ribs, aware of his warmth,
the scent of his skin. She trembled as his mouth inched hotly
down towards her breasts. Oh, God, what was she doing? Anxiety
had already begun to permeate the fog of pleasure when he rolled
them over, his body holding hers down, his hand sliding inside
the waistband of her pyjama bottoms. Hannah froze, unable to
control her reaction as she instinctively shrank from the intimacy
of his touch and fought against the press of his weight.

'Don't hurt me.'

* * *

Nic felt as if he had been doused in icy water. He swore under his breath when he saw the fear Hannah could not hide and forced himself to ease away, giving her some space. This never should have happened—wouldn't have happened had he been in proper control of himself. But he had woken up to find Hannah wrapped round him, looking at him as if she returned his desire, and he'd been too impatient, so caught up in his own need for her that he'd forgotten the unresolved issues.

'What is it?' she whispered, looking up at him through huge green eyes as if unaware she had spoken aloud. 'Did I do something wrong?'

Nic gathered her to him, his voice soothing 'No, of course not.'

'Then w-why?'

'Because you're not ready, *innamorata*. When our time comes, it will be because you want it as much as I do, not because you have to steel yourself to go through with it.'

Tears squeezed between her lashes. 'I'm sorry.'

'There's nothing to apologise for,' he admonished, tenderly wiping the wetness from her cheeks. 'Don't cry. Everything will be all right, Hannah, I promise you.'

Cradling her in his arms, careful not to crowd her, he soothed her until she calmed. When at last she was sleeping, he slipped from the bed and went to the shower, stripping off the rest of his clothes and stepping under the stinging cold barbs. He pressed his forehead against the cool tiles, fists clenched, waiting for his white-hot anger to subside. Anger at whoever had done this to her. More of the pieces of the jigsaw puzzle were fitting together and he didn't like the picture it made. He turned his face to the water, trying to drown out the image of Hannah's fear, the sound of her heartfelt plea. Jimmy's words came back to him, the older man's belief that something had happened to Hannah while she had been away from Lochanrig. The lump in his throat threatened to choke him. *Dio*, just how bad had it been?

Shivering, both from the cold and his thoughts, he dried

himself and wrapped a towel around his waist. Returning to the bedroom, he gathered up his things, careful not to disturb Hannah's restless sleep as he rescued his jumper and boots from the floor by the bed. He looked down at her for a long moment before moving quietly back to his own room, his mind troubled.

It was light when Hannah next woke and she discovered she was alone. She groaned as jumbled memories flooded back and she rolled over, burying her face in the pillow with an anguished groan. She was so embarrassed. Dear God, how could she ever face him again? Nic must think her the worst kind of tease, leading him so far and then acting like a madwoman and pushing him away.

Somehow she forced herself from the bed and after a quick shower she took her time getting dressed. As she left her room she heard noise and movement downstairs. Nic was in the kitchen. The aroma of percolating coffee filtered tantalisingly to her as she walked down the stairs, her legs unsteady. Trembling with nerves, she pushed open the kitchen door. Nic turned from the counter to smile at her. Wallace was bounding around the floor, playing with a toy mouse.

'Good morning.'

'Morning,' she managed, seeing neither censure nor pity nor amusement in his dark eyes. Just kindness.

'The coffee is ready and there's toast and honey. I was just making myself some scrambled egg. Would you like some?'

She shook her head and sat down before her legs gave way, grateful he was making this as easy as possible. 'You've been busy,' she remarked, looking at the breakfast laid out on the table.

'I'm hungry. I was up early for a call.'

'I didn't hear the phone! I'm sorry, Nic, it was my responsibility to go.'

'Hush, it's OK.' He silenced her with a smile, then his face became serious and her nerves knotted once more. 'I've had to admit Mary McFee to hospital. She has pneumonia.'

Troubled, Hannah set down her knife, her appetite deserting her. 'Poor Mary. I was out there before Christmas and both Shona and Debbie have been in since. What happened?' she asked, concern for the elderly lady pushing all thoughts of her own troubles aside.

'Carole MacLean from the farm said Mary's health worsened a couple of days ago but she refused to allow her to ring us. Carole has been checking Mary regularly and was so worried last night that she decided to look in on her very early when Joe got up for milking. Lucky she did.'

'I'll go in to see her in hospital later today.'

Serving up his scrambled eggs on granary toast, Nic set his plate on the table and sat down opposite her. 'Don't expect too much, *cara*.'

'I suppose I should have pressed for her to go into care,' she mused sadly, blaming herself for allowing things to get to such a state.

'It's not your fault. She was adamant, no, that she would not leave her home?'

'It meant a lot to her to stay there, even though it was totally unsuitable.'

'Then she would have been very unhappy to be moved.' He reached out and briefly covered her hand with his before continuing with his meal. 'You gave her the time she wanted.'

Despite Nic's efforts to ease the tension, Hannah was relieved when a call came in and she insisted on taking it, grateful to get out of the house for a while and put some space between them, although her thoughts weighed heavily on her as she travelled out to a village in their catchment area.

'I'm sure it's appendicitis,' Hannah confirmed a while later, smiling sympathetically at the twelve-year-old girl who lay uncomfortably in bed. She glanced up at the girl's mother. 'We'll need to get Karen to hospital, Mrs Dunlop. Will you and your husband be able to drive her in?'

Mrs Dunlop nodded. 'Yes, thank you, Dr Frost.'

'I'll sit with Karen if you want to make arrangements and pack some things.'

'That would be so kind,' Mrs Dunlop exclaimed gratefully.

'What will happen?' Karen whispered after her mother had gone.

Hannah held the girl's hand. 'They'll examine you and do a few tests, then you'll go to sleep and when you wake up you'll begin to feel very much better.'

'I don't like hospitals.'

Hannah's smile slipped several notches, but she brushed sudden memories of her own experiences aside. 'No, I don't think anyone does, but you'll be home again soon,' she said reassuringly.

Back in her car after the family had set off on the half-hour journey to town, Hannah was about to head home when the beep of her mobile phone announced the arrival of a text message.

'Hannah, Sgt Harris needs to see you about the girl you attended yesterday. Nic.'

Hell and damnation. What exactly had the sergeant told Nic? Anxious, Hannah texted back.

'I'll go there next and then see Mary McFee. H.'

A few moments later the phone beeped again.

'Joanne McStay has just rung, her mama's had a fall. I'm going there now. Nic.'

'OK. H.'

'See you later. Nic.'

That's what worried her, Hannah thought, putting the car in gear.

It was after lunch when she returned to the house but she had not long been in, briefly exchanging details on the progress of Mrs McStay and Mary McFee with Nic, when they were both called out again. Nic went to a tractor accident at a nearby farm while Hannah attended a young child with what turned out to be a case of gastroenteritis, before being called to a car accident on the hill road. By the time she came back it was already seven,

Nic was in and, she discovered, had prepared one of his quick but delicious pasta specials.

They talked of their day's cases over the meal and Hannah started to relax, feeling that maybe she had got away with things and Nic hadn't gleaned any unwanted information from Sergeant Harris. By the time Wallace had been fed and the washing-up done, she was looking forward to flopping out in front of the fire. She walked through to the living room and found Nic had apparently had the same idea. He had added more logs and drawn the curtains, and the room felt warm and cosy.

'There's nothing worth watching on TV,' she complained, tossing the paper down on the table.

'Good.'

She glanced at him, curled as he was at one end of the settee, a determined glint in his dark eyes. Silently, his gaze holding hers, he held out his hand. Hannah swallowed. Every instinct told her to run in the opposite direction, so why were her feet closing the distance between them? Confused and nervous, she hesitated, but Nic leant forward and took her hand, drawing her towards him. He shifted sideways on the settee, encouraging her to sit so that she was settled in his arms, her back resting against his chest. Silence stretched and she was painfully conscious of him, aware of his every breath, his scent, his whole being seeming to envelop her, making her feel secure despite her anxiety.

'It's time, Hannah,' he finally told her, stroking her hair.

She didn't pretend not to know what he meant. Instead, she stared into the flames, thankful he had arranged this so she didn't have to face him, a ragged breath escaping as she acknowledged she was not going to be able to evade things this evening. But she didn't know where to start, how to discuss events she had kept hidden for so long, things she had never told another living soul.

Sighing, her head dropped forward. 'I can't do this.'

'Yes, you can. And you're not doing it alone. I'll be here as long as you need me,' he promised, his free hand holding one of hers, fingers entwining.

'Nic…'

'Start with the police station,' he suggested softly. 'You were called to a girl who had been assaulted?'

Hannah nodded, closing her eyes as she remembered Suzanne's distress. 'I just find that kind of thing upsetting.'

'We all do. But you were shaking before you even left here, Hannah. Does it make you remember what happened to you?'

'Sort of,' she whispered.

'You were assaulted?'

'Not like that.'

Nic let out a slow breath. 'These last weeks I've been through the usual lost love, jilted for best friend, found out he was married, and so on, only none of that fits. But someone, at some time, has dented your self-belief that you are a beautiful and desirable woman.'

'That's not it,' she refuted with a frown. 'Not that I think I am beautiful or desirable, I know I'm not. I'm just, I don't know, frigid, I suppose.'

'You most certainly are not,' he corrected huskily with a shocked laugh.

'I don't enjoy it.'

'Sex?'

Dear God, this was awful. Unable to force the words out, she nodded.

'Someone hurt you? Physically?' he questioned, his voice controlled.

Hannah swallowed and nodded again.

'This man hit you?'

'No.' She closed her eyes. 'We had sex. I didn't want to, he—'

'He raped you.'

'It wasn't like that. I wasn't attacked in the street, he wasn't a stranger.'

'Hannah, if you said no and he didn't listen, it's rape,' Nic insisted angrily. 'There is no excuse. Ever. What happened, *cara*?'

Tears trickled down her cheeks as she remembered the awful night her two-year nightmare had begun. 'I'd been seeing this guy from the hospital,' she told him, her voice shaking.

'He was a medical student like you?'

'No, a junior manager. I'd had boyfriends before, but no one I wanted to take things further with,' she explained. 'I hated it in Birmingham but I was desperate to be a doctor, so I kept my head down and worked hard. Then this guy asked me out. He seemed kind, easy to talk to, I liked him. We went out, kissed a few times but I didn't feel anything, not like that, you know? He was just a friend, or so I thought.'

'I understand. What happened then?' Nic prompted, his thumb stroking distracting caresses around her palm.

'There was a party for Bonfire Night and he asked me to go. I wasn't that keen but I agreed. We hadn't been there long when I started to feel strange. I thought he was being kind when he said he'd take me home but he had planned it all, had drugged my wine. Indoors, he turned on me, said I owed it to him. I tried to say n-no, that I didn't want to, but I couldn't move or speak. He wouldn't s-stop.' She shivered, tears stinging her eyes, and Nic's arms tightened round her. 'I was so scared. He was really heavy, holding me down. I thought he was going to smother me. Outside fireworks were going off, people were laughing, but I couldn't call anyone. I'd never done it before. It was horrible. It really hurt.'

Nic swore in Italian, sounding shocked and furious. 'Oh, Hannah,' he whispered against her ear, his warm breath fanning her skin.

'It wasn't until the next day, when whatever he gave me was wearing off, that I realised he hadn't used anything and I was terrified I might get pregnant.'

'And did you?'

Hannah shook her head, her fingers tightening on his. 'No.

And subsequent HIV-AIDS tests were clear. For a while I thought I was physically OK,' she added, feeling him stiffen as he took on board what she said.

'But you weren't?' he murmured, his voice rough.

'No. That was just the beginning.'

She felt Nic's tension. 'Hannah?'

'I started getting terrible pains, feeling ill. One day I collapsed. He'd given me chlamydia, but it was incorrectly treated with the wrong antibiotics and I developed a serious pelvic infection.'

'*Maledizione*!' Nic breathed, his fingers gentle as he brushed the tears from her face.

'I went to a gynae specialist at a different hospital,' she continued in a rush, unable to stop now she had started. 'The pain was so bad I couldn't work and nothing was helping. I was told that I was probably infertile, that I may never have a family of my own. Not that I was ever going to love anyone or have a relationship after that.'

She heard Nic's indrawn breath, then he moved, turning them so he could gather her close but see her face. Her gaze met his and she saw the sympathy and shock and hurt in his dark eyes, the glisten of moisture he made no attempt to hide.

'What you went through was criminal,' he told her, his voice raw with emotion. 'Did you not tell anyone?'

'I couldn't.'

'Not even your parents?'

'Especially not them. They would have been so disappointed in me.'

He looked down at her, a frown on his face. 'None of this was your fault, *cara*. You do know that, don't you?'

'I suppose,' she murmured uncertainly, seeing his frown deepen.

'It wasn't, Hannah,' he insisted, pausing for a few moments

before he continued. 'So when you recovered, you decided sex must always be like that, that there was something wrong with you?'

Hannah nodded. 'I just remember the fear and the pain.'

'So work only for the rest of your life?'

'I wanted to come back here, where it was safe, and be a GP. I never met anyone, never wanted to, you know—' She snapped off the words, just managing to stop herself from saying 'until you'.

'And you really believe you have no sexual feelings?' he asked incredulously.

'I just don't feel anything.'

His fingers under her chin tilted her face up and she saw the mischievous twinkle light his eyes. 'Really? You feel nothing when I touch you?' he asked softly.

'Nic, I…'

Her words trailed off as he ran his fingers tantalisingly over her face, leaving every millimetre tingling before brushing across the curve of her lips and slipping his thumb between them when her mouth opened on a gasp.

'You feel nothing when I kiss you?' he teased, replacing his fingers with his lips.

Instantly fire licked through her and her lips parted further in welcome. Her pulse raced as he accepted the invitation, deepening the contact, kissing her with a sensual thoroughness that left her breathless and trembling all over. Helplessly she found herself pressing closer to him, a moan of protest drawn from her when he eased away.

'You still think you don't feel anything?' he murmured huskily, eyes nearly black with passion, a smile curving his far too sexy mouth.

Hannah felt a flush warm her cheeks. She didn't know what to think. Only that with Nic she felt things she had never felt before. As he cupped her face in his hands, his words turned her insides to jelly and brought a rush of fearful anticipation flooding through her.

'Don't worry, Hannah. When the time is right, I'm going to show you how beautiful making love can be.'

CHAPTER TEN

HANNAH was on tenterhooks as the days passed, the combination of fearful anticipation and nervous excitement fuelling her growing skittishness. Part of her was terrified of the day when Nic suggested making good his promise…part of her was inexplicably scared that he wouldn't. Talking to him about what had happened to her had been traumatic but had left her feeling calmer, as if some ghosts had been laid to rest at last.

Of course she didn't want him to make love to her! Did she? No, absolutely not, she told herself, but her resolve seemed shamefully weak, her words hollow ones, especially when even thinking about his touch made her flesh prickle with excitement. As for his kisses… Her eyes closed. Those deep, sensual, consuming kisses that took her breath away. He hadn't kissed her since that night yet she could still taste him, ached to do so again, and—

'Hannah!'

Kirsty's admonition startled her from her thoughts. Her eyes jerked open and she looked up, realising all the practice staff were gathered around the table, staring at her. 'I'm sorry,' she murmured, clearing her throat, trying to banish her sinful thoughts.

'Are you all right?' Kirsty frowned. 'You've been behaving very oddly lately.'

'I'm fine.'

Her gaze skittered down the table to where Nic was sitting and she saw him raise his coffee-mug to his lips to hide his smile. Dark eyes laughed at her. Dear God, he knew, damn him! He knew he was driving her so mad with confusion and expectation that she couldn't think straight any more.

Annoyed, she sat up straight and pulled her notebook towards her. 'Right, let's get on shall we?'

'That's what I said five minutes ago.' Kirsty sighed, shaking her head.

Hannah forced herself to concentrate as they worked through the agenda for the practice meeting, everyone contributing ideas and comments from patient care to general operational issues.

'You all know that Mary McFee was taken ill. I want to thank you all, especially Shona and Debbie, for your hard work caring for her. She's holding her own in hospital but is still very sick and it is unlikely she will go home if she does recover.'

There was general comment and discussion, and Hannah knew how sorry all the staff were in such cases.

'Any news of Mrs McStay?' Shona asked.

Hannah kept her gaze studiously averted as Nic filled them in on the latest update.

'She suffered a complicated break to her arm when she fell but it is mending slowly,' he informed them. 'However, her confusion has worsened considerably and she scarcely recognises Joanne now. I think Joanne knows it is impossible for her to provide the continuing level of help at home that her mother needs. I'm seeing her this week and will suggest the time is right to allow her mother to be moved to somewhere nearby where she can have twenty-four-hour specialist care.'

'I'm sure that's the right thing,' Debbie said, and everyone murmured agreement.

'It's very sad,' Morag sighed. 'Joanne's done such a good job.'

Nic nodded. 'She has, and it is sad, but Joanne is a young woman herself and has to think about her own well-being. I think we need to consider both their needs in helping her reach a decision.'

Hannah silently agreed with Nic's assessment, knowing how much time and effort he had put into the McStays' case and what a difference he had made to Joanne's outlook from that first meeting back in October.

'OK,' she said, moving on to the final subject on her list. 'One of the local practices that share out-of-hours cover have confirmed they are withdrawing their service, as the contract allows them to do.'

Kirsty tutted in disapproval. 'Well, that's going to cause a lot of difficulty, isn't it?'

'It might,' Hannah admitted.

Jane held up her hand. 'You'll be the one affected, Hannah. You're the one called out at nights and weekends. How do you feel?'

'In my experience, the vast majority of patients do not abuse out-of-hours calls,' she began, looking round at her colleagues. 'I'm very uneasy about the new system and I want to provide a continuity of care to our patients. If the other practices did pull out, it would release us from covering their lists and perhaps we could manage our own.' She tried not to glance at Nic as she continued, her voice faltering. 'Of course, it depends on the agreement of whoever else is working here as second doctor.'

She felt Nic's gaze on her but made a pretence of writing some notes on her pad. The thought of him leaving in a matter of weeks filled her with a cold knot of despair she really didn't want to examine.

'I have something I'd like to put forward,' Kirsty announced.

Hannah dragged her thoughts back to matters at hand and forced a smile. 'Of course.'

'It's not that long before we have to start thinking about a replacement for Nic. Finding the right locum is never easy, nor is it the most satisfactory solution for the patients. That continuity of care, Hannah,' Kirsty stressed.

'I agree,' Morag chipped in.

Hannah frowned. 'So what are you suggesting?'

'We all know why the decision was made to use locums at the time your father died. It was all too much,' Morag said with a sympathetic smile. 'But three and a half years on, maybe it is time to think about taking on a new permanent partner.'

'I see.'

Taken aback by the turn of the conversation, Hannah wondered how long her staff had been thinking this way and why no one had said anything before. She could see the sense of the argument. Her gaze strayed round the table, seeing the general agreement amongst the rest of the staff, although Nic was staring down at his pad, a frown on his face as he twisted his pen through his fingers. Hannah swallowed again, unable to imagine him not being here.

'It probably would be the best idea.' She cleared her throat, trying to ease the sudden roughness from her voice. 'Any feedback from patients, Kirsty?'

'From the comments I get, people would prefer not to have someone new coming and going every few months.'

'I've heard the same,' Jane confirmed.

Manufacturing a smile, Hannah began gathering her things. 'Right. Let me know if you have any more thoughts. Thanks, that's it for this morning.'

A few days later, Nic paused in the doorway of Hannah's consulting room, watching as she frowned down at something she was writing, the tip of her tongue peeping out between her lips. A rush of desire washed over him. He'd wanted to give her some time to come to terms with everything, but the wait was driving him insane. Learning about her past had been a shock and he ached for all she had been through. He wanted to track down the bastard who had caused her so much fear and pain, and take him apart piece by piece. Most of all he longed to do all he could to ease her out of the prison in which she had shut herself for too long. When she glanced up and saw him, he guarded his thoughts and stepped forward.

'Hi.'

'Hello,' she responded with a nervy smile, faint colour staining her cheeks, her eyes revealing her emotions, her confusion and her own flash of desire as her gaze involuntarily dropped to his mouth.

'What were you frowning over?'

Her brow puckered and she looked down at her desk. 'I'm trying to draft out an advertisement for Kirsty to place for a new permanent doctor for the practice,' she admitted, her voice uncharacteristically flat.

'You've decided, then?' he prompted, ignoring the knot in his stomach.

'It's what everyone seems to want.'

'And what do you want?'

Her gaze darkened as she looked up at him, making his pulse race. 'I, um, think it's the best thing to do. You wanted to see me?' she said, after a tense pause.

'Yes.' He struggled to draw his mind back to why he was here. 'I thought you'd like to know that I've had a letter this morning from the endocrinologist about the young man with gynaecomastia.'

Her smile became more natural. 'That's good. What's the news?'

'They'll be doing surgery,' he told her, sitting on the edge of her desk, noting how she clenched her hands together as if preventing herself reaching out to touch his fingers, which rested a few inches away.

'Right. I hope it's a success.'

He rose to his feet, edgy with tension and unfulfilled yearning. 'I'll leave you to get on.'

'Thanks.'

'Hannah…about your advertisement.'

Her eyes widened. 'Yes?'

'Don't forget to say they should be female!' he teased.

As fresh colour washed her cheeks, Nic went back to his own consulting room, his thoughts on Hannah. The time was flying by, he had only a few more weeks here. Frowning, he chased away the unsettling and alarming thoughts that started to nibble at the edges of his mind. The fact was, they didn't have too many more days—or nights—to waste.

Sitting on the rug in front of the fire that night, Hannah played with Wallace, trying to work out why she was so on edge. Nic had been quiet all evening, although when they had been preparing a meal earlier, he had brushed against her or elicited contact between them far more than usual, until she had been at screaming point. And with him dressed in his most disreputable, figure-hugging jeans and a black shirt that he seemed to have forgotten to button properly, her nerves were frayed.

Several times she had felt his gaze on her, but whenever she had looked round, he'd either been napping or reading a book. Was it just her wayward imagination playing tricks on her? It must be, because he seemed relaxed and unconcerned. As if aware he was the object of her thoughts, he closed his book and smiled, rising to his feet with a yawn, stretching in a sinuous way that drew her attention to the lithe perfection of his body.

This was ridiculous, she chastised herself, focusing her attention back on the sleepy kitten. From beneath her lashes she watched as Nic gathered up their empty coffee-mugs and went out to the kitchen, returning a few moments later and leaning in the doorway, looking at her. She glanced up, unnerved by the lazy speculation in his dark eyes.

'Having an early night?' she asked, anticipating some quiet time on her own.

'That's the plan.' He smiled, pushing away from the door. *'E siete venendo con me.'*

'What does that mean?' Damn him, he knew how much that irritated her.

'You really want to know?' he teased, whisking Wallace away to the kitchen.

'Nic, stop being annoying. What did you say?'

She thought he wasn't going to answer as there was a long silence before he surprised her by returning to the living room and walking slowly across to her. *'E siete venendo con me.'* He took her hand, drawing her to her feet.

'What are you doing?' She was unaccountably anxious, her stomach feeling as if it harboured a whole flight of butterflies carrying out acrobatic manoeuvres.

'You asked if I was having an early night,' he reminded her.

'I know.' Her heart started thudding. 'Y-you said yes.'

He gave her hand a gentle tug and started to lead her from the room. 'Then I said, "And you're coming with me."'

Oh, God! At the foot of the stairs she hesitated. 'You're not serious?'

'We're wasting too much time.'

He started up the stairs and, like a lamb to the slaughter, her heart hammering in her chest, she followed. She was trembling from head to foot as Nic led her inexorably to his bedroom.

'This is a bad idea,' she whispered, scarcely able to force the words out.

'You think too much,' he chastised softly. 'You look for problems where there need be none.'

He'd planned this deliberately so she wouldn't have time to worry, she realised. She looked at him, her breath locking in her throat. For years she had avoided this kind of intimacy, tortured by what had happened before, but in a few short weeks Nic had dismantled all her barriers until she now stood before him, on the brink of the most frightening and risky act of her life, her defences in tatters.

A tremble rippled through her as Nic pulled the pins from her hair, releasing the restraining knot so that the chestnut waves fell in a curtain around her shoulders. Cupping her face in his hands, he brushed his lips across hers, increasing the shiver that already ran along her spine.

'We're going to take our time, Hannah, and nothing will happen that you do not want. This I promise you.'

Many times he had told her and shown her how much he wanted her but no matter how aroused he was, or how capricious and beyond his understanding her behaviour, he had always let her go at once if she had said no. She bit her lip, drowning in the dark depths of his eyes.

'Nic...'

'Hush.' Turning, he picked up a shirt and handed it to her, giving her a gentle push towards the bathroom. 'Go. Put this on.'

Legs unsteady, she made it to the *en suite* and closed the door, leaning back against it for support. She held the shirt to her face, her eyes closing as she breathed in the lingering scent of him from the silken fabric. He'd known it would be too much for her to undress in front of him. Grateful for his sensitivity, but still scared, she started to take off her clothes in the privacy of the bathroom, her fingers shaking over the task. They fumbled even more as she drew his shirt over her bare skin, its touch making her tingle. Soon it would be his hands. She sucked in a breath. Slowly she did up the buttons. Now she had to walk back out there. Somehow.

She forced herself to open the door. The bedroom curtains had been drawn, the lights were out and candlelight flickered. The fire had obviously been set some time earlier as it exuded a gentle heat. The room looked cosy, warm...safe. Then her gaze strayed to the bed and she knew it wasn't safe at all. Nic waited for her. His clothes were draped on a nearby chair and it didn't take a genius to work out that he had very little, if anything, left on. Hannah's gaze flicked to where he lay under the covers, just part of his bare chest and his arms on view. Even that brief sight of his olive-toned skin drawn supply over muscle was enough to make her catch her breath.

He held out his hand to her. 'Come here, *innamorata*,' he instructed huskily.

Nervous, she moved forward. It seemed a ridiculously long way. Finally she stood beside the bed, her fingers feeling cool and unsteady as they were entwined with the warmth and strength of his. He partly drew back the duvet and she sat down, sliding her legs underneath before lying on her back, drawing the duvet up to her chin and staring straight up at the ceiling. Oh, God, what was she doing here?

Lying on his side, he watched her. He was still holding her hand, his fingers straying across her palm and over her wrist. Surely he must feel the race of her pulse. Her heart was thudding. The heat of him seeped into her. His scent teased her. Gently he encouraged her onto her side so she had to face him. One finger trailed a line of fire across her cheekbones, her eyes, her jaw line, her mouth. Her gaze met his and she saw the mix of emotions in his eyes, tenderness, understanding, passionate intent.

'Nic, I—'

'Don't be frightened, *cara*,' he gentled, voice husky. 'I'll look after you.'

She felt his breath fan her skin as he rained butterfly kisses over her face, the line of her freckles, her eyelids and then her mouth, teasing her with soft caresses. Hannah gasped as his tongue flicked out to trace her lips. He took advantage of her action, gradually deepening the kiss, sensually sucking on her lower lip before releasing it. Gently he nibbled round her mouth, driving her crazy. She could feel him smile, then his lips settled back over hers, cajoling, seductive, teasingly sliding his tongue lightly into her mouth. She heard her own whimper of desire, was unable to control her response as she kissed him back, involuntarily pressing closer to him. Nic took what she offered, kissing her with such intensity she didn't think she could stand it.

He drew her hand against him, holding her palm on his chest. Hannah revelled in the texture of his warm, hair-brushed skin and ripple of muscle beneath, allowing him to guide her hand slowly over him until she was confident enough to explore on her own, enjoying the way his body responded, his breath shortening, his heart thudding as she ran her fingers over the smooth solidness of his shoulders, his back and round to the breadth of his chest. She hesitated, too nervous and uncertain to go lower.

After what seemed an eternity, when she wanted to cry with frustration, he began touching her through the silken softness of the shirt, fingers working slowly down her spine before journeying back up her side, his thumb brushing the rounded curve of her breast. Hannah moaned against his kiss as he cupped her, filling his hand, shaping her. She protested when he drew back, opening her eyes to find his sultry and dark with passion before he bent his head, closing his mouth over one swollen, hardened nipple. Hannah cried out as his tongue rasped the dampened fabric across her sensitised flesh, her fingers tightening on him.

'Oh, God,' she murmured.

'You like that?'

'Y-yes.'

She arched to him as he did it again. And more. When his hand travelled down below the hem of the shirt, teasing over her bare thigh, she trembled. His fingers inched upwards, exploring the rounded swell of her rear, drawing her towards him, making her all too aware of his own arousal. Gradually his touch became more insistent and intimate as he eased one of her thighs over his and leaned in to her. Feeling more of his weight and the caress of his fingers, Hannah couldn't prevent herself from tensing, or hold back the whimper of alarm that escaped from her.

'Nic?'

'*Prendalo facile*,' he whispered. 'Easy, Hannah.'

As his words silenced her fears, he rolled onto his back, taking her with him, holding her close and kissing her until her arousal built once more. Easing her up to give himself room, his hands slid up under her shirt, caressing her, before moving round to slowly undo the buttons, opening her to him. She shivered as he tossed the garment aside and his fingers returned to trace her skin.

'You're so beautiful.'

Despite her doubts, he made her feel it. Her hands closed on the strength of his shoulders to steady herself as his mouth pleasured first one breast and then the other. She felt the tension in him, the restraint, saw the desire in his eyes he was trying to control. Sensitised to his touch, her own need burned through her, an ache of emptiness inside making her squirm against him, and his hands slid to her hips, moving her, letting her feel all of him.

'Please, Nic,' she whimpered, suffused with heat and unimaginable need.

'This is for you,' he promised, his voice rough, his breath ragged. 'Whatever you want. You're in control.'

She looked down at him, seeing the flush of passion on his face, knowing he was holding back to make this right for her. Brushing the fall of hair back from her face, he drew her head down for his kiss. Oh, God, she wanted him, Hannah acknowledged. Wanted to know what it might be like with him. Fighting her fears, she moved to accept him, hesitant at first, awkward, tense as she expected pain, gradually relaxing as she found none.

Nic helped her, his eyes closing, the breath catching in his throat as they were finally joined, completely, intimately. He thought he had forgotten how to breathe as she slowly and tentatively started to move on him. Keeping still was going to kill him. He opened his eyes, feasting on the sight of her, flushed with passion, lips parted, her beautiful breasts swollen from his caresses, the creamy smoothness of her thighs as she straddled him, her movements becoming less controlled and more urgent.

Unable to bear any distance between them, he ran his hands over her, one locking in the tangle of her hair, urging her down for his kiss. Her breasts pressed against his chest as he loved her mouth, his tongue mimicking what he wished to do to her. With his other hand he explored their joined bodies, unable to prevent himself moving, her moans of pleasure as her time neared exciting him. He fought desperately to keep control so this would be right for her, his heart pounding beneath his ribs as she went over the edge, crying out his name, and he let go, joining her in release. He held her as tears slid between her lashes, falling with her as her body spasmed deliciously around him.

Shaking, she lay on top of him, too shocked and amazed to move. His caresses gentled her, his whispered words in Italian soothing her. He eased them apart, moving her so she was lying more comfortably in his arms, cradling her head against him, wiping away her tears. She heard his breathing slow, his heartbeat calm.

'Thank you,' she whispered when she could manage to speak.

He stroked her with exquisite tenderness. 'Thank you, Hannah.'

'I'm sorry.'

'Excuse me?' He frowned.

'If it wasn't much good for you.'

He tilted her face up to look at her. 'You are joking, yes? Hannah, this was one of the most special experiences of my life,' he insisted, sincerity ringing in his words, warming her.

'I didn't know. That it could be like that, I mean.'

'There is much you still don't know,' he teased, smiling as she flushed. 'But there will be time.'

The husky promise made her shiver with anticipation. 'Nic, I—'

'Still,' he interrupted, lying back, his gaze mischievous. 'It is nothing to get bothered about. Just a mechanical act of procreation, no? Is that not right, *innamorata*?'

Laughter bubbled inside her as he cheekily quoted her words back at her. 'OK, so I might have been wrong.'

'Might have been?' he demanded with mock outrage.

'Perhaps I need a bit more practice to be certain,' she dared to whisper, her breath catching at the look on his face.

'You can have all the practice you want.'

His eyes darkened with desire as his hand slid across her face and into her hair, drawing her closer, his tongue tip tracing the outline of her lips, making her gasp. Dear God, how could she want him again so badly so soon?

'Nic,' she begged, as his mouth continued to tease hers. 'Please.'

Molten dark eyes watched her. 'Do you trust me?'

'Yes'

Hannah spoke without hesitation, knowing it was true. She trusted this man implicitly, as she had trusted no one else before. And, she realised, pushing thoughts of the future away, as she would never trust anyone else again. Knowing their time would be short, that he would be leaving, she didn't want to waste another minute. Holding his gaze, she rolled onto her back, inviting him to follow, to show her everything making love with him could be like.

'Are you sure?' he whispered hoarsely.

Nervous but excited, she nodded. 'Very sure.'

The passion she unleashed took her breath away as Nic's mouth and hands began a lingering exploration of her body that left her quivering with need. She bit her lip, her fingers sinking into his hair when his lips trailed lovingly over her belly. Then her eyes widened in shock as, instead of moving back up as she expected, his lips and fingers explored lower. He couldn't... Oh, God! The breath hissed from her lungs, her body instinctively arching to his touch as he took her to levels of pleasure she had never imagined existed. Just when she thought she couldn't bear it any more, he slid sensually back up her body, his hot, dark gaze holding hers as he joined them with one smooth, sure motion, driving her mad by pausing.

'Am I hurting you?' he whispered.

'No, no.' Her hands slid down his back, her hips moving under his, her legs wrapping round him. 'Don't stop. Please, don't stop.'

Groaning her name, he began to move, taking her on a wild ride that nothing could have prepared her for, leaving her, finally, panting and gasping, washed up entwined with him in some distant, foreign place she had never visited before.

'Hannah, are you all right?'

His husky words permeated the sensual cloud that enveloped her and she nodded. 'I'm fine.' Fine? What a ridiculously insipid word to describe how wonderful and incredible and amazed she felt.

She opened her eyes, seeing the concern in his change to amusement as she gave him a slow smile of utter contentment.

'I feel like a shameless hussy,' she whispered as he gathered her to him, moving so she lay in his arms with her head on his chest.

'Good.' She felt a chuckle rumble inside him. 'Hold that thought!'

Smiling, spent, Hannah closed her eyes, listening to the thud of his heart, feeling the rise and fall of his chest gradually begin to slow. Her smile faded as an aftermath of thoughts began to intrude. Constrained by the ghosts of her past, she had wasted so much time. Weeks of being with Nic had slipped by and now, when she had been given a taste of paradise, in all too short a time it would be snatched away from her again.

Hannah stifled a sob. Nic's touch had healed the painful wounds of her past, had opened her mind, her heart and her body, but soon he would go, and where did that leave her? With nothing. Tonight had worked because Nic was special…compassionate, generous, loving and, oh, so sexy. The spark had been firing between them from the first moment they had met and over the weeks she had fallen in love with him. The reality hit home with painful clarity. What a stupid thing to do. Only heartbreak lay ahead. Because Nic would be leaving. He had told her himself that he didn't do commitment, didn't put down roots.

I'll stay as long as you need me, he had promised. Only he wouldn't, would he? Not beyond his contract. Not for ever. And she was very much afraid that he had come to mean so much to her that even for ever would not be long enough.

* * *

Nic lay awake for a long time, savouring the reality of being able to hold her, in his bed, skin on skin. *Dio*, she was so responsive, like a new flower opening in welcome to the sun. He'd never experienced anything so perfect or intense in his life, learning all the places she was most sensitive, where his lightest touch made her squirm with need, hearing her call his name at the height of her pleasure, knowing she had never felt that before.

The knowledge that she had awakened to him but would one day move on after he left brought a searing pain to his chest. He couldn't bear to think of another man touching her. Closing his eyes, he steeled himself to face the fact that they had an agreement and he had to walk away from her when his contract was over.

CHAPTER ELEVEN

'Just be adult about it,' Hannah lectured her reflection in the mirror. 'You went into this knowing Nic was going to leave.'

It didn't make her feel any better. Neither did it stop the days marching by at an alarming rate. The nights, too. She closed her eyes, thinking of the nights in Nic's bed, a flush warming her cheeks at the memories of the things they had done. Continued to do. Not that it made the slightest difference in terms of easing the desperation of wanting him. If anything, it just fuelled the fire of passion between them. Hannah closed her hands over the side of the vanity unit for support. How could she give him up? They were halfway through February and next month he would walk out of her life for ever. And she couldn't hold him, couldn't beg him to stay, even if he would, because she couldn't give him what he needed, the family he so desperately wanted and had planned with Federica, the woman he still mourned.

'Hannah? We're going to be late.'

Nic's reminder floated up the stairs. 'I won't be a minute,' she called back, putting finishing touches to her appearance.

She wished they didn't have to go but Jane's Valentine's Day wedding was a long-planned event and she knew the young receptionist would be disappointed if they didn't attend the reception as promised. With a sigh, she picked up her bag and went downstairs.

'*Dio!*'

Nic's exclamation hissed out on a whisper of breath as she walked into the kitchen.

'What's wrong?'

'Nothing,' he denied, but she saw his Adam's apple bob as he swallowed, his gaze fixed on her.

'Nic?'

'I thought the jeans were bad.'

'What are you talking about?' She frowned at him.

'I've never seen you in a dress.'

Hannah looked down at her emerald green, above-the-knee dress. 'Is something wrong with it?'

'Yes.'

'I don't understand.'

Smiling, he sat down on a kitchen chair and drew her towards him. 'You look fantastic and you're driving me mad.' His hands slid down to the hem of her skirt and slipped underneath to glide over her thighs, above the tops of her stockings.

'Oh, God,' she breathed, her hands on his shoulders steadying her as her legs turned to jelly, an ache of desire knotting inside her. 'Nic…'

He stood up, holding her against him. 'Feel what you do to me?' he whispered hoarsely.

Hannah shivered at the touch of his hands on her, the evidence of his arousal, her eyes widening as she heard the faint hiss of the zip as he unfastened his trousers.

'We can't!'

'We can.'

He kissed her until she was reeling, dispensing with her panties, his fingers finding her ready for him despite her half-hearted arguments to the contrary. Smiling, he drew up her skirt and backed her up to the kitchen table.

'You said we were late,' she reminded him breathlessly.

'So we'll be late.'

'But—'

He grinned wickedly at her. 'We'll tell them something came up!'

'Oh, God,' she sighed again, her feverish gaze locked with his as she wrapped her legs around his hips in encouragement and welcomed him inside her.

They were late. Hannah felt she must have a neon sign flashing over her head, telling everyone what they had been doing, as she mumbled her apologies to Jane's family.

'An unexpected emergency,' Nic explained smoothly, laughter in his eyes as colour washed her cheeks.

They helped themselves to food from the buffet and circulated, Hannah trying to keep some distance between her and Nic, fearful she would give something away or disgrace herself. The man only had to look at her and she wanted him.

'Jane looks happy,' Nic murmured in her ear, and she started, taking a step away.

'Yes, she does.' She watched the young woman and her new husband, in full Scottish dress, canoodling before they cut the cake. 'So does Craig.'

'I'd never make a Scotsman—I hate whisky and I won't wear a kilt!'

'Not even for me?' she teased.

His eyes turned sultry and he leaned over to whisper in her ear. 'Maybe in the privacy of our bedroom, *innamorata*!'

'Nic, stop it!'

'How long do we have to stay here?'

Hannah glanced at him and grinned. 'Hours, I expect.'

'Don't,' he groaned. 'I can't wait that long.'

'Behave yourself.'

'It's your fault for wearing that dress,' he complained, his voice rough.

Warmed by his desire for her, Hannah forced herself to move away and chat to some of the other guests, not wanting to draw attention to her and Nic.

'How's it going, Doc?' Allan Pollock said, the jovial garage owner attending the reception with his wife, Dorothy.

'Fine.' Hannah smiled. 'How are you both?'

'Not so bad, Doc. The old knee's holding up. I did what you said and saw your physio for the exercises.'

'When I remind him to do them,' Dorothy added with an indulgent smile.

Hannah laughed. 'Well, you keep nagging him, Dorothy. And come back any time, Allan, if you're having problems.'

'Will do, Doc, thanks.' He paused, his gaze straying around the room. 'Shame Dr Nic will be moving on. He's settled in so well here, everyone likes him.'

'Yes,' Hannah managed, not wanting to be reminded of the fast-approaching day when Nic would leave.

'Aye, well, I'm sure you'll do your best to get someone as good.' Allan smiled before he and Dorothy were hailed by other friends and turned away.

'That won't be easy, will it?'

Hannah spun round at the sound of Kirsty's voice. 'You made me jump!'

'Sorry.' The older woman smiled. 'I overheard what Allan said and it won't be easy to replace Nic.'

'We always manage somehow,' Hannah pointed out, unwilling to be drawn, shifting uncomfortably under Kirsty's probing gaze.

'We'll see what the applicants are like when you start interviewing.'

'Indeed.' She glanced around for an escape and saw Jane smile and wave at her. Smothering her relief, Hannah turned back to Kirsty. 'Excuse me, I must have a quick word with Jane.'

She was halfway across the room when she felt a hand tap insistently on her arm and she looked down, recognising Debbie's seven-year-old daughter.

'Hi, Kim,' she said.

The girl pressed a set of keys into her hand. 'Dr Nic says can you get his bag from the car and go into the next room without letting everyone know there's a problem?' the girl repeated solemnly.

'Yes, of course.' Hannah ran a comforting hand over the child's dark hair. 'You all right?'

'I'm OK.'

'Good girl.'

'I've got to get Mummy now,' she said, heading off into the throng of wedding guests.

Concerned, Hannah collected Nic's medical bag from the boot of his car and hurried to the adjoining room.

'What's happened?' she asked quietly, finding Nic attending a woman who was sitting on one of the chairs. 'Oh, no, it's Patricia, Jane's mother.'

Nic grimaced, opening his bag to find his stethoscope and sphygmomanometer to take Patricia's blood pressure, wrapping the cuff around her arm, frowning as he recorded the measurement.

Hannah sat down, taking Patricia's hand in hers. 'I know it's scary, but try not to worry.' She smiled, suspecting a transient ischaemic attack, or mini-stroke. The woman seemed to be able to hear what was going on around her but had lost her speech.

'I saw her come in here and thought she looked strange,' Nic explained, taking off his stethoscope after listening to her heart. 'I decided to see if she was OK. She was very slurred, said she was dizzy, and then slumped over and couldn't talk. I've called an ambulance on my mobile and Debbie has gone to talk to Jane and her father.'

'It was lucky you were so alert.'

The next ten minutes were chaotic as Jane and her father came rushing in with Debbie, Craig close behind them, all understandably distraught at what had happened. While Nic concentrated on caring for Patricia, Hannah explained things to the worried family.

'We'll get her off to hospital and she'll be thoroughly checked out,' Hannah told them gently. 'I know it's very frightening but there is a good chance she'll be fine. The doctors will assess the problem, what might have caused it and what the extent of it is. It doesn't mean she will have a full stroke, OK? They'll advise on medications necessary and any future monitoring.'

Brian Thompson nodded and Jane held tightly to Craig's hand, tears glistening on her lashes. Hannah was relieved when the ambulance arrived and Patricia was safely on her way to Casualty, the family following behind.

'Hospital first?' Nic asked when they climbed into his car a short while later.

'Do you mind?'

His smile was wry. 'Of course not. I'm worried about them, too. Just keep your coat on,' he added as a teasing aside, lightening the subdued atmosphere.

Hannah smiled back, grateful for his compassion and his humour. Allan and Kirsty were right. It would be impossible to find another doctor with Nic's special qualities.

'You got off on honeymoon all right in the end, then?' Hannah said with a smile when Jane came back to work two weeks later.

'We did. A couple of days' delay, but it was fine. Thanks to you and Nic,' she added. 'Mum's doing really well and her speech is much better than it was.'

Hannah placed a hand on her arm. 'I'm so glad, Jane, but it's Nic you really need to thank.'

'I'll see him now, before the rush starts,' the young woman said, heading off to his consulting room.

Hannah herself scarcely saw Nic all day as they were both kept busy with surgeries, clinics and home visits. She was in the kitchen, preparing a meal, when she heard him come home, greeting an ever-more adventurous and growing Wallace in the hallway. She smiled as she heard him talking to the little cat, a shiver running through her when his footsteps approached behind her as she stood at the sink. His arms slid round her and she leant back against him as he kissed her neck, nipping the lobe of her ear. She held onto the sink, her legs feeling shaky as he pressed against her, letting her know how much he wanted her. Again. And, God help her, she wanted him, too.

Wriggling round, hands wet, she wrapped her arms around his neck, meeting and matching the hot intensity of his kiss. She wasn't sure who moaned loudest in protest when the telephone rang, but she dragged herself away from him reluctantly, not entirely steady on her feet as she went to answer it.

'What?' he sighed when she came back a few moments later.

'I'm sorry, I'm on BASICS call tonight. I have to go.'

'I know.' He cupped her face and dropped a kiss on her lips. 'Where is it?'

'The motorway.' She grimaced, struggling into her things as he collected her bag for her.

'You take care. Please, *cara*.'

'I will. It sounds like a bad one, though, so don't wait up.'

Much to her despair, her predictions came true, and it was nearly midnight by the time she arrived home, having been stuck at the scene of the multiple pile-up in fog for hours. Fortunately no one had lost their lives but several people had serious injuries. After locking up, she saw Nic had left her some supper in the kitchen but she didn't feel like eating. Having a glass of water, she spent a moment with a drowsy Wallace and then climbed the stairs to her bedroom and had a quick shower. Wrapped in a soft, fluffy towel, she hesitated before walking along the corridor to Nic's room, feeling quite shameless as she slid into his bed.

For a few moments she watched him as he slept, sprawled on his front, face turned towards her on the pillow. Her heart swelled with a mixture of love and despair. Slowly, her fingers trailed across his shoulders and down his bare back and he stirred, sighing as he instinctively reached for her.

'Hannah…' he murmured, his dark eyes opening, lazy and slumberous.

Drawing her close, his mouth found hers, his hands roaming to all the places that made her tremble and whimper with desire as he made love to her with exquisite tenderness. When he finally fell asleep again, Hannah wiped at the tears that trickled down her cheeks, knowing she didn't have much longer with him.

Edgy and unsettled, Nic finished a new mother and baby clinic with Morag then went in search of Hannah, finding her in her consulting room writing up her notes.

'Hi,' she greeted him, wedging the files back into the tray and searching through a pile of papers on her desk. 'I meant to ask you for a second opinion on a patient. Where is the wretched thing?'

'Hannah, I—'

'Just a second. Ah, here it is! Can you take a look?'

Sighing, Nic took the papers she held out to him. 'Sure. Hannah, I need to ask you something.'

'Oh.' He saw her swallow, her green eyes clouding. 'Of course. What is it?'

'I'm going to need a few days away,' he explained.

'OK. Is this to do with your next job?' she asked, and he could gauge nothing from her tone.

'Yes.'

'Right.'

Nic wished she wouldn't hide her emotions. She gave nothing away and he had no idea what she wanted, how she felt about them, if this was just a pleasant interlude for her. She had never once asked if he would stay, had made no secret about making plans for his successor, as if his rapidly approaching departure meant little to her. Wouldn't she be at all sorry? As he tried to search her gaze now, she looked away, shuffling through her papers.

'Hannah—'

'Let me know when you want a reference or anything.'

Disgruntled, he gave up. 'Thanks. I'll read up about your patient and get back to you.'

'Fine.'

He left two days later, his heart heavy, hating Hannah's apparent acceptance but so confused in his own head he hadn't been able to talk to her about things. Them. The future. He needed this space away. His past made him wary of putting down roots again. Even more wary of caring too much, because everyone he loved had been taken from him and he couldn't go through that loss again. But he already cared for Hannah. More than cared. He'd been drawn to her from the first moment when she had been so prickly and scared, an intriguing mix of warmth and reserve, compassion and coolness, experience and innocence. Her aloneness had intrigued him, her pain had affected him, but finding the real Hannah underneath her defences had been the most joyous experience of his life. Having faced her fears, she had blossomed so beautifully, been so heart-stoppingly responsive, but she remained determinedly independent. While embracing their time together, she had asked for nothing, refused to discuss anything personal, given no indication of her feelings.

He ran a hand through his hair, confused and troubled. Don't stay in one place too long. Don't get involved. Those had been the maxims he had lived by these last two and more years, always on the move, always travelling light, unable to commit, unable to risk his heart again. Now he had broken all his rules. Sitting by the graves of his lost family and fiancée, he acknowledged that the thought of leaving Hannah for good was more painful than he could ever have expected. He'd helped her exorcise her ghosts, but what about his own? He closed his eyes, tipping his face to the warm Italian sun, his throat tight with emotion. What was he going to do?

The days Nic was away were the longest and most miserable Hannah had ever known. The house was empty and lonely without him. Even Wallace's company failed to lift her spirits, and she realised this was just a sample of what things would be like when he left for good. She slept in Nic's bed, cuddling his pillow, breathing in the lingering scent of him, her thoughts torturing her. Where in the world he would go next? Which place would know his healing touch? Which woman? The thought made her feel sick and brought a searing pain inside her. She missed him so much. Missed working with him and spending time with him at home. Missed his humour, his compassion. Missed sunny days off, exploring the southern uplands on his motorbike. Missed making love with him. No way could she ever let any other man touch her, not after Nic. She would be back in the old prison, but for a different reason.

Even the surgery was subdued, Kirsty prowling round like a grumpy lioness. 'Nic's gone for an interview?'

'I imagine so.'

Kirsty glared at her. 'You're just going to let him leave?'

'Nic has his own reasons for moving on. There's nothing I can do about that.' Hannah struggled to maintain her composure, fighting away the tears which seemed ever present. 'We knew he was only here for six months, that was the agreement. Now we have to find a permanent replacement.'

'I'm sorry, Hannah, but for such an intelligent woman you can be incredibly stupid sometimes. That man is the best thing that's happened to this place in years...and to you. We need him. You need him.'

'Kirsty—'

'If you seriously think no one knows what's going on between you, then you're even sillier than I thought,' the older woman lectured without mercy. 'It's been obvious from the first moment you were made for each other. I mean it, Hannah, you'll be all kinds of fool if you let Nic go.'

Hannah drew in a ragged breath as Kirsty turned on her heel and stomped out, closing the door none too quietly behind her.

Of course she didn't want Nic to go. She loved him, for good-ness' sake. But it wasn't in her power to stop him. He wasn't hers to keep. He'd made it plain from the beginning that he never stayed in one place, had never pretended anything else. And even if things had been different, she wasn't right for him. He deserved someone who could give him the family he craved. No matter what it cost her, she was not going to beg. She would not spoil the last special days they had together. Then she had to set him free. Free to find some other woman who could fulfil his needs. She closed her eyes against the unbearable pain.

Tired and unhappy, and with the out-of-hours calls covered on the rota, Hannah went to bed early, taking Wallace up to Nic's room with her for company. She'd been alone before, had often chosen solitude, but she had never known this gut-wrenching, devastating emptiness. She tensed, hearing sounds in the house, her breath catching when she heard Nic's footsteps on the stairs and coming along the landing.

Colour washed her face as he came into the room, smiling when he saw her in his bed. 'Hi.'

'Hi.' She smiled back, voice husky. 'I had no idea you were coming back tonight.'

'I got a last-minute flight.'

He didn't question her presence there, rather than being in her own room while he was away. Instead, he dropped his overnight bag on the floor and shrugged out of his leather jacket.

'Did your trip go well?' She forced the question, dreading his reply. 'Have your sorted out your next move?'

'There are a couple of loose ends to tie up, but my plans are made.'

Disappointment and a burning sense of loss made her want to curl into a ball and cry. She was aware of a new calmness in him. Did that mean he was pleased to be leaving? 'That's good,' she murmured, her voice hoarse with reined-in emotion and bitter regret.

'I hate to deprive the little man, but I think Wallace would be better off downstairs.' Crossing to the bed, Nic scooped the sleepy kitten up in his arms. 'Hello, *uomo piccolo*, did you miss me?'

Hannah heard him chatting to Wallace as he left the room and she used the few moments alone to try and get her emotions back in check. She sucked in a ragged breath, overwhelmed Nic was home…for now. A frisson of excitement rippled through her at the thought of him being back in bed, making love with her. She had to extract every last second of pleasure she could to sustain her in the dark and dismal days that lay ahead when he left. When Nic arrived back in the bedroom, her pulse started to race. He looked rumpled and roguish, his dark hair mussed, a day or two's shadow of stubble darkening his jaw.

'I'm sorry,' she murmured, unsure how he felt about her sleeping there.

He paused in the process of taking off his boots and looked at her, one eyebrow raised in puzzlement. 'Excuse me?'

'For being in your bed. I wasn't expecting…' Her words trailed off at the heated, sultry expression in his eyes.

'Hannah, I wouldn't have wanted to find you anywhere else.'

His husky admission set awareness curling inside her. She watched, desire burning, as he slowly started to undress. Dear God, he was beautiful. Her fingers itched to touch him, her body tingling with the expectation of feeling him close again. Unselfconscious of his nakedness, he ran a hand across his jaw, glancing at her with a rueful smile.

'I'll go and shave.'

'Don't.' She flushed when he turned back, her voice a whisper. 'I like it.'

Eyes darkening, he walked towards the bed. Heart hammering under her ribs, Hannah slid over to make room for him, a sigh escaping when she felt the touch of his hands as he knelt over her.

'I think we should lose the pyjamas, cute as they are,' he

decided, his fingers unbuttoning her top with tormenting slowness before he tossed it aside and turned his attention to the bottoms.

She trembled as he undressed her, desperate to have his mouth on her, eager to touch him, to taste him. 'Please, Nic.'

'All in good time, *amata*.'

He teased her, making her wait for the touches she craved until she thought she would explode with wanting. Impatient, her hands sank in the thickness of his hair, urging his head down, her lips parting in welcome, meeting the invasion of his tongue. His mouth moved on, working slowly down her neck, before worshipping first one breast, then the other, the rasp of his stubbled jaw on her skin an exciting caress. Breathless and needy, her hands conducted their own exploration, loving the smooth suppleness of skin over muscle, the perfection of his body that, for now, was hers to enjoy, to love. She gave everything she had to show him, without words, what he meant to her.

On Monday, with Nic taking extra patients, Hannah conducted a condensed early surgery and then began the preliminary interviews for the short-listed candidates who had applied for the permanent post of doctor at Lochanrig. Her heart wasn't in it. All she could think of was how perfect Nic was, not just as a friend and a lover but as a doctor. However well qualified, none of the people coming to see her would hold a candle to him, she just knew it.

The day was as long and unsatisfactory as she had anticipated. The assorted doctors had been qualified, but there was no sense of anticipation to work alongside any of them. A couple were over-confident, one quite the opposite, and one brash young man had been written off in the first five seconds by flirting brazenly with her. A frighteningly intense and earnest woman, well qualified on paper, was concerned about the rural location and whether her husband would find suitable employment locally. The only vague possibility was a married man looking to move with his wife and two children, but he was adamant he would not do out-of-hours work.

'Thank God that's over,' she grumbled when Kirsty stuck her head round the door.

'You have one more.'

Frowning, Hannah checked her appointment book and shook her head. 'Not listed here I haven't.'

'Sorry. Must be a clerical error,' Kirsty apologised, a strange expression twinkling in her eyes.

'Send them in, then, and let's get finished. I can't stand much more of this,' Hannah sighed, knowing this one would be as inappropriate as all the rest.

Frowning, she began searching through the papers on her desk for the extra CV and application form, glancing up as Nic sauntered in and closed the door. Her heart clenched painfully at the sight of him. Since he had come back from arranging his next contract, their love-making had been even more mind-blowing than before. She, who had thought she would never love anyone, who had been terrified of sex and intimacy, had fallen in love with Nic, had given him all of herself despite the knowledge he would walk out of her life all too soon. He, too, seemed different, the calmness she had noticed on his return bringing a new warmth and intensity to his every look and touch.

She tried to school her features into a mask of cool unconcern, banishing her body's traitorous response to him. 'Did you want something? Only I have another interview in a moment. Kirsty is just sending them in and I can't find the bloody form.'

'I know.' Nic smiled and sat down.

'Nic?'

'I'm waiting.'

Hannah frowned, in no mood for this. 'Waiting for what?

'For you to interview me.'

'Don't be silly.' Her heart lurched in disbelief. Tears stung her eyes. 'Nic, if this is some kind of joke, I don't find it remotely funny.'

'You refuse to consider my application? You don't want me here?'

He looked uncharacteristically nervous and uncertain, and his vulnerability was nearly her undoing. 'You w-want to stay?'

'I can't leave Wallace,' he stated, amusement shining in his eyes.

She wanted to scream with frustration. 'Nic, be serious.'

'Hannah, I've never been more serious about anything in my life,' he said, his voice rough, his sincerity tightening her chest and bringing a lump to her throat.

'Y-you said you wouldn't p-put down roots or do commitment again.'

'I was wrong. I met you.' Dark eyes filled with hope and something she didn't dare interpret. 'You said you could never love anyone.'

Hannah swallowed. She had said that. But then she hadn't known how magical loving Nic could be. 'I was wrong. I met you,' she whispered back.

He rose gracefully and came round the desk, taking her hands in his and drawing her to her feet. 'I love you, Hannah. I can no more leave you now than I can stop breathing. I love this place, these people. I've put down the deepest of roots these last months and I never want to leave. It's time for us both to step back into life—together. Will you have me? Will you let me buy into the practice and be your partner in all ways…in the surgery and in your life?'

Somehow she forced out the words. 'I can't, Nic.'

'Why not?' He looked pale with shock, eyes full of pain. 'Hannah, please.'

'It wouldn't be fair to you.'

He frowned, his hands tightening on hers. 'What are you talking about?'

'I'm not right for you. You want a family. I c-can't give you children, I—'

Tears squeezed between her lashes and he brushed them away with the pads of his thumbs before cupping her face in his hands. 'You don't know that for sure. But anyway, I want you, *amata*.

There will be other Wallaces, other lives that need us, whatever happens. I need *you*. You are my family. All the people here in Lochanrig are my family.'

'You went away for another job,' she murmured, unable to believe this was really happening.

Nic shook his head. 'Not for another job. I went to Italy. It would have been Mama's birthday. I needed to get my head together, to exorcise my own ghosts and to say goodbye to the past before I could come back here, to you, for the present and the future.'

'I didn't know how you felt.'

'You think I could make love with you, the way we do, if I didn't feel anything?' he teased.

Hannah shrugged, a flush warming her face. 'I don't know. I've not exactly had a lot of experience in that department, have I?'

'But you are a delightfully quick learner!' Nic's dark eyes twinkled naughtily. 'And you can have all the practice you want— but only with me.' His expression sobered. 'I had no idea how you felt, either, if what we had meant anything to you. You gave nothing away, just planned for the day I would be gone. So I took a chance. I had to. I can't lose you. What do you say, Hannah? Please, will you marry me and let me love you for the rest of our lives?'

'Yes! Oh, yes, Nic! I love you so much.'

His kiss took her breath away. She wound her arms round him, pressing herself against him, giving thanks for the day this caring, sexy man had bulldozed his way into her life.

This special doctor with his healing touch had given her new hope and a rich new life filled with a love and a passion she had never expected to know.

A sneaky peek at next month...

By Request

RELIVE THE ROMANCE WITH THE BEST OF THE BEST

My wish list for next month's titles...

In stores from 18th May 2012:

❑ The Right Bed? – Kate Hoffmann,
Jule McBride & Wendy Etherington

❑ Fortune's Mergers – Peggy Moreland,
Bronwyn Jameson & Charlene Sands

In stores from 1st June 2012:

❑ Baby Business
– Karen Templeton

3 stories in each book - only
£5.99!

Available at WHSmith, Tesco, Asda, Eason, Amazon and Apple

Just can't wait?

0512/05

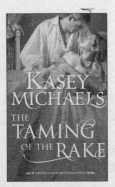

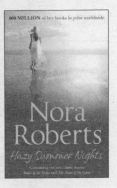

Have Your Say

You've just finished your book.
So what did you think?

We'd love to hear your thoughts on our
'Have your say' online panel
www.millsandboon.co.uk/haveyoursay

- 🌹 Easy to use
- 🌹 Short questionnaire
- 🌹 Chance to win Mills & Boon®
  goodies

Visit us
Online

Tell us what you thought of this book now at
www.millsandboon.co.uk/haveyoursay

YOUR_SAY